Wake Turbulence

Stilson Snow

EUPHRATES
PRESS

ISBN 979-8-9882544-0-9 (paperback)
ISBN 979-8-9882544-1-6 (Kindle)
ISBN 979-8-9882544-2-3 (eBook)

Book Cover by Far Shore Design

www.EuphratesPress.com

For Nancy Short, my wife, best friend, partner, supporter, and inveterate truth teller. It would be an understatement to say, 'without whom...'

ONE

"We could just kill him." The man in the right seat said. "What do you think?"

"What are you talking about?"

"Look, he's a scumbag. You know it, I know it, everyone knows it. He's of no earthly use to anyone. Why not just kill him?"

"Jesus. You're serious!"

"Well, why not? What does he contribute to the society, to the economy? He's a fucking leech. It would be a favor. We'd be doing everyone a favor. Wouldn't have to pay to support him."

"What about life, liberty, and the oath you took ... ah, never mind."

"What's the matter with you?" the man in the right seat continued. "Tell me one thing he's good for? He's worse than the bums in the Square. Shit, we ought to off them, too. Who would miss 'em, huh?" He looked in the back seat, then forward. "See? He's got nothing to say. Might as well dump him right here. Nice long drop."

The pilot shook his head slowly. "I'm delivering him as contracted. By your employer. And I'm going to enjoy the scenery. Why don't you?" He turned his head back to look out the window.

Griffin McNab never tired of flying; never tired of watching his country roll by below. He moved easily in the cockpit, tweaking the mixture, and checking the gauges. His movements had the unconscious economy of the professional. Gray was invading his black hair, though it should have started sooner. Pale azure eyes were bracketed with the crow's feet endemic to his career. He wore wrinkled khaki pants, a soft denim shirt, and frayed ancient running shoes. He had hated it when aviator sunglasses had become the fashion trend for salesmen and almost stopped wearing them. Most people would say he missed handsome by a hair. A few might mention a certain remoteness.

Huge, puffy cumulus crowded the sky. Darting in and out of openings on the way up through the layer of grey-bottomed fleece there was no way to know the beauty waiting above this lower level. Far above the small plane the mackerel sky of cirrus filtered the sunlight, dappling cloud formations as they explored this most transient of territories. There were tall crenelated spires, full and solid looking, streaked with grey and foreboding. There were wisps of white as if some non-Euclidian spider had hung her web in mid-air. Mostly there was the foundation of these ephemeral structures, as folded and cleaved as a glacier.

Through the occasional hole or thin spot in the cloud floor below, the ancient forest peeked through. Steep-sloped canyons and sharp ridges covered with fir and redwood slipped by, now seen through gauze, now in stark detail. Though they looked small at this altitude, the world's tallest and oldest trees still inspired the pilot. Disturbing the tranquility of his flight were bald patches on the slopes where the clear cuts, old and new, showed their scars. Each year there were more of them, and each year the ferocity of the battle between the corporate giants and environmentalists increased.

He prepared to bring down the twin-engine Seneca past just where the clouds ended. He looked over at the front seat passenger, about to say something, when suddenly the plane swung toward the left and started to drop.

"Dammit!" McNab stomped on the right rudder pedal and wrestled the plane level. Herman Pecheur, the deputy sheriff in the right seat, turned pale and gripped his knees until his knuckles went white. The prisoner chained to the deck in the back of the plane yelled a string of Spanish curses and pulled at the anchor bolt.

"Cut that out!" McNab yelled over his shoulder as he slapped his left knee.

He muttered to himself, "Dead foot, dead engine," following the standard procedure to identify correctly the engine that had failed. He pulled back the left engine's throttle cautiously to ensure he was cutting the power on the correct one. Then he shut down the engine and feathered the propeller. He looked out the window and saw oil streaming out of the engine nacelle to form a trail behind. The prisoner yanked at the chain, moving from side to side. The plane rocked. "Herman, stop him! He'll unbalance the plane!"

"Fuck. Fuck. Fuck..." The deputy didn't move but whispered the obscenity over and over. McNab leaned back and punched the prisoner with a right backhand. Blood spurted from the prisoner's nose, and he screamed again. He stopped trying to dislodge his shackles and reached up to hold his bleeding nose all the time swearing in Spanish. The pilot quickly returned to the controls to stabilize the plane.

Suddenly the prisoner lunged forward and kicked at McNab's seat back, screaming epithets in Spanish, then English. "Cavron! You are dead! Hijo de la puta! I kill you fuckin' ass!" He rolled from side to side, and McNab threw the wheel from side to side trying to keep the plane level.

"Herman! Stop him!"

McNab screamed over the rage of the prisoner.

"Fuck. Fuck. Fuck." The deputy continued to repeat.

McNab reached over and slapped the deputy. "Herman! Help me!"

The deputy shook his head and finally looked over at the pilot. "Stop him. Now!" Herman just looked at him.

"Shit!" McNab slapped on the controls for the autopilot, which was never meant for this situation. "Herman, if we start to go down, grab the wheel and hold it!" The pilot unbuckled his seat belt and turned to the raging prisoner.

"Dead man! You dead, man!" He kept flailing and yelling. McNab braced himself against the seat and waited for an opening as the plane rolled back and forth at ever-increasing angles.

Suddenly the plane lurched and McNab was almost thrown back into the controls. "Herman! Grab the wheel!" The autopilot's safety range had been exceeded, and it had shut itself off. As McNab regained his balance, the prisoner lost his, and the pilot saw his chance. He leaned forward and jabbed the smaller man twice in the face, stunning him, then followed with a precisely aimed blow at the solar plexus. The prisoner collapsed.

"Fuck. Fuck. Fuck." Herman was still chanting his mantra of fear. McNab wheeled around into his seat, almost kicking Herman in the head, and grabbed the wheel. Quickly he reduced power, leveled the wings, and pulled the plane's nose up to where blue sky was the predominant color.

"Thanks a lot, Herman." McNab finished up the lost engine procedure. The plane was running smoothly on the one good engine. "You'd better give him a handkerchief or something."

The deputy slowed his breathing and relaxed the death grip on his knees.

He looked over sheepishly at the pilot.

"Ah, sure, Grif." The deputy felt in his shirt pockets, then lifted himself slightly out of the seat to feel his pants pockets.

"Shit, Grif, I don't have one." He looked plaintively over at the pilot. McNab shook his head.

"Christ. Someone is going to pay to have that upholstery cleaned up, Herman. I can't ferry around people with blood on the seats."

He leaned back, reached into the pocket behind the deputy's seat, and pulled out some gasoline and oil-smeared rags.

"Here." He tossed them to the prisoner. "Hold them against the side of your nose."

The captive, now just recovering his breath, picked the rags up and held them to his bleeding nose. "You a dead man."

McNab ignored him and looked out at the forested hills, heavily checkered where the logging operations of Mountain Lumber, Inc. went on tirelessly.

"Christ. I was hoping for another couple hundred hours out of that engine."

He looked over at the deputy.

"You okay, Herman?"

Sweat was still beading on the slick, high forehead of the middle-aged deputy. His eyes were large, and his breathing shallow. He nodded in one quick jerk.

"We're not going to fall out of the sky." McNab sighed. "We can fly just fine on one engine. Besides, I just had the good engine overhauled three months ago. Cost me a lot. It'll just take us a little longer to get to Deak City. Relax!" Another short, jerky nod. "Jerkoff here will get more of a view of what he won't see again any time soon." The prisoner took the rags away from his nose long enough to spit toward McNab.

The sunset was particularly gaudy that night. Landing at Deak City airport, the closest field to the Hundray Maximum Security Prison, was uneventful. Prison officials were on hand to claim their delivery. No less than four vehicles and twelve armed guards stood on the tarmac when the plane taxied up. "Quite the reception, Herman. Who's our friend?"

The deputy unhooked his shoulder harness and seat belt. "Name's Manuel Tanaka. Big time drug dealer from SoCal. Supposed to be a big deal in the Culiacán gang." McNab gave him a puzzled look. "They move the drugs through Mexico for the Colombians." Herman sighed. "Real psycho. Supposed to have killed over forty people climbing to the top, and most of them weren't necessary."

"You mean this wasn't our normal milk run?" McNab looked over at Tanaka, who glared at him above the rags.

"Well, ah, I couldn't tell you. They wanted to move him quick and dirty. I mean, you know, so no one would know. His buddies tried to break him out when they transferred him from the courthouse to the county jail after his trial. Besides, you know, there's only one road up here. Lots of ambush places. Didn't you see it on the news?"

"I don't watch the news." The pilot motioned to Herman, and the deputy opened the door. "Imagine that. A real live celebrity." McNab and Herman climbed out and watched. Two armed deputies pointed pistols at Tanaka from the doors while a third undid the locks on the anchor bolt. A fourth, a sergeant, watched. Tanaka had to be helped out because his handcuffs prevented him from using all the handholds. He kept up a litany of cursing in his native tongue until they got him in the van with heavily meshed windows.

"What happened to his nose?" The sergeant asked Herman.

McNab cut in, "We had engine trouble. The prisoner panicked. He could have wrecked the plane. Herman wanted to talk him down, but I didn't want to take the chance. I had to pop him one."

The officer looked hard at McNab, then turned to Herman. "That how it went?"

Herman nodded judiciously. "Yeah.

"Then that's the way it was." The sergeant looked back at McNab a moment, then returned to Tanaka.

As they walked toward the sorry shack of a terminal building, Herman turned to McNab. "Thanks, Grif. Sorry about what happened up there. I just froze."

McNab nodded. "Yeah, I'd be scared, too, if I didn't practice engine outs."

"Give you a lift somewhere?"

The pilot looked at his airplane and then around at the now deserted airfield.

"I'm sure not flying anywhere real soon. How about taking me over to Gray's?"

Two

Gray's Boarding House and Eatery was located on a bluff overlooking Agate Beach, so named for the agates that could be found there among the gravel on the shore. Initially built by a lumber baron in the 1880s, it was considered a prime example of Victorian architecture and was a state historical site. Twenty-two years previously, Betty Jordan and her partner Griswold Emerson had bought it just before it was about to fall down and converted the hippie commune into a bed and breakfast. Seven sleeping rooms and a dining room kept them busy and happy.

Betty and Gris kept Gray's out of travel guides and off any list of B&Bs, took checks, but no credit cards, charged less than chain motel rates, and automatically turned away tourists in luxury cars. Betty owned up to being a reverse snob but wanted to do her part to keep her town from being devoured by the 'rapacious rich' as she called them.

McNab was on a short and informal list of those who could always find a room.

He kissed Betty on the cheek and got punched in the arm by Gris. Then he called Alonzo of Rodriguez Aircraft at home.

"Hey, Alonzo. That left engine went out on me today. How soon can you get me in the air?"

"Who's this?"

"Alonzo, don't give me that crap."

McNab could feel the sigh before he heard it. "Grif. It's Friday night. I'm just sitting down to dinner."

"Yeah, I know. But I figured if you left in the morning..."

"I got to take Maria to soccer. Call me Monday."

"Alonzo! I'm stuck in Deak City."

"Get a good rest, say hi to Betty, and I'll see you Monday. Good night."

"Wait! I have a charter on Monday morning. I'll lose it if —" McNab realized he was talking to a dial tone. He put the receiver down, muttering to himself.

As he came off the last stair into the parlor Betty patted him on the shoulder as she walked to the kitchen. "Things not going your way, Grif?"

"I have a charter on Monday and ... oh, well. What's on the menu?"

"Wild boar, elk steak, buffalo, and filet mignon."

"Right. Now, what is there to eat?"

"Pasta and salad."

They sat at the expansive carved table in the dining room. Griswold came in with the pasta bowl while Betty brought in the salad. There was one other guest, a thin man with a wispy white beard and intense blue eyes.

"Saigon Duphet." He pronounced it "Doo-fay." The man stood, leaned over the table, and held his hand out to McNab.

"Real name is Courtney, but since Nam they've called me Saigon."

Pasta was passed all around. "Where do you go from here?" McNab asked, putting salad on his plate.

"I'm on my way to Euphrates. Got a colony there."

"Colony?"

Betty served herself. "Mister Duphet is on a mission."

"That's right. I'm going for a world record. I'm going to visit every single nudist colony in America, and I'm going by bus. Not by car. Never by car."

McNab was speechless. After a moment he recovered and inquired. "I didn't know they had a nudist colony in Euphrates. Or is that a naturist resort?"

"Whatever you call it. It's listed, and if it's listed, I'm going." He picked up a piece of garlic bread.

"Where is it?" McNab was curious.

"Don't know. Has a P.O. Box and a phone number. I'm calling them tonight. In fact, if you'll excuse me?" He patted his lips with his napkin, nodded at everyone, and left the table.

McNab looked at Betty and Griswold. They shrugged in unison. Betty said, "We do have some interesting guests." Gris nodded and went back to his pasta.

A few minutes later, Saigon Duphet emerged from his room. He came back to the table, looking very glum. Betty enquired about his call.

"Bad news. Colony is up in the mountains, no buses. Thirty-eight miles up in the mountains. I don't know if I can walk it."

McNab finished a mouthful of pasta. "Where is it?"

"They said it's up the Blue River Road, about two miles past the Forest Service air strip."

"Oh, really?" Betty lit up.

"Mister Duphet, do your world record rules prohibit you from flying?"

"Airlines. Can't fly airlines."

"Grif?"

McNab shook his head. Betty wouldn't let go. "Mister Duphet, our friend here, Mister McNab, is a charter pilot. I'm sure he knows that air strip you refer to. Isn't that right, Grif?"

McNab shot her a dirty look. "That's true. Small strip."

Duphet's eyes came alive. "Really? Can you land there? Could I hire you?"

"Charter's not cheap, Mister Duphet."

"Call me Saigon. Don't worry. I have money." He reached into the pocket of his faded jeans and pulled out a wad of hundred-dollar bills. "I go by bus because I like it. I love bus terminals. All the interesting people. Great conversations. My daddy, he owned a telephone company in the Midwest, would never let me go anywhere or do anything. Sent me to a pissant liberal arts college. Wanted me to take over the telephone company from him. No way. Volunteered for Nam." Duphet looked down at his plate. "Not the best idea I ever had. By the time I got back, he'd died and left me the telephone company." He paused. "I left it. Been doing buses ever since." He looked at McNab. "You got a plane, you got a customer."

"Well, I haven't got a plane right now. Lost an engine coming in tonight. Maybe in a couple of weeks."

Saigon Duphet shook his head. "Can't wait that long. I'm heading for Euphrates day after tomorrow."

Betty put her hand on McNab's arm. "Grif, how about Charlie? He hasn't flown his plane in a long time. I'm sure you could work something out. Could save your charter on Monday?"

McNab brooded a minute. "I haven't seen Charlie in a long time."

"Charlie's been down since his heart attack. But he still talks about the way you saved his plane. Why don't you give him a call?"

"Charlie's got enough troubles right now."

"Well, he's there if you want him. Dessert, Mister Duphet?"

After dinner Saigon Duphet sat in the overstuffed chair in front of the fire, telling stories about his nudist colony visits, supposedly to Gris and McNab, who played cribbage in the bay window overlooking the ocean. It didn't seem to them that Duphet cared whether they were listening or not. Betty came out of the kitchen, glanced quickly at McNab, and then put another log into the big stone fireplace. After a satisfying burst of flame and sparks, Betty got a basket from the cabinet and sat on the couch near Duphet. She pulled out a round object, discarded the wrapping, an old Annette Funicello beach towel, and began work on an alabaster sculpture of a girl.

"Skunked again!" McNab looked dismally at Gris, who smiled. "You mind telling me how you beat me all the time?"

"I pay attention, Grif. To the cards. Want another go?" McNab nodded, and Gris began to deal when the phone rang.

Gris looked over at Betty, who was bent over her sculpture. He got up and answered the phone. "Charlie! How are you? Yeah? Us, too," he paused. "Say, Grif McNab's here. Want to say hello?" Gris ingenuously held out the receiver. As he walked to the phone, McNab glared at Betty.

In the morning, McNab came down the stairs with his worn canvas overnight bag slung over his shoulder. Gris was waiting at the door and pulled it open as McNab reached the bottom.

"Ready?" Gris pulled the car keys out of his pocket.

"Yeah." McNab poked his head into the parlor. "Saigon still around? I thought I'd say goodbye."

"He went out on a walk. Said he'd back before you left."

"Strange man. I kind of liked him. Well, say goodbye for me."

"Okay. We'd better go. Your bus leaves in a few minutes."

They drove to the Greyhound terminal quickly, and McNab jumped out of the car. "Thanks again, Gris." He closed the door and walked into the different world of long-distance bus travel.

As McNab found his seat, he flashed back to the limos he used to ride in. It wasn't the first time this ironic thought had occurred to him. The huge diesels rumbled alive.

THREE

"Please put your tray table in the upright position for landing." The pert, fifty-ish stewardess, blond with dark roots, whisked the plastic glass out of the monk's hands and plunged it into the clear plastic trash bag she hauled down the aisle. She repeated the mantra at almost every row of seats. Jamyang Rinpoche looked over at his two companions, rearranged his red and yellow robes, and sat back, gazing out the window.

If he allowed himself to forget, it almost looked to the monk as if they were above his far-off homeland. The cloud deck below the silver twin-engine commuter plane was rippled and folded with cumulus, white with some tinges of darker gray. Snow-capped peaks poked through the radiant puffs off to their right, grandiosely named Alps. As they approached their destination, the clouds thinned, and pools of conifers appeared below. Jamyang Rinpoche felt an ache of nostalgia as fir and redwood forest spread out beneath them.

The nostalgia turned toward grief as the bald swaths became apparent. He remembered too clearly the devastation of the invasion. Soon the clouds turned to wisps, and a patchwork quilt of mountains, trees, and shaved hills stretched as far as they could see.

The propellers' pitch changed, and the angle of the deck dipped slightly. The stewardess announced their imminent arrival at the Euphrates Regional Airport. In the 1930s Euphrates was one of the bastions of the movement to form a new state of Jefferson. Residents of an area bounded roughly by a line from the Pacific Ocean to Roseburg, Oregon, down to Redding, California, and back to the sea were tired of urban politicians controlling and, in many cases, laying waste their communities. They fought mightily, even inaugurating a "governor," but to no avail. Pearl Harbor put an end to the practical efforts, but, like all mythical lands, Jefferson became an inhabited state of mind.

When Jamyang Rinpoche and his companions, Ongdi Rinpoche, and Tenzing Rinpoche, monks of the soon-to-be-rebuilt Trangmar monastery, debarked, they saw a man holding a sign that said 'Trangmar.' Mohammed Erk, an Uzbek who had made his way into the redwood empire via Ecuador, now drove a cab for Delbert Simms. An apologetic note carried by the cabbie said that their putative hosts, Jim and Nunaluk Carlsen, had been suddenly called away.

Jim was a friend of the monastery and an accountant at Mountain Lumber.

Though they thought it strange that the Carlsens had made no other arrangements for them, the monks, being more used to living in the present than any of the people they had met, or would meet, on this journey, nodded. They asked Erk to take them to a place of lodging, which he did, for his usual 15 percent kickback. Erk knew that Vijay Najpool, proprietor of the Holiday Capri motel on One Street, the heart of the scummy underbelly of Euphrates, would be pissed off that the guests didn't want any dope or girls. He also knew they would fill a room and help with Vijay's overhead.

The city, so it goes, was named in a fit of frustration when the recent immigrant Ole Carlsen was trying to ship a load of elk meat from the motley collection of buildings by the bay that to date had no accepted name.

The none-too-bright second mate aboard the small schooner, who was trying to understand the old Dane, mistook his question, "You freight thees?" for the town's name, and so the small collection of buildings came to be known as Eufratees. Later, someone with a warped geographical bent changed the spelling.

The following day at 4:00 am, the monks awoke for their regular meditation and prayers, assuming that since they were in the West, a few hours of quiet were in store. However, earlier in the night, Larry the Pervert had scored an unusually high-quality bag, cut it, and resold most of it for a generous profit. He then enlisted the services of Lilith Serena, who was trying to get the money to finish her sex change operations and was, at the moment, a he-she. This was good, since it kept one more runaway boy out of Larry's clutches for a night.

Fueled by tequila and blow, Larry and Lilith didn't hit the Holiday Capri until 4:10 am, being assigned by the sleepy, hungover, and by now very pissed off Vijay to the room next to the monks.

Larry and Lilith specialized in furniture passion, preferring walls and dressers to beds or floors, and thus the monks were forced to seek another venue for their quiet spiritual rites on that foggy morning.

Henry Bouchard was sleeping in his cardboard box under the bench near the statue dedicated to the Fisherman of Euphrates. He thought his DTs were worse than usual when he awoke at dawn to low-pitched chants and the vision of three men in orange and red robes on the lawn in front of him. He emerged from his paper cocoon just as the monks were finishing.

Wiping the sleep out of his eyes, he wandered over to them to make sure they were real. "Hey!" he mumbled, "You guys for real?" Being not only polite but dedicated to easing the suffering of others, the monks asked if he could help them find an eating place and would he join them. Henry needed no more urging for a free meal and guided them to the Old Logger Cook House, which served their single-item menu of ham and sausage omelet, sourdough toast, and coffee that morning.

While Henry and Ongdi, the youngest monk, gorged on the all-you-can-eat fare, Jamyang asked him how to get to the Mountain Lumber Company, or ML as it was locally known. Henry, whose alcoholism had made him a few cans short of a six-pack, offered to take them there himself, for which they expressed great appreciation. He allowed as it was about a six-hour walk to the main offices in Mill City, the smaller town east of Euphrates. The monks told him they could take a cab, and Henry graciously offered to find them a reputable one. Within minutes Mohammed Erk was once again at their service, and the monks were on the way to Mountain Lumber.

"Why you guys going there?" Henry sat in the front seat while the three robed monks squeezed in the decrepit back seat of Erk's thirty-six-year-old Checker.

"We wish to meet with Mister Eric Hoffstader." Jamyang tried to bow while entrapped by the sprung seat.

Henry's salivary glands began to work overtime. He mopped his face. "Do you guys believe in the Devil?"

The monks looked at each other. Jamyang replied. "Not the same as Westerners believe. No."

"Well, you should. Because... you're going to meet him. In person!" Henry's voice started to rise. "He's evil. Evil incarnate! He's worse than Mao or napalm or Spam. He's—"

Erk put a hand on his shoulder. "Calm, my friend, calm. You are disturbing my passengers. Please."

Henry's mood quieted. "Yeah. Sure."

He turned back to the monks. "But you don't want to go there. Believe me, you don't want to know this man. You guys got a cigarette?"

Four

McNab's heart sank as he looked at the old Cessna 185 Skywagon. He and Charlie were pushing it out of the rusted T-hangar at the Euphrates airport. "Haven't flown it for almost two years. Damn FAA says it wants more information from the damn doctors." He spat a wad of something onto the pavement. "Damn bureaucrats. I'm in better shape than before the damn bypass. Walk four miles twice a day, chop my own firewood." He pronounced it 'far-wood.'

Grease stains streamed down the belly of the plane from the engine compartment. Bug splats adorned the windscreen, leading edges of the wings, and the horizontal stabilizer. Dust dulled the forty-seven-year-old oxidized orange and white paint.

"Always kept it hangared. Damn good thing, too." He stopped, and so did McNab. "Needs a little sprucing up. Just cosmetic. Take a look see. It ain't no space shuttle," he winked at McNab, "but if you think it'll do the trick, you can use her." Charlie ducked his head under the wing on the way to the pilot's door. He unlocked it and stepped back, waving his hand into the cockpit.

The gash in the felt fabric started just above the co-pilot's head, snaked its way back over the back seats, and ended just shy of the baggage door. It was only the inner lining to a safe hull, but the ruined airplane's headliner would not be comforting to a paying passenger.

McNab checked the panel. Dual navcoms, one with glide slope, encoding altimeter, ancient RNAV, and a jerry-rigged first-generation GPS. Definitely not a modern cockpit. Truly back to basics. "Everything work, Charlie?"

"Well, the radios worked last time I was out. Didn't use the RNAV much, don't know if it works anymore. If you're going to fly IFR it needs the whole check out. I always have Ed do my work."

"Good man."

"Whaddya think? Want to use it?"

"When was it last annualled?"

Charlie scratched his head. "Lemme see. Last annual inspection. Hm. It was some time after the damn earthquake. Oh, maybe four, five years."

"Uh, Charlie?"

"Yeah, I know. Supposed to be every year. But the last few years I hardly flew the damn thing. Probably didn't put twenty hours a year on it. Hell, those rent-a-plane places only have to check theirs out every hundred hours. Didn't seem right."

McNab shot him a look sideways.

"Geez, Grif. Give me a break. I know it's supposed to be every year, hours or not. But, damn, it was always hangared, always gave it a good pre-flight. You know me, I wouldn't put Marquita in any danger."

"Charlie, I appreciate the offer, I really do. But it'll cost me more than I have to bring it up to standards."

Charlie stood looking down at the ground. "Yeah, I should've kept it up better." They both looked out at the orange wind sock, twisting this way and that in the shifting winds coming ahead of the storm. "Tell you what, Grif. You'd be doing me a favor, using it. Cylinders probably got rust in them already. I'll have Ed throw an annual on it, do the Pitot-static and transponder checks, too. How's that for a deal?"

McNab turned to him. "Charlie, that's real nice of you, but—"

"You always look a gift horse in the mouth?!"

"Betty put you up to this?"

"Can't you ever just shut up?" He pulled the cap lower on his head. "Let's pull the damn battery and get it over to charge. Then you come home for dinner." It was not a question.

FIVE

Jamyang Rinpoche bowed as he accepted the cup of coffee. "Thank you very much."

"Our pleasure, I'm sure." Bryan Bofford, public relations director of Mountain Lumber, inclined his head slightly. He rubbed his longish chin and seemed to be in pain. He then ran his hands up his cheeks, careful not to muss the carefully coiffed hair. "Well, Mister Rinpoche," he gave a small embarrassed smile, "it seems as if Mister Hoffstader is tied up in a very important meeting and won't be able to meet with us today. In his absence I will serve you as best I can."

The monk nodded slightly while the two others sitting beside him did not acknowledge. "You are too kind, Mister Bofford. Are you familiar with our mission?"

"Mister Hoffstader instructed me to help you in any way I can. Perhaps you could enlighten me as to your particular needs." Bofford almost giggled. "Excuse me. Enlighten me. How stupid of me."

The monk smiled at him. "We come from Lo Mulang, a small kingdom that shares a border with Tibet and China. A very small, very isolated country. Our people practice Tibetan Buddhism though we are not Tibetans. The Dalai Lama is our spiritual leader, also. When China invaded Tibet they also invaded our country. We share a similar fate with Tibet. Most of our temples and monasteries were destroyed, most of the monks and nuns were killed. Those who were not killed were imprisoned and tortured."

"Oh, my, that's ghastly."

"Myself, and a few other monks were able to escape and to go to Dharmsala, in India, to be near Dalai Lama. Many years later Dalai Lama sent several groups of Tibetans to different parts of the world to establish centers of Tibetan culture so that the Chinese plan of eradicating our religion and culture would not succeed. I appealed to him to allow some of us to go and we were sent. I myself was in the second group. I went to St. Paul in Minnesota."

"Your English is impeccable."

"Thank you. I lived with an American family for several months. A few years ago China was forced through public opinion to allow rebuilding of a very few monasteries in Tibet. They use them as, what do you call them? Show pieces. Yes, they use them to show people that they are not terrible. Yet, it is only a few. When that happened we appealed to the Chinese to allow us to restore our main monastery at Trang-mar. They refused."

"That is just dreadful."

"One of your movie stars came to our region and made a documentary about our small nation which was broadcast on educational television."

"Really. That's fascinating. Who was it?"

"Mr. Tyler Benz."

"Oh. I didn't know he was political."

"The publicity helped us to get permission from the Chinese to rebuild our monastery."

There was silence. Bofford finally broke it. "And you want us to ... what is it, exactly, that we can do for you?"

"Our monastery's main hall was supported by a single

large beam of wood before it was burned. It had stood for over six hundred years since the last time we rebuilt it. In the past we had found the right tree in our own forests. However, the Chinese have forbidden us to go into our forests. They take all the trees."

"Ah, you need a tree!"

"Yes!" They both seemed happy to finally reach an understanding. "We were able to contact Mister James Carlsen who lives here. He is a friend to us. He works with your company and he suggested your Mister Hoffstader might be of assistance. Unfortunately, Mister Carlsen could not be here, either."

Bofford sat back in his chair and grinned. "Well, now, you are perfectly correct. There is nothing Mister Hoffstader likes more than to sell timber."

"Thank you, Mister Bofford. We would like to go to your forest to find the right tree."

"No need to do that Mister Rinpoche. We have hundreds of trees already cut. Just tell us the size you want and we'll just pack it up for you."

"Thank you, Mister Bofford, but we need to make sure it is the right tree. We need to see it in the forest."

"Well, why not? I can have Mac take you out tomorrow morning, if you like."

"That would be very nice."

"Fine. Where are you staying?"

"A very fine establishment. It is called... "Jamyang turned to Tenzing on his right and said something in Tibetan. "Ah, yes, the Holiday Capri Motel."

Bofford started. "Did you say the Holiday Capri?"

The monks beamed at him and nodded.

"I see." Bofford picked up his phone. "Get me Jacquye, right now." He turned back to the monks. "Perhaps you would like to stay closer to Mill City in some, ah, different accommodations?"

Jamyang whispered briefly to both of the other monks. "Mister Carlsen said we should put ourselves in your hands."

"Fine. Would you like another cup of coffee?"

"Do you have Coca-Cola?" Ongdi piped up.

"Ah. Yes. Certainly. Three cokes coming up!" Bofford left the office.

Henry Bouchard sat in the cab with Mohammed Erk, wishing he had a bottle of white port and some lemon juice. The other guys were always razzing him because he liked to do it himself. Kelly kept telling him that Thunderbird was developed after a survey showed that most winos liked lemon juice with their white port and that it saved a step. But Henry was a purist. Besides, Erk was no conversationalist. What Erk thought about him, Henry didn't know or care, he was sure. Henry spied the L&M Market, a neighborhood store a few doors down. "Gonna get something. Be right back."

Henry got out of the cab and noticed several other cars parked there with nattily dressed men and women standing around smoking and talking with each other. The vehicles had logos of different TV stations on them. Henry walked up to the group. "What's happening? Why are you guys here?"

The group tried to ignore him. "Hey! I'm John Q. Public! What are you guys doing out here in East Bum Fuck? Do you want my opinion of things? Go on your talk shows? I got opinions, too. Those gray haired old white men you got on there don't know everything." They studiously avoided noticing him. Henry walked straight into the crowd. "How about me? Want to interview me?"

Finally, one of the reporters took Henry by the shoulders and gently guided him out of the circle. "We're here because Hoffstader is in town and said he would make an announcement about the timber bill. Okay?"

"I was just asking. Say, aren't you the guy who was caught in the motel with the supervisor's wife?"

The reporter closed his eyes a moment and muttered something.

"What was that?"

The reporter sighed, "I said I thought I'd had my fifteen minutes."

Henry nodded. "Yeah." He lumbered over to the small, dark market and started looking for the wine but couldn't find any. Henry wandered up to the counter. "Hey, got any wine?"

Femily Dewey slowly came to the counter. She must have weighed upwards of three hundred fifty pounds and wore a faded mu-mu stained with various food groups. "Nope. Don't got no wine. Lost our license a year ago."

"Shit. Got anything sweet? Candy? Doughnuts?"

"Nope. No candy. They put us on cash only and we don't have no cash. Same with the bakery."

"What do you have?"

She thought for a minute. "I got a peach pie. Emily, she's my cousin, down the street, she made it. Said I could sell it if I could."

This seemed all right to Henry, whose blood sugar was dropping rapidly. "Okay, give it to me."

They haggled about the price for a minute and then completed the transaction. Henry asked for a paper bag and left the store to come out into the bright sunlight. He stopped and glanced over at the cab. He decided Erk probably didn't like peach pie and moved over to the side of the Mountain Lumber building to sit in the shade next to a door that hadn't seen paint in a long time. It wasn't like the front entrance, all done up in hearty logs. He opened the bag and was about to pull the pie out when the door opened with a loud squeak.

Henry jumped up, startled, and came face to face with a huge man. The man had a full head of tightly curled iron-gray hair and a severely pockmarked face. His mouth curved downward to the left, giving him an unbalanced look. An odor of garlic and stale cigarette smoke wafted from him. Just behind the massive shoulders stood the Great Satan himself, Hoffstader, and another man, an Asian, with the classic small wire-rimmed glasses, in a charcoal Brooks Brothers suit. Henry was speechless.

He had fantasized about accosting Hoffstader someday. Hoffstader had assumed the role of being all the evil in the world in Henry's view. Hoffstader had come from out of the east by way of a shrewd, and as it turned out, an illegal stock deal that had bought Mountain Lumber out from under its founders, the O'Briens.

The O'Briens were legends in Euphrates and, indeed, in the timber industry. They had shepherded their timber and cut less than the number of board feet grown each year. The O'Brien creed was that everyone and every creature depended on a healthy forest and what was good for the forest was good for the timber business and their community. They had treated their workers like family, and several generations had worked for them. It was a nineteenth-century company ripe for the barracudas of the new age.

Within days after the slick deal had closed, the O'Briens were gone, and the new era began. The cut was increased far above sustainable levels. There were junk bonds to be paid off. The forests shrank, and ugly scars of clear-cutting sprouted up all over the mountainsides. Crews were cut to the bone and beyond. Shift lengths increased. Injuries increased exponentially. Clear-cutting destroyed watersheds and streams were damaged by runoff. Fish died by the hundreds of thousands until the sport fishing industry was destroyed. The floods severely damaged several communities caused by excessive runoff from the naked hillsides. ML denied any responsibility and simply increased the cut and the workload. Some laid-off workers left the area, many went on welfare, and some ended up in the alleys with Henry. Henry hated Hoffstader.

The large man opened the door wider. Hoffstader and the Asian man shook hands, and the Asian turned to come out. They saw Henry and hesitated. Henry looked at the Asian, saw Hoffstader, and started moving forward. Hoffstader just said, "Karl." The big man came forward, put a massive hand on Henry's chest, and simply pushed Henry out of the door. Henry staggered back, arms windmilling, trying to keep his balance. He couldn't and hit the asphalt squarely on his coccyx. He yelped in pain. The Asian man walked quickly away toward a red car.

Henry jumped up and down and screamed insults at the closed door and its peeling paint. "You goddamn sonofabitch, Hoffstader. You fucking no good cock sucker fuck head shit heel bastard fuckface asshole motherfucker! Greedy rotten capitalist tree raping, baby killing, cock sucker asshole! Somebody ought to kill you, you fucker! I ought to kill you, you motherfucker!" He stopped a moment to catch his breath. As he took a deep breath, he brightened and turned around. The front door!

Henry reached the front of the building. The reporters were crowding around Hoffstader, who was speaking to them. "Yes. The new timber bill will benefit everyone, especially the people. This bill will give the families of timber workers a gift, the security of their jobs. That's sweet. And these people have needed something sweet for a long time. Thank you for coming." The camera crews shut off their equipment and started to pack up. A couple of reporters stood talking with Hoffstader informally.

Henry elbowed his way through the crowd. "I got something for you, Hoffstader! Something sweet!" Before Karl could get him, Henry had taken the peach pie from Femily Dewey's cousin Emily and slammed it onto the top of Hoffstader's head.

The reporters went into a frenzy, trying to get their equipment back up. Hoffstader stood, peach pie dripping into his face, with Henry yelling obscenities. It was the reporters that saved Henry's life. Karl had his hand on Henry's collar and was pulling back his fist when Hoffstader, seeing the possibility of cameras, yelled at him to let the man go. Karl pushed Henry and sent him sprawling. Henry sprang up and charged Karl. The large man swatted him, and Henry went down. Hoffstader was furiously whispering to Karl when Henry slithered over to Karl and bit him on the ankle. Karl yelled and was kicking Henry when Hoffstader grabbed the large man and pushed him toward the door.

Before the video cameras were ready Hoffstader and Karl disappeared back into the offices. Henry scuttled back to the cab. The reporters started to follow. Mohammed Erk started the cab and gunned it, heading out of the parking lot. He slammed on the brakes as a red car cut him off at the driveway, getting out of the parking lot first. Reporters were swarming toward them as Erk careened out of the lot. He turned to Henry. "You're crazy, man. But I like it. He's a bad man."

Six

McNab did the last turn on the oil pan drain when the phone rang. "Of course," he thought as he scurried out from under the plane. He got there on the fifth ring. "Euphrates Fly by Night Charter. Grif McNab." The voice buzzed in his ear. "Saigon! How are you?"

"I'm just fine, Grif, just fine. Got me down here on the bus. Got your number from Griswold. Hope you don't mind."

"Not at all."

"Well, I got to thinking. There's a lot of miles up that road and no bus and I can't use a car and, well, what Betty said came to mind. I'd sure like to add that colony to my list. Are you getting my drift, Grif?"

McNab chuckled. "Yes, I think I am."

"How soon are you heading up that way?"

"How soon do you want to go?"

"Well, I could get there in about an hour. If that's all right with you."

"That would just fine. You know where I am?"

"Saw that teeny little airport coming into town. It can't be so big I can't find you, I imagine."

"The sign's pretty big. See you soon." McNab put down the phone.

About thirty minutes later, the Euphrates Auto Parts truck drove up and disgorged Roy Dimas and a truck differential. "Tried to get here fast, Grif." Roy was about six foot four and weighed in at more than McNab cared to think about. He hefted the gearbox on his shoulder and brought it over to the plane. "Didn't mean to hold you up."

McNab wiped the oil off his hands. "You didn't hold me up. As a matter of fact, I got another passenger." Roy looked at him quizzically. "Guy wants to go to El Cielo. We'll drop him off on the way to your place."

"Why don't he drive?"

"It's a long story."

"We got time." He put the axle down.

"I met him when I had to overnight in Deak City. It seems as if—"

"Hi, Grif!" McNab turned around to see Saigon come into the hangar carrying a small bag. "Made better time than I thought. Good level ground around here." He turned to Roy. "My name's Saigon. Saigon Duphet" and stuck out his hand. Roy took the small man's hand and wrapped his around it, and nodded. "Whoa. You're a big fella. Well, Grif, are we ready to go?"

"Yeah. Roy here has a differential to get to his place back up in the mountains. We'll drop you at El Cielo first." He turned to the airplane to open the doors.

Saigon was silent for a moment. "Oh. I thought we'd be looking at the scenery."

McNab continued opening the doors and moving things for the cargo. "We'll still see plenty of scenery. This way, though, we're saving both you and Roy some money. Only one dead head leg instead of two. Okay, let's get loaded up."

Roy and McNab put the differential onto the floor in the

rear passenger area, and Roy got in. McNab put Saigon's bag in the cargo bay.

"Ever flown before? In a small plane?" McNab asked Saigon as he stood before the passenger side door.

"Oh, sure. My daddy had a couple of friends who owned planes. Little bitty things, like this one. Took me up a bunch of times. I liked it. They loved it. My mother was always deathly scared every time I went. Used to argue with daddy about it." McNab showed him how to fasten the seat belts and shoulder straps. He adjusted his earphones and mike and showed him how to control the volume on his side of the intercom.

Soon they were racing down the runway and lifting off into the light azure sky of morning. They went down the coast, rocky cliffs plunging into the ocean, crowned by firs and stands of birch. Inland, in the hills and folds of valleys, were alder, yellow swatches of scotch broom, and meadows of tall grass. Patches of early morning fog lingered in odd clefts in the landscape, catching the sun and trailing into the air like an ethereal cold forest fire. The ocean was clear, with spots of light and dark blue, kelp visible beneath the surface, and the undulating rock formations of this part of the continental shelf.

"Look at that!" Saigon Duphet pointed down. McNab banked the plane to see a pod of five grey whales meandering down to their birthing lagoons in far off Mexico. Two of them, younger, or at least smaller, seemed to be playing, breaching, and splashing. Duphet smiled and gave a thumbs-up sign. McNab returned the grin and leveled the wings. "You see that all the time?"

"Not as often as I'd like. My work usually takes me more inland. Executives going to bigger airports, cities. This is a bonus."

"How'd you get into this business?"

"Got lucky. Right place at the right time. Bought out an old friend who was retiring."

"Good thing, luck. Never know when it's coming. Or going."

"That's right. Look at my truck." Roy opined from the rear.

"You said it. I just got finished paying off the right engine in my airplane. Now the left one's gone. I'll need some luck on that."

"You're plenty lucky. Look at where you get to be." Saigon Duphet indicated with a wave of his hand the splendor of the sky, forest, and ocean spread out before them.

McNab nodded. "You're right. I get so caught up in my problems I sometimes don't see this." He reached to fractionally adjust the mixture. "How did you hit on the idea of visiting every nudist colony in America? By bus, even? Obviously you're a sun worshiper yourself."

"What?" Roy's astonished voice came at them.

Saigon paid him no attention. "Nope. I keep my clothes on. I just visit them. Chalk 'em up. Just thought it would be, ah, unique. Didn't sound any worse to me than collecting Barbie dolls, or pens, or autographed basketball jerseys. Takes more time, which is what I like. Get to see a lot more of the country and talk to more people. Like yourself. Don't have to worry about anything getting stolen. Unless they want my brain. I'd take exception to that. How far are we?"

"See that mountain off to the left of the nose of the airplane? The field is just to the right of it and on a little plateau. Called 'El Cielo.' Means, 'the sky.' Not a bad description. It drops off all around the runway. Looks scarier than it is. We should be there in about ten minutes." McNab started the descent to pattern altitude.

McNab set the plane down on the narrow, up-sloping runway. He taxied back down the runway to the parking area at mid-field and stopped the engine. They got out and retrieved Duphet's backpack from the baggage compartment.

McNab stuck out his hand. "Good to have you along, Saigon. You go up the road from here. There's probably a sign."

"Thanks, Grif." He handed some bills to McNab, taking his time. "Appreciate it. Have a good one. Where you going from here?"

"Over to Roy's." He waved vaguely toward the mountains. "Then home. Good luck." McNab turned away, then back. "Keep in touch."

Saigon looked up at Roy, who had come around to get in the front seat. The big man was over a head taller and a foot wider than the wiry white-haired vet. He opened his mouth to say something, hesitated, then said, "Sure thing."

McNab and Roy took off, leaving Saigon standing on the runway. "Nudist colonies?"

The pilot shrugged. "You meet a lot of interesting people in this business."

Roy snorted. A while later, he slightly tightened his grip on his knees as the tree tops came level with the window.

"Yeah, Roy, pretty soon you'll have to trim them or fell them if you want me to get in here." McNab didn't take his eyes off the dirt road that would serve as the runway for this delivery. Roy's head jerked up and down in one brief acknowledgment.

McNab put in the last notch of flaps, adjusted the elevator trim one more time, and let the single-engine plane float to the start of the straight stretch of dirt road. Easing back on the yoke, he brought the Cessna's nose up to make a full stall landing. They fell the last six inches, landing with a resounding "kerplop." Quickly the pilot retracted the flaps. He kept back pressure on the yoke. Moments later, as he applied the brakes, the plane came to a stop just where the road turned right and dipped into the redwood forest that surrounded the clearing. McNab popped open the window and went through his shutdown procedure. The propeller stopped spinning, and Roy let go of his knees. Grif opened his door and pushed his seat back as the sounds of the woods crept into the airplane cabin.

A hawk came from the north and circled the open space, crows cawed, stellar jays flitted at the edge of the trees, and insect songs buzzed. The hot sun was directly overhead. McNab pulled his cap down and turned back to the business at hand. "Let's get that thing out of here." He opened the cargo door. Roy came around the back of the plane and helped him wrestle the differential out of the cargo hold.

"Hold on, Grif, let me get it." Roy walked off toward the barn that sat a few hundred feet away. Grif could see into the open doors and the outline of a truck up on blocks visible in the shadows. A few hundred feet to the left of the barn was a simple wood cabin.

Twenty minutes later, McNab and Roy sat on the cabin's porch with lemonades. Squirrels were investigating the tires of the plane. "Thanks for coming so fast, Grif. If I didn't get this fixed before ... well, you know how it is way back here. I'd sure be in a mess. Guess I'd better see about those treetops, too."

McNab looked over the place. He couldn't see the generator shed, chicken shack, or the cistern around the back. Neither did he pay attention to the complex of hoop greenhouses just at the side of the clearing where Roy grazed his few head of cattle. Roy didn't get many visitors, and he didn't want many. Grif put his empty glass down on the floor. "No problem. Any time. Thanks for the drink." He stood and stretched, getting the stiffness out. Not for the first time Grif wondered if age was gaining on him. "If I want dinner I'd better get a move on."

"Need any help turning the plane around?"

"Thanks, that would help." Roy nodded.

McNab walked down the cabin's steps and crossed the hay field to the plane. Roy'd get one more harvest done before the rains, he thought. He and Roy took opposite struts. He pulled, and Roy pushed. Soon the plane was headed back the way it came in. There was a pronounced downslope to the road. It was the only way to take off.

As McNab turned toward the pilot's door, Roy put his hand on the pilot's shoulder. "You be careful. I don't know about guys that go to nudie places."

McNab tried not to smile. "Okay, Roy. I'll be careful."

"I mean it, now."

"I know." He got into the plane, strapped himself in, and went through the starting procedure. Grif did his run-up, set twenty degrees of flaps, ran up the engine, and popped the brakes. The old 185 waddled down the road, picking up speed. McNab pushed on the yoke to get the tailwheel airborne as soon as possible. As soon as the tail wheel came off the ground, he pulled slightly back on the yoke to get the plane off the road. He leveled off, flying inches above the roadway. He built up speed until the airspeed indicator read best angle of climb speed and pulled back on the yoke, holding the airspeed. The wall of trees rushed at him. McNab held the airplane in the same attitude and watched the top of the trees slowly descend in his windshield. As he passed over the tops of the nearest trees with whole yards to spare, he wondered how long he could keep coming into Roy's before the tree tops made it impossible. Or the Feds raided him.

SEVEN

Sunlight filtered through the branches dappling the site. Jamyang Rinpoche led the prayers as he and his fellow monks stood next to the soaring trunk of the gigantic Douglas fir. Chanting and sprinkling herbs on the tree, the monks blended their voices to form a sonorous harmony of deep-throated sounds rising and falling in entrancing rhythms.

Boyd Williams stood off to the side of the small clearing waiting for the signal to fell the giant tree. He wasn't sure what to make of this ceremony. He'd seen news stories of Buddhist monks before but never expected to see them in his woods. He and Stan would have some stories to tell down at the 'Green Chain' tonight. What a sight. Three weird guys wearing red and yellow robes mumbling shit in front of a goddam tree. Jesus Christ. It was bad enough with the goddam environmentalists and the fucking college kids. Now they had the goddam monks running all over the place.

The monks finished their prayers and turned back to the small group gathered there. Jacquye (she pronounced it 'Jackie') Ormus, acting deputy assistant director of public relations for ML, ran up to Jamyang Rinpoche and gushed at him, "That was so wonderful. It was so ... so ... spiritual, if you know what I mean. It's like Our Lord Jesus Christ himself was right here watching and blessing all of us. You must be so proud."

Jamyang Rinpoche bowed to her. "Thank you very much. It is an honor to be in this forest. We thank you for your help." He bowed again.

"This is so wonderful. All of us out here, communing with nature and all. And it is just so wonderful that as a woman I was asked to be a part of this spiritual, ah, thing you're doing, even if women in your country are so repressed and have to wear veils and can't worship Jesus Christ."

"Jacquye?" Bryan Bofford, assistant to Hoffstader, came walking up from the company land rover that had just arrived. "I think you may be referring to Iran, not Tibet... or wherever they're from."

The lacquered blond looked startled. "Am I? Oh, my goodness. You know, I just can't get all those countries straight. They all look alike to me." She put her hand up to her mouth. "Oh, gee. I guess I shouldn't say things like that." She turned to Jamyang Rinpoche. "I am *so* sorry. I was just promoted last week and I have been *so* busy that I just can't think straight. You know how it is; so much to do and no time to do it!" Jacquye turned back to Bofford. "I am *so* sorry Mister Bofford. I am just *so* embarrassed. I'll fix it up all right and the press release will just knock your socks off."

Bofford brushed by Jacquye and went straight to Jamyang Rinpoche. "Mister Rinpoche, I am afraid I have bad news. Our attorneys informed me just a few minutes ago that this tree you want is right on the border of a parcel that the government leases to us and that the lease has just become the subject of a lawsuit. Accordingly, we are not allowed to cut any timber on this, or the adjoining parcel for, oh, at least several months until we get this all worked out." He got out a handkerchief and wiped his forehead. "I'm afraid that means we all have to go back to town now and think of some other solution for you." He pocketed the handkerchief and grinned at the Rinpoche. "We're all just terribly sorry. Isn't that right, Jacquye?"

"Oh, my, yes. We are *so* sorry, Mister Rinpoche." Jamyang Rinpoche looked at them a moment.

Ongdi, just in back of him, suddenly spoke up. "Rinpoche means 'Precious One' and is given to great teachers."

Jamyang Rinpoche waved him silent and spoke to Bofford. "Forgive him, he is young." He looked around, back at the tree. "When do you think this unfortunate problem will be settled?"

Bofford rubbed his jaw with intense concentration. "You know, Mister Rinpoche, we just don't know. The wheels of justice turn very slowly sometimes. It could be a few weeks or maybe a couple of years or more."

"I see." He looked back at his companions. "This is unfortunate. We shall have to decide what to do."

Bofford gathered them up and herded them towards the vehicles. "We are terribly sorry about this."

"Yes, we are so sorry."

"We'll get you back to town and then we can have a meeting soon. Our most profound apologies, Mister Rinpoche."

"We are just heartbroken. This was *so* spiritual." Jacquye dabbed at the corner of her right eye with a tissue, not ever quite touching her skin.

As the people moved toward their vehicles, Boyd Williams turned to his boss. "Are you shittin' me? We aren't going to cut? That mean we're laid off again?"

Bofford looked at the receding monks. "Don't get all steamed up, Boyd. We aren't laying anyone off. That lawsuit could be over real soon."

EIGHT

McNab crossed the Square feeling relaxed. Tall cumulus built up over the range of ridges to the east and reflected the dull copper of the unseen sun, which was covered by dark, forbidding clouds. They promised another onslaught of rain. The effect, tonight, was as if the sun were setting in the east, a most unsettling feeling.

Otto was pushing his shopping cart along the edge of the Square, green garbage bags hanging off both sides and the front. It seemed odd that new garbage bags could look sordid, but on Otto's cart they did. As always, Otto carried on a vociferous conversation with himself that few other humans could understand. A long-ago stroke and massive amounts of antipsychotics in the mental hospital had left him with tardive dyskinesia. In addition to his head palsy, his tongue would snake out from his gaping mouth every few seconds and barely wet the salt and pepper mustache and the beard on his lower lip. He barely wore an old bomber jacket with a faded red patch on the back. Looking out from under his stained Greek fisherman's cap, he appeared like some dark oracle, head shaking from side to side, tongue lashing his lips, guttural sounds emanating from his always open mouth. Tourists ran from him, but locals paid him little mind except to say hello and give him food or money every so often. Fear, loneliness, and need poured out of his eyes, and few could meet his gaze for long.

Otto saw McNab and started to steer the overburdened cart his way. McNab moved on and waved at him, not stopping. Ahead he saw his roommate, Pat, give some change to another of the street people, Henry Bouchard, back at his regular station after his adventures, and then head toward the wharf and Luego's bar and restaurant. McNab quickened his walk.

As he approached the gazebo Henry, just back from his mission with the monks, came up to him. "Repent! Repent! All is not lost! You can be saved!"

"Henry, give it a rest." McNab stopped as the ragged man shambled up to him. Henry grabbed onto the front of McNab's windbreaker.

"Ask not what your country can do for you, ask what you can do for your Henry." He held out his hand.

"You already nicked Pat."

"How'd you know?" He scratched his chin. "Yeah, Grif, but that was earlier." He wiped his nose on the sleeve of his moth-eaten army greatcoat. "I need a cuppa coffee. French roast." He looked around furtively. "Mingus said he'd let me in. If you came with me?" The last words were on a rising note, just edging into a whine.

McNab grimaced. "Not today, Henry," and started to walk on.

Henry reached out and grabbed his arm. "C'mon, Grif." McNab shook his arm loose and wheeled to face him.

"Henry, I've told you about touching people." Henry backed off a moment, hearing the chill in McNab's voice.

McNab started the turn to leave when Henry spoke up. "Nice jacket, Grif." He pointed to McNab's faded 49ers windbreaker. "Can I have it?"

"No, Henry. I like it." He started off again.

"But Grif, I need it." Henry pointed to his dissolving coat.

McNab stood for a moment. The jacket was at least eight years old and not wearing well anymore. He shrugged out of it. "Last time, Henry." He handed it to the wino.

"Yippee! I got a new jacket!" Henry danced around McNab, showing off the jacket. Henry stopped, swiftly took off his own tattered coat, and put on McNab's windbreaker. "How about some coffee, Grif? To celebrate?"

McNab put up a hand. "I'm tired Henry. The answer is no."

"I'll tell you a secret." He looked at McNab with a bright, sly look.

"Have fun with your secret, Henry." As he tried to move on, Henry grabbed him again.

"I got a secret. I got a secret." The ragged man was singing in a grotesque parody of a four-year-old, pulling on McNab's arm. McNab tried to pull his arm away. Henry held on tighter still. "I got a secret. I got a secret. You don't know it. You don't know it." Now he was circling the pilot, swinging on his arm like a maypole. "You want to know it. You want to know it. Wanta have some coffee. Wanta have some coffee." Henry's voice pitch was rising, and the circling was going faster. "I got a secret. I got—" McNab shrugged him off, and Henry suddenly collapsed on the ground holding his stomach and groaning. The pilot stood back while he continued to moan. "Why'd you hit me, Grif?" He gasped. "Why?" Henry clutched his stomach again and then yelled out to the other people in the square who had stopped to watch. "He hit me! Grif hurt me! Grif McNab hurt me!" Then he rolled over onto his back and started to keen.

Several people ran over. One older woman bent over Henry and tried to soothe him. Her companion, a young woman, possibly her daughter, wheeled on McNab while backing away from him. "You didn't have to hurt him. He's a sick, harmless old man. Why don't you pick on someone your own size?" She didn't wait for a reply but bent down next to her mother and tried to calm Henry down. The other spectators looked at him blankly.

McNab started to open his mouth and then thought better of it. He walked off a few paces, then stopped and turned back to watch the scene. The two women were trying to pull Henry, who was still howling, up off the pavement. Henry stopped his moaning and looked toward McNab. The two women turned, glaring at McNab. Henry looked straight at McNab, flashed a grin, and winked.

NINE

Luego's was a watering hole for a disparate clientele. Located on the wharf, two blocks down from the Square, it had started years ago as a breakfast place where local fishermen ate early breakfasts. Eventually, it evolved into a tourist dinner house with lousy food and high prices. The fact that not many tourists came to Euphrates didn't seem to bother the owners. Not surprisingly, it went bankrupt and was taken over by Mingus.

The decor was a mélange of tacky nets, glass balls, starched blowfish, fake distressed wood, and brass nautical stuff with a lot of green around the edges. Mingus had run out of money — what little money he had — at the faded blue velvet flocked wallpaper left over from the previous owner.

It became home to a bunch of gregarious loners who drank coffee, sucked on beer bottles, and ate Mingus' cooking, which was surprisingly good. The fishermen came back to eat breakfast. Bookstore clerks, clothiers, lawyers, street people, accountants, and the odd pilot came to eat, drink, and schmooze. The decor was weird, the food pretty strange, the coffee great.

"Ah, the spiritual descendant of the great Lindbergh,

gracing us with his presence. What's this? Where is your formal 49ers jacket? Are we dining informally today? Do you mean to flaunt the dress code?" Mingus was an inch shorter than average, but his energy made him seem bigger. Thick black curly hair over what could only be called a Neanderthal brow, bright black eyes, a mouth that was oddly sensitive, and a chest of steel wool bulging out of a denim shirt a half size too small, he was repellent and attractive at the same time, a trait he knew and cultivated. No matter how sarcastic and caustic he got, no one deserted Luego's. Everyone had to have their daily ration of abuse from Mingus, kind of like vitamins.

"I've already had mine today, Mingus." McNab walked past him and found the booth where Pat was sitting, looking out over the harbor through the large windows. He sat down and looked for the waitress.

McNab signaled to Myrna. He looked at Pat and assessed her as already pretty far gone. Myrna, Mingus' most stable waitress, came over and put a shot of Aquavit and a Carlsberg beer in front of McNab.

"It's what Pat's having." Myrna could only be described as anorexic, bordering on cadaverous. She almost always wore black leotards which hung on her. Long black stringy hair, fish-belly white skin, and black nail polish completed her usual ensemble. Mingus, in a strangely Puritanical move, drew the line at piercing, or the thirty or so holes in her ears and nose would have sparkled. Myrna did, however, watch out for her regulars.

McNab put a quarter in the jukebox selector bolted to the wall. Jimmy Smith's 'The Sermon' came on softly.

"Goddamn women." Pat picked up the shot glass, and in one swift move, the clear liquid was down the throat. "Myrna!" Hand circled in the air. Almost immediately, another shot and another beer appeared.

McNab picked up the beer. Pat's sleeve intervened.

"My turn." Pat lifted the glass, "Goddamn women. Who needs 'em?"

"You already said that." McNab waved at Myrna again.

"Ya give the bitches everything and then they dump you!" Pat upended the glass.

"Right." More booze came.

"Fuckin' Tanya." Pat poured down another. "I really loved her."

"I know." McNab waved off the next round. "You were together a long time. I kind of liked her."

"I did, too." Pat started to cry. "Why'd she have to dump me?" McNab handed over a napkin. "Shit. Crying in public, too. Goddamn her."

They were in a back booth and shielded somewhat from the crowd. McNab looked across at his friend. Her long blond hair was coming loose from the barrette and hanging down close to her face. She was in a thirties period. Today she wore a suede ensemble, stone blue with a lace effect at the throat and sleeves, and a navy vest underneath. Pat reached into her purse and pulled out some Kleenex. "Nice timing, McNab. Haven't seen you in a couple of days, and you have to come just when Tanya runs out. Shit." Pat blew her nose. "Just what you needed, a crying woman on your hands." Pat dabbed at her eyes.

"You've pulled me through a few, too, if you recall. Remember Lureen?"

"Oh, Christ! You didn't—"

"No. I promised you I wouldn't call her, and I haven't." Grif hesitated a moment. "She did leave a message a couple of days ago, though."

"You asshole. You didn't tell me!" She pushed back her hair. Her high cheekbones, long nose, and wide mouth set off her hazel eyes. Pat had been pursued for modeling jobs. She was happy practicing law. "Well?"

"I was busy, you know, and—"

"Bullshit. You were going to call her, weren't you? Just waiting for the 'right time,' right?" She took another swig of her beer. "You think I don't know you."

"Well ... "

"Well, what, Mister Sleaze? Remember what I told you?"

"No."

"That's a load of crap. I told you, that if there was a choice between calling Lureen and shooting yourself, you should shoot yourself. Remember? Hmmm?" She leaned over the table, putting her face almost into his.

McNab pulled his hand down over his face. "Yeah, I remember."

"Well?"

"Okay, I won't call her."

"Ha!" She took another drink. "Look at me! You told me this would happen to me. It didn't matter that you liked her. You knew she'd dump me. But would I listen? Nooo." Pat looked over toward the bar. "Shit."

McNab followed her look. Curly was sitting at the bar.

Pat turned back to him. "Great. Curly. Hope he doesn't see me like this."

"You know him?"

"Sort of. Seems like a nice guy." She looked out at Curly. "How do you know him?"

"I see him around."

"What's that supposed to mean?"

McNab shrugged. "I see him around."

"Oh. That." She pushed back against the table to sit upright. "Doesn't it drive you crazy to be so compartmentalized? I mean, what if you ever had a real sweetie? Could you tell her about all that shit from the past? Could you? I mean, could you even admit you had a past?"

McNab waved a circle at Myrna and got a nod in reply.

"How do you think that would make her feel? Not being able to know all of you?"

The next round arrived. "I guess if she loved me she'd understand. That the past was part of me, too."

"Grif, are you going to let that stuff run you all the rest of your life?"

"Got no choice, Pat. It was part of the deal." He threw down the shot. "Besides, it doesn't affect the personal side of me."

Pat snorted in derision. "Ha! Do they know about me? Your live-in lesbian girl friend?" She laughed.

"You're drunk. Next subject."

"Ooooh, classified shit happenin' here." She giggled and started to sing softly, "Secret agent man, secret agent man, given you a number, take away your name ..."

"Cut the crap, Pat." He put his glass down on the table. "Maybe we should talk tomorrow."

Pat started singing again. "Tomorrow, tomorrow, I love you, tomorrow, you're only a day away..."

"You're dating yourself."

"Look who's talking." Pat pushed hair out of her eyes. "Where's Myrna?"

"Let's go home."

"You go home. Spoil sport. Crap head. Wet blanket. Party pooper. You know what, Grif McNab? You're no fun. That's right. You're no fun."

"This is fun?"

Pat opened her mouth with a comeback, then stopped. "No. It's not very much fun." She stopped and closed her eyes. Then she opened them blearily. "You're right. Let's go home."

TEN

McNab looked down at the manual, then back up to the LCD screen in front of him. He reached up to the brand-new Global Positioning Satellite receiver and punched a series of numbers on the pad next to the screen. The screen blinked back at him, the icon that meant "Coordinates entered." He let out a sigh of satisfaction. He flipped through the pages until he came to the next entry. He ran his finger down the page until he found the set he needed. He raised his hand toward the panel when he heard the footsteps turn the corner into the hangar. He peered over the aircraft's glare shield into the sun and saw the silhouettes of two men approaching the plane. He couldn't tell who they were.

"Grif? Need to talk with you a minute." The lead man's identity became clear through his voice.

McNab climbed down out of the cockpit, turning off the master switch. "Hi, Herman. What's up?"

The sandy-haired skinny deputy came up to him. "You met Aaron, yet?" McNab shook his head. "Aaron Grogan, Grif McNab. Aaron's just come on board. Used to be LAPD."

McNab stuck out his hand. "Glad to meet you." Grogan,

a heavyset man, but compact, with thinning dark brown hair, looked non-plussed, finally taking the pilot's hand.

"Aaron's getting used to small towns."

"Yeah, takes a while." The new deputy seemed out of his element.

Herman turned back to the pilot. "Got a couple of minutes?"

McNab looked at both the deputies for a brief moment. "Sure, come in the office. Got some coffee brewing." They moved from the hangar into the small closet that McNab referred to so grandly. The pilot squeezed himself behind the tiny desk. Herman sat down in the chair that didn't have the pile of manuals on it. Grogan tried to take his cue from his partner but, not getting one, hesitated. McNab saw the game being played and motioned for the deputy to put the books on the desk. Grogan did so and moved his chair over to get some room, effectively blocking McNab behind the desk. Finally, they were sitting down.

"You guys want some coffee?" McNab pointed at the pot sitting on top of the file cabinet next to the desk.

"No, thanks, Grif." Herman took his hat off and looked at McNab. Grogan did the same. Herman looked uncomfortable.

After several moments of silence, McNab asked, "What's up?"

Grogan leaned over the desk. "Where were you last night around midnight?"

McNab looked at Herman. "Is he serious, Herman?"

Herman turned to the new deputy. "Let me handle it this time."

"That isn't the way we do it in L.A. You got to—"

"Aaron. We aren't in L.A."

"He a friend of yours or something?"

"Yeah, or something. Cool it." He turned back. McNab noticed that the new deputy was not taking this very well and was certainly getting no fonder of McNab. "You had any trouble with Henry Bouchard lately?"

The pilot rocked the chair on its two rear legs, leaning the back up against the wall. "Did those women make a complaint?" McNab was incredulous. He brought the chair down on all four legs and leaned across the table. "Herman, is the sheriff sending two deputies out here to question me about Henry's antics? Did Henry make the complaint or was it the two women?"

Grogan shot back, "So, you admit you had an argument with him. And roughed him up? Just how mad were you?"

McNab kept his gaze on Herman. "Where did you find this guy? I thought LAPD were pretty thorough in their screening, or did he slip through and they had to get rid of him?"

"Watch it, asshole! If you think you—"

"Hold it! Both of you." Herman raised his hand. "Grif, Henry was found dead this morning."

McNab couldn't respond for a moment. "What? Henry? Dead?" He looked out the door for a moment. "Damn. How'd he die?"

Grogan said, "He was found dead along with one," he looked down at his notebook, "Lawrence Billingham the Third."

"Who?"

"Larry the Pervert. It looks like Henry and Larry got into a knife fight in the alley behind Luego's," said Herman

Grogan continued. "There was a complaint that someone had beaten Henry up on the Square earlier yesterday. The description and the use of your name narrowed it down pretty good."

"You know Henry. We all put up with his little scams and if he remembers to take his medicine he's okay. But when he doesn't he gets out of control and scares people who don't know him. We talked about it and he agreed not to touch people. Well, yesterday he went over the top while he was grabbing me and I tapped him in the chest. You know Henry, he's the world's best victim. He went into one of his better acts. You know what he does around people he thinks he can scam."

"Ever handle a knife, McNab? Maybe he got on your nerves once too often? Thought you might straighten him out permanently? Take out a witness, too?" Grogan waded in again.

"Cut it out." Herman raised his voice, then turned back to McNab, who glared at the new deputy. "For the record, Grif, where were you last night?"

"At home. Alone. Watching X-Files reruns."

"Oh, right." Grogan sneered. "Come on, Herman, this guy stinks."

Herman ignored him. "Which one?"

"'Dwayne Barry.' Came on at eleven."

Grogan came back in. "How do we know he was watching T.V.?"

"Because I watched the same show," said Herman. Grogan started to open his mouth. "Before you say anything more, that wasn't the show that was listed in the T.V. guide."

McNab asked, "Does Pat know? She was very fond of him."

"Not yet. We're still looking for next of kin."

"I doubt there would be any. Pat may know. She talked to him more than anyone."

Herman pulled out his pad. "Right. We were going get a hold of her later today if we didn't find anyone else to call. Do you want us to tell Pat?"

"I'll tell her. Better me than Bozo here."

"Just watch it, McNab."

"Threats, deputy?"

"All right, both of you, just stop it. Come on, Grogan, let's go." They got up and were moving out of the small space.

Grogan glared at McNab and left first. Herman went to the door, called out to him that he would be right there, and came back to the pilot. "Jesus, Grif, you're not making my job any easier. I know he's a pain in the butt, but I've got to work with the SOB. He's still Department. Okay?"

"Okay, Herman. You're right. I shouldn't have let the little prick get under my skin."

"You still want to come over for barbecue tomorrow?"

"Sure."

"I'll tell Carol. She'll be happy to see you. By the way, how are the charters coming?"

McNab sighed. "Still way slow. Got a couple of fishing trips lined up. Farley Luscombe's one. A Fish and Game supply run. If it doesn't pick up pretty soon I don't know how I'll pay for that engine. How is Carol's store going?" Herman's wife owned a used baby clothes shop.

Herman put his hand out, palm down, and wiggled it side to side. "It's going, sort of. I'd better get in gear. See you tomorrow."

ELEVEN

McNab pulled off the narrow winding road into a driveway that ended abruptly thirty feet in at a metal gate. After pulling his truck through and locking the gate behind him, McNab drove slowly up the dirt lane. He noticed that the ruts from the tires were getting deeper, and the grass in the center was brushing the underside of his vehicle. Time to grade it again, especially before the rains. Fir, redwood, and alder trees half-covered the road with their canopies. On his left was a small ravine in which the creek ran. Sometimes he just stopped along here, turned off his truck, and listened, but not tonight. Rhododendron bushes lined the drive as it curved. Pat had bought it from Jedidiah Hansen, a retired nurseryman who had used it as a growing place for his more exotic varieties.

Some of the branches were insinuating themselves into the truck's path. Time to get Sheldon out here. McNab didn't know a thing about pruning or much about gardening at all, but at least he knew he didn't know.

As the drive curved left, he glimpsed the pond off to the right. He had worked hard to sculpt that just right and to make sure the flow in from the rest of the land and the flow out to the creek was enough to keep the koi alive. Now, if he could just find a way to keep the raccoons from eating his fish, he would be happy. Each time he came home, he loved the transition from the fairyland entry road into the large open clearing. The house, even though a two-story Victorian, was dwarfed by the redwoods and fir surrounding it. Still today, the sight made him catch his breath.

Pat's car was parked by the shop building. McNab pulled his into the slot beside it. Every so often, he wouldn't use the back door as he usually did but would walk up the front stairs to the heavy carved door with its beveled glass. Jedidiah had told him of finding all his treasures, including this door. That had come to him when a fire had destroyed the Carlsen mansion in the forties, and they were just trying to clear the site to build another, grander house. The door had been rescued off the scrap pile by one of the workers and sold to Jed for the price of a case of half-decent bourbon.

He opened the heavy door and walked into the entryway and a different world. Although Pat loved rustic houses, she wanted to move into a more modern age. She kept the hardwood floors and sprinkled them with richly patterned rugs from India and Persia, mostly from her grandmother's parlor. What she did love was fine wood furniture. Pat could only afford a few good things, so the place was a combination of almost museum-quality pieces mixed with some he himself had picked up at yard sales. One of his girlfriends had compared it unfavorably to a Salvation Army showroom. It had been their last date.

"It's me," McNab called up the staircase. An unintelligible acknowledgment came down from above, but he was already on his way to the kitchen. Snack time. He dumped his flight bag on the chair nearest the kitchen door and walked over the starkly modern linoleum floor to the refrigerator. He peered inside and poked through the dense forest of plastic bags. Ha! He withdrew the bag with the slices of leftover pizza from last Monday. He knew it would be better if he used the oven in the

Wolf range, but he was in a hurry. The microwave would do. While it whirred, he went back to the refrigerator for a drink. He flipped on the small boom box over the sink. The local non-profit station was playing their international music hour, this time featuring music from the Middle East. A couple of minutes later, he was sitting at a table of undetermined wood he had bought at a yard sale in Grigsby, on a paint-stained chair he had picked up in Morgan's Creek. Reheated pepperoni, sausage, and broccoli pizza and a Reed's ginger brew. Heaven.

"You had a call from Darcy at the airport. Some sort of charter request." Darcy managed the airport part-time as one of the duties of her county job. Pat walked in carrying a mug and crossed over to the coffee pot on the counter. She poured some and came and sat down at the table. Holding the mug with both hands circling it, she commented, "Cold today." She brushed her long blond hair out of her eyes. "She called three times today." She brought the cup up, took a sip, and held it close to her chest. Pulling her feet up on the chair, she tucked them inside her quilted robe.

McNab waved at his mouth and chewed for a moment. "I'll call her. I haven't talked with her for a while." He took a swig of his ginger ale. "Three times? That's more than she's called in the last six months. Maybe business is picking up." McNab shrugged. "Who knows?" He took another bite of pizza.

"Tanya might come by tonight." Pat held her mug in her lap and looked out the window at the lawn where it met the forest.

"Not done yet?"

Pat sighed and took a sip. "I guess not. Christ, I wish I were done. It gets really depressing."

"Yeah, I know." McNab thought a moment. "You should really..." He dried up. "Never mind. None of my business."

"What? Come on, McNab, spill it."

He wiped his mouth with the piece of the paper towel he had ripped off the roll on the way to the table. "I was just going to give you some advice. Then I remembered how well I took advice when you gave it to me." They both laughed. McNab stopped laughing. "Uh, I bagged a trip with ML tomorrow and...," he paused. "Uh, Pat..."

"What?" She looked over at him, alerted by his change of tone.

"Herman and his new partner came by to see me today."

She waited a moment, then moved her hands in a pulling motion. "Yeah?"

McNab looked up at the ceiling, then back at Pat. "They told me Henry got killed last night."

Pat froze for a moment. "What?"

"Henry got killed last night in a knife fight. Evidently he and Larry the Pervert got into it and they killed each other."

"No!" The sound was a wail. She staggered. McNab started toward her. Pat regained her balance and held out her hand to stop him. Quickly she left the room.

Bewildered, McNab followed her into the living room. She sat stoically on the couch, streaks of tears running down her cheeks. She wiped them away and started talking, not looking at him.

"He was a peaceful man, Grif. He wouldn't have gotten into a knife fight." Pat wiped more tears away. "He was a loon, but he wasn't violent."

McNab sat beside her on the couch. "He was acting pretty strange yesterday. He was grabbing on to me, even though I had talked to him about that. He was kind of manic. You know, he could have..."

"No! He couldn't have." Pat's fists tightened around the tissues she was holding. "He would not have gotten involved in a fight. He would have run away. Henry was pretty fast."

McNab shrugged. "Pat..."

"No, Grif. I knew Henry. Better than anyone else. It's impossible."

"Why?"

"It's how he got to where he is."

"What do you mean?"

She pursed her lips. "I can't... Christ, he's dead now, what difference can it make?" Pat looked at Grif. "You ready for this?"

"You want something to drink?"

Pat sat back. "No. Maybe coffee later." She exhaled deeply.

"Did you know that Morrissey was my married name?"

"What?" McNab was stunned. "No. You never told me you had been married."

"I don't tell that. To anyone. My birth name is Bouchard."

McNab sat back heavily. "Jesus Christ."

"Well, not Jesus Christ, but, well, I'm out of flip comments right now. Yes, Henry is, was, my brother. He didn't want anyone to know. I couldn't tell anyone I'd been married because then I'd have to tell my maiden name somewhere and, you know. Besides, everyone here only knows me as a lesbian, so there was no real hiding to be done."

"Why didn't he want anyone to know?"

"That's the question, isn't it?" She took a deep breath. "About fifteen years ago, Henry was a lawyer, in love with the law. He badgered me to be one, too. So I did. He was working in Los Angeles in a small firm that did a lot of personal injury. He was very good at what he did. Worked hard, a perfection- ist. Too much of one. His partners were always piling more work on him, stretching him thin. Well, one day, he took on one case too many. He got sloppy on it." Pat took a sip. "It was a boy who had been paralyzed in a fight outside a nightclub with a sitcom star. Usual story, a coked-up star throwing his weight around, an ordinary guy in the wrong place at the wrong time. The star was shoving and slugging everyone around, and Nathan, the kid, got hit and bounced off the curb on his neck.

"Now the kid was back living with mom, who had a shit job that barely gave her enough to eat, and now she had him, too. Medicaid said he was stable and sent him home, even though the doctors said he could recover some function with intensive rehab. There is no money for rehab if you don't have insurance, and not much even if you do. The kid was suicidal. The mother was cracking up under the pressure.

"The star's agent got the best law firm in the city, and they were fighting the whole thing, trying to make it look like the kid's fault. They wanted to do damage control, save his career. Anyway, Henry really cared about this kid and wanted to do right by him. The star was doing a beautiful P.R. job, contrite about the 'scuffle' and 'concerned' about Nathan, but denied having done anything wrong.

"As trial approached the witnesses suddenly got memory loss. There was one piece of hard evidence, though, a piece of videotape from an apartment security camera that showed enough to do the guy in. Henry took the tape home one night to review it. He shouldn't have done it. He was so tired, he accidentally left it at home. Then he went on a two day deposition trip. Guess what? An unsolved burglary, with the one of the missing items being the tape."

"What happened?"

"He lost. The boy got one of his friends to smuggle him some pills, and he committed suicide. The mother went over the edge and committed suicide, too. The star won an Emmy and became the spokesman for 'Entertainers Against Violence.' Henry started to drink." Pat reached for a Kleenex. She stopped a sob with a visible effort. In a moment, she took a deep breath and looked out the window. "Within six months Henry got fired. He wouldn't try therapy or A.A. A few months later he was on the street. About a year after that he showed up here, crazy." She turned to McNab. "I need some coffee, now."

McNab got up and went to the kitchen to make coffee. Pat followed him in and leaned against the doorway. "It really shook me up. He was so far around the bend I knew he'd never get back. That didn't stop me from trying, though. I hooked him up with Social Services, tried to get him in the mental health system, got him a place to live. But it was no use. He couldn't forgive himself. He drove himself to suffering. That's what I meant about him not getting involved in a fight. It wasn't that he hated fighting because of the case, it was because he knew he had to suffer, to atone. That was the only way he could figure out to do it."

She accepted the mug that McNab offered her. "He trashed the apartment I found him and was on the street in a matter of days. When he was lucid, which wasn't very often, he would beg me not to tell anyone we were related. He was concerned that some bad thing would happen to me because of him. Shit, I didn't care. But he did, and finally I knew that keeping my name out of it was the only thing I could do for him that meant anything to him." She sipped from the mug. "Good coffee, McNab."

Pat led them back to the living room. "I don't care what the sheriff said. Henry wouldn't have gotten in a knife fight. He could have died and that would have ended his penance. He could never have allowed that to happen."

"I don't get it. Henry, as I've known him for the last ten years was a kind of goofy, wacked out guy. These are pretty sophisticated ideas for, for a…"

"For a wacked out wino?"

McNab, embarrassed, just nodded.

"It's those sophisticated ideas that sent him around the bend. What he had done was unforgivable to him. He was unfit for society. He looked for the God he deserted years earlier and didn't find Him. Since there couldn't be a God who could let such things happen, Henry had to take His place. And punish Henry. Forever." She took another deep breath. "Sometimes he would rant at me about these things and nothing I said would make any difference. There was no way out for him. Not even death."

They stood next to the bay window overlooking the front meadow. "At least it's over for him, now. I'm almost grateful to whoever killed him." She took another sip. "That's not true. He's dead, he's out of his pain, but I don't have a brother. There's something else going on, Grif."

"You mean, why would anyone go out of their way to murder a crazy street bum?"

"Yeah. Why?" They were silent for a while.

Pat set her mug down on the lamp table and turned to McNab. "How long have we known each other, Grif?"

"A long time."

"I've never imposed on you, have I, Grif?"

"Nope."

"Well, I'm about to." Pat looked away from him, then bent down and picked up the two cups. "I need a favor."

"What is it?"

"I think you know." McNab made no response. She put the cups down again. "You once told me that when you were in the Air Force you spent time in some investigative unit or something like that? You were always pretty evasive about it."

"Yes, something like that."

"I need to know why Henry died."

TWELVE

Pat got off the phone with the police. She sat down in her grandmother's leather armchair, looking out over the front lawn. She couldn't seem to face McNab. "There's one other thing." She paused. "I'm supposed to identify him. I don't think I can do it alone."

"When do you want to go?"

"Oh, soon, I guess."

"Are you sure? I could do it for you."

Pat sighed. "No. Legally it has to be me. Besides, I owe it to him."

McNab didn't know quite what to say. "It won't be pretty or easy."

"What is, these days?"

Their drive was silent. The morgue was a shared room of Heavenly Pines Mortuary, down in the basement. On the outside it was like a somber Swiss chalet, but no Hansel and Gretel here. The amenities of city morgues were absent. The viewing room was little more than a curtained-off portion of the larger space. Aluminum-legged chairs with black molded plastic seats and institutional green tile made for slight comfort. The scent of industrial-strength antiseptic hung in the air.

It took only a momentary flip of the sheet for Pat to nod and turn away. Henry's face was almost unrecognizable from the lacerations. McNab put his arm around Pat and guided her out to the hall, where live people walked. A few minutes later, the orderly brought them a package wrapped in brown paper and tied with string. "His belongings," he intoned softly as he gave them to Pat. It was then that Pat started crying for real, and McNab felt as helpless as he had ever felt. Taking the package and putting it under his arm, McNab walked Pat through the mortuary and up to the parking lot. Neither noticed the drizzle as they walked to his car and drove away.

THIRTEEN

"Did Darcy get hold of you?" Bill James, one of the P.R. men at Mountain Lumber, fidgeted by the side of the plane.

"Yeah. Tell me about this Bryan Bofford character. One of yours?"

"No. He's something to do with Hoffstader. Did you find out what he wanted?"

"No. He wasn't there." McNab wiped off the dipstick, screwed it down, and closed the flap on the cowl. "Where to, today?"

"Two Forks. Got a couple of outside P.R. types who want to see 'real' redwood country." He laughed but didn't seem to be enjoying himself. "Hoffstader's really got his tit in a wringer on this one. He's trying to reclaim the Two Forks clear-cut. But it isn't working. They took too much and waited too long to fix it." Bill James shook his head. "These frickin' guys. They'll fly in, fly out, then go back to their little cubicles in the glass towers and write loads of bullshit about how wonderful ML is in conserving the forests. Shit." James had a wife and three daughters in high school.

"Should I fly them over the Big Rock clear cut?"

"Jesus, no. We take them over only green shit. You know that."

"You a little nervous today?" McNab finished his walk around and stood by the open passenger door of the plane.

James pulled at his face. "Ah, Maggie's at the clinic having some tests done. She hasn't been up to par for a couple of months. She'll be okay." The creak of the hangar door announced the arrival of Jonathan North and Brett Sandler, assistant V.P.s of Corporate Relations for Mountain Lumber, headquartered in New York.

North, the taller and slimmer of the two, with sandy hair with high widow's peaks, was decked out in a complete Eddie Bauer outfit, so new that the fold marks were still in the wool shirt and khaki pants. Brett was short and dumpy, with black hair and acne scars. He was stiff in his new wide-wale corduroys and Timberline boots, the plastic loop that once held the price tag still dangling.

"Jonathan! Brett! Glad you made it!" James' eager smile made McNab wince. "Meet Grif McNab, best pilot in the country. Grif, this is Jonathan and Brett." They shook hands all around. The two P.R. men looked at the ratty plane and then at each other. North was opening his mouth to say something when McNab moved to the passenger door of the Skywagon.

"Just a step up and into the back, gentlemen. Be sure to strap yourselves in good and tight. There are headsets for you. That will enable you to talk while we're in flight. There might be some turbulence going over the mountains. Bill will take good care of you." James got into the front passenger seat.

Shortly the plane pulled them into the air arcing over the small field, and headed for the Alps and the camp at Two Forks. James worked the intercom and adjusted his David Clark headset. McNab could hear him giving them the pitch as they climbed to eighty-five hundred feet.

"Boys, this is the biggest restoration project ML has going.

We take our responsibilities to the community and country very seriously, as you'll see. No one is doing more than ML to conserve the environment for our children and their children."

"Yeah, Bill," Jonathan North said, "we got the scoop from Bofford. Hoffstader's going to be the darling of the environmental movement by the time we get done."

"That's right." Brett pitched in. "We'll do a number on Two Forks that's so good that no one will even think of Big Rock. James' face dropped. McNab didn't crack a smile. "Are we going over Big Rock?"

"Well, actually..."

"Let's do that. If we have to do a counterattack, we should see what the fuss is about." McNab looked over at James, who just shrugged. The plane turned northeast.

Twenty minutes later by plane, which would have been over three hours by four-wheel drive, they passed over the Big Rock clear-cut. It was as if a giant electric razor had buzzed down the slopes of Big Rock canyon. The tree line was straight up the hillsides to the crest of the ridge on both sides of the creek in an almost perfect rectangular swath. A towering pile of 'slash' was burning down near the stream itself, the smoke plume rising above the airplane and blowing southeast. Downstream of the cut, the creek water had turned brownish red and continued its discoloration for several miles. Stumps, leftover branches, and underbrush littered the moonscape. Logging roads cut the slopes at odd angles. Some heavy equipment still stood near the top, ready to move out.

"There's a storm system supposed to move in late tomorrow night." Bill looked at McNab.

"What's that mean?" Jonathan looked down at the red water in the crevice of the hills.

"We could have a lot of runoff and landslides. Maybe block the creek, maybe just send a lot of dirt down it. Could impact Nero."

"What's that?" Brett chimed in.

"Little town down the valley about ten, twelve miles. About a hundred and fifty people. Used to be a mill town, but now a fishing resort. Not many fish left, though."

"Any press around there?" Jonathan looked over at James.

"No. Too far in. They'd only come if the whole town was wiped out."

"Fuck 'em. Let's get to Two Forks." James shrugged, and McNab turned the aircraft to the new course.

Another fifteen minutes got them above the valley of Two Forks, where the restoration project was in progress.

Bill started into his spiel. "You can see from here the extent of the commitment ML is making to the environment—"

"Thanks, we know." Jonathan cut him off. "Hoffstader is spending three million bucks to keep the mud from going into the Two Forks National Recreation Area and pissing off the half million tourists a year that swim in the river and who vote for Congressmen who vote for timber leasing and subsidies. Let's get on the ground and see how we can make this pig of a project irresistible and patriotic."

McNab dropped the big single onto the tiny newly graded airstrip. As he taxied over to the wide space where the muddy Bronco driven by Bruce Snade was parked, he popped open the side window. Down in the valley, it was hot and still. Snade, the project manager, was all teeth and rustic bonhomie as he led the group to the ML vehicle.

McNab opened all the doors and windows. He walked over to the project shack with the Two Forks name stenciled on it. A large cooler rested in the shade of a redwood. McNab popped open a soda, sat down, and pulled out his mystery novel. It could be hours before they came back. Ah, the glamorous life of a charter pilot, he thought, as sweat started to roll down his neck. He tried not to think about Henry.

Fourteen

McNab sat at the kitchen table with the bundle in front of him. He was glad Pat was at her friend Elizabeth's. Several of Pat's circle of women friends were gathering there for her support. He hesitated a moment and then cut the twine that held the brown Kraft paper that encompassed the entire estate of Henry Bouchard, failed lawyer, confirmed eccentric, dedicated drunk, and brother of McNab's best friend. There was a slight rustle as the paper opened and sat like a dingy lotus blossom with the detritus of Henry's life at its center.

He separated the clothes from the rest. Henry's pants smelled. The shirt must have been too bloody to save. For some reason, there wasn't much blood on the 49ers windbreaker that McNab had given him a few days previous. There was eighty-six cents in change, two quarters, two dimes, two nickels, and six pennies, a wallet that looked like it had been issued in the trenches of World War I, a cheap knockoff of a Swiss Army knife, two buttons, one red and one white. McNab opened the wallet. Sixteen dollars, a five and eleven ones, a driver's license that had expired twelve years previously, the stub from his last welfare check of two hundred and forty dollars for the month. A three-by-five index card with several phone numbers, including Pat's. The rest were from social service agencies or churches known to give out free meals or shelter. Other than a few wadded-up pieces of paper, there wasn't much else to sum up Henry Bouchard.

What was he supposed to do with this, he thought? Although he didn't particularly want to do it, he started to unfold the scraps of paper. The first was a religious tract that zealots handed out to street people. The chief message seemed one of forgiveness for the sin of being poor. There were a few scribbles in pencil on the back, but McNab couldn't figure them out. He set that one aside. Maybe Pat could enlighten him on their meaning. The next several were receipts from various liquor and grocery stores with a numbing sameness, down to the same brand of cheap wine and the price.

The next to last one was a return receipt for registered mail. The green card was folded and wadded, but it revealed that Henry had sent a registered letter to Hoffstader. The receipt showed that it had been signed for by someone whose name McNab couldn't read. Why would Henry send Hoffs-tader a registered letter? He put it aside. The last one was a photocopy of a newspaper photograph. The picture showed Hoffstader standing with the Chinese premier in what was obviously Beijing. A group of Chinese men was in the back-ground, a step or two behind Hoffstader and the premier. One face in the group had been circled in blue ballpoint. McNab looked at the caption. It merely identified Hoffstader and the premier and said that a large forest products deal had been signed between Mountain Lumber and the People's Republic. McNab vaguely remembered hearing about that a year or two ago. He looked closer. The man who was circled seemed to have on some sort of uniform, but he couldn't tell if it was military or not. He turned the piece of paper over. Nothing on the other side. He turned back. The name of the paper was cut off in the copy process.

McNab put the wallet, religious tract, the return receipt, and the picture aside and then retied the bundle. Pat would be home soon. He went to the refrigerator and got himself a cold soda water. What was Henry's obsession with Hoffstader about? As if anyone could figure out what was going on in Henry's mind at any one time. McNab finished the drink and put the plastic bottle in the recycling bin. He didn't want Pat to become unglued over recycling again. He went to his car.

FIFTEEN

Boyd Williams got out of the company truck along with five other men. The crew boss was already there. The boss motioned them over to the tree that the monks had selected.

"All right. I guess you know what's happening. The lawsuit has been settled. Just this morning. We've got three days to get this parcel cut. Any questions?"

Boyd thought a moment and then asked. "We doing anything special with the tree for the monks?"

"Did I say we were doing anything special?"

Boyd shook his head. "No. Just asking."

"Did you hear me say that the monks were getting the tree?"

"Nope."

"You're paid to cut, not ask. Understood?" He looked at the men. "Anyone not understand? Good. Everything gets cut. Just like always. Let's get moving."

Sixteen

McNab was walking through the Square on his way to Luego's. Two of the local street people were sitting on the lip of the fountain with a brown paper bag between them. As he passed close to them, he overheard one of them say, "Henry was great! A generous man. He gave away a whole peach pie!"

McNab stopped. He didn't want to approach the men directly. Looking around, he saw a bench within earshot of them.

"Peach pie. Yessir. A whole peach pie." The older one with the sailor cap went on, "What a waste. I mean, the fucking guy is worth billions and someone gives him a peach pie. Just ain't right."

"What the hell you talkin' about, Shorty?"

"Old man Hoffstader got hisself a peach pie. Hee hee, sho 'nuff. A whole peach pie, Marvin."

"You drunk this early in the mornin'?"

"Not me, no, sir. No way. Sure wished I could've seen it."

"Seen what?"

"The peach pie, you sumbitch! Didn't you hear me?"

"You done flipped, that's what."

"You ain't seen it, that's what."

"What?"

"I done told you, the peach pie."

"I ain't staying around to listen to this shit. I'm going back to the mission."

"You miss a good story."

"Stop that! Make some sense! What is this peach pie?"

"A couple of days ago, Hoffstader was coming out of his office and Mister Bouchard, Henry to you, was standing right there waiting for him. He just wanted Hoffstader to understand what was happening now that the timber is almost all gone. But Hoffstader, he didn't want to listen. So ol' Henry reached into his sack and pulled out a peach pie. A whole one. Then he made a gift of it to Mister Hoffstader. Instead of just handing it to him, though, he slapped it down on top of his head! Hee hee! Old man Hoffstader just standin' there, peaches dripping down off the top of his head, that old pie pan balanced on that pointy top, sun reflecting off the tin, peaches and juice just runnin' down his face and onto his three thousand dollar suit. Sure wish I hadda been there. Hee hee."

"You're not serious."

"Serious as a heart attack, man. Jody told me. He heard it from Clyde, who heard it from a guy who saw it. Shit, it was in the paper, too. A little bitty article. Sure wish I coulda been there. Woulda done me good."

"Whatta ya know. Old Henry did somethin'. Good for him!"

"Yeah. Old Clyde, he tells me that Hoffstader was mad. Just steamin'. He looked at old Henry and if looks could kill ... whoooey! Probably could've cooked the whole damn pie all over again, the way he was boilin'. Wish it'd teach him a lesson. But it won't. Those folks, they never learn nothin'. All they do is go git some more. Like that's all there is. Never learn."

The two old men sat there for a while, savoring Henry's Last Stand. "He'd've gotten at least ninety days, don't you think? Probably more, since it's Hoffstader. Would have got him out of the cold for a while. Three hots and cot. Sounds good to me. Ol' Henry. God bless him. I'd like to do somethin' like that before I check out. Think old Hoffstader wants any more pie?"

They fell on each other, punching each other's arms and slapping each other on the back, howling at the sky, glad to be alive.

McNab waited a minute, then got up and went over to them. "Hi, guys. What's happening?"

The men looked at him suspiciously. Marvin muttered, without hope, "Spare any change?"

McNab got a couple of dollars out of his pocket. Marvin suddenly brightened. "I'm a, I was a friend of Henry's. I'm trying to find out where he was the last couple of days before he died."

Marvin reached for the bills. McNab kept them just out of reach. Marvin put his arm down. "Why you want to do that?"

McNab shrugged. "He was a friend."

"You? You was a friend of Henry's? Now I've heard everything."

McNab pulled out a few more bills. "Any information about Henry in the last few days."

Marvin looked at Shorty. "Well, I didn't see him, myself, but I know that Larry was looking for him. Guess he found him."

"How do you know Larry was looking for him?"

"He axed me. That's how."

"Did he seem mad?"

Marvin thought for a minute. "No, as a matter of fact, he didn't. He looked happy. Said he wanted to take Henry to a party." Shorty started to laugh. Then Marvin joined in. "Like

Larry could get invited to a party!" They started laughing again.

"How long ago was this?"

Marvin finally calmed down enough to answer. "Day they found them in the alley." McNab gave them the money.

SEVENTEEN

"How's it going, Herman?" McNab sat down in front of the deputy.

"Hi, Grif. Want some coffee?"

Herman was sipping from a clear mug of viscous black liquid whose odor would have stripped varnish. "Not right now, thanks. Got a minute?

"Sure. What's up?"

"Henry Bouchard."

"What about him?"

"That's what I'm wondering. You got anything new on the case?"

"What case? He got in a knife fight with Larry the Pervert and they killed each other. End of story."

"Yeah, I know that's what it looks like."

"That's the way it is." There was a harder tone in Herman's voice. "Two bodies, both killed by knife wounds in 'Score Alley.' Booze and drugs around. Each other's finger-prints on the murder weapons." He took another sip. "You see, we do our homework. No evidence of anything else. Nada. Two street bums going at it over a jug or drugs."

McNab drummed his fingers on the desk. "Autopsies?"

"Sure." There was an awkward silence as McNab just looked at him.

"Can I see them?"

"Not filed yet."

"Oh."

"You can get a copy from the coroner in a couple of days. Or rather, Pat can. She filed as next of kin yesterday."

"I know. I mean, I didn't know Henry was her brother myself until yesterday." McNab looked around the deserted squad room. "Why the hard ass, Herman? We've worked together a long time."

Herman squirmed. "Look. This is strange stuff. Let it rest."

"What does that mean? Didn't I help you get Mandy Reynolds when he was fleecing those old folks with that phony retirement home? How about the time I saved your butt in that Hmong gang investigation? Without those videos you would have been left sucking your thumb and they would still be running coke in here."

Herman looked quickly around. "Luego's, half an hour."

"Gentlemen, gentlemen. How good of you to come." Mingus was wearing a leather apron that probably hadn't been cleaned since the Middle Ages. "Civic pride swells my heart. Our wonderful constabulary hard at work, consorting with known fly by night operators. Got that plane out of hock yet? Business going down the drain?"

McNab looked at Herman. "To think I pay to come here."

Mingus waved to a fairly empty room. "Wherever, gentlemen." They sat in a booth near the back, sheltered from the street.

Myrna sauntered over to them. "Whaddya want?" They both ordered coffee.

Herman leaned toward McNab. "Sorry about this morning. I couldn't tell you in there. Shouldn't be telling anyone, but this sucks."

Their coffees came. Herman doctored his with cream and sugar. "At least I get a decent cup of coffee here."

McNab sipped and made a face. "You call this decent?"

"You kidding?"

"Guess not. What is going on?"

The deputy stirred his coffee, taking time. "I'm not sure. It's got a bad feel to it, though." He hesitated, then seemed to make a decision. He reached into his jacket pocket and pulled out a folded square of papers. "I really shouldn't be doing this. It'd be my ass if they found out." He handed it to the pilot. "Henry's autopsy. They just put a clamp on it. No release for a while."

"Why?"

"Beats me. Nothing in it. See for yourself."

McNab opened up the folded report and skimmed it. "Cause of death, multiple stab wounds to the chest and stomach. Bruises, cuts, and abrasions on head and face. Bit of gravel in a couple of the face wounds." He flipped the page over. "Toxicological ... point one four alcohol, he was legally drunk, probably just normal for him, no other psychotropic drugs." McNab flipped back and forth between pages a few times. "You're right. Nothing. Why try to suppress it?"

"Ongoing investigation." He snorted. "What investigation? We got word from on high, close this one up. Now." He drank some more coffee. "Beats me. We got an open and shut case and we're closing it down, but we can't release the autopsy yet because we have an ongoing investigation. Makes no sense."

"Who ordered the shut down?"

"Don't know. I just know that with all the other stuff going on this just came down as fact from wherever. No one is saying anything."

"Any ideas?"

"No. Not yet." He waved at Myrna for more coffee. "Oh. You're going to love this. You know after your last prisoner transfer? Where I, uh, well, you know. Well, they took me off of prisoner transport."

"Why? How did they find out you froze? I didn't tell anyone."

"That fucking doper prisoner ratted on me to the State prison boys. Asshole. Wish I could get my hands on that little fart."

"Too bad. Who's going to coordinate prisoner transfer now?"

Herman looked down. "Sorry, Grif. It's Aaron Grogan."

"Oh, shit."

"Yeah. Oh, shit is right. He doesn't like you much. Don't know why."

McNab sat back against the booth. "Jesus. The transfer biz is a big part of my regular flights."

Herman looked uncomfortable. "I know. Grogan has already started to get quotes from the other guys.

"I have a contract!"

"He's saying your plane isn't safe and that you can't be trusted because you didn't bust me. Could void your contract."

"How did he get that job?"

"After a few patrols, no one on the street would work with him, so they shoved him over to administration."

"Great. Just what I need. The overhaul... Hope I can... How did Mingus find that out?"

"Who knows where Mingus gets his information."

He looked down at the autopsy report. "Can I keep this for a couple of days?"

"It's yours. I made you a copy. For Christ's sake don't let it out of your hands. Burn it when you're done."

EIGHTEEN

McNab walked through the large glass doors of the new, state-of-the-art Euphrates Public Library. He was not a regular customer. Pat volunteered here and kept him up to date on the latest skullduggery. It was a well-known but little-publicized scandal that the land on which the library now sat had been purchased from an individual who made significant campaign contributions to most of the officials that made the decision. That they all were members of the same exclusive club was coincidental. Also coincidental was that the contractor was also a member of that same club, and the cost overruns, though substantial, were never seriously questioned. The mistake was that the state government provided the construction funds, but the overruns came out of the county budget.

This meant, of course, that the library now had no money to buy books and, indeed, ranked last in the state in per capita book buying. New additions to the library were most often donated by the Friends of the Library, primarily gray-haired ladies with no political clout. The politicians wrung their hands over the terrible problem and came up with the solution that since there weren't as many books, they needed fewer librarians, and since there were now fewer librarians, they couldn't keep the library open as much. So, after spending millions on building the library, it now had inadequate stock and staff and was open only thirteen hours a week. Meanwhile, the city's leaders wondered why businesses weren't eager to relocate to beautiful, illiterate Euphrates. McNab endured many evening lectures from Pat about the situation. Pat's favorite quote had come from one of the most corrupt supervisors. "Hell, you got a lot of volunteers. They can run the library."

He walked across the luxurious green carpet to the reference desk. There a harried young woman answered telephone calls one after another. Hermione Braithwaite, a pillar of the Friends, shuffled back and forth between the stacks and the desk with requests. Finally, she came to McNab. "Morning, Grif. What can I do for you?"

"Busy day."

"You said it. All Marcia can do is answer the phone. Doris is out sick today. She volunteers with me on Wednesdays. Pleurisy. Sounds bad." She pushed her large glasses, with the curved temples attached to the bottom of the lens frame, back up her nose. She wore a white sweater with beads and sequins over a blue patterned dress. Her white hair was perfectly done. Hermione's father had owned a small logging operation in the forties. McNab knew she had helped out by being a camp cook in the skid towns that followed the loggers through the woods. All the bunkhouses and service huts were built on large wooden skids. When an area had been cut, all the loose items were mounded on the hut's floor. Either a tractor or the oxen that pulled logs were attached to the skid houses and dragged them all through the mud to the next site. When her father, Don, died, Hermione ran the operation for a couple of years before selling out. Hermione was tough.

"You got anything on an incident out in Mill City? I heard that Hoffstader got hit with a pie."

Hermione fixed him with a withering look. "Another

worthless piece of tomfoolery. Yes. There was a small article in the paper. Thursday a week, I think. Let me look." She took off into the back. A few minutes later, she had a copy of *The Euphrates Sun* in her hand. "Page five. More attention than it deserves." She handed it over to McNab.

He sat at a gorgeous wooden library table, which cost one thousand eight hundred seventy-seven dollars and sixty-three cents apiece. The article was, indeed, on page five. It was a small story, full of 'alleged' and 'reported.' A picture along with the article showed a cab starting to pull away from the parking area and just missing another car also leaving the parking area. McNab couldn't tell if Henry was in the taxi or not, though the article said the prankster left by cab. McNab took the paper over to the coin-operated copy machine and made an enlargement of the photo, then returned to the reference desk.

Hermione was still there but helping another customer. McNab waited. Hermione looked over at him and then called to the back, "Marcia, front!"

Marcia, young for the Friends, had long black hair and a round, moonlike face. She looked at Hermione, who indicated McNab with a nod. She came over. "Can I help you?"

"Yes, I'd like to turn this back in." He pushed the newspaper toward her.

"That's fine, sir." She reached for them and paused. McNab turned away. "Oh, my."

McNab turned back. "Is anything missing?"

Marcia looked sad. "Oh, no. Not at all. It's just that... Never mind."

McNab started to turn away, then turned back. "Please tell me."

The woman sighed. "It's just... well, that poor man, the one who got killed? The street person. Henry? He always came in here. I helped him."

"Tell me more."

Marcia looked over at Hermione, who was still talking with a customer. "I'm not really supposed to. You know, confidentiality."

McNab could see she was dying to tell someone. "It's all right. He was a friend of mine. I was shocked, too."

She looked over at Hermione again and then leaned over the counter. "He was so nice. When he was clear-headed, that is. You could never tell. I mean, half the time we had to ask him to leave. He'd start shouting and disrupting the library. Other times he was just as nice and sharp as a tack. Mostly he'd look at environmental things. You know, all those reports the government puts out, or those organizations." She leaned closer and whispered. "The ones that Hermione hates so much? He'd make copies and take them over to Pike Rambus."

"Marcia?" Hermione was standing beside her. "We have confidentiality of library records. We don't break the law here."

"I'm sorry, Hermione. I just thought that since he's dead and all... "

"It doesn't matter."

McNab stepped in. "It's my fault, Hermione. Henry was a friend and I'm curious."

Hermione made a harrumph sound. "Well, we still aren't supposed to do it."

"I understand. Thanks for your help, Hermione." McNab winked at Marcia and turned to leave.

NINETEEN

McNab pulled open the door to his fifteen-year-old Jeep and climbed in. He looked at the enlarged copy of the photo from the *Sun*. By squinting at the picture, he could almost make out the company number on the cab, but not quite. He put the photocopy down and started the car.

Ten minutes later, he was in the *Sun's* office at the desk of Dewey Phelps, reporter, and community gadfly. The tall, gangly reporter had made several vain attempts to interview McNab. McNab had artfully turned what could have been an ugly confrontation into mutual respect. "Dewey, how are the birds?" Dewey was trying to farm emus on his two-acre lot, much to the dismay of his neighbors.

"Christ. One of them froze to death last night. It was hardly freezing, for Christ's sake. If I lose any more I won't have enough to breed worth a shit, much less have eggs or meat. What's up, Grif?"

McNab hauled out the photocopy of the cab and handed it over to Dewey. "I'm trying to find out what happened to a friend of mine who, I think, was in that cab. Do you still have the original of that? Maybe I could read the number of the cab and find the driver."

Phelps took the piece of paper and glanced at it. "Sure, I think so. What's it about, Grif? Anything I can use?"

"You interested in the murder two street people?" McNab asked. Phelps looked at him. "A friend of mine knew one of the guys who was killed. Wants me to look into it."

"What about Herman? He's the sheriff's homicide guy. He looking into it?" Phelps' curiosity seemed to be coming alive.

"Yeah, Herman's on it. It's going nowhere. They've got a lot to do over there, and I have some time."

"Yeah, I heard about your plane."

McNab just shook his head. "The grapevine is faster than light."

Phelps shrugged. "So, nothing for me?"

"I don't think so, Dewey."

"Stay tight for a minute." Phelps got up and went down the hall. McNab looked around. The newsroom, a highly overblown name for this small-town rag, looked like it was from out of time. The furniture hadn't been changed since the sixties, or early seventies. The only concession to modernity were the computer screens on all the faded, scratched, and oversized wooden desks. The high ceilings still had the giant globe and fan fixtures. Institutional green walls hadn't seen a new institution for decades. Brown patches and streaks marked where moisture had dissolved airborne nicotine.

"Here you go." Dewey returned with the photo.

McNab looked over the enlarged picture, an eight by ten. Now he could make out the name of the cab company and the number of the cab. He wrote them down in a small note-book in his shirt pocket. "Thanks, Dewey. I owe you one."

"You find out anything good, let me know?" Phelps called to McNab's retreating back.

McNab was at the headquarters of Euphrates Taxi within fifteen minutes, talking with the owner, Delbert Simms. Delbert was dressed in dirty khaki slacks, Redwing boots, a blue and green plaid shirt, and thinning gray hair that just covered his bald spot. "So, Delbert, what do you say? Who was driving that cab?"

"Well, let me see. This is confidential information, you know. Trade secrets, like? I'm not sure I'd feel comfortable disclosing trade secrets. If you catch my drift."

McNab nodded. "I catch your drift, Delbert." He pulled out a twenty and held it out. "A man of your busy schedule. Your time is valuable." Delbert reached out for the bill, and McNab pulled it back, arching one eyebrow.

"Mohammed Erk."

"I beg your pardon?"

"Mohammed Erk. E. R. K. Hasn't been here that long, a few months or so. He'll be coming in around four." McNab handed him the bill.

By four o'clock, McNab had eaten fish and chips at Klyde's Korner, a small three-stooled shack of no more than sixty square feet perched on the edge of a parking lot near the Square and the taxi place. Clyde sold fish and chips and pizza. McNab always regretted not bringing antacids when he ate here. He had finished the last fry and was poised on the sloping seat of the red vinyl-covered stool when Mohammed Erk sauntered by.

Though McNab had never seen him before, he thought it might be Erk because he was wearing the only jelabbah he had ever seen in Euphrates. McNab slid off the stool and called out to him. Erk looked back and stopped.

"Mohammed Erk? I'm Grif McNab. I was a friend of Henry Bouchard." Erk looked at him blankly. "The man who threw the pie at Hoffstader."

A large smile spread across Erk's face. "Yes! A good deed, indeed." The smile disappeared. "But so sad."

"Yes. I'm trying to find out about Henry's movements after that. Buy you a cup of coffee?"

They sat on Klyde's stools and drank the wretched brew

that masqueraded as coffee. "It was very strange. When Henry put the pie on Hoffstader, the reporters all got out their cameras and took many pictures," Erk laughed. "All the parking lot had its portrait taken. But not Henry." He took another sip of his coffee. "I was so very angry with him, you know. I had to get him out of there and then come back for the funny men."

"Funny men?"

"Very strange fellows. All dressed in orange and red robes. Monks they said they were. So very strange. Henry could not pay the fare, of course. So I had a round trip from Mill City with no fare. But it was very funny. The pie, I mean. But it worked out well. When I returned, the monks were just coming out of the door. At least I didn't lose all the fares."

"Where did you take Henry?"

"He wanted to go back to the Square, but I was so angry I was going to drop him at the bus terminal. But he was so funny," Erk shrugged. "I took him to the Square. I did not see him after that." He took the last of the coffee. "It was too bad for him. That Larry, though, he was not a good man. I don't know why Henry would be with him."

"I don't know, either." McNab put the money on the counter. "By the way, where did you take the monks?"

"First to the Holiday Capri Motel. To pick up their things. Then to the Queen Victoria bed and breakfast in Mill City."

"What was Henry's connection to them?"

"I do not know. The monks, they seemed to like him, though. They asked about him."

TWENTY

The offices of "Friends of the Forest" were in a rundown storefront off the Square. Huge posters and bumper stickers covered the windows. Displays of books and tracts were prominent just under the posters of the endangered Spotted Owls, Coho Salmon, the Marbled Murrelet, and Port Orford Cedars. Next to them was a woefully long list of less sexy species also under siege. Inside there were more posters and bumper stickers, buttons, hats, T-shirts, sweatshirts, baseball caps, notebooks, pens, key chains, in short, every merchandising angle known. On one wall, several large maps indicated forest areas in danger. An impressively extensive research library took up most of the space.

Among all the material chaos, there were several desks with people of mixed ages. They were mostly on telephones. Sitting at a vast old desk in the back was Pike Rambus, either patron saint or arch-enemy, depending on where you stood on environmental issues. He was in his thirties, but gray was creeping into his thick black hair and beard. He wore thick-lensed black-framed glasses and exuded a sort of manic energy. He was talking intensely on the phone, obviously to some media person.

"Yeah, that's it. They clear cut the west slope. Two months later the rains came, washed a lot of mud into the creek. Damned it up until the pressure blew the damn away. The wall of mud came through Sitwell and took out eight houses, killed a seven-month old baby and a bunch of cows. That's right. Wiped out eight homes. Yes. That's right. ML land. They deny the clear cut had anything to do with it. Okay. I'll send you pictures. Thanks." He hung up and sat back in the wooden banker's chair. "Okay, people, the San Francisco Chronicle is going to follow up on the Sitwell thing. We need pictures! Linda, you get them together. Mike, you organize the print stuff. Anything else we need? Okay. Let's go." He got up and then noticed McNab.

"Welcome to 'Friends of the Forest.' What can we do for you?"

"Could I have a word with you?"

"Sure." He indicated an old chair in front of his desk. They both sat down. "Start talking, Mister..."

"Grif McNab."

"McNab... you're the..."

"All in the past." McNab looked around the room. "So, this is the dreaded organization which will bring the end of the world to Euphrates."

Rambus laughed. "Yes. We're the dreaded commie, pinko, eco-Nazi, liberal, anti-American scum whose only purpose is to destroy the economy of the United States and hand the country over to the slathering Asian barbarian hordes. Did I miss anything?"

McNab had to smile. "I don't think so. I don't know what Hermione Braithwaite would say though."

"Hermione! I haven't seen her for months. She used to babysit me, did you know that? We usually have dinner a few times a year. I can usually gauge how effective I'm being by how much she scolds me, and what she serves me for dessert.

Asks me all the time, 'This house made of wood, Pike?'" He laughed. "What can I do for you?"

"I have, or had, a friend by the name of Henry Bouchard..."

Rambus interrupted. "Christ that was awful. Henry was a pain in the ass a lot of the time, but he was a decent guy. What about him?"

"Someone at the library told me he would bring things to you."

Rambus shook his head. "Yeah, he did that, all right. It was so funny. You could never tell with Henry. One minute he was as lucid as you or me. When he was like that he could bring in the most wonderful stuff. Arcane studies and articles that I never heard of. Good stuff. He provided some of the backbone research for a couple of our most successful lawsuits. But, the next time he would be out of his skull with all kinds of bullshit. He especially liked conspiracy theories. When he would go into that bag it was just bizarre and we would have to ask him to leave. It got worse in the last few months. We had to have a meeting to decide if we could even allow him in the office at all anymore. The consensus was that we couldn't reach consensus."

"Was there anything lately that stood out?"

"Oh, yeah. He was on a Hoffstader thing like you wouldn't believe. I mean, I'm no Hoffstader fan, as you well know, but this was beyond, well, beyond." He leaned close to McNab. "You know, if Hoffstader would only keep the cut within reason we wouldn't have a problem with him. But the way he's going there will be no more timber at all on his land in fifteen years, even by his own figures, and all the timber workers that support him now will be out of their jobs, all of them. That's why..." He stopped himself. "Sorry, I have to come out of that mode."

Rambus paused a minute. "Henry became convinced that Hoffstader was in an international conspiracy that involved

China invading the western United States. Last week he was in here waving a picture of Hoffstader standing with the Chinese premier as proof. The picture was from the New York Times, for Christ's sake. It was so bizarre. He claimed that Hoffstader was in secret communication with the Chinese premier and that the invasion was coming soon. We had to throw him out. That was last week, in fact, a few days before he was killed."

"So he didn't have any information about Hoffstader that was of any use to you?"

"Right. God knows we get enough just by Hoffstader's own actions. He's clever, though. He's got his PR down cold. Every time something goes wrong, it's our fault. The last time world pulp prices dropped and he laid off three hundred people? He blamed the layoffs on 'sabotage by environmentalists.' Us in particular. Anyway, enough of that. It's not like we don't have kooks, too. But Henry? Really fucked up. Fundamentally, he was a good guy. But lately? No information that meant anything."

TWENTY-ONE

The next day McNab was at the hangar working on Charlie's plane. He changed the oil and did a few cosmetic things to the cabin. Mostly it was busy work. He couldn't stop thinking about Henry, and the busy work wasn't helping.

Finally, he climbed out of the plane and went into the office. He called Mountain Lumber in Mill City. After several transfers, he found himself talking to Jacquye Ormus in the PR department. "Mountain Lumber Community Relations, can I help you?"

"Perhaps you can. A little bit ago there was an altercation out at your site between Hoffstader and a street person. It involved a peach pie, I think."

There was a distinct silence on the other end of the line. "To whom am I speaking?"

"My name is Grif McNab."

"Well. There was an ugly incident in which *Mister* Hoffstader was assaulted by an environmental terrorist? Is that what you mean?"

McNab sighed. "I guess so."

"What is it, exactly, that I can help you with?" The upward lilt of her voice was not pleasant.

"I was just wondering if anyone there knew what happened right after the, ah, pie incident. I mean to the man who threw the pie, that is."

There was another silence. "I don't have any information on that?"

"Is there anyone there that might?"

"I don't think so? We don't keep track of environmental terrorists? I'm sure you can find out at 'Friends of the Forest' or other subversive organization of its kind? Is that all you want?"

"Well, yes, that's all I want. It seems as if the peach pie man found himself dead in an alley and I was trying to find out all I could about him."

"Are you some sort of reporter or something?"

"Or something would be more like it. I knew the man and was just trying to find out what happened to him."

"I'm certain I wouldn't know? I'm sorry to hear he passed on? I will pray for his soul to go to the Lord, Jesus?"

"Thank you. In the meantime is there anyone else there that might have some information? I would really appreciate it."

There was a pause. "There isn't anyone here right now that could help you? If you would give me your name and number I'll see that someone will contact you?"

McNab thought a moment. "Sure." He repeated his name and gave the hangar office number.

"I will do my best to see that you are contacted? Thank you for calling Mountain Lumber?" The hang-up was swift.

McNab went back out to the plane. How was he going to kill more time? God, he felt useless. Charters were slow, and he didn't know where the money for the overhaul was coming from. Charlie hadn't kept the plane up very well. There was a lot to do if he wanted. Why not start by cleaning the whole thing from propeller spinner to tail? That should take quite a while. Just as he was reaching for the bucket, the phone rang.

"Mister McNab? My name's Bryan Bofford. I work for Mountain Lumber?"

"Hi." He let the silence build.

"You called regarding the man who was involved in the unfortunate incident with Mister Hoffstader?"

"That was fast. Yes, that's right. I was trying to help out a friend of Henry's to track his movements over the last few days before his death. I was hoping someone there might have some information about what happened to him immediately after the peach pie thing."

"There's not much we can say, Mister McNab. The man in question disappeared and we don't know where. The sheriff was called but Mister Hoffstader decided not to press charges. Other than that, we have no idea. I'm sorry we couldn't be of any help to you."

"Thanks anyway." McNab paused. "By the way, what is your position there?" But the phone was dead.

McNab pulled out Henry's receipt from the Post Office and punched the number for the Euphrates Post Office. After several minutes of truly terrible music, he was able to talk with a human. "Hi. I'm trying to determine when a registered letter of mine was actually delivered? Yes, I have the receipt number." He read it off. "The date of delivery wasn't put on the return receipt, and I can't read the signature of the recipient." He gave the number to the postal clerk. "Sure, I'll wait."

McNab tossed paper clips into a chipped coffee cup on his desk. He figured he was doing well, two out of five. "Yes? Okay. And the signature? You have it as Bofford? Thank you."

He looked down at the scribbled information. The letter was received two days before Henry died and was signed for by Bryan Bofford, even though it was sent 'addressee only.' So, what did Henry think was so important that he spent his meager money to send registered mail? Henry was obsessional, but was he deranged in this way? Even if he was, what did it have to do with his death? With nothing to lose, McNab called ML and asked for Bryan Bofford.

He listened to Bofford. "Yes, Mister McNab. I did sign for a registered letter from Mister Bouchard. If you will pardon me, it was just another crank letter. The same as many we receive from all over. They are so boring, so repetitive in their accusations. Yes, we do save them. I can give you a copy of it, if you like. He accused Mister Hoffstader of plotting with the Chinese Communists to take over the world and subjugate the United States under their rule. He sent a picture of Mister Hoffstader standing next to the Chinese premier as proof. The photo, I believe, was published in the New York Times, that bastion of subversion."

"Was this the only letter than Henry sent Hoffstader?"

"Oh, no. He was quite prolific. We have quite a file. He certainly had a way with invective. Of course he isn't alone. There are several others like him." McNab thanked him. "No, no problem at all. It's one of my jobs. Thank you for calling."

McNab poured himself some coffee from the pot in the corner and went out to the hangar. The large door was open, showing him a view of the runway and the adjacent pasture. The wind sock swung aimlessly, meaning essentially calm conditions. McNab looked past that to the gently rising ridge of fir, alder, and redwood, houses peeking out of the green foliage.

Twenty-Two

McNab was disappointed. The Queen Victoria Bed and Breakfast innkeeper said he'd just missed the monks.

"They are the strangest little men. But so nice. They never complain about anything, keep to themselves. You hardly know they're around. They just sort of glide about. Then, oops! Suddenly one of them is standing right next to you with a question. And polite? They are so polite." Regina Osterwald was in her sixties, ample of girth and sporting iron-grey hair. She wore a spotless white apron. McNab thought that with that clean an apron, she couldn't have been the cook. "Sometimes I see them in the early morning, sitting cross-legged on the lawn under the Japanese maple over there." She pointed to a tall willowy tree with purple-red leaves. "They'll already be there when I get up to start the biscuits, around five or so."

"Do you know when they'll be back?" McNab asked without much hope. He changed his mind about Regina.

"I just can't say. From what I hear in the neighborhood they just love the woods. Walk in them all the time." He knew there were scores of miles of logging roads in the forest behind Mill City. "They might be back for dinner." Regina leaned close to McNab. He could smell the talc on her face.

"That little Ongdi, the young one? He's a hoot. Always laughing. Loves Coke. The old one, Jamyang, I think he's called. Pulls a face when Ongdi asks for it, but never says anything. It's funny. He likes butterflies. Chases them all over the yard, just like a kid. He laughs a lot, too. The quiet one, Tenzing? Never says much. But the children just seem to gather around him. He doesn't say much to them, but they just like being around him. He laughs, too. They all do. Wish I knew what the joke was. What was it you wanted to see them about?"

"They were with a friend of mine a couple of days before he died. I just wanted to find out more about him."

"I am so sorry. Sometimes they eat here, sometimes not. There's a few Buddhist folk around here. They take them for food sometimes. You know Matt Cawdly?" McNab nodded. "He and his wife wanted to take them to that vegetarian restaurant in Euphrates. I forget what it's called. But they didn't want to go there. They wanted to go to McDonalds." She shook her head. "I can't figure it."

McNab thanked her and left. On the way back to town, he kept glancing at the sun going down over the mud flats of the bay, marveling at the grooves and canyons carved by the tide. He didn't see the flashing lights in his rearview mirror until the tap of the siren alerted him. He pulled over on the shoulder and turned off the engine. The patrol car stopped behind him. It was a Euphrates sheriff's car, not the Highway Patrol. The cop got out and slowly walked up to his window.

"You know the drill. Driver's license, registration."

"And a good evening to you, deputy Grogan."

"Cut the shit. Just hand them over."

"What's the infraction?"

"You know the speed limit here?"

"In this section, I believe, it's sixty miles per hour." McNab handed over the documents.

"No, asshole. In this section, starting a hundred yards back, it's fifty five."

"And I was going, how fast, deputy Grogan?"

"Sixty-one. On the gun."

"Mercy me."

Grogan started writing the citation. "You know, McNab, you're a real pain in the ass." McNab said nothing. "This county has a sheriff." He kept on writing. "You could get in a lot of trouble trying to muscle in on their job."

"If they did their job, you mean. By the way, I heard they don't allow you to go out on patrol. You playing hooky?"

"Fuck you, McNab. Let me give you some helpful advice. Keep your fucking nose out of sheriff's business. You hear me? There's no end of shit you could get in to. You understand me?"

"I'll keep it in mind."

"Do more than that, asshole." He threw the ticket through the window and went back to his cruiser.

TWENTY-THREE

McNab fiddled with the radio to put the oldies station on and got out the drip pan to change the oil in the plane. He heard footsteps in the doorway of the hangar. He looked up to see a smartly dressed man silhouetted against the opening. The man held out his hand and approached.

"Bryan Bofford, Mister McNab. We've spoken on the telephone."

McNab shook his hand. "Mister Bofford. What can I do for you? Excuse me, let me turn down the music."

The man's hands seemed to be everywhere, on his jacket, smoothing his hair, brushing imaginary lint off his sleeve. "Beautiful day isn't it? Not often we get the clear sunshine is it?" McNab didn't reply. "What a lovely airplane you have! It must be very exciting to fly about all over."

McNab indicated an upturned milk box and sat on a stool. "Oh, yes. Very exciting."

Bofford craned his neck around the hangar. "You know, there aren't many pilots like yourself with a large amount of experience in many types of aircraft." McNab grunted neutrally. The statement was patently untrue. "We were just thinking, that is the aviation manager at our headquarters was thinking, that there might be some sort of opportunity for you at Mountain Lumber."

"Really?"

"Why, yes. Our operations are flung all over the world, and we have our own flight department who are always looking for the right sort of person." He flicked some more imaginary lint from his jacket.

McNab nodded again. "And I am that right sort of person?"

Bofford stroked his chin. "Yes, we think so. Mister Hoffstader is always looking out for the communities where he has interests. Likes to do the right thing. Hire locally. That sort of thing. We were just bandying around a new position that has come up and your name popped right up."

"Did it, now?"

"Yes, yes. You've done a splendid job with Bill James in our PR department. It's not gone unnoticed." He paused. "Our subsidiary down in Venezuela has an opening for a chief pilot to take charge of all our South American flight operations. Bit of flying, bit of administration. We hear you've had some experience in that. Sort of an all-around kind chap, that's what they say about you."

"Who is 'they'?"

Bofford appeared flustered. "Well, you know. Other pilots and service chums of yours. Those sort of people." He paused. "In any case we have this opening. You would be headquartered in Caracas but fly almost everywhere in South America. Our planes fit your Air Force experience, though they aren't quite as exciting. Some bush things, too. We understand you like that sort of thing. No intrigue, I'm afraid." He lowered his voice to a conspiratorial level, "We know of your Office of Special Investigations experience. Not the usual things, though? Am I right? Little cloak and dagger stuff, eh? We don't need that, but it adds another dimension to your qualifications."

"Really?"

"Top salary." He mentioned a figure that made McNab's eyes widen. He could have the engine replaced in no time. "First rate airplanes. Exotic country. Lovely senoritas. Great food."

"When does this position need to be filled?"

"Well, actually, we need someone right away. Someone on the top rung. We could get you on your way day after tomorrow." He held up his hand. "I know. It sounds very fast and how could you possibly straighten out things by then? Am I right? Just leave that to me. My staff and I would take care of everything, down to shutting off your newspaper subscriptions and getting a year's supply of your Swedish toothpaste. We really do take care of our people, Mister McNab, and especially our top flight ones. What do you say?"

McNab looked at Bofford for a long minute, then stood up. He held out his hand. "Thank you for thinking of me, Mister Bofford. But I have a business to run right here and some things I need to do that will take longer than a day and a half. Your offer is very tempting, but I don't think so."

"I know this must seem overwhelming at first." He paused. "It's the money, isn't it?" He wagged a finger at McNab. "We were warned that you are a shrewd bargainer, Mister McNab. Well, let's just say that the salary was simply a first offer. We know the worth of true talent and are willing to pay for it. Say, increase it by a third?"

"Mister Bofford, it isn't the money. It's my business and my home that are here."

"But your business is failing, Mister McNab."

McNab stilled himself into cold motionlessness. "Really?"

"It's widely known. Come, Mister McNab. I meant no offense. Forgive my eagerness to have you on board. It's a little character flaw that I have, impatience. Please don't let that color your decision in this gravely important matter."

"Mister Bofford, thank you, again, but no thanks. I appre-

ciate your offer and your concern, but I am happy right here."
He bent down to pick up the oil pan. "If you'll excuse me, I
have to change my oil."

"Mister McNab?" His tone was different, and his hands
were still. McNab straightened up. "Mister Hoffstader insists
on having top people in his organization. As you can tell by his
offer that talent is rewarded, and rewarded better than
anywhere. He also prides himself on getting what he wants.
He really wants you to join us."

McNab walked close to Bofford, standing no more than a
foot away from him, hands on his hips. "You can tell Mister
Hoffstader that I am content right here."

Bofford was silent for a moment. "Mister Hoffstader has
made you an extremely generous offer. I suggest you take it. It
can become unpleasant to insult Mister Hoffstader."

"It can become very unpleasant to threaten me, Bofford."

The man's hands were back in motion, hair, sleeve, jacket.
"Oh, dear me, Mister McNab. Please excuse me for causing a
misunderstanding. Mister Hoffstader has only the highest
regards for you and your abilities. If I misspoke, the fault was
surely mine. Please don't let my clumsiness be an impediment
to an important career decision."

"It's not. There's no decision to make. Nice talking to
you." He turned to the oil pan.

Twenty-Four

McNab sat at his desk in the small office off the hangar. Everywhere he looked on the desk were bills. He pushed them over to the side and put his feet up. Charlie sat across from him, sipping his coffee.

"Thanks, Charlie. You saved my charters. Roy thanks you for his axle, too."

"Hmmm." Charlie wasn't very verbal.

"Got another one today. Farley Luscombe is taking a couple of city friends up to Rangeford Lake for steelhead."

"Good fishin' there."

"And on Thursday I go to Rebellion Island. Fish and Game personnel transfer and some supplies."

"Hmmm."

The phone rang. "Fly by Night Charters, Grif McNab speaking." He listened for a minute. "That's Okay, Farley, I understand. You have a good time." He hung up. "Farley canceled. Got a cut rate from Brophy. Less than half of what I could do it for. I didn't think he could fly that cheap."

"He can't."

"Well, he must be able to because he's doing it." He paused. "That wouldn't even pay for my gas."

"He in trouble like you?"

"I didn't think so. Fact is, we both charge just about the same. Operating costs are pretty close, I would assume. He picked up some of the business when Wade sold out to me, so he's not in real bad shape. At least I didn't think so."

"Sounds fishy to me."

McNab took his feet off the floor. "That's the way it goes, I guess. You want some more coffee?"

"No, thanks. Got to get on."

Just as they reached the open hangar door, the phone rang. McNab went in and answered it. Through the window he watched a student pilot bounce a plane down the runway before wobbling back up in the air. McNab came outside. He scratched his head.

"Who was that," asked Charlie.

"Fish and Game. They canceled for Thursday. Didn't know when they would reschedule. Said I might want to rethink my bid."

TWENTY-FIVE

Strains of 'The Bugle Boy From Company B' were audible as Mingus approached them. "Ah. The distraught duo. So much love, so little sex. What can I get for you pining people tonight?"

Pat turned to McNab. "Do you want to hit him or shall I?"

"Be my guest. If you think it would do any good."

Pat turned her attention back to Mingus. "Did anyone ever tell you that you are one of the most disgusting excuses for a human that ever existed?"

"Flattery, flattery. We have a wonderful special tonight, Sea Slug with raspberry mint sauce."

She looked at McNab again. "He's not even going to respond. Do you think anyone ever orders one of those horrors he's always telling us about?" She looked back at Mingus. "Just send Myrna over here. And give us a discount for the emotional abuse you inflict, you creep."

McNab brought Pat up to date on his efforts, including his conversation with Bofford.

Pat twirled the straw in the drink Myrna delivered. "Why are you concentrating on Hoffstader?

"That's all I've got, Henry's movements in the last few days of his life. I don't know where this investigation is going. All I know for sure is that Henry was killed in the alley. He committed assault on the leading citizen of the community, or at least the economic baron of the community. He's been in a cab with an Uzbek driver and some monks from the neighborhood of Tibet. He sent a crank letter to Hoffstader. Evidently not the first. He's tolerated at 'Friends of the Forest.' He got killed. No witnesses. No evidence at all that things didn't happen just as Herman said. Nothing other than your belief that Henry wouldn't let himself be killed and some strange behavior at the sheriff station."

"I'm sorry, Grif. I didn't mean to criticize. It's just so frustrating."

"I know."

"Do you think this is just pointless? Should we call it a day?"

"It's your call, Pat. I don't mind nosing around some more. Some leads may show up."

"Yeah. Like videotape of Hoffstader killing Henry because he threw a pie at him." She laughed at that.

"Good one, Pat." McNab chuckled.

"Yeah. If it weren't for black humor, I wouldn't have any humor at all." She looked down at the table. "I feel foolish, sort of. I don't know why I think that things didn't happen the way the sheriff says they did. I just don't think so." She took another drink, got something in her mouth, and discreetly put it in her napkin. "Do you think I'm crazy, Grif? Is it that I just can't accept his death was what it seems, the inevitable tawdry demise of a street person?" Her voice was starting to quaver. "It just seems so senseless."

"Death usually is."

"What do I do, Grif?"

McNab drew imaginary figures on the table with his

fingers. "Tell you what. Let me look around a little more. If I get nothing in a week, we'll talk about it. Okay?"

Pat nodded as their Sea Slug with raspberry mint sauce arrived.

Twenty-Six

"I need a favor." McNab sank into the grungy leather couch.

Rico Hakaku Amadoro looked up from his book, out over his half-frame glasses. "Fuck you." He bent his head down and continued to read.

McNab looked over the room while he waited for Rico's head to surface from the depths he was in. It hadn't changed in fifteen years. He remembered helping to paint the walls a brilliant white and the floor a dusky burnt orange. Now the walls were more like dingy gray marred by scrapes where Rico had reached out when he fell, which he did with great regularity. The floor was scratched and pitted, bare spots of the underlying wood peeking through. Rico's paths to the kitchen, bathroom, and computer room were worn with parallel potholes from the walker.

"You don't call before you come over?" Rico's head was still bowed to the book.

"Didn't have time. I was over at..."

Rico looked up and just stared at him. His face was thin, like his body, olive-skinned, and a slight epicanthic fold showing his Italian-Japanese heritage. He had been born late to two survivors of World War II devastation and sometimes joked that if he could find some German ancestry, he could be a one-man Axis. He bore several scars over his eyes along the bony ridges of his cheekbones and along the jaw line. He looked like he had endured a long career as a third-tier fighter. McNab knew they were all from the falls he took. More than once he had been called to rush Rico to the emergency room to stop the bleeding and get him stitched up.

McNab stared back at him for a while. "I know you don't like that."

"And?"

"I'll call from now on."

"Thank you." Rico closed the book and threw it on the couch next to McNab. It was a dog-eared copy of a thick NASA document about a manned mission to Mars. "You want to borrow it? He couldn't keep the corner of his mouth from twitching upward.

"You know I'm not into that stuff anymore. You say this shit all the time to me, Rico. Why is that?"

"Lighten up, man."

McNab just shook his head. "You got something for me or not?"

Rico nodded. "Come on back." He reached for the walker and pulled it to face the chair. McNab just sat while he watched Rico begin the painful process of getting out of his chair. He knew it would be about five to seven minutes before they would be back in the computer room, some thirty feet away. Just as Rico attained his walking position, he shook his head and turned to McNab. "Gotta piss. Go on back."

McNab just nodded and started for the back room. He knew it would now be about fifteen to twenty minutes before they could get down to business. He went through the door and down the hall to the next room. He should be immune to it by now, he thought. The kayak accident was over 17 years ago. But he wasn't immune, and it still cut him to see his friend suffering, knowing it would never end. Rico rarely said anything about the arduous minutiae of his everyday life, having to plan hours in advance just to get to the grocery store or the cleaners. He never spoke of the random frustration about the immense effort it took for him to do the things others took for granted or about how unconscious people generally were. A few times McNab had started to say something, but Rico was not interested in his pity. "It's my karma, man. I got to deal with it my own way. I appreciate it when you help, though."

Rico's main computer was on and running some program behind a screen saver showing the current president involved in a prurient act with the preceding first lady. McNab always marveled at the setup Rico had constructed. There were several computers with two printers and a plotter. Several scanners, a video camera, an audio system, a digital still camera, and various other devices that McNab could only guess at made up the rest.

McNab had been part of a group of friends that gently helped Rico escape a state of terminal despair after the accident. Rico had endured a year of painful physical therapy, finally coming up against the limitations beyond which he could never go. When he eventually overcame his hospital-induced drug addiction and showed some interest in living, they helped him find something to do from his home. Rico took to computers more rapidly than anyone had expected. At first he did piecework and word processing for some of the charitable foundations and non-profits in town. Slowly he graduated into online research and then web page design. Then he found more arcane areas of work. Rico became known as 'The White Crane,' the translation of his middle name. He found a community that didn't care about his physical limitations. Now he did McNab informational favors from time to time. McNab didn't ask how he got the information. Rico did similar work for others, but McNab pointedly did not ask him about that.

McNab turned when he heard the sound of a printer powering up. The input light flashed, and then sheets started to eject into the output tray face down.

"No, no, no." Rico sang as he stood in the doorway, crouched on his walker. "Remember curiosity and the proverbial cat."

"Rico..." Exasperated.

"I know, Grif, you want to, but you wouldn't. If I really thought you would, you wouldn't be back here." He motioned to the swivel chair next to the main console. McNab sat, and Rico hobbled over to the padded Swedish custom chair on rollers, one of the two in the house, the only ones he could sit in for more than ten minutes at a time.

Rico faced the console. "Hey, mother fucker!" he yelled. The screen saver blinked off, and a giant hand appeared with the middle digit raised. It dissolved into the picture of a genie that bowed low, and out of the speakers came a sepulchral voice, "Your wish is my command, oh Master." The genie then morphed into the Terminator.

"You like it, Grif?" Rico turned to him. "I've got a beta of the military's latest voice recognition system. Cool, huh?"

McNab shook his head. "Does it get dates for you, too?"

"Of course." He turned back to the monitor. "Baby Cakes, where are you?" The Terminator morphed into Beyoncé. Before the new picture could speak, McNab reached over and hit the Escape key on the keyboard, and a standard interface popped onto the screen.

"C'mon Rico."

Rico shrugged. "Print 'Search Program McNab Fifty-three.'" The printer powered up again, and pages were soon deposited into the tray. McNab arched an eyebrow at Rico.

"The top ones are mine. You can look if you want."

McNab got up and got the pages. The top five were lists of Buddhist websites. He took them off and put them face down on the desk. He started reading the last seven as he walked back to his chair. They were price quotes on remanufactured engines and engine overhauls. Just as he sat down, he heard the back door open, and light footsteps walk in. The rustling of paper, a couple of thunks, the sound of the refrigerator door opening and then closing, cabinet doors opening. McNab read on—the padding of steps back and forth across the kitchen and the back porch.

A dish was put into the sink and some silverware, then a voice. "Is that you, Grif?"

"Yeah." The footsteps came closer and then into the room. "Hi, Jen."

"Hi, Grif." Jennifer was just coming into her forties, small spots of grey in her auburn hair. She stood leaning against the door frame, slight, fatigue etching tiny lines around her light blue eyes.

"Is he flashing Baby Cakes at you?"

"Does the pope crap in the woods?"

"Jesus, Rico." Her face showed the exasperation in her voice.

Rico gave her an innocent look. "Give me a break. I am just allowing the man to make up his own mind about art."

Jennifer rolled her eyes. "Stay for dinner, Grif?"

"Thanks, no. I gotta get back. How about next week? I'll bring some pizza."

"Great!" Jen turned around and went back to the kitchen. McNab turned back to Rico.

"Do I get that favor?"

"Motherfucker. What is it?"

"You hear about that double murder in the alley behind Luego's?"

"That was something."

"Turns out one of the guys was Pat's brother."

"No shit!"

McNab nodded. "She doesn't believe the story. She asked me to look around. So I've been looking around and every time I turn around I run into Hoffstader." Rico arched his eyebrows. "Yeah, it sounds really weird. But that's what's happened. I don't think he's involved, but his presence is everywhere. Then I realized that other than knowing he's been a real prick in this neck of the woods I don't know much about him. What his other companies are, what shape he's in."

"So?"

"So. I'm going to do some library work for the public stuff. Could you do your magic thing and find out what else is going on with him?"

Rico looked off toward the ceiling. "Financial?"

"Yeah."

"Government influence, lobbying, like that?"

"Yeah. Anything you can get."

"Give me a week."

"Okay. Bye." Rico waved with one hand. McNab looked down the hall and saw it was empty. "You ever going to ask her on a date?"

"C'mon, Grif, we've been through that. She's just a friend. And yes I asked her out a long time ago and she rejected me."

"How did you ask her out, with Baby Cakes?"

"I did it my own inimitable way."

"No wonder she said no. If you'd... ah, what the hell."

"I wouldn't talk, if I were you. Or should I mention Lureen?"

McNab leaned over and hugged his friend. He walked back through the kitchen. Jen was stirring something on the stove. "Jen, you want to have some coffee later?"

"I don't know. I'm kind of tired. By the time I get his dinner done, I'm done."

"Double cappuccino at Luego's?" Jen looked at the pot. "With biscotti?" Pause. "Chocolate almond biscotti? I'll even have Mingus serve it with his mouth shut?"

"You're terrible, McNab. But, all right. About an hour and a half?"

TWENTY-SEVEN

"Could you pass the sugar?" Jennifer brushed a strand of hair out of her eyes. There were several that had escaped the haphazard braid she had thrown together. "I thought you were going to have Mingus keep his mouth shut. 'Cripple chaser' for God's sake. A new low, even for him." McNab passed her the sugar. "Have you brought up the wheelchair again?" She tasted her concoction, nodded slightly and took a bite of her biscotti.

McNab finished his swig of Steelhead Ale and pursed his lips. "Nope. Thought you might have."

"Chicken!" Jen turned and shook her head. "And I thought you were such a brave pilot. Afraid of a skinny crippled guy."

McNab snorted derisively. "Oh, right. Rico's a wimp because he uses a walker." He paused, "If it doesn't take any courage, why didn't you talk to him?"

"Touché." She leaned over to him and put her hand on his.

"Iron man. When he goes into a wheelchair it'll be a real bad day for him."

Jen squeezed his hand. "Yeah, but how long can he hold

out?" She pulled away. "Do you know how many times he's fallen in just the last week? Four!" She punctuated her comment with four fingers held high.

"I only knew about two of them." McNab put his hands in his back pockets. "Did you have to take him to the ER?"

"No, thank God. But that was just the luck of the draw…" She took another sip of her cappuccino. "And where were you? Never mind. But, Grif, he needs a live in helper. You know that."

"Yeah. I know. You know. We all know but Rico. Sounds like a jingle."

"Or a mantra." She shook her head. "How long are we going to have to put up with his stubbornness? How long can we go along like this?"

"You're not serious, asking how long he can be stubborn, are you?" He reached for his ale. "How long have you known him? Fourteen years? Give me a break."

"But we've got to do something. The next one might do him some more serious injury." Jen clenched her fists. "That goddamn arrogant, stubborn…"

"Hey, hey! Hold on. You know, Jen. It's his will that keeps him going."

Her fury collapsing, she drew away. "We've got to do something!"

"Okay. Tell you what. He was talking to me about needing some more rails in the bathroom and down the hall. I'll get Fred and Ray and we can do it next weekend." McNab paused as if in the middle of a thought.

"What is that silence I hear?"

"Uh, he'll have to stay somewhere for a couple of days while we do the bathroom part."

"And?" Jen put her hands on her hips and waited. "Oh, no. No, you don't. I'll help him at his place, but, no. Not in my house."

"Well, Jen, whose house? Mine? You know what mine is like. Too many stairs. There's no way. And who else is there."

"No. Absolutely not. No way." She stirred her drink furiously.

The silence lasted for a few more minutes. McNab sipped his beer slowly. Finally, he said, "Scared?"

"Of what?" Jen's head snapped up; her tone soared, blue eyes were hard and glittering. "You... you..." A fleck of spit arced in the air. They both watched it as it reached its zenith and descended to land on McNab's left collar.

There was a moment of tense silence. Jen and McNab both started laughing together. After some minutes they stopped and looked at each other.

"Okay. I'll take him for two days. Only two!" McNab grinned. "And he sleeps out in the living room. On the fold out." He grinned wider. "It's lumpy and he can lump it. And stop that stupid grinning."

"Okay, okay. I'll call Fred and Ray and we'll start Friday night."

"Saturday morning!"

McNab almost gagged on his beer. "Okay, Saturday morning."

Jen stirred her coffee for a long time and took a sip. Calm now. She looked at McNab. "It won't work, you know."

"What won't work?" McNab looked at her with wide, innocent eyes.

Twenty-Eight

McNab sat at the small desk in the cluttered hangar office. Outside, the rain was lashing the runway. Inside, the old tin roof reverberated with the uneven pelting of the drops as the wind rose and fell. The old wood stove radiated its dry warmth. Mississippi John Hurt sang softly in the background.

He picked up the telephone and dialed an almost forgotten number. "Colonel Matthews, please." He drummed pen on the faded green blotter. The smell of engine oil wafted through faintly. "Doug? Grif McNab. How the hell are you?"

Doug Matthews chattered in his ear about Julie and the kids, Rachel and Brad, for a few minutes and bitched about bureaucracy in the Pentagon. They reminisced a bit about old friends.

"What's up, good buddy?" Doug's voice reverted to that southern drawl McNab remembered so well. "What can I do you for?"

"Doug, I have a puzzle here. I was wondering if you could help me solve it."

"No aliens, Grif. I swore off of them."

"You know Eric Hoffstader?"

"We don't exactly travel in the same circles."

"I mean, Doug, do you know about him?"

"Just what everyone knows: rich, arrogant, shithead."

McNab paused. "Something curious happened to me a little bit ago. One of Hoffstader's flunkies wanted to hire me to fly for them. This guy knew about me."

"Well, why not, old buddy? You're one hot pilot."

"Doug, he knew a lot about me. Emphasis on the 'a lot'."

"What does that mean?"

"He knew my brand of toothpaste, Doug."

"So?"

"He knew about OSI, and hinted at a certain cephalopod."

There was a long pause. "Grif, this line isn't secure."

"I'd like to know how he found out about me, and why."

"I'd sure like to find out how, too. You'll have to figure out why." There was silence. "Give me a few days. I'll call you. You still in that fleabag town?"

"Yeah. Thanks, Doug."

TWENTY-NINE

Pat looked down at her hands curled around the mug for warmth. Gray light seeped through the windows, and buffets of wind sent drops to their death against the glass. "This thing has kicked up some stuff for you, hasn't it?" She swirled her coffee and looked at McNab. His eyes were unfocused. He was somewhere else. "It's her, again, isn't it?"

McNab came back to earth. "What?"

"Tell me about it."

McNab put down his coffee and looked out the window at the pier. "You already know about it. Besides, it doesn't serve any purpose." McNab picked up the mug and took another sip. "Well, I've got to go." He set the cup down and started to get up.

"No." It wasn't quite a command. McNab sat back down. "Tell me. Please. All these years and you've never told me how it was for you."

McNab shifted uncomfortably. "You were great then, Pat. You were just... there. I couldn't talk about it. You understand that."

"Yes. I do. Maybe we're different, Grif. I know that this

pain about Henry is so huge I can't contain it. I talk with some of my girlfriends. I talk with you. It helps. Some." She crossed her legs, sinking into the oversized soft chair. "I don't think you talked about Cindy at all. I think it's still there, and Henry's death has reawakened it."

"It's in the past. It's gone. Dragging it up won't help."

"Shoving it down won't. Look, Grif. She was my friend, too. She stood up for me when it wasn't popular. It meant a lot. She meant a lot to me, too."

"You know all this stuff."

"I know about the accident. How Cindy and your mother were killed by a drunk driver. How you were hospitalized for months. How your career deteriorated. I don't know how you felt."

There was a long silence. McNab gave out a great sigh. Pat didn't say anything. McNab took another drink from his mug. "What's there to say? It was the worst time of my life. Just before the accident I had gotten word that I had been put into the launch rotation. I was going to be an official astronaut, not just one in training. I'd worked my whole life for that. My dream was coming true. And then... I was in the hospital for two months. When I got out I took all the leave I had or could wangle."

"Grif."

"What?"

"Please tell me."

"You know. It was the first time the two of them had met. I told mom that we were going to get married. She was thrilled. She and Cindy got along real well. It was great. It was the easiest time I'd had with mom in years. Then that drunk came around the curve and hit us head on. When I came to, I was in the hospital and both Cindy and mom were dead." He paused.

McNab looked down. "I left here as soon as I could walk,

then spent the next four months drinking as much as I could as often as I could. I think that's called 'poor coping skills.' One of my old C.O.s, Bill Norville, called one morning near the end. He wanted to know if I was still going to be alive when my leave was up. I told him, 'not if I'm lucky.'

"We met for lunch. That was the earliest in the day I could be coherent. Bill told me what I already knew and didn't want to hear, my injuries washed me out of astronaut class. He offered me a job. It was with a small, special group within the Air Force Office of Special Investigations that investigated things that were, well, out of the ordinary. The name of the unit was... "McNab stopped and looked out at the pelting rain. "I'm not supposed to tell you even that much. Let's just say that we had training over and above what the normal investigators do."

"We didn't hear much from you in those days. How long were you in this unit?"

"A bit over four years. I re-upped once more. I didn't know what to do or where to do it. I had no one or nothing else."

"Sounds like you're still carrying a load around."

"If you say so."

Pat was silent. "You know Elizabeth." McNab nodded. "When she was in therapy about the death of her father, the therapist had her write him a letter. Just to get the stuff out. Have you ever thought about writing Cindy and your mother a letter?"

McNab exploded out of his chair. "No! I don't want to write another fucking letter to someone I can't talk to on the phone. Especially to someone who's deader than shit. I've done enough of that. Goddam Air Force shrinks told me to do that." He was breathing hard.

"I wrote dozens of letters. I could make a whole damn book of letters to corpses. They told me I'd feel a lot better. Well, maybe for a couple of days, but not for long. Felt like I was pissing up a rope. Write the damn letter. Go to the fucking cemetery. Read the damn letter. Burn the damn letter. Where was the chorus? The epiphany? The sun breaking through the clouds? The voice that said, 'You're Okay, now,'?

"There was never a goddam chorus, no sun, no forgiving voice. Shit, I thought, must have fucked up, again. Didn't do it right. Again. Well, shit. Write another goddam letter. Get more honest. Or at least more brutal. Use harsher words. Try to cry, harder. Maybe this time it'll do it. Drive down to the cemetery, again. Read it, again. Tear it up. Wait. Drive back. Hole up in the house, looking at the writing pad. Write another goddamn letter. Maybe I should dig them up and shoot them. Make sure they're dead."

Pat was stunned. McNab paced the room for a few moments, then sat down, still breathing hard.

She changed the subject. "You were never very clear about why you left the Air Force."

"Let's just say we had different priorities." He looked at the floor, the ceiling, and the walls.

"Oh. Now I understand completely. Thanks for the illumination." She crossed her arms.

"You're welcome."

"Asshole."

"Snoopy bitch."

"I told you about that word."

"Yes, you did."

"Well?"

"Well, what?"

"Jesus Christ, McNab. You don't give up a thing, do you?"

"Why should I?"

"Are you so fucking damaged that you can't even have a friend?"

Silence.

McNab massaged his jaw. "I'm not ready to talk about it."

"Oh, really?" Sarcastic.

McNab laughed. "Give me a break, Pat."

"Why should I?"

"You're not my mother, you're not my analyst, you're not my confessor, you're just my goddamn landlady. Now, let's drop it!"

Pat put down her cup. "You got it, tenant. Speaking of which, tenants aren't allowed to leave their fucking muddy shoes in the entry way or to use more than half the fucking refrigerator for their fucking beer or to abuse the landlady with fucking profanity. Asshole."

"Oh, really?"

"Yeah, oh, really." Pat's face contorted. "You're such a child."

"So are you. And by the way, do you swear at your clients the way you swear at me?"

Pat collapsed into her chair. "God, I don't know why I put up with this shit from you."

McNab's stony face softened, and he sat back. "I don't know why you do either." He put his hands to his face and pulled them down as if to wipe off something stuck there. "Cindy used to say the same thing. How I wouldn't 'let her in' as she put it. It was becoming a problem for her." McNab laughed without mirth. "Maybe it wasn't just her problem." He turned to Pat. "Why is it so important that you know this stuff?"

"Just built that way, I guess. I just want to know."

"Know what?"

"Just know."

"Very illuminating."

"Okay." She sighed. "Truce?"

"Truce."

"I'm hungry. Do you want anything to eat?"

"Sure. Let's..." McNab paused. "It was Norway."

"What?"

"Norway. That's why I left the Air Force."

"You don't have to."

"Yeah, I know. But it's time." He picked up his coffee and raised an eyebrow at her. Pat nodded. McNab went to the kitchen and brought back the pot. "I was in the SCUID. We pronounced it 'squid' and that's what we felt like, most of us. The acronym was for, well, it doesn't really matter. It was enough that it drove those Navy pricks wild. We were a separate department under counterintelligence at OSI. What we did mostly was keep an eye on attempts to get unauthorized Air Force information. This turned out to mean, mostly, people who were convinced we had captured UFOs, and aviation buffs who wanted to know about secret research planes."

"That must have been fascinating."

"Sometimes. A lot of the time, it was a shit assignment. It was someplace to put me after the accident where I couldn't make a complete mess of things. I was pretty messed up, and they didn't want to boot me out, and they didn't want me in a responsible position yet. Their idea was that I would regain my emotional balance and have 'the right stuff.' Mainly it was tedious. We dealt with people who were a bit unbalanced and obsessed and who didn't take no for an answer. It was my job to document their illegal activities and then convince them they would get into trouble if they kept up.

"In most cases it was repetitious, doing and saying similar things. If they got out of hand, we turned them over to the legal people. Then there were those few who were perfectly lucid and quite persistent. We gave them very serious attention.

"As I came out of my hole, I got to work with the more serious stuff, some hard core COINTEL. I got pretty good at it. But there was always the mandatory rotation on the kook patrol." McNab stopped a moment. A plane droned overhead. He returned to Pat. "Then one day I got the case of Norway

Submer. You know him?" Pat shook her head. "Curly? We saw him at Luego's? Curly red hair? He hangs out with Ellie?"

"Of course. He fixes the computers at the office. I was afraid he'd see me drunk that night."

"That's him. Anyway, one day, I'm in the office and his name appears on the case docket. I can't believe it. I'm two thousand miles away and here's his name, and I get to investigate him like he's some sort of dangerous spy.

"He'd tried to do some computer hacking into a database at Wright Patterson. Very common for UFO freaks. Anyway, this new colonel gets a wild hair up his ass and says we have to make an example of him. Make a big splash, prosecute to the full extent, and all that horse shit. Lots of publicity, he says." He finished his beer and raised his eyebrow at Pat, who shook her head.

"I tried to tell him that I know this kid, that he's harmless, and what we got was one incident that we didn't even have any hard information on yet. I pointed out to him that a better case would be someone with a long pattern of abusing the system and where we have a lot of proof. He thinks that if we made a big splash about a small fry, then we scare off a lot more people, and then we don't have as high a workload. What he doesn't say, of course, is that means that he gets credit for shrinking a budget and gets a promotion. I counter that all this will really do is comfort the more sophisticated ones. They'll think that they haven't been noticed and the attempts will get more numerous and bolder. The colonel doesn't think much of my idea. He tells me to get the goods on Norway Submer, who is suspect, it seems, because he has an unusual name. He's my boss, I don't like it, but I do what he tells me.

"I get all the info they have and come out here to investigate Curly the terrible spy. Well, the stuff they give me is crap. They don't have a hard piece of evidence anywhere. It was his account that came up on the server that tried to break into

Wright-Pat. But no serious hacker I ever heard of would use their own name and leave a trail like that. They all spoof addresses. Also, it turns out that Curly had a decent enough alibi for the specific time period." McNab looked out of the window.

"The colonel wouldn't let it go. He saw his name in lights, and all it would cost him would be the future of a little geek in some jerkwater town. But I knew Curly slightly and his family, this being a little jerkwater town, and I knew he didn't do it. I got mad. We had a go-round. He pulled rank. I still argued. He threatened to bring me up on charges of insubordination. He ordered me to prepare the case against Curly. I refused. He called security. I started screaming at him. When they arrived, we were both screaming at each other. He called me a nut case that the Air Force didn't have the guts to can me. I lost it and popped him one, thus proving his case. The Air Police grabbed me, and I was in the clink. After some deliberation, the Air Force decided that 'for the good of the service,' I would be allowed to resign quietly.

"About that time the insurance companies finally paid off for the accident and it let me come here and buy out Wade Gustafson. So, here I am, failed astronaut, failed investigator, failed charter pilot and businessman, and subject of Hoffstader's curiosity."

Pat nodded. "So, what are you going to do now?"

"Don't you ever lay off?"

"Do you want me to?"

"If you weren't a lady—"

"Don't give me that macho bullshit."

"Touchy, aren't we?" McNab smiled. "I'm going to find out how Hoffstader knows so much about me and why."

"I'll drink to that."

McNab thought a minute. "Not to change the subject, but have you seen Otto on the Square lately?"

"Come to think about it, no, I haven't. He usually panhandles me every morning."

"I haven't seen him either. I think I'd like to talk to him."

"How? No one understands him. Do you?"

"I could try. It just seems a little odd that he isn't around. He's been holding down that corner for years."

THIRTY

Jamyang Rinpoche came into the Prince Albert suite at the Queen Victoria Bed and Breakfast. Ongdi and Tenzing were looking out the window facing a hillside, half of which had recently been logged. He moved to them and looked out also. "We must find another company to help us. Mister Hoffstader has cut our tree."

Ongdi asked, "How do you know this?"

"Remember when we went to the yoga center? The space is used for several groups, including the Tibetan Buddhists, as you saw. I was just there speaking to one of the members of the meditation group. He is a feller, a cutter of trees, for Mister Hoffstader's company. He told me that the day after we saw the tree we wanted, that the entire grove was cut down."

The two younger monks sat with this a moment. Tenzing said, "That is not right."

"It is their karma, not ours. This was not our tree. We must find a different one."

"Where?"

"Our friend told me about a small company, a small one, but one that respects their heritage. We will go see them."

"What about Mister Hoffstader?"

"I am sure that he thinks we do not know this information."

Ongdi asked, "Why would he tell us to wait for something that will never happen?"

"I do not know. But we must find our tree. Come. We have an appointment."

Mohammed Erk was waiting outside in his cab. "Hi! You crazy guys! Where we go today? Bright lights, big city?" He laughed.

Jamyang took out a small piece of paper from inside his robes. "McGinty Lumber."

"Oh, sure. No problem. McGinty. He rides with me sometimes from airport. Big man. Red face."

A bit later, they pulled up in front of what appeared to be an outsized two-story log cabin. The name of the company was emblazoned over the doorway in yellow block letters. The monks got out and went inside.

Derek McGinty stood about six foot four and weighed in at around three hundred pounds. Not much of it was fat. As Erk had said, he was ruddy with a fuzz of reddish-gray hair and clear blue eyes. "Good to have you guys here." He ushered them into his office. Giant leather chairs faced a monstrous redwood burl desk, behind which was another huge leather chair. "So, I hear you've been had by Hoffstader. Sorry for that. No consolation that you're not the first and won't be the last. What can I do for you?"

Jamyang outlined their mission to find a large tree that would serve as the center beam of their monastery restoration in their now Chinese-dominated country. He sketched, quickly, the relief they felt at finding a good tree and their disappointment at how it was cut down.

"So, he really did that, just like they said? That's a new low, even for Hoffstader. Oh, do you boys want some coffee or tea or something?"

Ongdi spoke up, "Do you have any Coca-Cola?" Jamyang made a face.

"Sure thing." McGinty picked up a phone. "Laurie, bring us in some cokes and some of my tea." In a few minutes, Laurie showed up with cans of coke and a tea cozy with a delicate bone china teapot and cup and saucer.

"This is my wife, Laurie. Laurie, the boys." McGinty didn't wait to see if they looked at the teapot. "Love the stuff. Decaffeinated, though. Not like it was. Used to drink Scotch out of that teapot. Thought I was fooling people." He chuckled. "So, you need a tree. You do know that laminate is better and stronger?"

Jamyang nodded. "Yes. That has been explained to us. Our tradition is to have one large beam."

"Thought you might say that." McGinty thought a minute. "Well, we do have a grove that is scheduled for thinning in about six months. We could go take a look up there. It would be a special operation, though. Cost you more." Jamyang nodded. "Not much more, but some." McGinty took the china cup into his large, rough hand in a precise and delicate maneuver and took a big gulp of the decaf tea. "We don't clear cut here. We can't afford to. We only got so much land with timber on it and it's got to last us. We pick our trees, never cut more than forty percent of a stand. Costs more. My grandfather would spin in his grave if he knew how much. Anyway, that's not your business, you want a tree. Well, I think we can help you out. Can you be here day after tomorrow? Six AM? We'll go do some scouting."

THIRTY-ONE

Frank Johnson, head of the County Board of Airports, and Darcy's boss, walked into the hangar. McNab was just finishing filing away the updates on his instrument approach plates and looked up. "Hi, Frank. How you doing?"

"Just fine, Grif, just fine. Got a minute?"

"Sure, have a seat. Coffee?" McNab waved at the chairs in front of the desk.

Johnson poured a cup, sat down, and took an envelope out of his jacket pocket. He tapped it a couple of times on his thumbnail and then handed it over to McNab. "Bad news, I'm afraid, Grif."

McNab looked at him and then opened the envelope. He shuffled through the sheets a moment and then back up at Johnson. "Double? My rent's doubled?" He looked back down at the papers. "Safety concerns?" McNab put them all back down on the desk. "What's up, Frank? Why are you doubling my rent and citing me for safety violations?"

Johnson pursed his lips, put a finger to the side of his nose, and massaged his jaw. "Well, Grif, that's the way the new Board of Airports is handling things now. I thought I'd better come here personally, what with you taking over from Wade and all."

"I don't understand. Regulatory boards usually don't raise rents by that amount."

Johnson looked more discomfited. "Let me put it this way, Grif. There have been a few new appointees and they look at things differently."

McNab looked down at the papers again. "Here is a safety citation for storing dangerous chemicals. What chemicals, Frank?"

"It's all in the paperwork, Grif."

McNab looked at the papers more closely. "Oil? Solvent? WD40 for Christ's sake? Frank, how could anyone operate an airplane, or a car for that matter, without these... chemicals?"

Johnson crossed his legs, then crossed them the other way. "Well, Grif, you see, all these chemicals are on the government's list of dangerous things, and you know, well, the County airport isn't too keen on losing federal funds and besides, you know, there's the liability issues."

McNab sat back. "Frank, what is really going on?" He looked back at the paperwork again. "This week? All chemicals have to be removed this week? How am I going to work on my plane, Frank?"

"Ah, there are special exceptions made, but application has to be made for them. You can make application for them, Grif. 'Course it'll be a few weeks before the Board meets again..."

"Who's on the Board, Frank?"

Johnson named the Board members, "Webster, Huggins, Lucian, Pimental, and Bofford."

"Bryan Bofford? Hoffstader's poodle?"

"Now, Grif, don't go making any trouble. Mister Hoffstader does a lot for this county and a lot of folks think he's doing the right thing by getting involved in our local issues. Lots of folks."

McNab thought a minute. "Frank, are these going out to everyone?"

Johnson looked up at the ceiling. "Well, I guess so."

"What does that mean, exactly?"

"Well, let's just say that you're the first." He re-crossed his legs.

McNab picked up a pencil, tapped the blotter's eraser, then reversed to tap the point, and then repeated the motion. "When will the rest be sent out?"

"Oh, I don't know. When we get more clerical staff, I suppose."

"Budget's pretty tight, isn't it?" Johnson nodded. "So, clerical help isn't likely to come any time soon is it?"

"You know how things are, Grif. People want smaller government."

"Uh-huh." McNab kept tapping his pencil. "You were a good friend of Wade's."

Johnson uncrossed his legs. "Yeah. Wade was like family. We were sure glad when he sold out to you, instead of someone else. You kept the heart in Wade's business."

"I don't suppose an appeal would work, would it, Frank?"

"Let's just say that this new guy, Bofford, is running the appeals board right now."

McNab put down the pencil. "Is there something going on here I don't know?" He chuckled. "Of course there is, or I wouldn't be asking. Anything you can tell me, Frank?"

Johnson leaned forward over the desk. "All I know is that Bofford, and that means Hoffstader, wants to give you a whole lot of grief. Why, I don't know." Johnson reached over to find his coffee cup and knocked it over on the desk, the liquid flowing over the notices. "Damn. Just ruined that notice. I don't think I could rightly serve that, wet as it is. Let me take it back and get it re-typed. But what with the clerical shortage and all, it might take some time. If that's okay with you, Grif?"

THIRTY-TWO

McNab picked up the phone. "Mister McNab, my name is Bruce Smith. I'm with the FAA. Did you receive our letter?"

"No. What letter?"

"We received a complaint about you a few days ago and sent you a letter informing you of that and that we would be out today to inspect your facility and records. We'll be flying in about two o'clock and we wanted to be sure you would be there."

"Complaint? Who made a complaint? What's this about?"

"It's in the letter, Mister McNab. We'll see you at two o'clock." The phone went dead.

McNab looked at the phone before he put it back on the cradle. The clock said 11:30. Paperwork. They were absolute sticklers for paperwork. He had two and a half hours. He picked up the phone and dialed. "Darcy? Can you get here fifteen minutes ago? The FAA is coming at two. I need you." He hung up.

Darcy arrived ten minutes later, and they started in. Within ninety minutes they figured out that what was missing was the emergency locator transmitter battery check on Charlie's plane. Twenty minutes later, Ed had replaced the bunch of D-cell batteries and entered it in the airplane log book when the FAA Learjet turned on final approach.

Just then, Frank Ordley, the postman, dropped the mail at the office. On top was a certified letter from the FAA. McNab signed for it and ripped open the letter. He read for a few moments and then put it down. Darcy looked at him. "Well?"

McNab opened his mouth and shut it again. Four FAA men were walking across the tarmac toward the hangar. "An anonymous complaint that I flew too low over Deak City. It was the day the engine failed."

The four men, all dressed in cheap blue suits, white shirts, and thin ties, walked in. One approached McNab. "Are you John McNab?" McNab nodded. "I'm Bruce Smith. Where can we talk?" McNab indicated the office, and they all trooped in. Two of the men had to stand in the doorway.

"First I need to see your airman certificate, personal logbook, your aircraft's airworthiness certificate, aircraft logs, and maintenance logs. Where are they?"

"Mister Smith—"

"Just show us the paperwork, Mister McNab. You can have your say later."

McNab pointed at the filing cabinets. Smith nodded to the two standing in the doorway. There was a few seconds of dancing as McNab tried to leave the office as the two tried to come in and access the cabinet. Finally, McNab and Smith were on the outside of the office. Smith gestured to McNab to hand him his licenses. McNab pulled out his wallet and handed over his ATP certificate and medical certificate. Smith glanced at them and handed them back. "Logbook?"

McNab indicated the desk in the office. Smith went back toward the office.

McNab and Darcy moved out by the plane. Darcy looked up at him. "What's this all about, Grif?"

"I don't know. This is very strange. If you fly too low they usually send you a letter asking for an explanation or schedule a hearing at some time in the future. Usually it takes weeks or months with lots of certified letters. But this? Four inspectors on a special flight? Tear apart the whole operation on one anonymous complaint? Reminds me of Bob Hoover. I should be flattered."

"Who?"

"Years ago a couple of FAA types decided that Bob Hoover, one of the best and most experienced air show pilots in the world was unfit to fly. No basis in fact whatever. But they put the whole weight of the bureaucracy down on him. Revoked his medical certificate. Despite passing every medical exam they gave him, they refused to certify him. He got a legal team on his side. Still, it took him three years to get back what should never have been taken away. Made the FAA look very bad. Evidently it didn't stop them."

Three hours later, Smith came out, obviously frustrated. McNab and Darcy were sitting outside the hangar watching a student pilot do touch and goes. "What do you say about the low-flying, McNab?"

"As you saw in my log, I had engine failure over the mountains. Nevertheless I kept to standard approach procedures, including altitude. There was no low flying."

"Our source says differently."

"Who is your source?"

"That's not your business."

Darcy started to pipe up. "Wait a minute. He's entitled to confront witnesses. It's in the Constitution."

Smith turned to her. "This is administrative. Doesn't apply." He turned back to McNab. "Well?"

"I've got two witnesses, including a cop who was in the plane."

"We'll see about that." He turned to walk away. "Paperwork's in order." He called to the men who were now coming out. "Let's go." They boarded the jet and were soon in the air.

"What's going to happen?" The sun was starting to go down. Darcy shivered.

"Don't know. I sure don't like the feel of it."

Thirty-Three

McNab glided to a smooth touchdown at Deak City airport and taxied to the fuel pit. Jerry Hibbard, the line boy who worked for flying lessons and dreamed of an airline job, started filling the right wing. McNab pulled out the hard boxes of bank records he had been hired to fly up to the branch by the First Bank of Euphrates and set them on the tarmac. Jerry finished with the right wing and moved his ladder to the left wing. As he put the nozzle into the tank, he turned to McNab.

"Don't leave those out too long. You won't see them again."

McNab set the last one down. "Don't worry, the bank guy will be here in about," he checked his watch, "ten minutes or so." He finished lining them up next to the tail of the plane. "Are you having problems here that you didn't before?"

"Ah, not much. There's just been a couple of weirdos hanging around. Sleeping in the bushes over by the edge of the runway. We chase 'em out but they always come back. They don't steal much, mostly food, a couple of tarps. To sleep in, I guess."

"Too bad."

"Yeah. Actually I feel kind of sorry for this one guy. He's

so pathetic. Must have been one of the ones kicked out of the mental hospitals years ago. Can't understand a word he says. Just sort of puts his head on one side and makes noises, tongue sticking out. Scared the hell out of us when he first showed up. But he's harmless, just scared. Only comes around if he thinks no one's here. Me and Mike surprised him a couple of times and he ran off. Now he comes around us. We give him some food and off he goes."

McNab's attention sharpened. "How long ago did he show up?"

"Few weeks. I really don't remember. He looks so... sad, if you know what I mean."

"Does he wear an old bomber jacket? With a big faded red patch on the back?"

"Yeah. You know him?"

"Used to hang around the Square in Euphrates."

"What the hell's he doing up here? Be a hell of a lot better pickin's down there."

"You know where he is now?"

Jerry finished the fill-up and got down off the ladder. "Not really. I think he stays around the trees off the approach end of runway three zero. But I sure haven't looked. Put it on account?"

McNab was momentarily lost. "What?"

"On account? The gas?"

"Sure. Yeah." There was the sound of a car approaching, and the neon purple and pink Geo of the bank's messenger swung into view. Ginky Dawes, an early twenty-something with green spiked hair and more piercings than a dart board, leaped out of the car.

"Hi, Grif. This all?" McNab nodded, and Ginky swiftly put the boxes in the car, carefully arranging them to travel well and not scuff his interior. "Hey Jerry, 'Dead Salmon' at the Weed Patch tonight. No cover. See you next time, Grif." The car peeled out.

McNab looked at Jerry. "Dead Salmon?"

"New group. Some of the guys from the fishing boats. There's no salmon anymore, so they got to do something. They're trying Zydeco. They're pretty bad. That's why no cover. At least they're live. We don't get much in the way of big-name groups up here." He handed McNab a chit to sign and returned to the fuel shed.

McNab walked to the plane, got in and taxied it over to the tie-downs, got out, and locked it. Then he headed for the approach end of runway three zero. The trees were about a hundred yards off to the east side of the runway, a small stand of cypress. The underbrush was pretty thick around the base, and as he approached them, several snowy egrets flew out of the tops of the cypress, tucking their necks close to their bodies and slowly flapping those great wings.

A faint trail led into the brush. McNab followed it until it got near the trees. He saw a small opening partially blocked by an uprooted bush. He approached the opening and started pulling away the bush when he heard feet scraping on dirt, trying to get purchase and brush breaking. McNab called out, "Otto! Is that you? It's Grif from the Square. Pat's friend." The noises stopped. "Otto, I need to talk to you. It's about Henry. Otto, would you come out? I won't hurt you." No sounds emanated from the bush. "Otto, I'll bet you're hungry. Remember the pastry Pat used to give you? From Luego's? I don't have any right now, but I can get something. Otto?"

There were the sounds of twigs breaking and a soft scuffling noise, and the branches parted to show the seared, haggard face of Otto. His head leaned over to the side, a pink and black tongue showed out of the side of his mouth, and his head wobbled as he made sounds that McNab couldn't at first make out. McNab sat down in the dirt in front of the opening, and Otto looked all around and then came out to sit in front of him.

When McNab had been with Pat on the Square, he had

made some headway in understanding Otto. Not many had tried. Fewer had the patience to be with him long enough to make any sense, and even fewer had made the commitment to communicate with him. McNab hadn't made the total commitment to being a link from Otto's world to the larger one outside of his twisted existence, but he could make out some words.

Otto kept making sounds, 'awking,' Pat called it. He became more and more agitated. McNab slowed him down and then could understand about every fifth sound. Finally, he held up his hands. "Otto, how about we go get something to eat and talk about this there? What do you want to eat?"

Otto's eyes widened and started gabbling in a furious rush of sounds, then started to get up and move toward the hole in the vegetation. McNab, panicked, yelled at him, "Okay, Otto, okay. I won't take you anywhere. How about I come back with some food? Okay? It'll just be a little while." Otto looked at him suspiciously. "I'll come alone and I won't tell anyone else you're here, okay?" Otto finally nodded. McNab got up slowly and said, one more time, "I'll be back soon, with food. No one else will come. Okay?" Otto nodded again, and McNab turned back to the airport.

About an hour later McNab returned with four orders of hamburgers, fries, and soft drinks. Otto fell to and devoured them all. It was a painstaking business, what with his spasms, noises, and half-masticated food that dribbled out of his mouth. At times McNab forced himself not to look away.

Otto was calmer after he had finished eating. McNab got a primer on communication. Otto stuttered, his grackly speech required McNab's concentration and a socially unacceptable focus on Otto's mouth.

Often McNab would ask Otto to repeat things until McNab was sure he understood them correctly. A number of times McNab repeated things back to Otto, including a full recitation by McNab to which Otto finally nodded his assent. It took a few hours, but a story ultimately emerged.

According to Otto, he had been asleep in the alley behind Luego's, burrowed under some flattened cardboard and other detritus that happened to be there. This wasn't his usual spot. Someone else, bigger, stronger, had appropriated his place under the loading dock of the abandoned fish cannery. He heard some voices.

Larry the Pervert was calling someone. Who was it? Otto saw Henry stop at the mouth of the alley and sway a little and slowly move his head around so he wouldn't get dizzy. He heard the name again but couldn't figure out where it was coming from. Then he figured it was down the alley.

Otto heard Larry call out, "Henry! Want some? Got us a jug." Larry waved at him. "Come on!"

Henry wiped his mouth with the greasy sleeve and headed for the entry to the alley. "Who is it? Jelly, is that you?" The figure retreated into the dark.

"Got some meth, too." Henry moved more quickly, but put out his left hand to steady himself as he went into the darkness.

"Larry?" He moved further into the dark. Up ahead there was a slit between buildings, and a bit of the street light from One Street filtered in. Larry was with someone standing there with a jug. "Larry! What's up, man?"

Larry the Pervert held up a large wine bottle. "Come on, man. Let's party!" Henry moved toward him. Henry and Larry had had a falling out when Larry had grabbed that thirteen-year-old Native American runaway boy off the street and taken him to the abandoned warehouse where Larry did his pervert thing. Henry and Otto had heard that Larry did dirty things but hadn't ever seen them. Later, when Henry had yelled at Larry about it, the pervert had hit him and threatened him with the big Buck knife he carried in his boot, and Henry had nursed his broken nose and shut up. Why was

Larry so friendly, offering to share his jug and pills? Otto wondered.

He weaved up to Larry. "Yo, Larry! How's the man." Henry looked around, anxious. "No hard feelings?" It was tentative.

"No, man. Hey, I'd like you to meet some friends of mine." Three men came out of the shadows. They weren't from these parts. They had suits on. Nice suits. The short one in the back of the other two wore an Armani, said some old, deep memory from Otto's past. The two in front grabbed Henry and pinned his arms behind him. The shorter one in the back came forward. A moment of awareness came over Henry just before he saw the glint on the hand that came rushing toward his face.

Otto heard Larry cackling as the fists crashed into Henry's face, stomach, chest, and balls. The two men braced him against the wall while the short, dapper man smashed his face into a red smear, his rough ring tearing chunks of flesh from his cheeks and chin, blood rushing between his shattered teeth mixing with the grease and mud on his coat. Suddenly it was over. The hitter gave a signal, the two goons let go of him, and he slumped to the ground, moaning.

"Man, you sure did him good. That was some work over!" Larry took a swig from his bottle. "Where's my money?" The men turned to him.

"You'll get what's coming to you, Larry," the larger of the two men said softly. The man reached into his pocket. Larry looked with greed at the hand in the pocket. The man pulled out something that looked like... a knife? Larry's eyes widened as his arms were pinioned behind him. The large man lunged at him with the knife and buried it in his chest. Larry tried to scream, but a hand was over his mouth. The large man was smiling now, at least on one side of his face. The man withdrew the knife and stabbed him again, and again, and again, finally leaving the knife in him. Larry dropped.

"Now let's finish it up." The smaller of the two goons rifled Larry's body until he came up with the big Buck knife from his boot. He turned toward the prostrate Henry.

Otto closed his eyes and covered his ears, trying to keep out the sounds of the knife repeatedly plunging into Henry, sometimes making sucking noises when it came out. He was very careful not to make any noise. When the suits had finished, they sprinted down the alley, one of the men limping. Otto peeked out from the boxes just in time to see a Jeep four-wheel drive come to a stop at the entrance to the alley. It looked reddish brown (Otto pointed to McNab's jacket) and had one green fender (Otto pointed to the tree leaves). The men jumped into the vehicle and sped away.

Otto waited a long time and then carefully got out of his hole. He looked over the bodies and decided it was no time to be in the alley or, indeed, in Euphrates. He wasn't very verbal, but he wasn't stupid, either. This wasn't the ordinary street violence he saw all the time. This was something different, and he wanted no part of it. He sold whatever he could and bought a bus ticket as far as he could get, which was only to Deak City. He was still afraid of the suits and was trying to get money to go farther.

"Did you recognize any of the suits?" McNab kept prodding.

Otto gabbled and shook his head. McNab thought he might be holding back. The question seemed to terrorize him further. Finally, when McNab figured he couldn't get any more out of him, he stopped. He gave him some candy bars he had secreted in his jacket. "I'll be back in a few days, Otto. Bring you some more food. Take care of yourself." McNab walked slowly back to the airplane.

THIRTY-FOUR

"Where's Herman?" McNab stood at the door to the detective's office.

Aaron Grogan looked up, then went back to his paperwork. "Not here."

McNab waited a moment. "When will he be back?"

"Don't know."

"No idea?"

Grogan threw down his pen and swiveled his chair to face McNab. "You hard of hearing or something?"

McNab visibly controlled himself. "Would you tell him to call me?"

"Sure." Grogan turned his chair back to his desk and picked up the report he was reading.

McNab debated about saying anything else, then decided not to. As he was turning to leave, Herman walked in. "Hi, Grif." He went to Grogan's desk. "Here's the Uppman file you wanted." He handed Grogan one file from those he was carrying and then went to his own desk. "Come on in, Grif. What can we do you for?"

"I didn't think you were in." McNab sank into the chair in front of Herman's cluttered desk.

"Just went down to records."

McNab shifted in the seat. "Got something you might want to know about."

"Concerning... ?"

"Henry Bouchard."

Grogan snorted in the background. Herman looked uncomfortable. "That case is closed. We cleared it yesterday."

"You might want to reopen it."

"That would take a lot, Grif."

"This might be a lot." McNab told Herman about finding Otto in Deak City and of getting his story about witnessing Henry's killing. When he finished, he sat back in his chair amid an uncomfortable silence. McNab looked over to find Grogan had unashamedly turned his chair to face the two of them.

"What a crock!" Grogan was vehement. "You take the word of this wacked out street wino? How did you even understand him? No one does, do they Herman?"

Herman looked very ill at ease. "Well, Grif, you have to admit that not many people can make anything out of what Otto says. Matter of fact I don't know any."

"Yeah. How come you're the only one who can understand him?," Grogan sneered.

"I spent time with him. I got used to hearing him."

Grogan shook his head in disgust. "You're a piece of work, McNab."

"Grif. Aaron's got a point. You're telling us what Otto said. Otto isn't even in our jurisdiction anymore. I'd have to convince the captain that this is a credible lead just to get him to reopen the case. Then I'd have to convince him to spend the money to send someone up to Deak City. Then we'd have to find Otto. Then we'd have to find someone, other than you, who could understand him. Then we'd have to find corroborating evidence, like some way of identifying these guys."

"It's a good lead, Herman."

Grogan snorted again. "This is too rich for me. I got to get some fresh air." He picked up some files and left the office, leaving Herman and McNab alone.

Herman looked at McNab. "You really want me to go to the captain and tell him he has to reopen the case because you said that Otto the Weird, that no one can understand, told you that three suits went hunting for Larry the Pervert and Henry the wino? I'm taking the lieutenant's exam next month, Grif. The captain's going to be on the examining committee. I haven't had a promotion in four years and Carol wants to move out to Glen Aire, get the kids into schools where gangs aren't. Am I making sense to you, Grif?"

McNab sighed. "Yeah, Herman. I get your point. What about the description of the car? How about an APB on the car?" Herman didn't answer. McNab stood up. "I'll have to track this down myself."

"Grif, don't." Herman was agitated. "I know how you feel, but this case is closed. The department doesn't want any stuff stirred up."

"Is there stuff to stir up?"

"Look, Grif. I thought there was some weird things going on here. Maybe there were. But I kept my eyes and ears open and I didn't find out anything. As far as I can tell it wasn't any weirder than some of the other stuff that comes down."

"Uh-huh."

"I mean it." Herman hunched forward across the desk. "Remember two years ago when the mayor's wife got arrested for shoplifting in the toy store?"

"Yeah."

"Well, there was some weird things going on then, too. But they couldn't keep it under wraps. Too many people knew about it. Well, same thing here. If there is anything happening here it'll come out. Too many people know too much. All the time. Everywhere. If there is something strange happening it'll come out. With the mayor's wife, we could feel the pressure of something building all around us. We didn't know what it was, but we knew it was there. With this thing the weirdness was over quick. No pressure building." He stopped a moment. "Look, Grif. I want things on the up and up as much as you do. But I won't stick my neck out for no reason, and I don't see any reason here. Let it alone, Grif. It's sad, but it's over."

He stood up. "Good luck on the exam, Herman."

THIRTY-FIVE

McNab pulled up to the house and shut off the engine. The last light of the day was filtering between the trees and projecting strange and glorious patterns on the walls and windows. It felt like those ephemeral patterns were about all he had. He couldn't remember being this tired or lost.

He climbed out of the truck and went into the house. Pat wasn't home yet. McNab could hear the beer calling him from the refrigerator and decided to quiet the noise of the brews by drinking one. With his beer and his newspaper, he plopped down on the couch and prepared to spend some time in mediocre escape.

The front section had nothing he wanted to pursue. Nor did the sports, or the 'Living' section, or travel, or classified. He put the paper down in disgust and picked up the remote for the TV. News and weather; that would do it, especially if the news was in Korean or Farsi. When he lived in the big city, he would unwind by tuning in to the small station that carried multiple programs in a variety of tongues. That he couldn't understand anything they said was the point. Unfortunately, there were no foreign-language television shows in Euphrates.

After a few minutes of the latest tornado disaster, he gave

up. It seemed to him that the news folk had an endless supply of disaster tapes and simply grabbed one to plug into whatever new horror had just happened. He thought of a new quiz show, *Name That Disaster*, similar to *Jeopardy*, where the contestants would select categories of natural disasters such as hurricanes, floods, tornadoes, blizzards, fires, etc., and then be shown news footage to identify. Prizes could be helicopter tours with the governor of the next natural catastrophe and a cot in a Red Cross shelter, followed by lengthy interviews with disaster relief bureaucrats. McNab shook his head. He was getting close to the edge.

He got up, liberated another beer from the refrigerator and headed into the den. On the way he put on Bach's Concerto for Two Violins. The crumpled brown paper package of Henry's things was lying on the floor by the closet. McNab picked it up, took it to the dining room, and sat at the table. Slowly he went through the package, piece by piece, again. He fingered the knife and the index card with phone numbers and put them down. The religious tract with the penciled scrawls turned out not to be Henry's writing at all. He put that down. The only thing that still puzzled him was the picture of Hoffstader with the Chinese premier and the circled face of an unknown Chinese, one of several in a phalanx behind the premier. Why would Henry circle this one face? Was the circle on the copy he sent to Hoffstader? If so, why? Certainly, Hoffstader would know who it was. Or maybe not. Maybe he didn't care. Why would he care? This was a nationally published photograph, nothing secretive or clandestine about it. Was this Henry's shabby "secret," a photo from the New York Times?

He picked up the phone and called Bryan Bofford's private extension at ML. "Bryan? Grif McNab. You must work late a lot. Got a minute?"

"We have a rush project on, Mister McNab. I can give you just that minute. How can I help you?"

"Sorry to bother you, I'm just trying to make some sense out of this thing about the death of Henry Bouchard. I appreciate your patience. Remember when I called you about the letter Henry sent Hoffstader?"

"Mister Hoffstader."

"Right. Mister Hoffstader, excuse me. You said he sent a picture along with it. I think I have a copy of the same picture and in it one of the men in the background is circled. Does that mean anything to you or to Mister Hoffstader?"

"Could you hold for a moment? I'll need to get the file."

"Sure, I'll hold." Syrupy music wafted out of the earpiece as McNab waited for Bofford to retrieve the file. Finally, Bofford came back on.

"Thank you, Jacquye. Mister McNab? I have the file here. I'm afraid the picture seems to have been discarded, but I don't remember seeing anyone circled in it."

McNab thought a moment. "Well, thank you for trying. I appreciate it. Sorry to have disturbed you."

"It was no disturbance at all. However, I trust we have answered all of your questions?"

"Yeah, I think so. Thanks, again."

Thirty-Six

Pat took the phone from her ear and yelled to him. "It's for you."

"Got it!" McNab stopped typing momentarily, picked up the receiver, and jammed it between his left shoulder and ear. "McNab."

"Hello, Grif."

"Who is this?"

"Isn't my voice familiar?"

McNab frowned. The male voice was muffled. He couldn't quite place it. He fingered the computer keyboard absently. "I know a lot of people."

"You used to know me very well."

McNab rocked his chair forward and spoke intently into the phone. "I don't know who the hell you are, but you only have about five seconds to tell me."

There was a low chuckle from the other end. "Ah, Grif. Always the pragmatist. Listen to me. What do these things have in common? *Dibranchia*, and the finest burger in Sandtown. When you figure it out, call me at home. Be sure to mind your manners, though. You don't want to offend anyone.

Especially unintentionally. Oh, and don't try 'star 69.' It won't work." The line went dead.

McNab looked at the phone a moment and then punched 'star' 69. He got a recording that it wasn't available for that number. After a long pause, he sat back in his chair and stared out the window where a swallow had built her nest.

He watched as the petite swallow flew in, fed her babies, and left, only to repeat the pattern over and over. As the shadows lengthened, he heard Pat moving around, starting to fix some supper. The sun was down over the horizon, and a ghostly orange twilight touched the trees and the house. He reached for the phone and dialed. "Bob? Still overloaded with tuna? Could I grab some of that tonight? Thanks."

THIRTY-SEVEN

He pecked Jennifer on the cheek and put the bag on the counter. It was starting to darken with the blood from the tuna. "I brought some tuna. Rico in back?"

"Yeah. Go on back."

"How's it going?"

"You mean for me or for Rico? Or for him and me? Hmmm?"

McNab paused, then shook his head. "Sorry."

"It's Okay." Jennifer brushed her hair back from her forehead. "I knew better. I just hope we don't lose the friendship." She came over to him and put her head on his chest, and let out a long sigh. "Am I supposed to tell you 'I told you so'? Or are you supposed to tell me that? I forget now who was supposed to do what to whom."

McNab hugged her. "I think it was my bad idea. How can I help?"

"Just be here, okay?" She pushed back from him. "You'd better go back." She turned back to the kitchen.

Rico was bent over his computer. "You still don't call, do you? Be just a minute." He finished poking some keys, hitting the last one triumphantly. "Ha!" He swiveled his chair toward McNab. "Just made four hundred bucks!"

"I brought some tuna. How you doing?"

"Pretty good." Rico's eyes slid off toward the floor.

"How about Jennifer?"

Rico picked up and twirled a pencil and looked directly at McNab. "The sun's been out. I've been working on my tan." Still looking at him, he raised his arms, uniformly shark-bait white. "What do you think?"

McNab looked down and sighed. "Okay." He brought his gaze back up. "I need a favor."

"Motherfucker." Rico sat upright. "Okay. Shoot."

"I need a phone that can't be traced to me."

"Just buy a burner phone at the mall, Grif."

"I want no witnesses and I want one that can't be hacked."

Rico grinned. "Why, Grif I'm surprised. This is sounding a little, shall we say, clandestine." He brought the tip of the pencil up to his mouth. "I can do part of it. I can get you a phone that won't trace to you, but every call is logged onto some computer and cross referenced with the calling number. There's no way I can fix that." McNab drummed his fingers on the desk. Rico fidgeted with his pencil. "Tell me this, Grif. Do you just want to make some untraceable calls or do you want to make some untraceable calls that can't come back to you even if they found the phone on you?"

"You're fast, Rico."

"That's what you pay me for, man."

McNab gave him a sour look. "Right."

"How soon you need it? Never mind, yesterday. Am I right?" McNab nodded. "Give me a couple of days." He twirled the pencil in his mouth. "Are you going to be using it where cell coverage is, shall we say, spotty?"

McNab thought a moment. "Maybe."

Rico grunted. "Couple more days, then. Oh, by the way,

your Hoffstader stuff is taking more time than I thought. I'll get it to you as soon as I can." McNab nodded. Rico twirled the pencil in his mouth again. "Graphite tastes shitty, man. Don't get the habit." McNab stood to go. "Jen's fine. It's me. I just can't do it."

"Rico..."

"Look, it's okay, it's really okay. I just hope I don't blow her off totally."

THIRTY-EIGHT

"Nine sili nebesniye..." "The acapella voices of the Chorovaya Akademia swelled in religious praise, echoing through the airplane hangar. McNab reveled in Russian liturgical music. Rich baritone and bass chant filled the rusted temple of aviation he had created. He tried to sing along with the CD, grateful that only he could hear himself. Nevertheless, the low tones resonated in his chest and opened him.

Fog still steamed off the forests on the hills. The cattle next to the airport were half hidden in a mystical gauze. A snowy egret glided over the runway, then extended its legs and unfolded its head as it glided to a landing in the little creek bordering the field. Soon it was peering into the shallow water, looking for breakfast, its head darting this way and that. Low clouds were breaking up, and McNab saw sharp shafts of light piercing through the holes in the walls of his principality, illuminating trays of tools, islands of spark plugs, carburetor parts, the unbuttoned cowling of the 185, rags, wires, two tires, oil, the grease-stained rough lumber workbench lining the back wall.

"Slava vo vishnikh Bogu..." The sun broke through the clouds just above the eucalyptus trees and spread its wings of light.

Two more egrets, now dazzling white, glided over the brilliant green grass in formation to take up their own positions along the sparkling creek. Light reflected off something at the end of the field. McNab looked down toward the beginning of the taxiway. He squinted, then turned off the sacred music, put on some Modern Jazz Quartet, and went back to work on the fuel pump inside the plane's engine compartment.

Tire hiss was barely audible over the harpsichord and vibraharp as the black Mercedes halted in front of the hangar. A door opened and slammed shut, then the staccato sounds of high heels coming across the hangar floor hesitantly.

"Are you Mister McNab?" The voice was as tentative as the walk had sounded. McNab pulled his head out of the engine compartment and looked at the woman before him. He wondered if he was hallucinating. She was dressed entirely in pink. Pink bolero over a pink blouse on top of a pink pleated skirt with pink patent leather pumps. A small pink leather purse hung from a pink strap over her right shoulder. A pink pillbox hat topped her platinum blond hair, which was held in place by a material that McNab wished he could use to glue his airplane together. "Excuse me? I'm Jacquye Ormus?" She stuck out her hand. "I'm acting deputy assistant director of public relations for Mountain Lumber in Euphrates?" Every statement came out as a question.

McNab took her hand and gave it a perfunctory shake. "How can I help you?"

"Well, Mister McNab, I... didn't I meet you before or talk to you about something? Excuse me, but I just can't seem to remember where it was we encountered one another?"

McNab calmed himself, "Yes, I spoke with you for a few minutes on the phone about the death of a friend of mine." Jacquye looked puzzled. "The one who threw the peach pie."

Her eyes widened. "Oh, my, yes. That was so unfortunate. Mister Hoffstader had to throw away his suit? He said it couldn't be cleaned enough? Poor man."

"Hoffstader?"

"Well, yes. I mean, it's too bad about your friend, too, of course." She squinted at McNab. "He was a friend of yours? He was supposed to be a street person?"

"Yes, he was." McNab offered no more explanation.

Jacquye looked around at the disheveled grease stained shop. "You must get awfully dirty working here."

"You can, too, if you want."

She turned to look at him, puzzlement on her face. "What did you say?"

"I said if you wanted to get dirty in here, too, you could. I wouldn't mind, I'd just continue working on my plane." He turned back to the engine compartment.

"Excuse me?" Her voice rose. "Are you insulting me?"

McNab turned back. "Only if you think so. I have a fuel pump to fix. Is there something I can help you with?"

McNab didn't know you could flounce while standing still, but Jacquye was doing an excellent job of it. "If I didn't have orders..." She opened her purse and fished for something. "I was sent here on behalf of Mister Hoffstader himself? He wants to fly to the Two Forks Reclamation Project tomorrow? He would like to hire you to fly him?" She pulled out a slip of paper. "Mister Hoffstader knows this is short notice and would be willing to pay double your usual charter fee if you would do that? I have a purchase order for that?"

McNab took the paper and looked at it. "Fine. What time?"

"About eleven o'clock?"

"I'll be here with bells."

"Well, thank you? I'll be going and tell Mister Hoffstader? So nice to meet you?" She stuck out her hand.

McNab took it in both hands and brought it to his lips, planting a big wet kiss on the back of her hand. "Enchanted, I'm sure."

Jacquye flinched and backed off. She went to her car, and

McNab started to wrestle with the fuel pump. The music stopped, so he returned to the small system and put back the Russian religious music. He thought he heard the sound of a car cranking but dismissed it. The chorus swelled, filling the hangar with glorious music as he reached inside the cowling for the recalcitrant pump.

"Mister McNab? Mister McNab?" Her voice barely made it above the music. McNab pulled his head back out and stared at her. "I've... could you turn down the music?" He nodded and went to the CD player, and stopped the disc. He came back toward her. "Oh, you didn't have to turn it off? I just love the Chorovaya Akademia myself? I just can't compete with their volume?"

"You know Russian music?" McNab was dumbstruck.

"Oh, yes. I love religious music. It makes me feel closer to my Lord?" McNab's heart sank. "You were playing the Modern Jazz Quartet when I first came in? It's very spiritual music, too? I think music is God's greatest gift to us, don't you?"

"You listen to the MJQ?"

"Why, yes, and Sonny Rollins and Miles Davis and Laurindo Almeida? All sorts of wonderful people, the Mormon Tabernacle Choir, Mozart, Aaron Copland. I must confess, though, I never understood Charles Ives or Ornette Coleman. But I like Sun Ra, do you? It's so sad he died?"

McNab was almost speechless. "What... why are you here?"

"Oh, I almost forgot? My car won't start? I was wondering if I could use your phone? To call the auto club?"

"Yeah, sure." Jacquye started for the phone. "Wait a minute. If you want I'll take a quick look at it. Save you some time." She nodded. "Keys?" She walked over and handed him her keys. McNab picked up a whiff of *L'air du Temp*. He had a sudden flash of his dead wife, Cindy. "Be right back. You can sit in the office if you like. Turn on the music."

A few minutes later, McNab came into the office. The Russian liturgy was being played at a lower decibel level. Jacquye was sitting in his chair, shoes off, feet on the desk, jacket askew, eyes closed. He stood in the doorway for a moment, looking at her and seeing a softness he hadn't seen before. McNab kicked the door softly. Jacquye opened her eyes, focused, and took her feet off his desk quickly. "I'm so sorry? I was just carried away?" She turned down the volume.

"No gas."

"I beg your pardon?"

"You're out of gas."

"Oh, shoot. I knew I was pushing it?" She reached down and put her shoes on. "I'll just call the auto club and they'll bring me some? They'll be mad, though? Fourth time this year? They'll probably charge me some outrageous service charge? That music is so pretty? Do you listen to music a lot?"

McNab started wiping his hands off on the rag he had in his pocket. "Yeah. I listen to all sorts of music. Not a lot of modern, though."

"Most of my friends only listen to two kinds? Country, and western? Isn't that funny? A joke, you know? I love country and western, but I like a lot more? Like jazz from the fifties and sixties and Gershwin? A little bebop? Gregorian chant, Wagner? Like that? All mixed up?"

McNab finished cleaning his hands. "I'll give you a lift to get some gas, if you like."

"You're not such a mean guy after all, are you, Mister McNab?"

"Sorry about earlier. Call me Grif."

"Well, all right, Grif. Let's get us some gas."

They jumped in his truck and headed toward town. "Carl Perkins." McNab barked.

"Missa Luba? The original one from the sixties? It is *so* spiritual?"

"Oscar Petersen."

"Chuck Berry?" Jacquye laughed as she said it.

"Miriam Makeba. Can you do the click sound?"

"No. Can you?"

He gave an ersatz click. Jacquye giggled. "Cole Porter," McNab said over his shoulder as he turned toward the Square. The full gas can had been secured in the back of his truck.

"The Fabulous Wailers? Where are we going?"

"Reggae?"

"Not reggae? This was a two album group from the fifties? Nice looking boys in black framed glasses and sport coats and ties? Pretty good rock 'n roll, though?"

"It's getting toward dinner. Have you been to Luego's?"

"No, I've never been there? I don't know if I should?"

"Your call, Jacquye. Lord Kitchener?"

"I love calypso? And Soca? No one carries much of it anymore? Do they have seafood?"

"They have what Mingus calls seafood. He's the owner and chief obnoxious person."

"I love breaded fish sticks? The kind they sell frozen in the super market? With lots of homemade tartar sauce? You know, mayonnaise and pickle relish all mixed up? Or ketchup with horseradish spooned in it?"

McNab pulled into Luego's parking lot. They were still talking about music when Mingus walked up.

"My God, McNab, what have you done? Kidnaped the Cotton Candy Queen for 1956?"

"Shut it, Mingus, just get us a table."

Jacquye whispered to McNab, "Did you bring me here just to be insulted?"

"He's insulting to everyone."

Still whispering, she said, "I'm not everyone?"

Mingus grabbed two menus and started walking toward the back, talking over his shoulder, "I'll bet it's all polyester. Did they even have polyester in 1956? We got a booth in the back. Where no one can see you. Be grateful."

"Grif? He is being nasty?"

"Yeah. But don't notice or you'll just encourage him. Treat him like you would a rabid skunk. Edge around him and don't call attention to yourself."

"No wonder I never came here?"

Mingus waved to one of the customers, "Yeah, no wonder. Christ, McNab, I have a reputation to uphold. Polyester!"

"Was he swearing? He was swearing?" McNab grabbed her by the hand and pulled her toward the back booth.

"Come on, it'll be fun."

As they turned the corner toward the darker back, McNab saw Pat sitting in a small booth, eating dinner with her best friend, Elizabeth. She looked up as McNab approached and smiled. Then she saw Jacquye behind him, and the smile turned into a knowing grin.

McNab continued on to the back. "They have a great jukebox." They got to the booth and sat across from each other. "Look." McNab pointed to the jukebox selector bolted to the wall at the table. "Only four of the booths have this. Sometimes they work. Take a look."

Jacquye flipped the pages with the metal handles sticking out of the bottom. "Who was that beautiful lady we passed? Who smiled at you? That was a gorgeous jacket? All that silk braid work on fitted black crepe? I'd just die for a coat like that? One play for a quarter?"

"Inflation. That's my friend Pat."

"Oh?"

"You remember my friend, the street person who got killed? That's his sister."

"Really?" Jacquye went silent for a moment. "Oh, that's so sad? I hope she doesn't feel too bad? I never thought he might have a sister? Or a mother? Is his mother still alive? Goes to show you, everyone has a mother?"

"I don't know if she's still alive. I know that Pat loved him very much."

"Look at this? They have the good Morgans! Helen, Lee, and Frank? This is wonderful, Grif?"

"Whaddya want?" Myrna stood over them.

"I'll have the usual. Jacquye hasn't seen the menu yet."

"Oh, I don't need to? Grif said you had seafood? Do you have those little breaded fish sticks with some tartar sauce and cole slaw? Maybe some cocktail sauce on the side? Do you have decaffeinated iced tea?"

Myrna started to roll her eyes when McNab kicked her under the table. "Ow! I don't think we have those, ma'am. We do have a special of *Coquille St. Jacques*, scallops in cream sauce. That's as close as we can get, I think."

"What do you think, Grif? I get so confused? It sounds like my name, don't you think? Jacquye and Jacques?" She slurred the 'j' of her first name. McNab preemptively kicked Myrna again.

"I think that's good." He looked up to murderous eyes. "That's what we'll have. And a liter of white." Myrna stomped off.

"She's kind of weird? Don't you think? Oh, my, I should powder my nose. Where is...?" McNab pointed to the restrooms. "Why don't you pick out something to listen to? I'll be right back?"

Myrna came back and slammed the carafe of white wine and two glasses on the table, spun around, and left before McNab could say anything. He poured wine into both glasses and took a sip. He flipped through the music selection, took a few quarters, and put them into the jukebox.

Jacquye slipped back into the booth. "Well, how do I look? All powdered?" She took a sip from her glass.

"You look... so... pink."

"You like it? I have my periods? Oops!" She giggled. "I mean, I wear different colors at different times? For a long time? You know, like Picasso's Blue Period? This is my pink period? I also do powder blue, forest green and," she paused for effect, "midnight?" Jacquye tossed down half of her glass of wine in one swallow. "This is good wine? You were right about this place, even if that man is a real jerk?"

"Well, Mingus is well, yeah, a jerk sometimes."

"You're in luck." Myrna appeared with the food. She plopped a plate down in front of Jacquye. It was breaded scallops with a cup of mayonnaise. Next came a bottle of sweet relish and, finally, McNab's food. Myrna refilled both their wine glasses.

"Oh, look at that? There are those funny men? The monks, I mean?" Jacquye pointed. McNab turned around to see Derek McGinty walk in with the three monks dressed in orange and red robes. Mingus sat them near the door.

Myrna looked over at them. "Do they wear those dresses all the time or just special occasions, do you think?"

McNab started to get up. "I need to talk with them. I'll be right back."

Jacquye put her hand on his arm. "Why don't you talk with them tomorrow? Our food's here, and it'll get cold?" He hesitated and then sat down.

"I don't know where to find them." McNab started to get up again.

"Darling? Don't you worry? I have their address at work? I'll let you know?" He could see Mingus putting a large Coca-Cola in front of the young monk. McNab looked at the monks, then at the woman smiling up at him, and sat down.

They both dug in and ate and drank heartily, talking about music. They were laughing a lot. Jacquye was in the middle of a description of sneaking into a Chuck Berry concert in Honolulu. "...and I just looked at him and said, 'Why I don't know what you mean? My friend has my ticket,' and I pointed over to one of those really big Hawaiian guys? About two hundred pounds bigger than this teeny-weeny little guard? And he just went away? It was so funny? I just about died?" They both started to laugh again.

"Hi, Grif." They both looked up to see Pat standing at the table. Jacquye frowned a moment.

"Jacquye Ormus, this is Pat Morrissey. Pat and I share a house together. Pat, Jacquye."

Jacquye looked puzzled, then recovered. "I am so pleased to meet you?" She stuck out her hand. Pat, momentarily nonplussed, finally shook it. "I didn't know Grif had a girl friend?"

"Actually, he doesn't. I'm a lesbian. We just share a house."

Jacquye opened her mouth to start to say something and then closed it, then opened it again. "Oh."

Pat looked speculatively at Jacquye and turned to Grif. "Did I tell you about the charity board meeting?"

McNab paused a moment. It was their code. If the reply was yes, then it meant that, yes, the answerer was bringing someone home and that the questioner should be prepared to be discreet. "Well, I think I may recall something about it."

"Is that a yes or a no?"

"Ah... yes."

"Unbelievable. Well, I must be off. It'll be a long meeting." Pat turned to Jacquye. "I'm *so* pleased to meet you. Have a nice dinner."

"What did she mean, unbelievable?"

McNab poured her a glass of wine. "Probably my lousy memory. Want some more wine?"

"I really shouldn't." Lee Morgan's 'Sidewinder' started to come out of the speakers. "Well, maybe just a little?" McNab poured her some more wine. Jacquye hunched forward over the table. Keeping her eyes fixed on McNab's, she took a sip. "Do you have many CDs? At home?"

THIRTY-NINE

"Karl, leave us alone for a minute." Hoffstader said. The huge man got out of the front seat of the plane and walked across the narrow, dusty strip to the shade of a redwood. He sat down next to the shack that had "Two Forks Reclamation Project" stenciled on it. He never took his eyes off the plane. Hoffstader sat back in the rear seat and addressed McNab, "Nice landing on a short field."

Up close, Hoffstader seemed less than he was. He was short and balding. He still had a fringe, but cut it so short it was almost shaved. Hoffstader dressed impeccably. McNab could well believe that his suits cost over three thousand dollars. It seemed incongruous that someone this well-dressed would be sitting in McNab's old, borrowed plane. But it was the eyes that McNab paid attention to. No matter the mood: hearty, charming, deadpan, matter of fact, the eyes never varied. They were pale, colorless eyes, like a winter sky, windows to a calculating machine, but behind them something burned.

McNab inclined his head, acknowledging the compliment.

"People tell me you've been asking questions about me."

McNab shrugged.

"If you have questions about me, ask me."

"Did you have Henry Bouchard killed?"

Hoffstader's eyes flared briefly, then went pale again. "You're being rude, Mister McNab. I'll overlook it this time."

"That's very gracious of you."

"Don't try my patience, Mister McNab. Life can get very difficult."

"So I've heard."

"But that's not why I wanted to talk with you." McNab arched his eyebrows. Hoffstader looked around the tiny airplane cabin, patted the worn seat, and traced the tear in the ceiling liner. "I hear you've had some problems with your regular plane."

McNab pushed his cap back on his head. "Nothing that can't be worked out."

"New engines cost a lot of money."

"Depends on your perspective."

"Fifty thousand dollars is a lot of money in any language."

McNab thought about the article he'd been shown by Pike Rambus. It was an architectural magazine featuring Hoffstader's new home in Los Angeles. The writer had gushed about Hoffstader's closet having over $600,000 in custom woodwork. "As I said, it depends."

Hoffstader put his large hand against the Plexiglas window. A colossal ring dominated the hand. A massive gold band was topped by a ragged stone that looked quite ordinary, like rough gravel. He noticed McNab looking at it.

"Like it?" McNab shrugged. "A present from NASA. When we completed the work on the launch pad eleven weeks early. Saved them a lot of money." He looked at it almost clinically. "Moon rock. A real piece of the moon." He pulled his hand back down to his lap. "Ever want to own a piece of the sky?"

Hoffstader leaned forward. "I could use a man like you, McNab. You think, you innovate. Your own plane is down, but here you are. Still in business. A piece of shit bucket of bolts, but what the hell, it flies. Am I right?" The pilot just looked at him. "Ingenuity. I like that." He paused a minute. "I also like a man who knows the limits. I mean, you wouldn't deliberately fly right into the heart of a thunderstorm, would you? It would tear this tin bird apart. Scatter little aluminum pieces over half the county. Right?" McNab didn't respond. "A man like that could be very valuable."

"What, exactly, are you saying?"

"I don't need another full time pilot. I have a Gulfstream and a crew already. But, ML could use regular service into their smaller strips. That is if the plane could make it in and out and carry enough to make it worthwhile. Do you get my drift?"

"I must be a little slow today. Why don't you fill me in?"

"Well," Hoffstader flexed his arms in front of him, "this puddle jumper can take, what, two, three people plus you and maybe some baggage? Maybe? If it isn't too hot and the runway is long enough? Now, if you had a Cessna Caravan or something like it... carries eight, nine people? Lots of cargo. Turboprop, lot of power, good short-field performance? A lot better than this piece of shit. How much do they cost? Two and a half million plus or minus? You could get a lot more business than you have now.

"I figure it would be a good investment for ML. We get first call on your service with a reliable plane. ML doesn't want to be in the charter business, but we can use a reliable man. We buy the plane, pay you to fly it for us and you get to use it when we don't need it. Direct operating costs only, no capitalization."

"Sounds too good to be true."

"A good businessman looks at the long term and looks at all the possibilities." McNab didn't respond. "A good businessman also has the sense to recognize a good deal when he sees it."

McNab took a breath and let it out. "Well, I guess I'm not a very good businessman."

Bruce Snade, the project manager, was walking toward the plane, clearly impatient. Hoffstader motioned him away. "Pissant. He fucks up the project then wants me to come bail him out." He leaned forward. "Look, McNab, I know you don't have the money to pay for that engine. You're in a lot of trouble. I'm offering you a way out."

"At what price?"

"Price? Did I say anything about price? You just fly for me when I need you, that's all."

"I don't think so."

There was a moment of silence. "You're running away from a good deal, just like you ran from the Air Force." McNab started. "You think I don't know about you? Astronaut, car accident, OSI, SCUID. Then you cut and run to this jerkwater place. Shit, you don't even try here. Won't even be a big fish in this fucking little pond. You just quit." He paused. "You're a loser, McNab. Your plane is down, you don't have any money, you're becoming a joke in the sheriff's office. He leaned back and softened his voice. "Let me help you, Grif. A man like you should be in the thick of it. You need me, McNab. Think about it."

McNab looked out at the frustrated project manager. "Your pissant wants you."

Hoffstader reached for the door. "Look, McNab. If it's personal animosity I can handle that. It doesn't have to affect business. Christ, I talk to Pike Rambus and he hates my guts. You wouldn't even have to fly me around. Think about it. Call me if you change your mind. I leave for L.A. tomorrow afternoon. You can call me before then or call Brian Bofford later. But don't take too long." He paused. "In the meantime, stay out of my business."

FORTY

Gray skies put little cheer through the skylights in the kitchen. Pat stood in the doorway as McNab opened two beers.

"You're really stupid, McNab."

"Thanks for the support." He continued to pour their beers.

"He may be a scumbag but at least he has money and could be of some help. You could have at least told him you'd think about it, for Christ's sake. What a jerk. Give me a beer." Pat folded her arms across her chest and glowered at him.

"Is that all?" He handed her a glass.

"No, that's not all." She took a sip. "How stupid can you be? He's the richest, most powerful man in the county, shit, the whole fucking state, maybe the country, and you not only refuse his help but insult him in the process. Shit for brains." They moved into the living room. McNab sat on the hearth and drank some of his beer. "You've got a plane that needs a new engine, no money to pay for it, and you blow off the best offer you've had since you got here. Stupid little shit."

"Any more?"

Pat sat forward in her chair. "Yes, goddamn it! Charlie isn't going to lend you that wreck of a plane of his forever. Even if he did, you aren't making the kind of money that could pay for the engine anyway. Especially now that Grogan is out to get you. I thought you were supposed to be bright."

"Maybe."

"Well, what's the story, anyway? You want to crash and burn? Sorry, bad analogy." Pat's voice was rising, her hand motions came perilously close to knocking the beer off the lamp table next to the chair. "Well, do you? Jesus, Grif, you came here with just enough to get started and you've worked your ass off to build what little you got. Are you going to sit there and watch it all go under because of your stupid fucking pride? What are you thinking?" McNab took another sip of his beer. "Don't you have anything to say?"

He smiled at her. "I didn't know you cared."

"Fuck you, McNab. Asshole. Stupid... oh, never mind! Of course I care for you. Men are so stupid."

"What would Tanya say?"

"Watch it."

McNab set his glass down on the bricks. "You still seeing her? Never mind. Look, I don't want his money, Pat. He's not trying to help me. He's trying to buy me off."

"What do you mean, 'buy you off'?"

"He knew my whole history. Why would a man like Hoffstader give a shit about me?"

"What does he want?"

"I don't know. It makes no sense."

"Are you a threat to him?"

"I don't know how I could be."

"Have you joined Friends of the Forest or the Sierra Club? Or written letters to the editor?"

McNab laughed. "Sure. Like that would bother him." He paused a moment. "I asked him if he had Henry killed."

"You did what?" Pat just looked at him. "I don't believe you."

"Yeah. He still made me the offer. You know, Hoffstader

said he had his own crew and a Gulfstream and didn't need another pilot. He also didn't need to hire me. He could have hired Brophy or Peter. They both have STOL planes, and in a lot better condition than Charlie's."

"You think this was a set up?"

"It did give him an excuse to talk to me casually."

"Does Hoffstader needs an excuse for anything he does?" Pat said.

"No, I guess he doesn't. But, something doesn't feel right."

Pat laughed. "I'll say. Broke doesn't feel right at all."

McNab made a sour face. "Will you just listen to me?"

"Sorry."

"It felt wrong. I have no love for Hoffstader, as you know. I think he's the worst thing that ever happened to this part of the country and Euphrates especially. But I respect his intelligence and his power. What he offered doesn't make sense, unless he wants me beholden to him. Under his control. The question is why?"

"He's right about one thing, you've been asking a lot of questions about him lately."

McNab nodded. "Is he that paranoid? If so, why? And if so, why go to all the trouble and expense? Why be this elaborate? If I'm a real threat, why not just kill me?"

"And you think Hoffstader's paranoid?" Pat brushed the hair out of her eyes.

McNab smiled. "I got a little far out, didn't I?"

Pat got up and went to the window. "You don't get it, do you, McNab?"

"What do you mean?"

"You came back to this town thinking yourself a failure. People around here think you're a hero." McNab started to say something. "It's your turn to shut up and listen." She assumed the pose McNab defined as 'closing argument.' "You're delusional. I haven't been here my whole life like you have. I'm a newcomer. I've only been here twelve years. When

I've been here thirty years, I'll just start to be accepted. Second generation gets accepted here. That's not the point, though.

"The point is that you're a home town boy who made good and didn't forget where you came from. You were an astronaut..." McNab started to say something. "Just shut up and listen. You're born and bred Euphrates. The kid who worked on the family ranch. You bucked hay, milked cows, did rodeos. You and Herman were co-captains on the high school championship football team. You survived your father's death and took care of your mom. You graduated first in your class and then you became a hotshot Air Force pilot. They don't care about the strict rules that you never went into space. You were in the program; that makes you an astronaut. As important and meaningful as John Glenn and Neil Armstrong to them. More important. You're one of them. One of us."

"But..."

"Don't." She sat down and faced him directly. "The accident was a terrible tragedy, and it hurt everyone here. You could have stayed in Houston or wherever you could have stayed, and people would still care about you. But, eventually, you came home. And you didn't try to capitalize on your fame. You didn't become a tout for some slimy real estate developer or some other humiliating thing. You came back and just lived here. Among us. You suffered along with the rest when the Creamery Co-op failed, taking the life savings of a lot of farmers, including your parents'. You weren't remote. You were one of them. These people aren't very good about telling you they love you, but they do. They're very proud of you.

"Hoffstader knows that. It could be part of his plan to get himself accepted here. Or if not accepted, at least barely tolerated." She grinned impishly, "He won't kill you, stupid. You know too many cops." Pat got more serious. "But he would try to destroy you if you got in his way. But what are you in the way of? Nothing. It's not conspiracy, and it's not pity. It's a good business move for him and for you. Hold your nose and take the deal, Grif."

"It doesn't feel right, Pat. Something's not right about this."

"You're such a shithead. You're not even consistent. Christ, you're fucking that bubble-headed little twit that works for him. Did you know she looks a lot like Lureen? Did that ever occur to you, Chief Thinks-With-His-Dick?"

"You leave her out of this."

Pat put her head in her hands. "Tell me this isn't happening. I know this isn't happening. This is a dream, a very, very bad dream." She looked up. "You're not falling for Miss Cotton Brain, are you? Tell me it ain't so, Grif."

McNab fidgeted. "I thought we were talking about Hoffstader?"

"You know your problem, McNab? You're cross wired. You're not a regular man. Your dick is connected to your heart. I don't believe this." Pat got up and paced the floor. "You're paranoid about Hoffstader, but you're sleeping with his oily assistant's assistant. You want to run your life by your gut instincts and you're falling for the witless wonder. Yes, she's pretty... in pink, polyester." She turned to him. "I'm sorry, that was low, but you've got to admit this isn't one of your shining romantic moments. Not that you've had very many shining moments, as you'll admit." McNab gave up and sat back as Pat kept going. "I haven't either, God knows, but, please, not this one. I'm sure she's nice."

"Pat—"

"Shut up." She paced some more. "Let's think this through. You're paranoid about Hoffstader. You think he's up to something. I don't, in this case, but let's give it the benefit of the doubt. Let's say he's working some weird plot behind the scenes. You say he knows more about you than he should. Why wouldn't he know about your love life? Why wouldn't he know that you're a hopeless romantic shithead that always falls for the most inappropriate woman around? Now, here you are, alone, vulnerable, your world is falling down around you and suddenly, standing before you, in a cloud of pink haze, is a pretty, vacuous, and available... employee."

"It wasn't like that, Pat. She knows music. My kind of music."

"Well, of course she does. If Hoffstader really knows all the shit you wouldn't even tell me for years, he would never know what music you listened to. He certainly wouldn't prime Miss Polyester, would he?"

"It was not like that."

Pat sat back down in her chair. "I know it wasn't, Grif. That isn't the point. You're too paranoid in one area and not enough in your love life. Christ, I don't even know this woman, Grif, but I've known you long enough to smell sex disaster looming.

"I promised myself I wouldn't tell you. While you were in the shower she was out in the kitchen. Cleaning my coffee pot." McNab put his hands over his eyes. "Yes. My coffee pot!" Pat opened her eyes very wide and made her voice higher and squeakier. "'I hope you don't mind? I learned this little trick? If you put five ice cubes and some vinegar and some salt? In the coffee pot? It'll clean it right up? Isn't that just the neatest thing?" She paused. "Take the deal, dump the broad."

McNab kneaded his chin for a minute. "You're right about Jacquye, cute spelling and all. She isn't as dumb as she seems. You're right, we'd be going nowhere. But I'm not going to be part of Hoffstader's whorehouse."

FORTY-ONE

McNab got off the phone. Wind whipped outside the hangar and through the holes and cracks in the metal siding. He was on the tenth marketing call of the morning. There was no actual selling going on, but he had decided to touch base with everyone who had flown with him in the last two years just to stay connected. He also knew he was avoiding the one call he had to make.

He got up and got himself another cup of coffee. McNab started to the phone and hesitated yet again. Coward, he told himself. Afraid of a pink polyester woman. What a wimp. He didn't need Pat to tell him this was wrong. Loneliness had gotten him into more trouble than he cared to remember. Then the litany started: all the women he'd been involved with where the relationship had been doomed from the start and how he hadn't wanted to know that and, therefore, didn't know it until it was too late not to know it and then paid the price for not knowing it sooner because he was just too goddam lonely.

She wasn't the worst he'd ever had, not by a long shot. McNab shuddered, remembering some of the choices he'd made. There were women far worse for him than Jacquye.

This ruminating, though, was not going to change anything. He had to bite the bullet.

Just as he reached for the phone, he heard a car stop in front of the hangar. He walked over to the Judas gate, the person-sized door at the side of the large one, and peeked outside. Jacquye was just emerging from the black Mercedes. She wasn't pink. She was wearing a smart, dark green business suit that flattered her figure. It made her look both more professional and sexier. The wind tossed her hair, which was down now, softer and more natural. She closed the car door, turned, and saw McNab. The sight of him seemed to startle her a little.

McNab held the door for her and she came into the hangar. The wind blew up the hem of her jacket, revealing a dark green silk blouse that caressed her waist. Jacquye clutched her rich, dark brown leather purse tightly and kept away from the embrace that McNab had not made. Inwardly, McNab clenched. He motioned her to the office. Jacquye went in without a word.

"Coffee?" McNab gestured to the pot. Jacquye shook her head and kept standing. "Seat?"

She shook her head again and clutched the purse even more tightly. Finally, she said, "Grif, this is very hard? You're such a nice man? I like you, I really do? But I don't think we should see each other anymore?" McNab didn't say anything. "I really enjoyed the other night? The whole evening was so wonderful? I had a little too much wine? And I did something I don't like myself for very much? I think I led you on? Made you think there was more going on than there was? You know what I mean?"

McNab shrugged. "No. I don't think I do."

Jacquye was massaging her purse and not looking straight at him. "I don't sleep with men I don't love? I hardly sleep with anyone at all. It's a sin against the Lord? I know you think that's old-fashioned, but it's just the way I am?

"I tried to make it feel all right? I tried to pretend it was all right? I tried to be nice to your friend? Good Lord, what she must have thought, some crazy woman out in the kitchen cleaning her coffee pot and babbling on like some sort of lunatic? She sure looked at me strange? Don't you tell her I said that?" She looked down at the floor, hands fidgeting.

"But it's not right, Grif, it's not right at all? I don't love you?" Her knuckles were turning white. "I'm sorry to hurt you this way, but I just can't do it like that? Like you want? I'm sorry." She bolted for the door. McNab heard her high heels clicking over the concrete floor and then the slam of the small door.

McNab just stood there for a minute, blinking. Then he turned to the coffee pot and poured himself another cup. He sat down at the desk. He took a sip and frowned. It didn't taste very good. He didn't know whether to start more marketing calls or not. Well, he could file some of this stuff on his desk. Or he could look at the fuel pump again. All this could distract him. He reached for some papers and a file folder. "Shit." He threw them back down on the desk. No paperwork today, please, dear God. Tools. Yes. That was it. The cool feel of metal against his skin, the precise fitting together of parts, the order and predictability of a good running engine. McNab picked up the coffee cup and walked out to the hangar. There were lots of mechanical projects to keep him busy. He went over to the bench, looked at the array of tools, and felt comforted. It was going to be all right. Then he heard the Mercedes start and drive away.

He stood a minute, stunned by this whirlwind. The wind picked up and hurled sand and some gravel against the metal walls of the hangar. Over the pelting noise he heard a vehicle stop in front of the building. He hurried toward the small door. As he approached it, the door opened, and a brown uniform came through. "Package for Mister McNab?"

He thanked the delivery man and took the package to the

office. He didn't remember ordering anything. McNab found a box knife and opened the parcel. Under several layers of bubble wrap was a smaller box and a note. It read, "Happy Hippopotamus Day, Rico." Opening the smaller box he found what appeared to be a bulky cellphone.

McNab checked the phone and then called Pat's office. "Pat? You have that 'star 69' thing? When I hang up, try it. If I don't hear from you right away I'll call back. Okay?" He flipped the phone down and waited. After two minutes of silence, he called her back. "No go, huh? I'll tell you later."

Then he dialed a long-distance number. It was picked up on the second ring.

"Hello?"

"Hi, Doug."

"Took you long enough."

"I had to make some arrangements."

"I think we need to get together. There's been some interesting things happening."

"Like what?"

"Better in person. You been to Elko?"

"That's where they tested the Stealth Fighter, isn't it?"

"Yeah. We're doing some work out there. There's a civilian field there on the outskirts of town. How about I pick you up there day after tomorrow? Bring along what you know about the friend you told me about."

FORTY-TWO

McNab was back in front of Hermione Braithwaite at the reference desk in the library.

"I'm looking for anything you might have on Hoffstader."

"Personal or business?"

"Anything."

"You going tree hugger on us, Grif?" She looked at him hard. "Timber supports this economy, you know. You don't live in a plastic house, do you? You like your redwood deck?" She paused. "Well, we throw away the *Sun* after a week or so. Check with them. Don't have the money to microfilm it. We have the New York Times and LA Times on microfilm. Do you want either of those?"

"Both. Say about ten years back?"

"Okay. Be right back." A few minutes later she came back to the desk with a stack of microfilm reels. "We probably won't be able to renew our subscription next year. Want to join the Friends of the Library, Grif? Only twenty bucks."

"Gee, Hermione…"

"Don't waffle on me, Grif. Yes or no."

McNab hauled out a twenty and handed it over. "You're a saint, Grif." She swiftly moved to the next customer.

He went to the viewer and fed in the first reel. Over the next seven hours McNab came up with a profile of Hoffstader. There were a few stories in the early editions, more later, as Hoffstader's star ascended. There were a couple of overview articles among the more specific ones about large business deals. McNab found a series of articles by the same writer who appeared to be less idolatrous about Hoffstader. His writings seemed to dig more. McNab began looking for Grafton Leamus' byline.

The tenor of the articles was that he was simply a billionaire shark. Like a shark, all Hoffstader seemed to do was eat and shit. He would eat companies and eliminate people. There seemed to be no other interests in life for him other than the accumulation of power and wealth. His infrequent visits to the world of art and culture came across as transparent frauds.

He appeared to be an anomaly. Lower middle-class background, loving parents, though very poor. Father a mechanic, mother a hairdresser. They lived in rural Indiana in a small town where nothing ever happened. Always restless, a few scrapes with the law when he was a teenager. Didn't drink to excess, never used drugs. He was too focused. Dropped out of school and hustled. Encyclopedias, cookware, magazines, anything with a big commission and a relaxed view of ethics. Crew chief within a month of joining wherever he went. Considered too young to be a manager, he was always the best producer.

He was among the last ones drafted into the army before it went all-volunteer. While serving in Germany in the quartermaster corps he became the subject of an investigation of a ring that stole from the military and sold to the German black market. His underlings were caught and punished, but he escaped prosecution, was rotated back to Kansas and out of the quartermasters.

After the army he started to trade penny stocks and made

a lot of money. He got into a power struggle with one of the senior managers when he was passed over for a management position. The stated reason was that his competition had a college degree. So, he went to night school to get a degree, seeing it as an entry ticket to higher manipulations. He still led the company in sales and commissions. Everyone saw him as a shining example.

After his degree, he quit pots and pans and got a job selling computers. He sold the computers almost faster than they could make them and grew impatient with the company. He quit and set up his own company to broker computers and computer time. He also came to dabble in oil and gas. It was here he started to buy small companies, combine them, and sell the combination for more than the sum of the parts. He would keep some and sell some. He phased out of computers and focused on energy, building materials, construction, insurance, and real estate.

Soon Hoffstader Industries was one of the roaring conglomerates, more interested in manipulating companies and industries than in producing anything. Like most successful businessmen, he saw the economics of politics. Over time, money invested in politicians paid a higher return than any other investment. Hoffstader forged alliances with local politicians and then moved on to state and national ones. One picture of his office showed a wall covered with photographs of Hoffstader with various politicians. He married the daughter of an east coast banker with the right pedigree and had the requisite two children, who Hoffstader rarely saw. He was going places.

When the oil and gas boom fizzled, timber came to his attention as a dwindling national resource. If he could control enough of it, he could inflate the price. So began his spree of gutting the timber industry. He bought Mountain Lumber in a patently illegal stock manipulation. Unfortunately, by the time this became public, the deed was done and couldn't be undone. His attorneys, the best money could buy, sold all juries on reasonable doubt.

He spread out into Canadian timber, then into South American operations, moving some of his pulp mills down where labor was cheap. He tried to make deals in Asian markets for pulp and even whole logs. He met with indifferent success, but gained international contacts. There were many pictures of Hoffstader with the various ministers of different countries, primarily dictatorships. McNab even saw the picture of Hoffstader with the Chinese premier that Henry had had in his pocket when he died.

No area of influence was overlooked by Hoffstader. He got connected with DOD through base closures and some military construction. He then came full circle into high technology. He bought several small electronics companies and merged them into one, Odin, to bid on the entire array of aviation electronics, including esoteric government contracts. He won contracts for foreign and domestic airlines and also military craft. His domestic political contributions and international contacts were serving him well.

Then clouds appeared on the horizon. His oil and gas businesses came under scrutiny in price-fixing schemes. Aspects of his real estate, insurance, and his construction empire were involved in bribery scandals. Unflattering articles appeared about his predatory business practices and ruthlessness. His reckless timber cutting got him into trouble with environmentalists and government agencies. World pulp prices plummeted, and some operations had to be shut down. Profits were disappearing. He put more energy into the defense electronics portion of his realm.

The last article McNab found was that Hoffstader's electronics company had lost out on the biggest single military contract for electronic warfare hardware so far, the development of radar to detect stealth aircraft and the countermeasures to it. The military suspected that Russia and China were desperately trying to develop this technology not only for their own use, but to use to enlist client states, like Iran and North Korea.

Hoffstader's bid was too high, but not by much. The article speculated that Hoffstader had spent much more than the seed money the government had given to developing the bid. He had gambled on doing more of the actual research work up front in order to present a more credible technology for the bid and to offer a shorter timetable. The winning company had a somewhat more sophisticated, though speculative, technology, a somewhat longer timetable, a marginally lower price, and, most importantly, more powerful lobbyists. According to the article, the vultures seemed to be circling. However, in his last interview, Hoffstader didn't say anything about losing the bid and waxed rhapsodic about the economic future of his enterprises, especially electronics and timber.

McNab shut off the viewer and rubbed his eyes. Nothing there to throw any light on why Hoffstader would want anything from a broken-down pilot in a backwater town. Maybe Hoffstader's deal was on the level. Maybe he could have a good plane, hold his nose while flying it, and keep his way of living. Other people had settled, and they didn't seem to suffer. Often they seemed happier than he was. What was his problem? He was getting older, and it was time to plan for retirement. What retirement? Almost all his retirement money from the military had gone into the business. He just couldn't pour any more money or effort into a failing business. He could hear his mother saying it now, "Grif, you've got to plan for the future. There'll be no one there to help you but you."

Or maybe he could get a job with the airlines. His military experience should give him an edge. He shuddered. Besides being too old, driving an air bus over the same route day after day, following those tight-ass company regs, made him nauseous. Safe flying was one thing; company bullshit was another. He'd done his time in the military to get what he wanted. He didn't get it. He had to get out. Hadn't he had this internal conversation plenty of times? Hadn't the result always been the same? If he couldn't stand airline rules, what made him think he could stand Hoffstader's rules? He shook his head and took the reels back up to the desk.

FORTY-THREE

Derek McGinty was waiting for them when the monks arrived at his office. They all climbed in his blue Toyota four-wheel drive and headed for the forest. Ongdi clutched the McDonald's bag with the Big Macs and fries. Tenzing carried the Cokes. About three hours later they were bouncing over a heavily rutted logging road. McGinty gestured off to their right.

"We got about fifteen thousand acres from here to just the other side of those ridges. Most of those are second growth, about sixty to eighty years old. Won't be ready for a while yet. Up ahead is a mixed grove, some old growth, some second, kind of unusual. From what you tell me, your tree could be there." He downshifted as they came to a rise. "Just over the top here."

They went over the top of the hill and turned down another road. This ran on the side of a ridge. Off to the left, the ridge rose higher and higher, roads meeting theirs from time to time. McGinty was explaining about the early days of oxen and wagons when he looked to his left and muttered to himself, "Who's that?" Down a smaller logging road that intersected the one they were on barreled a brownish-red Jeep.

Its right front fender was a dark green. McGinty squinted at it a moment and then stopped his truck in the intersection. "Wait here a minute. I want to find out who this is. Not supposed to be here, whoever it is."

McGinty got out of the truck and stood by the door directly in the path of the oncoming vehicle that he now recognized as a Jeep of some sort. Suddenly it accelerated right at McGinty and his four-wheeler. All McGinty was aware of was that a heavy-duty bumper was aimed right at him. He screamed, "Get out of there!" and dove to the side of the road into a thicket. The Jeep rammed the Toyota, sending it off the ridge road and down the steep slope. The blue four-wheeler rolled and tumbled down the hillside for about a hundred feet and came to rest on its side, stopped by a second growth redwood planted by McGinty's grandfather some seventy years previously.

The Jeep backed away from the edge of the steep slope and turned down the road McGinty had just come up. McGinty was trying to disentangle himself from a patch of ferns and underbrush. He got up just in time to see the truck disappear over the top of the ridge he had come down.

McGinty ran to the edge and looked down. Smoke was coming from the Toyota's engine compartment. He leaped down the slope as fast as he could. His foot caught a root and tripped him, sending him down face first. McGinty recovered after about a fifty-foot skid and pulled himself upright, and continued on down.

The backseat door opened up to the sky, and Tenzing Rinpoche struggled out, blood running down his head onto his orange and red robes. McGinty got to the four-wheeler and hauled himself up on the side of the car and pulled Tenzing out, and then set him down on the ground next to the vehicle. McGinty went back just as Jamyang's head appeared in the opening, bloody and dazed. Jamyang proved more difficult to pull out, but soon both monks sat beside the car, bewildered and bleeding.

McGinty climbed back onto the car and put his head into the passenger compartment. It was too dark, so he went in head first. Ongdi was on what was now the bottom of the car, his head twisted at an unnatural angle, sightless eyes open to the shattered windshield. Big Mac wrappers had fallen to his side. McGinty felt for a pulse.

McGinty pushed his way out of the wreck. Jamyang and Tenzing looked up at him. "I'm sorry, boys. He's dead." Immediately the two monks struggled up to the top of the car. Jamyang tried to climb down in the cab. McGinty tried to stop him. "Hold on, now, you're hurt."

Jamyang gently pushed his hand away. "We must do *phowa*. If we do not help him, Ongdi may be imprisoned in this violent death. We must help him to move on." Still bleeding, he held out his hand to Tenzing, who lowered him into the truck.

Jamyang maneuvered himself until he was next to Ongdi. He bent down and started whispering into his ear. A few minutes later, Ongdi's eyelids fluttered open, and he looked at him. Jamyang paused, then began chanting in a low voice. Very soon, Ongdi's eyes closed for the last time, peacefully.

FORTY-FOUR

"Elko traffic, Cessna Six Foxtrot Zulu turning final, runway two three, Elko." McNab finished his turn, lined up on the center line of the runway, and put in the final notch of flaps. The tower was closed for the night, and there was no other traffic in sight. He followed the Visual Approach Slope Indicator lights down, landed just beyond the numbers, and then taxied off to transient parking. Ten minutes later he was in the restaurant looking for Doug Matthews, who was not in evidence.

McNab grabbed a booth and ordered some coffee. It was two and a half hours back to Euphrates from whenever this meeting ended. McNab remembered the café well. He had come here often when he was coming to or from the so-called secret base where the Stealth Fighter had been test flown. He'd done a lot of disinformation about that in the area. Just as the coffee came, Doug walked through the door, dressed in civilian clothes. He waved at McNab and went to the booth. "How are you, Grif?"

"Good to see you, Doug."

"Decaf for me." Doug ordered as the waitress appeared

with menus. "How's it going? Still doing Fly By Night Charters? Business good?"

"Still doing it, business could be better. Though that could change."

"Great."

"It's the change that worries me."

"Hoffstader?"

"I'm so glad I don't have to spell out everything."

"We did good in the old days."

"Ah, yes, the good old days."

"Right." Doug made a face. "I've got some information on Hoffstader for you. Sort of strange, too."

"How so?"

"Do you want to hear our specials?" The waitress was suddenly standing at their table.

The two men looked up at her. "No thanks, just give me a mushroom cheeseburger, medium well, fries, well done, root beer." Doug looked over at McNab.

"Same for me, but make it bacon, mushroom, cheese and a diet Coke with my coffee."

"Diet Pepsi, Okay?" McNab nodded, and the waitress disappeared.

"No sense wasting good cholesterol. You were saying something about strange?" McNab sipped his coffee.

Doug hunched over the table. "I'd been doing some looking around and getting nowhere. There wasn't a lot I could do officially and, you know, need to know." McNab nodded. "Then a couple of days ago General Carter came in. He's in charge of Special Projects. Right now that means the contract for DOSAP."

"DOSAP?"

"Detection Of Stealth Aircraft Project. It's been in the papers, especially the aviation press. We're developing a radar that can detect stealth technology, just in case anyone else develops it, or steals it from us."

"I read about it."

"Hoffstader's defense arm, Odin Electronics, was one of the bidders. He lost out to Littlefield Technologies a while ago. Rumor has it he bet the company on getting the contract and is in a lot of trouble."

"So?"

"So, Hoffstader still has a lot of supporters in DOD and in Special Projects. There's been a lot of pressure on Carter to make Littlefield give up some of the components to Odin. So far, no one is going for it. Hoffstader has been spreading around a lot of money, or so they say." McNab looked at him blankly.

"Cheese with bacon." The waitress put the burger down in front of Doug.

"No, he's got the bacon."

"Oh, sorry." She switched the plate. "Mushroom cheese only." She set the plate in front of Doug. "Root beer, Diet Pepsi." The glasses were plunked down on the table. "Straws?" They nodded, and she put them down. "Anything else I can get you?" She was off before either could react.

They launched into their meals. "So, why are you here?" McNab asked with a mouth full of fries.

Matthews finished chewing his first mouthful. "Damn juicy burger. It's one of the reasons I like coming out here." He wiped his mouth. "General Carter came into my office and said I had to get out here right away. This is where the stealth planes were based before they became public knowledge and this is where we'll be testing the new radar, as it's developed. Well, it seems there was a breach of security out here. Ketchup?" McNab shook his head as Doug poured some on his fries. "A staff sergeant was found with some secret documents. Very technical stuff from the heart of Littlefield's designs."

"Who's he working for?"

"We don't know. Could be Russia or a lot of others. Iran,

China, North Korea, Syria, Russia, India, Pakistan." Doug shrugged. "Hell, it could be anybody. But, you're going to like this. There was something else in the sergeant's room. A full dossier on one John Griffin McNab."

McNab stopped eating. "What?"

"You heard me, buddy. Your complete Air Force file." He drank some root beer. "Now, he was caught with the Littlefield stuff as he was coming out of the secure document area."

"Meaning he hadn't already taken them out."

"Bingo." McNab held both palms up and raised his eyebrows. "He isn't talking. At least not to us, only to his lawyer. A civilian lawyer. A very expensive civilian lawyer."

"How did he get my file?"

"Don't know. All we know is that already he had it."

McNab went back to his sandwich. "Who on earth would want my file? I've been out of the game for a long time. Makes no sense."

"No it doesn't. But I thought you'd want to know soonest. When I get back to Washington I'll nose around a bit more, see what I can scare up. My hunch is that not much is going to be there, but I'll let you know."

McNab thought a moment. "Okay. But if you find out something just leave a message at the hangar. Say you're calling about a fishing trip to Lake Henry."

"You got it, good buddy." They ate in silence for a few more minutes. Doug broke the silence. "You seeing anybody?"

"Not right now. You know how it is. I got a lot on my plate with the business."

"By 'not right now' I assume you just got pounded by another one?"

McNab wiped his mouth. "No. She was nice, Doug. We just didn't fit."

"You got to let go, Grif. You got to move on." McNab started to say something, but Doug kept on. "I know. This time it was different. Just like all the other times were different.

You want some advice? Don't answer that, because you're going to get it anyway. Keep it in your pants for at least six months. Okay? Cindy was one in a million. I'll never know how you even saw her, she was so good. You go for the worst ones. Not bad women, just bad for you. Get all heated up, jump into bed, and you're gone. Don't see you until you're ready for the ICU. The accident wasn't your fault. Stop punishing yourself." He chewed on a French fry.

McNab looked over at him. "You finished? You have anything else you want to say?"

"You still living at Pat's?"

"Yeah."

"You can't hang on to Cindy by hanging on to her friend."

McNab said, "You're right. This is the finest burger in Sandtown."

FORTY-FIVE

McNab walked onto the plush, green carpet. Ben Cabot looked up from his desk across the vast expanse of green and waved at him. McNab crossed the distance, surrounded by large white pillars that held the vaulted ceiling. The pillars were grooved with gold paint and had ersatz Corinthian caps. A vaguely Renaissance painting covered the ceiling. The First Bank of Euphrates did not stint on its appointments.

Cabot got up from behind his large rosewood desk and motioned McNab to sit in the large, upholstered chair. "How are you, Grif?" His handshake was firm. Light reflected from his bald spot. McNab wondered why some men had such clean, shiny skin on their bald pates. Cabot was tall and very trim, small black mustache and thin gold-framed glasses. He ran marathons regularly and was active in all the local athletic endeavors. He was also McNab's loan officer.

McNab sank into the chair. "Not bad, Ben. I got your call. What's up?"

Cabot sat back in his high-back leather executive chair. Spreadsheet calculations were arrayed on his desk. "Well, Grif, as you know, we've been pretty good about giving you some grace on the loan payments on your plane."

"Don't think I don't appreciate it, Ben."

"We had a meeting of the loan committee yesterday. We have those weekly. Mostly to deal with new loan applications. Sometimes we look at loans that are not performing as well as they should."

"And I'm in that category?"

"Frankly, yes, Grif. Your loan has been on the 'watch' list for some time. We know you've had some problems and we're trying to be helpful. However, you've missed the last two payments and it looks as if the pattern is deteriorating rather than improving."

McNab looked up at the painting on the ceiling. It was a pastoral showing Florence in the background. He looked back at Cabot. "It's true I've had some problems, Ben. There was the overhaul on the right engine a couple of months ago. That set me back. And the left engine just went down. It's waiting for overhaul now."

"Yes, I heard about that scary landing in Deak City."

"Ben, it wasn't scary. It's what I'm trained for."

"Be that as it may, Grif, we're concerned. We hold a lien on that plane and right now it isn't producing any revenue for you. No revenue, no loan payments. Am I right?"

"That's true. But I've managed to borrow another plane to take up the slack. It'll take a little while, but I'll be back on my feet. You'll get your money."

Cabot twirled his gold-plated pen in his left hand. "Grif, the committee is very concerned. We've been running our numbers, and they don't seem to pan out. Your actual revenue doesn't match your projected revenue. In fact, it falls seriously short." He sat forward and put the pen on the blotter. "Confidentially, Grif, we're hearing rumors that you've been having a lot of contract cancellations. Is that true?"

McNab closed his eyes a moment. "I have had a few small cancellations. But they haven't affected the business seriously."

"I hear that your prisoner transfer and Fish and Game

contracts are gone. That's a significant part of your cash flow projections."

"Small towns." McNab muttered under his breath.

"I didn't catch that, Grif?"

"Sorry. Just talking to myself." He hitched himself up in the chair. "Ben, I need a little more time. As soon as I get the engine overhauled you'll see a big upswing."

"You mean the plane you borrowed isn't capable of fulfilling your current flying obligations?"

"No. I didn't mean that. I meant that I'll be able to haul more people and cargo at one time than I am now. Right now it just means that I have to make more trips if I get a large cargo order. But the operating costs are much lower on this plane so it sort of evens out."

"I heard you're losing business to Brophy."

"You've been talking to Farley Luscombe." Cabot shrugged. "That's only one isolated flight, Ben."

Cabot sat back. "I'm sorry, Grif. The committee's decided we can't continue to give you the grace we have. We need you to be current as of your next payment."

"You mean I have to come up with three payments right away?"

"By your next payment date."

"I can't do that, Ben. You know that." McNab sat forward. "For Christ's sake, Ben, give me a little time." He drummed his fingers on the edge of the rosewood desk. "Can you at least spread that out over the next two months?" Cabot slowly shook his head. "Why are you doing this, Ben? You know me. You'll get your money back."

"Grif, it pains me to do this. But I can't buck the committee. It's their decision."

"Ben, what are you going to do with a broken plane? It'll cost you more money to fix it and sell it than you'd get if you stuck with me and let it make money."

"I'm sorry, Grif."

"Who's on this committee?"

"It won't do any good, Grif."

"Who's on it?"

Cabot sighed. "There's the President of the bank, Ted Hollingsworth, myself, Fred Loftsgordon our senior VP on the loan side, and one of our outside directors."

"Who's the outside director?"

Cabot paused ever so slightly. "Rosemary Willis. She's local counsel for ML."

FORTY-SIX

"Yesterday you wore black, today, yellow. Why don't you put them together and be a fucking bumble bee?" Mingus waved Pat to the table where McNab was sitting.

"Why, Mingus, you want me to sting you?" She bit him on the cheek.

"Ouch! Why'd you do that?" Mingus pouted. "Never mind. Fucking lawyers."

McNab raised his beer bottle in a toast when she slid into the booth. "Great work. If only it would help."

"Right." Pat picked up the menu and closed it as quickly.

Myrna came up to the table and raised her eyebrows. "Usual?" She glanced at each of them, got affirmative nods, and left.

Pat rummaged in her purse and pulled out some papers. "Here's what I got. Unfortunately, there's not much you can legally do. They've got you by the cojones, my dear. About the best we can do is appeal personally to the president of the bank."

"I don't think that's going to help. When I talked to Ben Cabot I got the impression that the pressure was coming from up the line."

"What do you mean?"

"He kept deferring to the loan committee. That's not like him. It's what you do to avoid being personally responsible. Ben's always been a straight shooter. You might not like what he tells you, but he tells you straight."

Pat looked out the window to the harbor. The overcast almost reached the tops of the masts of the sailboats moored there. "Sounded pretty straight to me: pay up or else."

"Yeah, but it felt strange. Especially when I cornered him into telling me who was on the committee. One of the committee members is Hoffstader's legal counsel."

"Rosemary Willis?" Pat asked. McNab nodded. "That's really too bad."

"Why?"

"I don't know what her agenda is, but whatever it is it's only good for Rosemary." McNab raised an eyebrow. "Story goes that she's a local girl." Pat paused. "Do you know her?"

"She was a year behind me. Pretty. Her father had a chain of feed stores and then morphed them into nurseries. Ran with the rich boys."

"Well, the story goes that she got into law school and didn't do all that well. Got hired at a cheesy San Francisco law firm that specialized in auto accidents. A real mill. Couldn't cut it there and ran through a few more firms in the city until her reputation preceded her. Finally, she gave up and came back here and hooked up with Bentlow and Sperry."

"Aren't they about the top for this town?"

"Yes. She's done better with them, got to partner quickly. She had lots of family contacts, brought a lot of business into the firm. Rosemary still hankers for the big city. It was a real feather for her to be named lead attorney for Hoffstader's business here. The local gossip, ever since she landed Hoffstader, is that she wants to make an impression on him so she can get to the big time."

"So if she makes it out of here, do you get her clients?" McNab smiled.

"Bentlow and Sperry wouldn't let squat out of their office." Pat frowned. "Besides which, I can't seem to hang on to my own clients." McNab looked at her quizzically. "Two of the contract logging companies that have been my clients for a couple of years just gave me notice. I asked them why? What I had done or not done that displeased them, but they didn't say anything that made any sense to me."

"That's too bad."

"Yeah. But I may get a new client, or rather two of them. Very interesting."

"Good ones? Lots of billings?"

"Hardly. It's a *pro bono* case. Jed from the D.A.'s office is referring them to me. Did you see that story where one of those not quite Tibetan monks got killed in the truck accident?"

"I heard about it. In fact, I've been trying to talk to them. They were with Henry a couple of days before he got killed. I don't think they can give me anything, but I still want to talk to them. Do you know where they are?"

"No. They're supposed to call for an appointment. When they do I'll let you know."

"What were they here for? To get wood for a monastery, or something like that?"

"A single tree. For the main beam. Whatever. Well they're here with no money, of course. At least not enough for all the mortuary and cremation charges and, you know, on and on. I've been enlisted to help them with any legal stuff. I meet with them tomorrow. It won't pay any bills but it'll be interesting. I wonder what their story is."

"Strange, whatever it is. Anyway, let's talk about Henry for a minute, okay?"

A shadow descended over Pat's face. "All right."

"I'm getting nowhere. Everywhere I turn there's nothing

directly about Henry or his, um, murder. The only thing I have that disagrees with the sheriff's version is the description of the murder from Otto and the sheriff won't listen to him."

Pat's fist came down on the table, hard. "Grif, he wouldn't have gotten himself killed, I know it."

McNab took a deep breath. "I believe you. I'm talking about hard evidence. Something the cops will believe. Okay?"

"I'm sorry. It's just so frustrating with no direction."

"I'm just telling you like it is, Pat. I know how hard this is for you." McNab sighed. "I think what I'm going to do next is to go back to Otto and try to get him in front of someone who will verify what he tells me and take that statement to the cops. It's all I can think of to do right now."

"Okay. I'm just..."

"What?"

"You've been an investigator. You've seen what happens when the momentum of a case gets going in a certain direction. Trying to get the river to change direction is tough, even if you have good, hard evidence. Do you really think that an affidavit from Otto, our local schizo, is going to work?"

"What else do we have at the moment? If you have any other ideas, any at all, please tell me."

Pat hesitated. "I'm not trying to run your investigation. You've been wonderful in taking it on. Especially since everything's turned to shit since it started. I'm just not sure this is a good strategy."

McNab swirled the water in his glass. "I didn't say it was a good strategy, I said it was the only one I have right now."

Pat wiped her mouth with her napkin. "I'm sorry, Grif. I just feel lost. We're not getting anywhere and it feels like we won't. Maybe we should just chuck it all in."

"No one said anything about giving up, Pat. We just go with what we got and hope it can lead somewhere else. Sometimes it does." He tried to sound hopeful.

"You really believe that crap?" Pat's face was wan as she

looked out the window. "Never mind. I'm getting cynical. Imagine that!" She made a bright, false, happy face and then slumped. "You're the expert, Grif. That's why you get the big bucks. Go for it. But let me help, if I can. Okay?"

"Take care of the monks. Generate some good karma."

FORTY-SEVEN

"Top her off and check the oil. Eleven quarts." McNab finished giving his instructions to Jerry, the line boy at Deak City airport. "I'll be back in a little while." He hefted the pack over his shoulder and headed for the cypress grove where Otto had been camping. Feeling a bit neurotic, he patted the pack again to make sure he had the video camera and the small tripod. Looking for aircraft traffic, McNab crossed the runway and headed for the brush.

It was a longer walk this time, or so it seemed. There was the pack, but that didn't seem like it. He walked on. Snowy egrets nested in the tall trees, and some flew away as McNab approached. There was a sound coming from the opening that McNab had gone through before. It wasn't quite artificial, but it wasn't that familiar in nature, either.

The sound got louder as McNab approached. It wasn't quite a buzzing. Hesitating a moment at the opening to the hollow that had become Otto's home, he wondered why the opening didn't have a plug of brush in it. "Otto? It's Grif McNab. Is that you?"

There was no answer, just the almost subliminal roar or buzz of whatever was going on in the brush shelter. Suddenly

McNab knew and pushed into the shelter. A massive cloud of black flies rose up from what had been Otto and engulfed McNab. The stench was awful. Otto didn't leave a beautiful corpse. McNab batted at the flies and then beat ineffectually at the air around Otto's body to drive off some of them.

Otto was spread-eagled face up, hands clutching at his throat, or where his throat would have been. McNab could see the huge gash and the brown stain where the blood had seeped into the ground next to the body. Trying to breathe through his mouth, McNab looked quickly around the brushy hovel Otto had called home. Otto hadn't let McNab all the way in the last time he'd been here, so he couldn't tell if there had been a significant change. Some rags had been thrown around the dirt floor, and crusted cooking gear was heaped to the side.

There was a tinkling sound, and McNab looked up to see a small chime with five small corroded brass tubes surrounding a bell. A plastic angel hung from the bell. The breeze blew in the door and moved the small sign of home. McNab took another quick glance and retreated.

Too late, he looked for footprints around the entrance. There didn't appear to be any but his, and the ground showed some signs of having been brushed. McNab cursed briefly and started to head back out to the plane. He stopped about ten steps away and set down the pack. He opened it and took out the video camera he had planned to tape Otto with.

McNab went back into the shelter and shot everything he could see in wide and zoom, including the wind chime. Satisfied that he'd gotten what he could, McNab packed up and headed for the airport and the sheriff's office.

Forty-Eight

Pat put the last period on the document, saved it, and turned off her computer with a long sigh. Out the window glowed the lone streetlight on Rachel Lane, next to the firm's office. She glanced up at the clock on the wall. At first she thought it was wrong. It couldn't be 11:30. She ached all over. Pat was now the leading expert in Euphrates on transporting cremated remains to the remotest regions of western China. What a useful arrow in her legal quiver.

Luego's was closed by now, so no relaxing drink until she got home. Actually, she shouldn't go there anyway. The number of clients leaving her had accelerated, and money was starting to get tight. For the hundredth time, she wondered why they were going elsewhere. The last call she had made was the most alarming and most mysterious. Bob Wilson, proprietor of Wilson Supply, which provided hauling chains and other equipment to the dwindling timber industry, had taken a non-payment suit away from her just before it went to trial. It was unusual, especially since he had been a client of the firm for over seventeen years.

"Pat," he said, "I hate to do this, but I've got no choice."

"What does that mean, Bob?"

"I've got my business to think about."

"I don't understand, Bob."

"Word's out, Pat. You're taboo."

"What word? Who's saying I'm taboo?"

"I've already said too much. I'm sorry, Pat. I really am. Good-bye." The phone went dead as Pat yelled into the receiver.

That had been several hours earlier. What was going on? In the morning she'd call a meeting with her partners and see what they could find out. Meanwhile, home and a stiff drink. Or... No. No Tanya tonight. It was tempting when she felt low, but no. Besides, how could she be superior to McNab if she called her nemesis?

One by one she turned out the lights. She picked up her large leather purse, which doubled as her briefcase, and her ankle-length checked-wool duster and walked out the door, locking it behind her. The night was cool and bracing. She took a deep breath and started down the street toward the small lot where her car was. Pat didn't like walking there late. The dirt lot, with scabrous spots of tough grass sticking out of the gray and beige gravel, was between a couple of abandoned warehouses that transients used. It was the only place she could park for free and be within walking distance of her office. She got along with most of the street people, usually, but she still felt vulnerable at night.

She reached the end of one of the warehouses and saw the driveway ahead. Pat checked out the lot and saw three other cars, fifteen-year-old big American gas-guzzling ones that only the poor seemed to drive, and a van parked next to the driver's side of her sensible five-year-old Japanese spam can, now starting to sprout rust marks. A light was flickering in the van, like a candle or weak lantern. More vans were used as bedrooms than Pat cared to think about. It made her nervous. She took out her keys, went to the passenger side, and started to open the door.

Just as she got the key in the lock, she heard footsteps on the gravel behind her. She looked back and saw two men, one large and with a limp, coming toward her out of the shadows. Frantically, she twisted the lock and tried to pull the door open. It came open just a crack when her bag slipped down her arm and hit her hand. By then, the first man, the smaller one, grabbed her and spun her around.

"Fucking lesbo bitch," the man started to say as Pat brought her knee up into his crotch. The man screamed and doubled over. She swung her purse as hard as she could against the side of his head, and he went down. The large man had reached her by this time. Pat was turning to face him when he smashed the side of her face with his fist. She fell against the car and almost went down. Bracing herself against the side of the car, she pushed off at the man and started to scream at the top of her lungs, fingernails clawing at his face.

The man was experienced and ready for her. He ducked and slammed her in the stomach with a hard left. Pat doubled over, and the man pounded her on the back and sent her to the ground. By this time, the first man had gotten up. He staggered over and started screaming at her. "Fucking queer bitch. Lesbo dyke fuck head! Get out of this town." He started kicking her in the side. As he tried to kick, the pain from his crotch made him pull back, so he didn't get the full force into the kicks. "Goddamn whore slut." He kept kicking her.

Pat curled up as best she could to protect her face and front. She pulled her bag up to hide her face. The second man kicked her on the other side and tried for her head. He connected on a couple, gashing her temple and forehead. Her bag intercepted several others. Finally, he stopped. The first man kept yelling and trying to damage her on the other side. The other man told him to stop, but he wouldn't. Finally, the second man dragged the first one off and pushed him against the car. "Stop it. Wait here," he said.

He went back to Pat, who was still curled up, grabbed her

hair, and pulled her head up. Pat looked into the face of a ski mask. "This is a warning, dyke. Stay out of this or you'll get what your brother got. Understand?" Then he hit her in the face, and she blacked out.

Pat awoke to wetness on her face and voices in the dark. "I think she's coming around."

"Yeah?"

"Her eyes flickered."

Pat moaned and tried to pull herself up, but a hand held her down. "You're in bad shape, lady." She opened her eyes. The light hurt her eyes. She couldn't focus. All she saw were shapes of light and dark. There were vague signals of something terribly wrong in her body, but she couldn't say what. She did know that the shock would wear off soon, and then it would really begin. Finally, she got her hand up to block the bright light. Her eyes started to clear, and she saw the light coming out of the open side door of the van.

"Don't try to move, lady. We'll get some water." One of the shapes moved toward the light. Momentarily the light darkened, then lightened again. In a few moments she felt water on her face.

"Call for help, please."

"Sure, lady. Uh, we got a problem, though."

Pat's vision cleared enough to see two young men, one bearded, dressed in tie-dyed clothes, with rainbow-colored knit hats on their heads. "Just get me to the hospital." She started to get up.

"Hold on, lady," the one with the beard said. "Don't try to get up. They gave you a good work over. Something might be broken." He turned to the other tie-dyed man and whispered at him for a minute. "We'd call the paramedics, but we've got to be away from here when they come, you know? Otherwise they'll think we did it. And we'll be all night in the cop house. And we don't want to do that, you know? Besides—"

Pat interrupted him. "Yes, I know. They'd want to take a

look in your van. I used to be a public defender." The pain was starting to come on now.

"This isn't a rip off, you know, but, like, we don't have gas to get very far, if you know what I mean."

The pain was coming in waves now. "My purse is over there. Take the money and drive away, but please call."

The two hippie wannabes looked at each other, then back at her, and nodded. The bearded one brought out a blanket and put it over Pat. "We'll just take a little gas money, you know?" Pat nodded and passed out.

FORTY-NINE

"Hi." McNab held onto her hand and looked down at Pat in the hospital bed.

"Hi, yourself." She was barely conscious, then faded out completely.

McNab tried to keep himself from wincing as he thought about what lay under all those bandages. Pat's face was wrapped so that only one eye showed, and it was almost swollen shut.

The doctor had said she had four broken ribs, and it would be touch and go about her spleen and kidneys. Another seventy-two hours and they would be able to tell if she was going to recover fully. "Probably be two to three month convalescence time. This is what the kids don't know about. That violence has a very big price tag." He was shaking his head as he walked down the hall.

There was a quiet knock at the door. Herman and Grogan walked softly in, holding their hats. McNab glanced at Grogan, then spoke to Herman. "Find out anything yet?"

"Not really. Mostly what came over the 911 call. There had been a van in the lot that night. We're pretty sure that's who made the call. Probably didn't want us searching their van, so they split before they called." Herman looked at the sleeping woman. "She going to be okay?"

"Won't know for a while." McNab indicated Grogan with a nod of his head. "What's he doing here? I thought no one would work with him."

The color rose in Grogan's neck and he tensed, but didn't speak. Herman shook his head. "Grif, the sheriff himself sent us down here. He's taken a personal interest in the case."

"What does that mean?"

"We haven't had much in the way of hate crimes here, as you know, and the sheriff doesn't want them to start." McNab nodded. "So we're here to find out what Pat can give us so we can clear this thing pronto. Send a message. You know, no gay bashing in Euphrates. Besides, it's Pat. She's been a good friend to the department. We haven't always agreed, but she's always played straight with us."

"She's sleeping right now. You want me to call you when she's awake?"

"Do that, would you, Grif?" Grogan moved toward the door first. Herman looked as he opened the door and went into the corridor, then leaned over to McNab. "Give the guy a break, Grif. He volunteered on this."

"Why?"

"Beats me. Look, Grif, don't go looking the gift horse in the mouth. It's another body we can use for leg work, okay? Ease up a little." Herman started for the door, "Let me know when we can talk to her."

McNab felt a squeeze on his hand. He looked down and saw Pat's one working eye open. "They gone yet?" He nodded. "Thank God."

"You're supposed to be asleep."

"I have to tell you something."

"Later. Rest. Now."

Pat tried to pull herself up. "God dammit, McNab." She didn't make it and collapsed back onto the bed. "Listen to me.

This wasn't a gay bashing. Those guys in the van didn't hear what this guy said to me at the end."

"What do you mean?"

"I mean the guys in the van only heard the twerp who was swearing at me about being gay. The guy who punched my lights out said something else to me, real close."

"What did he say?"

"He said, 'Stay out of this or you'll get what your brother got.' That's what he said to me."

"Stay out of what?"

"I don't know. But whatever it is, that's the key." Pat stopped for breath. "It means I was right. It wasn't just some skid row knife fight. Henry got himself into something he couldn't deal with." Her voice was almost shaking. "God, I'm tired." Pat tried to get up again. "This is the proof, Grif. We're on the right trail!"

McNab gently pushed her back down into the bed. He took her hand and held it. "Listen, Pat. It's over."

"What do you mean?"

"Just what I said. It's over." Pat started to speak. "Listen to me. This is way out of hand and way out of our league. You are right. Someone killed Henry. Either Henry knew something he wasn't supposed to know or was at the wrong place at the wrong time. In either case, Henry probably didn't even know what it was they thought he did. But whatever it was, it cost him his life, and has almost cost you yours."

"But that's the point. They can't get away with it."

"They can and they have, Pat."

"No. This is not fair..." She tried to pull her hand away, but McNab held onto it.

"That's right. It isn't fair. But it's what's happening. Maybe it's time to say what we haven't wanted to say out loud. Ever since we've been trying to solve Henry's murder we've been blocked at every turn. Not only blocked, but our lives have been seriously messed with." Pat looked away from him.

"Doesn't it all make sense, now? My business is in the tank. Cancellations all over the place. FAA inspection. Loan called. Your clients are quitting. This isn't coincidence. You know that."

"But—?"

"Who's the most powerful man in the region? Who controls timber and all its allied industries around here? Who has national defense contracts and is connected in the government? Take a wild guess."

Pat said nothing.

"What else makes sense? What's the old Sherlock Holmes thing? Once you eliminate the possible then only what remains, however improbable, can be true. For some reason this rich bastard felt threatened by a wino and had him killed. Then he had to stop the investigation or it might uncover what it was that he wanted to keep secret. Right?"

Pat nodded.

"He is so threatened that he almost killed you tonight."

"Almost."

"Yes, almost. But don't underestimate him, Pat. If he wanted you dead, you'd be dead. He doesn't want an investigation into the murders of a brother and a sister. Especially the sister that has the support of the sheriff. Remember what you said to me about why Hoffstader wouldn't have me killed? You're a big fish in a little pond, too."

"So, we have some leverage."

"No. We don't have anything. We're out of it. The next time you'll be dead, and I won't have that on my conscience. We're through. Finished. Out of it. Over."

Pat turned her bandaged face toward the curtained window. "No. We can't give up now. We can't."

"This isn't the movies, Pat. We're aren't the plucky little guys who bring down the big bad man. We're nothing to him. He's got all the cards. He's won. If we stop this investigation, if we give up, we will be allowed to live. If we don't, we'll die. Just like Henry, just like Otto."

"What? Otto?"

"I got back too late to tell you. I found Otto with his throat cut in his hovel in Deak City."

Pat started to cry, "Oh, God, oh God."

McNab held her hand, then handed her some tissues. "Please understand, Pat. What good will it do to find Henry's killers if you're dead?" He held onto her hand tightly. "I'm sorry, Pat. I won't go on with this investigation."

"Chicken shit."

"Maybe. But I won't stand in that morgue and identify your body over this." Pat drew her hand away from his. "This is the real world, Pat. We all have to make compromises, and staying alive isn't all that bad." She turned away from him.

FIFTY

McNab sat at his desk, looking out at the hangar. He heard a plopping sound and looked down at the papers. "Shit." The ceiling patch hadn't worked. Rain was leaking from the spot just over the right edge of the blotter. He got up, got a mangy old coffee carafe from underneath the bookshelf, and put it on his desk. The rain drip worked like the proverbial Chinese water torture.

He was waiting for the call and didn't know whether to hope it came or not. Now there was a syncopated sound as another leak made its presence known, this time on the hangar floor. McNab slowly put his feet back on the floor, heaved himself back up, and ambled out to the hangar. He wandered around looking in various buckets until he found a small white one that didn't have too many parts in it, emptied the parts on his now useless workbench, and put it under the offending leak.

Now the phone rang. McNab sprinted to it and picked it up. The voice came from out of the past and surprised him. "Grif? This is Rosemary Willis, from Bentlow and Sperry."

"Hello."

"I remember you from Euphrates High. I don't know if you would remember me."

McNab paused a moment. "Yes, I do remember you."

"That's nice." There was a brief pause. "Brian Bofford asked me to give you a ring. He said he'd gotten a message from you saying you would like to accept ML's offer to join their local operation and help them purchase a suitable aircraft. I'm afraid I just got the preliminary call and don't have all the details, but am I right so far?"

McNab looked at the rusted ceiling and the droplets forming over the moldy old coffee carafe. "Yeah, that's the gist of it."

"That's just wonderful. I know you'll just love working for Mountain Lumber. They've been very good to our community. But enough of that. Brian is messengering me the details this morning. I thought it might be good to talk informally over lunch. Are you available today?"

McNab looked out at the hangar with Charlie's borrowed plane, water dripping into the buckets and the rain sheeting over the runway. "I could make myself available. Yes."

"It will be good to see you, Grif. It's been years too long."

"Um."

"What?"

"I said, you're right. It's been a long time."

"How about the Euphrates Hotel Grill Room around 12:30?"

"How about Luego's, one o'clock?"

There was a slight pause, then, "Fine. I'll see you at Luego's."

Mingus grabbed two menus and looked at McNab sideways. "Since when did you start fraternizing with lawyers?" He started walking toward the tables.

McNab, looking straight ahead, said, "Pat's a lawyer."

"Yeah, but not a very good one. She's human. Sometimes. Don't tell her I said that."

"About not being a very good lawyer."

"No. About being human. Sometimes." He looked back at Rosemary. "You slumming, or what, counselor? I thought you were the Grill Room type. Didn't like to associate with us proles."

Rosemary replied, "Do I know you?"

"I hope not." Mingus threw the menus down on the table. "Special's boiled barrister. They're too mean to grill," and he walked away.

Rosemary slid into the booth, putting an expensive brief-case on the seat next to her. "Nice friends you have."

"You don't remember him? He was a year ahead of me."

She looked puzzled. "Really? No, I don't remember him and I think I'm glad."

Myrna glided up to them and then wobbled, putting her hand on the table to balance herself. She looked inquiringly at McNab, who looked up at her. "Myrna, did you get taller?"

"It's the rollerblades." McNab looked down and saw she was, indeed, wearing rollerblades. "It took a while, but finally Mingus said it was okay. I'm still a little wobbly but I think I'll be faster. Usual?"

McNab looked at Rosemary. She didn't look at the menu, but said, "A green salad, no dressing, and some iced tea." Myrna arched one eyebrow at McNab. He nodded. Myrna skated away, saw she was about to collide with Armando, one of the bus boys, tried to stop, flailed her arms, and went down. Armando helped her up, and she rolled slowly toward the kitchen.

"Great entertainment." Rosemary brought her gaze back to McNab.

McNab looked at her consciously for the first time. Some of the characteristics he remembered from high school were still there. Her red hair had toned down, and her freckles

were muted. Prettiness had succumbed to a becoming matu-
ration, and her bearing was no longer cheerleader bouncy. He
keenly remembered that bounce and those freckles and
flaming red hair, the ache in his chest when he used to look at
her. He went to every game he could, though he didn't pay
much attention to the scores. He remembered having to walk
home to save bus fare and watching her ride by in the
convertibles of the rich boys. He still fantasized that sometimes she had looked back at him. Today she wore a beige
cashmere dress under an elegant black coat. "Yeah. Myrna's a
trip."

"It's good to see you, Grif." He smiled without saying
anything. "I'm sorry to hear you've been having trouble."

"It happens."

Rosemary removed her coat and put it on the seat beside
her. McNab could see that the dress fitted her still slender
form very well. "I need to say something before we go any
farther, though I probably shouldn't. I'm aware that you know
that I'm on the loan committee at the First Bank of
Euphrates. Last week, when your loan came up for review, I
wasn't in the room at the time it was reviewed. Mister Bentlow
had me called out of the meeting to attend an impromptu
press conference concerning the timber bill. I didn't have
anything to do with not extending your terms."

"If you say so."

"I was afraid of this." She looked out the window for a
moment. "I do say so. It's one of the reasons I wanted to meet
informally before we got into business matters. I don't know
who pulled the plug on you and, frankly, I don't want to know.
What I want you to know is that it wasn't me."

"Why are you so concerned about this? I'm just making a
business deal with Hoffstader. It's true I wouldn't be doing this
if I could have kept my loan going, but that's the breaks.
What's it to you? If you'll pardon my asking."

"You always were direct." She paused. "You're the town

hero, Grif. You almost went to the moon or Mars, or wherever."

"Ah. The celebrity factor. In Euphrates, media center of the universe." McNab looked around. "I don't see any reporters, or paparazzi, or groupies. I don't get it."

She ran her hand through her hair. "You sure don't make it easy on a girl."

"Make what easy?"

Rosemary took a deep breath. "We've gotten off on the wrong foot, here. Why don't we call a truce and just have lunch?"

As if on cue, Myrna skated up, balancing the tray on one shaky hand. Somehow she managed to put the food down in front of them without dumping it in their laps. She nodded with great satisfaction and pushed off for the kitchen. Armando saw her coming and dived into an empty booth until she passed by him.

McNab took a bite. "What about the deal? I thought we were going to talk about the deal?"

Rosemary paused to compose herself, then reached under her coat for her briefcase. "You're right." She pulled a piece of paper and glanced briefly at it. "As I see it, this is a fax from Brian Bofford. You will be hired as the chief pilot for small aviation operations in this area of ML's timber interests. ML will purchase an aircraft that will serve their needs. Blah, blah, blah. During the times when you're not actively piloting for ML you will have full use of the aircraft for your own charter operations, provided that you pay the hourly pro rata share of direct operating costs, no equipment capitalization or indirect costs. Blah, blah, blah, in addition, you may be asked to make a few public relations appearances for ML."

"Public appearances? No one told me about public appearances. I don't do public appearances. For anybody. I don't do them for me and I certainly won't do them for Hoffstader."

Rosemary looked back at the paper. "It's not clear from this summary whether Brian said that was part of your discussions or not. I can check it out."

"You do that. No PR."

She put the papers back into the briefcase. "Okay. I'll ask him to clarify." McNab stared stiffly out the window. Low clouds scudded across the bay. "Grif? I said I'd check it out. We aren't negotiating this deal today."

He turned back to her. "Give me a break, Rosemary. There is no time during negotiations when you're not negotiating. It's an axiom."

"Why are you so hostile? ML is doing you a huge favor and you're almost spitting in their face."

"You don't get it, do you?"

"Get what?"

"Never mind."

Rosemary pushed her half-finished salad away. "This isn't working for me. I think I'd better leave." She pulled some money from her purse and put it on the table. "This is on Bentlow and Sperry. I'll be in touch about the papers." She stood up and put her coat on.

McNab put his hand on her arm. "Please. Stay. Sit down. I've been pretty edgy lately. About the business. This was, ah, rude of me." He paused. "I think I remember seeing that press conference on the news. Something about negotiations breaking down between the timber owners and the Department of Interior?" Rosemary stood a moment looking at him and then sat down, still in her coat. McNab continued, "They have great desserts here."

"I don't eat dessert."

McNab fiddled with his fork. "Not ever?"

"No."

"Never?"

"Never." She looked out the window.

"I seem to recall you used to like hot fudge sundaes."

Rosemary looked back at him. "What?"

"Mingus makes a good one."

"How did you know I liked hot fudge sundaes?"

"Remember the 'Sweet Sixteen' coffee shop? That fifties café on 16th and Edgewater? Got torn down shortly after we graduated?"

"Yes."

"Some weekends I worked there as a dishwasher. Mingus was the cook's helper. Sometimes you'd come in with the football crowd after a game. You'd always sit in the corner seat, under the pink kit-kat clock, and order a hot fudge sundae."

"You remember that?" Rosemary was incredulous. McNab shrugged. She looked down at her half-eaten salad. "I don't know what to say."

"Say you'll have a hot fudge sundae with me."

"How could I refuse a sophisticated line like that?" Rosemary shrugged out of her coat. She paused a minute, then looked up at McNab. "The reason I sat in that corner was because that was the only seat in the place where you could peek into the kitchen."

FIFTY-ONE

"You did what?" Pat weakly threw down her magazine on the living room floor. "Tell me it ain't so, Grif. Oh, shit, there I go again. Never mind." She picked up her magazine and started to read. "Did you see this amusing story about piranhas? It's *so* fascinating." She threw it down, again. "I can't believe you. I'm in the hospital a few days and what happens to you? You go out and find another Lureen! You're hopeless, McNab, just hopeless." She put out her hand as if to shut him up. "Never mind. I'm sorry. I know I shouldn't do this." She put her hand down. "But you're such a dumb shit!" she yelled, falling back into the chair.

"Look, Pat, I know what I'm doing. She isn't involved with Hoffstader's stuff. She's just someone looking out for herself. Like you. Like me. It's just business."

Pat arched her eyebrows at him. "Just business. Right. It's just business to have a three-hour lunch and then to sign up for dinner the next night." She got up, raised her arm as far as it could go, and limped around the living room talking in a falsetto. "Oh. It's just business, just business. Really, it is. Truly it is. I always spend hours and hours of my time with the paid assassin of my worst enemy. On business. Yes, business. Where

would we be without business?" She began to sing, like
Maurice Chevalier, "Thank heaven for little business..." She
stopped. "Do you know what you're doing? Do you know this
is unethical behavior on her part?"

"Well..."

"Don't 'well' me, you dipshit. Christ." She dropped back
into her chair. She picked up the magazine and put it between
her and McNab. From behind it, McNab could hear her
mocking voice, "'I know what I'm doing. I'm Grif McNab. I
know what I'm doing. I have such a good track record with
women.' Shit."

"Are you through?"

"No."

"Well, get through. I want to talk to you."

Pat threw the magazine down again. "I'll never find my
place again, you creep. So, get to it."

"You are such a ... a ..."

"Don't say it."

"Do I do this to you? You never like anyone I go out with.
Is this some sort of jealousy thing or is there no one in the
world that could meet your criteria? What would it take for
you to not be so judgmental?"

"It's simple. Go out with someone who's not a jerk,
McNab." She pulled at her robe, smoothing invisible wrinkles.
"Besides, yes, you do it to me. So don't get all self-righteous on
me." She finished her smoothing and looked up at him. "So,
go on. What do you want?"

"Will you look over the papers for me, when they come?"

"You are such a jerk. Of course I'll look them over. Is that
it? Is that all you want?"

"What's eating you? You're always acerbic, but not like
this."

Pat slumped. "I know I'm not acting well. I just can't
accept that Henry's killers won't get caught. I just can't accept
it. Then you go and hire on with the number one asshole of

all time who we know is involved somehow." She put up a hand towards him. "Don't remind me of our last conversation, where I defended him." Pat exhaled. "Now there's this, this cheer leader prom queen. This isn't high school, McNab." She pushed herself up in the chair, wincing with the residual pain. "Watch out for her, McNab. She is a piranha. Maybe a Mayberry piranha, but a piranha nonetheless. She can do damage."

"I'll be careful. I did check on that press conference. She was there. She didn't do me in at the bank."

"Then who did?"

"I don't know. It doesn't really matter at this point, does it? Somehow Hoffstader got to them and put the squeeze on. If I resist I'll lose everything and have to move on, to God knows where. If I go with his plan, at least I'll be here when he makes the big mistake."

"Sounds good. Is the pep talk for me or for you?"

"Maybe a little of both." McNab got up and went toward his room. "I'll let you know what happens."

Pat looked at McNab's back, retreating down the hall. "Be careful. Asshole."

FIFTY-TWO

Fred and Ray had removed portions of sheetrock to attach the rails directly to the studs. Cover plates would make it look all right. They were banging away in the bathroom while McNab and Jen checked the hallway, measuring the width. Rico had to be able to maneuver his walker between the rail and the other wall if he wanted to. Rico had talked about 'wall walking' before, where he would lean up against the wall and slide down the hall. It scared Jen and McNab much more than it did Rico.

"He really didn't want to come to my place this morning. He said he had a lot to do for you." Jen held the tape for McNab.

"Um." McNab marked a measurement down on the notepad.

"Rico sounded worried."

"About what?" McNab reeled in the tape. "Do you think he needs anything in the computer room?" They walked into Rico's domain. All the equipment was dark. "Not enough room. He's got too many gizmos." McNab laughed.

"He's worried about you."

McNab turned back toward the kitchen. "He say that?"

"He wouldn't say that. I just know him."

"Not to worry."

"Come on, Grif. We've all been close for too long for you to start brushing me off now."

They got to the kitchen. "He didn't ask for rails in here. Do you think he needs them?"

"You are so irritating. Do you like being ignored?"

"All right. Why is he worried about me?"

They leaned against the counter. Jen brushed the hair away from her eyes. "I don't know. He mumbles, you know, and sometimes I'd hear him say something like 'holy shit' and 'what's he getting into?' So, what is it you're getting into?"

McNab looked out the kitchen window. "I don't know."

Jen shook her head. "Okay. Just tell me it's none of my business. I can handle that." She paused. "Does it have to do with what happened to Pat?"

McNab tossed the tape measure from hand to hand. "Why do you say that?"

"Because you didn't say a damn word about Pat until I asked you." Her face was red, nostrils were flaring. "If you're getting into something weird, that's your business. But if you drag Rico into it, that's not okay. He can't defend himself the way you can." Jen smoothed her dress with stiff, rapid motions. "Promise me you won't get him into something that could hurt him." She turned to him. "I mean it, Grif. I want you to promise me that."

"I promise."

FIFTY-THREE

Jamyang Rinpoche and Tenzing brought their cloth bags down the stairway of the Queen Victoria Bed and Breakfast. Mohammed Erk waited for them at the curb. He put the bags in the trunk of the old Checker and slammed the door. Regina Osterwald waved at them as they pulled away. They left Mill City on the straight, well-paved road they came in.

Erk soon turned off the highway onto a winding road that followed the river. Alder and cottonwood crowded the shores. In isolated clearings, Jamyang and Tenzing saw small farms and houses. A few cows and horses grazed in small pastures overlooking the gravel bars and meandering path of the waterway.

The cab turned onto a gravel road that traversed the forest. When it emerged from the dense grove, the lane climbed a hill. On the plateau sat a sprawling old wooden lodge surrounded by lawn, hundreds of rhododendron bushes, and several ponds. In the distance, the monks could see the ocean. Erk brought them in around the circular drive. On the steps, waiting, were Derek and Laurie McGinty.

Erk took out their bags. McGinty picked them up. Laurie

tried to hug the slightly startled monks as they were trying to bow. Gesturing with Jamyang's bag, McGinty welcomed them into his grandfather's house.

FIFTY-FOUR

Rosemary lived on the bay, out past where the fishing fleet used to tie up, when there had been a fishing fleet. Now that there were no salmon and few other fish closer than 200 miles from shore, the docks were almost ghostly, and the pleasant noises of the fishing fleet deeply diminished. Her bedroom was on the second floor, and huge windows overlooking the water. An occasional boat sailed by, but these were mostly pleasure craft now.

McNab had to admit that if he had the money, he would probably have a house like this. Hardwood floors with oriental throw rugs, light walls, skylights, lots of glass, king-sized bed, down comforter, and puffy pillows. Not the autographed photo of Eric Hoffstader, though. Sunrise filtered through patches of morning fog. They were drinking coffee, snuggled under the down.

McNab kissed her neck. "Never did I think I would actually be in bed with you. You were the unreachable star."

Rosemary burrowed closer to him. "I always thought about how strong you were, how determined and focused. It intimidated me. I liked the parties. The way you worked was, well, work." She wiggled against him. "God, you're good."

McNab caressed her arm, then kissed her head. "How did you get to work for Hoffstader?"

"Do we have to talk business? This is too yummy."

"Hmmm." They were silent for a while.

Rosemary put her cup down and rolled back to him, half covering his body with hers. She started kissing his chest and stomach and then moved lower. "Talk about yummy." She threw the blanket off them as sun came through the skylight.

Later, McNab was cooking eggs, tomatoes, basil, and Parmesan in the kitchen. Rosemary made more coffee and sourdough toast. They took their breakfast out on the deck and sat under the umbrella at her glass topped wrought iron patio table.

Rosemary bit into some toast. "I followed your career, you know. No, you wouldn't know. But, I did."

"Not much of it to follow."

"See. That's your problem, right there. You don't give yourself credit. Life's about credit, Grif. You got to go with all you got." She put her toast down. "You had more credit than almost anyone ever did that came out of Euphrates. I was so jealous. I was!"

"You're joking."

"Nope. First you got that after-school job with Wade Gustafson and started to learn to fly. You got that Air Force ROTC scholarship to UCLA, graduated with honors and then became a fighter pilot. One thing I got to say about the Air Force, they do know how to do PR. Your name was in the paper regularly, with all your promotions and awards. It was so exciting. Not like here."

"But you went to law school. That must have been exciting."

"Damn near killed me. I never worked so hard in my life. Got my cheer leader buns kicked all over the place. They show no mercy. I barely graduated. Excitement was getting more than four hours sleep at a time. Then it took me five times to pass the bar."

"Bar's a pretty tough exam."

"Each time you don't pass, though, the offers drop off. Finally I got a crummy job in a crummy firm handling personal injury claims." She laughed a bitter laugh. "Bright lights, big city. I wanted to be in the big time so bad. Every night I'd dream about being in a big firm handling spectacular cases. Then in the morning I'd be in a cramped little cubicle talking with someone who couldn't speak English who'd wrecked their Hyundai." She got up and poured them more coffee. "What was it like, Grif? In the big time. When you were an astronaut. Did you meet Congressmen and Senators? The Vice-President? Go to great parties? There must have been a lot of parties."

"A few, but not really. By the time I'd been accepted for the program most of the glamour had worn off. There wasn't a lot of political capital in space anymore. Except when a contract came to a Congressman's district. Then we had the limos." McNab laughed the same bitter laugh that Rosemary had. "The big time. Let me tell you about the big time. The only time you count is when you have something they can suck out of you. We did have our press conferences and Congressional meetings. Mostly they were photo ops for the hometown papers of the Congressmen, who then had to go do something really important. Parties? Thank God they're over. You weren't human, you were a thing. A totem, something to touch, to get juju from. There wasn't a single moment of reality in it. I hated every minute of it."

"Why did you do it?"

"I did it so I could be strapped to five hundred tons of high explosives and be blown off the face of the earth."

"That isn't a very good answer."

He paused a moment. "You remember that Episcopalian

priest that spoke at the ecumenical assembly a couple of years ago for the college?

"No, I don't think I do."

"He was part of a panel of ministers that talked about faith and their own ministry. Someone asked him how you did you know you had the calling? He talked about the interview process they went through to get into the seminary. There was a board of priests that you came before and they asked you questions. The most important one was: Why do you want to be a priest? Father Gill said that the best answer, the truest answer, was a kind of befuddlement that trailed off into an uncomfortable silence. He said the calling was something that couldn't quite be put into words. He said that the slick answer, the 'religiously correct' answer about saving souls or some such horse shit was always suspect. That made sense to me. I can't really put my feelings into words. I just know that I wanted to explore space so bad I could taste it. I wanted to be a part of it. The others I knew in the program felt the same way. It was something we didn't talk about a lot. It was too personal, too private, too... spiritual, if you will. Besides, we didn't have the words. There was no language for it. We just knew, and we knew each other knew. For me the 'big time' was simply the bullshit I had to endure to do what I wanted." McNab looked embarrassed, suddenly. "I guess I got a little out there."

"No, no." Rosemary finished her coffee. "But it still must have been exciting to be around those powerful people at launches and things like that. I mean, it takes those kinds of people to get the money to do that."

McNab looked at her. "Yes. You're right. It does."

FIFTY-FIVE

"Does this mean what I think it means?" McNab brought the contract over to the couch where Pat was sitting.

She picked it up, "Where?" He pointed at a paragraph on page six. Pat read a moment. "Jesus Christ."

"It does mean that."

"I don't believe this. Was this part of your discussion?"

"No, it wasn't."

"You've got a great sweetheart, McNab. Wasn't she Queen of the May? Wasn't she…"

"Enough! Enough! I'll talk to her. This has to be a mistake."

Thirty minutes later, McNab settled into the oversized leather chair in front of the massive wooden desk. The walls of the office were paneled in muted dark woods. Other expensive furniture littered the sitting area behind him. Across the desk, Rosemary finished scribbling something and looked up. "I'm glad this part's going to be over." She picked up a file folder and started around the desk. McNab looked at her in her tweed suit and thought it was the first time he had felt tweed sexy. "Let's sit over here. It's more comfortable." She led the way to an oversized leather couch and sat down. "You had a question."

"Yeah, I did." McNab opened the contract to page six. "Here. What it says here is that as part of this deal I have to sign my airplane over to Hoffstader. Am I right?"

"Mountain Lumber, actually. ML would be the owner of your airplane. Your broken airplane."

"Yes, my broken airplane. Which means if this deal ever falls through I have no airplane, right?"

"You also won't have the debt to pay off."

"This wasn't part of the deal, Rosemary."

She poked her teeth with her pen and smoothed her skirt. "I got instructions from Bofford just before I sent the draft over to you."

"You didn't call to tell me about it?"

Rosemary shrugged. "It was late. I didn't think it was that important."

McNab looked at her. "You didn't think that taking away my airplane was important enough to tell me? Or did you think I was so smitten that I would just sign something without reading it?"

"What difference does it make, Grif? You have to do the deal. It's the only way you can make it. You can't make enough money with that old wreck you're flying to pay off the debt much less buy a new engine. The plane's useless to you. It's a way out."

"But it wasn't important enough to tell me about it before I got to see the language buried in a subparagraph? Or wasn't I supposed to see it until they came for the plane?"

"That's not it, Grif. I... I was... I just didn't know how to tell you."

"So you don't tell me at all?"

Rosemary got up and started pacing in front of him. "Grif, I need this deal. Bofford told me that when this deal is done

I'll be going to the corporate office in Los Angeles. I've been waiting for this chance for a long time."

McNab put the contract down on the floor. "LA? What about us?"

"It's not that far away, Grif. Not really. You'd be flying in all the time on ML business. It wouldn't affect us. It would be fun."

"Fun."

"Please, Grif. This is real important to me. To us."

"How is it important to us?"

"It's the big time, Grif. I need it. Just like you needed to be in space. I can't stay in this cheesy little town forever. I'll die."

"You were in San Francisco."

"Not like this. I'd be somebody. I'd be in a big town, a big corporate department with a fabulous reputation. No one messes with Hoffstader. People would look up to me. I wouldn't be small town anymore, Grif."

"I'm small town."

"No you're not. You're Griffin McNab, astronaut. You could be big again, Grif. I know it. In a couple of years we could be in the circle. You could make a lot of money on the lecture circuit and soon I'd be on my own, getting high profile cases. It would be so good, Grif. There would be good restaurants. Theater. Stores. We'd be out of the crappy rain and fog. Sunshine. Think about, Grif, sun! We could do it. All we need is this little tiny deal."

"And we'd both be right where Hoffstader wants us. He could pull the plug any time he wanted."

"Why would he want to, Grif? He's a great man. He looks out for his people."

"Tell that to Henry or Otto."

"Who?"

"No, Rosemary. I won't do it."

"What? What are you saying?"

"I was willing to sell my acquiescence, not my life."

McNab shook his head. "Jesus. I can't believe I almost went for it."

"What are you talking about?"

"Get real, Rosemary. If you can't see what this guy is about, I feel sorry for you."

"You're not making any sense!"

"Pat was right. Here in Euphrates it would be harder for Hoffstader. But in South America?" He let out a deep breath.

"What are you talking about?"

"Forget that, Rosemary. Just look around you. This is your home. Soon there will be no more timber, no more fish. It'll be just wasteland."

"Are you some kind of tree hugger? Is that what you're telling me? You? You left this shitty little town to go into space, somewhere were there aren't any trees, or anything living at all. Don't lecture me."

"My father was a rancher, and a logger. He did it right, he respected his work. He was for real. It's this shitty little town that's real, Rosemary. I'm real. You're real. All the people here are real. It's Hoffstader who isn't real."

"Oh, yeah? Well, Hoffstader makes things happen. That's what's real. What do you do? Fly around in a forty year old moth eaten airplane, being noble, starving to death. What a crock of shit. You had the chance. You could have been some- body. But you gave it up. You could have been somebody in Euphrates when you came back. But you didn't even try for that." She stopped herself. "I didn't mean that, Grif. What I mean is that we could be somebody, Grif. Is that so bad? Is it really so bad?"

"Good-bye, Rosemary." McNab dropped the contract on the floor and stood up.

Rosemary put her hand on his arm. "Hoffstader's very serious about this deal."

McNab turned to face her. "You've talked with him, directly? Not just with Bofford?"

She nodded. "I didn't want to tell you. He said you had something against him, but he'd overlook it if you went for the deal."

"You did cut off my loan." It was a statement.

She shook her head. "Hoffstader arranged it. He spoke directly to Hollingsworth, the president. I didn't lie to you, Grif."

"You just withheld the truth."

Rosemary nodded and looked at her lap. "You're right about Hoffstader. He's dangerous. I don't know what you did to piss him off, but I would think twice before turning down this deal. If you don't sign it he'll destroy you."

"He said so?"

"He didn't have to. I've been around him long enough to know. I was trying to protect you. Protect us."

"Us?"

"I need this deal, Grif. It's my ticket out. It's our ticket out. We can go away from here. Be somebody. Please, Grif. Don't throw away this chance, too."

McNab stood there a moment looking at her, memorizing her. He turned and walked out.

FIFTY-SIX

McNab sat on a stool in the empty hangar. The office was too claustrophobic right now. He reviewed his options. They weren't good. He'd just rejected the only feasible financial deal he had. Alonzo Rodriguez wasn't going to keep his airplane forever waiting for him to come up with enough money to overhaul the engine. Rosemary was right. There weren't enough charters he could do with Charlie's plane to pay for the new engine, especially, as it now seemed true, that Hoffstader was behind the contract cancellations. McNab may be a hometown hero, but it would be hard to resist the will of someone like Hoffstader if he held your economic fate in his hands.

Hoffstader's political connections were everywhere. The Fish and Game contract was political, as was the sheriff's. Who knows about Farley Luscombe. He was a printer. Maybe he did a lot of business with ML.

That Hoffstader was somehow involved was beyond doubt. But why? There was no evidence to tie Hoffstader directly to Henry's death. Why would Hoffstader want a street bum dead? That had been the conundrum all along. The leads were so few, but all came back to Hoffstader. But what to do now? Maybe, finally, patch the hangar roof properly. As if he would ever have need of the hangar again.

McNab got up and started for the toolbox when he heard a knock on the Judas gate. He turned as it opened, and suddenly there was Jacquye. "Hi." Her voice was soft and shy. She looked around the hangar nervously. "I was hoping you'd be in? Do you have a minute?"

"Sure. Come on in." He motioned toward the minuscule office. "There's only one stool out here."

Jacquye shook her head. "That's okay, I'm not going to stay long?" She paused. "I don't know why I'm doing this? I've been praying real hard on this? I'm not sure where to begin?" McNab watched her. She clutched her purse closer to her stomach. "I shouldn't be doing this? Oh, this is no good." She turned to go out.

"Jacquye, wait. Please." She stopped and came back toward him, stopping a few feet from him. McNab took a deep breath. "It's good to see you."

"It's good to see you, too? Did you see the Gyoto monks are coming to give a concert next month? They're the monks from the Dalai Lama's monastery? They're going to do chants?"

"No, I didn't know. Are you going?"

"I wouldn't miss it for the world? How about you?"

"Now that I know..." there was an awkward pause. "Do you..."

Jacquye interrupted him. "That's not why I came?" McNab just stood there. "Do you remember when you called Mister Bofford? About the letter your friend sent to Mister Hoffstader? The one with the picture in it?"

McNab looked confused. "What?"

"You asked Mister Bofford if there was a picture in the letter?"

"Yeah. What about it?"

"Well. Mister Bofford asked me to get the file for him?

While you were on the phone? And Mister Bofford said he'd lost the picture?"

"Yeah."

"Well, that's not exactly true?"

"What do you mean?"

"I was standing there when he opened the file? The picture was right on top? He was looking at it when he told you he lost it? Then he crumpled it up and threw it away?"

McNab took a step closer to her. "Are you sure about this?"

"I most certainly am. I don't know. I mean why? Why he did that? I don't know why I'm telling you about it, anyway? It just didn't seem right to me? That's all." She clutched her purse tighter. "Excuse me, I've got to go now." She turned to go.

"Jacquye."

She kept on walking. "I've got to go." The door closed behind her.

McNab was still standing in the center of the hangar when the phone rang. He picked it up. "Fly by Night Charters, Grif McNab speaking."

"Grif? This is Saigon Duphet."

"Saigon, how are you? Where are you?"

"I'm just fine. Still up here at the nudist camp. They don't call it that, of course, at least on the signs. Call it Alderwood Naturist Retreat. What a deal. Can't even call it what it is. Enough of that. You still for hire?"

"Sure. What do you have in mind?"

"The folks here told me of another colony, up in the Trinities. Told me it's way back up there. Not a day camp, take too long to get there, even with a four wheel. More like a summer camp. Long term stay. Thought I'd like to do that. All this traveling's sort of got me tired. Could use a rest. Might even take off my clothes. Probably not. Anyway, they got a big pasture out there they use for a landing strip for member's planes. You interested?"

"Yeah. When and where?"

"Well, almost any time. I'm ready when you are. You tell me and I'll be at that little air strip you dropped me off at."

McNab did some quick mental calculations. "How about tomorrow morning? It's a little late in the day to make all the legs in daylight today."

He could hear Saigon debating with himself. "Well, maybe. I guess that's okay. I could walk back up there. I'm at a little store about four miles from there. How about this? I'm going to need some things if I'm going to be up there for a while. Why don't you come pick me up today, go back to Euphrates, and then we'll go on to the other place tomorrow? I can get a room in town tonight. How about it?"

McNab thought a minute. "Hey, it's your money. I could be up there in about an hour. Did they give you a map?"

"Yep, they gave me a map. No problem. How about you make it two hours?"

"That'd make it close to sunset up there." He looked at his watch. "No later than two hours."

"See you then." McNab hung up and shook his head. What a life.

FIFTY-SEVEN

He brought back the throttle and looked down from his left window. If the coastal fields were fogged in, El Cielo, this small Forestry Service strip was the only real alternative if anyone wanted to be within a hundred fifty miles of Euphrates. He noticed that down from the portable toilet there was a little shack off the tarmac that hadn't been there before. He lowered the first notch of flaps and settled into the landing pattern.

The turn onto final was smooth and he was aligned with the center of the short, upslope runway. Grif waited for the buffeting and was not disappointed. The drop-off on all sides made air burble all around it. He put a little more power on to counteract the increased sink rate, lowered the left wing a bit, and put in some right rudder to slip it down the centerline despite the crosswind. Power off, float, and the wheels touched down with a slight squeak just beyond the numbers. The plane slowed as he put on the brakes and passed the small parking area mid-field. He swung the aircraft around near the far end of the runway and taxied back down the runway. He turned off into the parking area, shut down the plane, and got out.

McNab walked toward the opening in the fence and

stopped. No Saigon Duphet. He looked at his watch. Then he looked at the horizon. The sun dipped below the mountains. He stood around for about ten minutes and started back to the plane. If Saigon didn't get here very soon, he'd have to go back. As he approached it, he noticed a spreading stain under the nose. He ran to the plane and bent down. Gasoline. Quickly he opened the cockpit door and shut off the fuel tanks that fed the gas to the engine. He grabbed his flashlight from the glove compartment and came out.

Outside, he unbuttoned the cowl and looked inside. Fuel was leaking from where the gas line was attached to the carburetor. Soon, the fuel that was left in the gravity-fed line leaked out and it was dry. McNab peered closer at the break. He was so stunned that he almost hit his head on the cowl as he jerked upward. There was a fine, straight cut on the top of the small hose.

A chill ran down McNab's back. The cut looked to be just deep enough to keep on feeding fuel without a leak until vibration opened it up. If he'd been in the air for much longer, he would either have run out of fuel or the leaking fuel would have caught fire from the engine heat. Either way, he would have been over some of the most rugged and inhospitable terrain. No naturally level places for miles around. It would have been remarkable if he had survived.

He closed the cowling, shut off the flashlight, and dropped it into his pocket. Just then, he heard the sound of a car approaching. Saigon? He was supposed to be walking here. McNab ran to his right and took cover behind the shack he had seen from the air. If whoever was in that car wanted to catch McNab out, they had done a good job of it. He spied a small hillock further to his right. If he could reach that, he could make it down off the hill into the brush and be virtually impossible to find.

He hesitated. What was he worried about? Other than Saigon Duphet, who knew he was here? And why would they want to mess with him? He didn't have an answer, but why would anyone come out to this deserted airstrip at twilight? Headlights swept over the darkening parking area as the car came around the bend.

The car motor stopped. Doors creaked open and slammed shut. "Don't turn off the lights." McNab didn't recognize the voice. He heard boots scraping the asphalt, one pair going for the open gate in the fence, the other moving more slowly away down the parking area toward the portable toilet.

"Grif!" The voice, loud, came from near the car. "It's Saigon Duphet. Where are you?"

McNab started to respond to him, then stopped. He wasn't sure quite why. He saw a man shining a flashlight into the window of the plane. McNab was completely visible if the guy turned around and pointed his light toward the shack. Slowly and quietly McNab stepped around the shed and came up on the parking lot.

He could see Duphet standing by the car, looking out toward the plane. McNab came up on his side, out of the headlights. "Saigon," McNab said softly enough that the man by the aircraft couldn't hear him.

Saigon Duphet jumped in surprise, then turned to him. "Grif. Wondering where you'd gone. Got lucky, found me a ride down here. You ready to go?"

McNab didn't answer him right away, then he said, "Why is he looking in my plane?"

"Shit, I don't know, Grif. Maybe he wants to be a pilot. Let's get on out to the plane, get out of here before it gets too dark." He started to move.

"Something puzzles me, Saigon."

He stopped and turned to McNab. "What's that?"

"If you're going to get that Guinness' record for going to all these nudist camps only by bus, why are you riding in a car?"

Duphet didn't answer for a moment. "Well, I guess you

caught me, Grif." He started to amble toward McNab. "I'm sort of ashamed of myself. It hasn't been as easy as I thought it would be and, well, I guess I've cut a few corners. I hope you won't tell anyone."

When he was about five feet from McNab, the second man came into the headlights. "Fucker's not around here. We're gonna have to..." he saw McNab and stopped. Saigon took his eyes off McNab to look at his partner.

As soon as Saigon looked away, McNab dashed for the cover of the shack. McNab turned from the back of the shed and sprinted for the hillock. He could hear running behind him. McNab turned the curve of the small hill and went down the slope. It was open for about another fifty feet for a fire break. Halfway there, the two men came up to the crest. McNab didn't slow, but sprinted for the brush. He heard the shot and then the buzz as a bullet whizzed close by his ear. Then he was in the bush and running blind.

"Take the left!" Saigon waved at the other, and they both plunged down the embankment.

McNab ran ahead, the way nearly indistinguishable. Branches scratched his face, legs, and arms as he bored down-hill into the forest. He stopped, chest heaving, trying to muffle his breath, sounds of crashing brush some yards behind him, also on the left. McNab tried to remember the hillside as he had seen it from the air so many times. There should be a ravine to the right. He reached into his pocket for the flash-light. Since it was a cockpit flashlight, it had two lenses, one a red lens which, he hoped, wouldn't be as noticeable. A few quick bursts of red light and he started to the right, picking his way around a tree.

"Over here! He's got a red light!" From behind. The white light lanced through the ferns and caught him. He ducked just as another shot went by him. Head down, he barreled through the forest, avoiding only the darkest shapes. The sound of brush being trampled behind him, light piercing the darkness above him. He couldn't make out the shouting now, only that he had to run. The ravine should be close. His foot was supposed to hit the ground. Instead, there was air. He plunged over the edge of the ravine, almost breaking his leg as the steep slope came up on him. The leg crumpled under him, and down he went, head over heels, scraping brush with his back, face, and arms. Tumbling down the ever-steeper slope, he flailed his arms out, the right one hitting a tree, flaming with pain. McNab pulled it in, increasing the rotation of his roll. More brush, blackberry thorns tore at his clothes, his hands, his face. And then there was the shock of a sudden stop and coolness. He breathed in a mouthful of water and choked and spit it out. He was in a small creek at the bottom of the ravine. There was no way to quietly cough the water out of his lungs, and he hacked several times. Then he got to the 'whooping' stage of recovering his breath.

Panting, looking up the slope, he could hear voices, though they seemed muffled and far away. He couldn't see the flashlights at all. At least he figured they wouldn't come down that hill looking for him for a while. They probably thought he was at least injured and maybe dead. McNab did a quick physical inventory. It seemed a miracle that he didn't at least have a broken bone or two. He felt a lot of bruises, scrapes, and thorn cuts. When the adrenaline wore off, he knew he would be very sore. But what to do now? He quieted down and listened some more.

The voices barked back and forth unintelligibly at one another for several more minutes. Then there was silence. McNab thought they had gone when he heard something crashing through the brush above him. There was a big thudding noise, and then the sound started escalating, coming directly toward him. McNab leaped to his feet and bolted downstream in the middle of the creek just as an old log bounced through the last few bushes and landed in the middle of the stream just where he had been. At the same moment, he tripped, twisting his ankle. A branch sticking out into the creek slashed his right brow just above his eye. He went down with a yell. McNab staggered over to the bank and collapsed onto it holding his now bleeding face. Christ, he couldn't run, could hardly see anyway, and now there was blood in his eye. They would be coming to finish him off, and there was nothing he could do.

He felt around for some dead branch or rock or something. In the dark, he came up with a fist-sized stone and a two-foot piece of a fallen branch no more than an inch thick. He was done for.

McNab waited, but they didn't come. Finally, as the adrenaline drained out of his system, he passed out on the bank, his injured foot dangling in the cool creek.

FIFTY-EIGHT

Chittering, buzzing, babbling, cawing, and skittering pulled McNab back into consciousness. His right eye refused to open, but his left one blinked into focus upon a red-speckled spider crawling on the fern leaf close to his nose. He sat straight up and gasped in pain. He remembered what had happened. Quickly he looked around for the men who had tried to kill him, but saw nothing. He pulled his foot out of the water. He felt freezing. McNab grabbed his jacket close around himself and drew up into a sitting fetal position. Light was just now seeping into the ravine where he sat.

McNab tried to stand and almost fell over. The strained foot was now also asleep. He sat back down and started to massage his foot. Needles of pain shot through his foot and calf but he kept on. It was less swollen than he feared. Probably the cool water running over it while he was out. Feeling came back, and it was not that sensitive to his touch. Pulling himself up gingerly, he found he could stand. A few faltering steps showed that he could walk if he didn't push it.

McNab looked back at the log in the creek and shuddered. He raised his head to look up toward the lip of the ravine. He could see the swath of brush taken out both by himself and the log. If he took it easy, that was the best way out of here. At least he wouldn't have to hack his way through the undergrowth. Slowly he started up the hill.

Almost an hour later he peeked out from the edge of the brush surrounding the fire break just down from the runway. No one. He circled around toward the far side of the runway to come up on the opposite side of the parking area. A half-hour later, he had crawled up to the edge of the level part of the runway and looked out over the pavement. There were no cars in the parking area, and only his plane was on the tarmac.

McNab waited another ten minutes to be sure, then got up and hobbled to the plane. The pilot's side door was open. Inside, his flight case had been ransacked, as well as the glove box and the baggage area. Quickly he checked the ignition and instruments and found them all right. He sighed in relief. More confident now, he limped over to the parking area and looked all around there and around the bend to the road beyond. Deserted.

He pored through the items spread around the plane and found the electrical tape he always carried. It sure wasn't perfect, but it would last until he got home. Forty minutes later, after the most thorough pre-flight he'd ever done, he was in the air and headed for Euphrates. He didn't radio in, breaking safety protocol. He hoped the field wasn't still fogged in. It wasn't, but visibility was marginal; for which he gave thanks. After he landed, McNab taxied over to an empty hangar and put the plane in it.

In the office, Darcy looked up as he came in and let out a little exclamation, "Yikes! What happened to the other guy?"

McNab limped over to the vending machine, fumbled for some change, and got out some M&Ms. He tore open the package and threw half of them into his mouth. Coming back to the counter, he leaned over to Darcy. "If anyone asks, you haven't seen me or heard from me since I took off yesterday, okay?"

Darcy looked at him. "Are you all right?"

"Just tell me you'll do it."

"Okay." Not happy.

"That means anyone and everyone. Even your boyfriend. Right?"

"All right, Grif, I get it." She made a pouting face.

"Also, and this is very important, tell Ed I need a new fuel line now. I mean now. Tell him that he hasn't seen me for days. You got it?"

"I'm not dumb."

"I know, Darcy, I'm a little stressed right now." He drummed his fingers on the desk. "Does Ed still have that clunker car he keeps to loan his visiting pilot friends?"

FIFTY-NINE

Grogan asked him again, "So what were you doing up there?"

McNab patiently said, "Like I told you the first time, I was doing some practice landings. El Cielo is up in the hills, at a higher altitude than the fog, and is where we all go when we can't get into Euphrates County airport. I hadn't been up there in a while, and I was just getting in some landings. It's a little tricky, what with being on top of a mountain and that upslope runway."

"So, you're up there just minding your own business and two goons just try to off you. Do I have that right?"

"Yeah."

"For no reason."

"None that I know of."

"Gun shot sounds carry a long way. Neighbors were pretty spooked."

"So was I."

"So why didn't you report it? Why did you wait for us to track you down? We had a hell of a time making Darcy give up that you came in from there."

"I told you. There wasn't anything to tell. I don't know who they were, what they were doing there, I couldn't identify them if they were standing in front of me." McNab looked around the decrepit interrogation room. "Besides, you wouldn't believe me. You don't now, do you?"

Grogan sat on the edge of the table. "Rumor has it that El Cielo is used by marijuana growers to fly out special shipments. Maybe you were doing that? Maybe you were trying to diddle them and they caught you?"

McNab wiped his hands down his face. "You're a piece of work, Grogan. What's with you? You've been on my ass since you came here. Trying to nail something on me. What's your story?"

"Fuck you, McNab. This whole thing stinks. First you're involved in that bum's death. Everyone knows you're in deep financial shit. There's a lot of money in grass. Now you're involved in a gunfight at an air strip used by dope growers. This isn't rocket science, McNab."

"If you're so damn smart, how does Henry's death tie into all this other shit? Tell me that."

"Larry the pervert was a known dealer. You and Henry are friends. Henry and Larry get into a fight and kill each other. Over what? What is the one of the biggest reasons for street fights? Booze and drugs. Am I making myself clear?"

"Jesus, Grogan, what have you been smoking?"

"I've seen it before, McNab. Some guy gets to be buddies with the local cops. All good feelings, great guy, does the cops a lot a favors. Turns out he has shit going on. Diverts attention. Works great. For a while."

"Someone like that get to you, Grogan? That why you're not in L.A. anymore?"

Grogan jumped up and grabbed McNab by the shirt, pulling him to his feet. "Look you cheap asshole, I know you're dirty. I'll get you, don't think I won't."

"Touched a sore spot, Grogan?"

Grogan pushed him back down into the chair. "You're a loser, McNab. I know about you. You had it made. My brother was Air Force. All he could talk about was astronauts, you and the others in your class. He'd have given his eyeteeth to be an astronaut. I'll bet you got his spot. Then you had an accident and you just gave up. You didn't have the guts to go on. You fucking quit and dropped out of sight. You've got to be dirty. No one gives up something like that and just drops out. They've got to have something going on. I know you've got something going on, McNab. Your act is just too damned shiny. I'll find it, too. You can bet on it. I'll find it and I'll put you away."

"Can I go now?"

SIXTY

McNab turned the pages once more. "Nothing on Saigon Duphet?"

Rico shook his head. "Nada. He doesn't exist. Not under Saigon, not under Courtney. He's not listed anywhere. If you want, we can go to the next level, but it'll take a while."

McNab nodded. "Do that." He turned to the next stack. "According to this, Hoffstader is up to his eyelids in debt and," he turned back to one of the pages, "if the analysts are correct, he's got maybe 90 days to six months to turn it around or he'll have to go Chapter 11. Is this true?"

Rico nodded. "There are red flags all over the international financial community. These are summaries of the best ones I found. IMF, World Bank, Japanese banks, German banks, Wall Street. They're all scared pissless that he's over the brink. They don't dare say anything or it'll start a panic. Or at least that's what the confidential reports say. The man is in serious trouble."

McNab leaned over the desk. "Now here's something. Hoffstader's been to Singapore at least three times in the last six months. Then, twice in the last three weeks. That right?"

"You got it. In fact, if you look at the timing of the trips, the last two came just after his defense firm, Odin, lost the bid for DOSAP. You know, to detect stealth aircraft. Now, that may be coincidental. After all he does have contracts there, logs, pulp, like that. But those are low level stuff, hardly the things for CEO visits in mid-contract."

"What are you thinking?"

Rico shifted in his chair. "You tell me. You were the Air Force investigator."

McNab shrugged. "I don't know. Let's see. Singapore is the financial capital of Southeast Asia. Hoffstader needs money. This doesn't require a lot of deep thought." McNab flipped through the papers again. "I'm wondering if Singapore has the kind of money that Hoffstader needs. Asia is having its own problems right now. Why would they fund Hoffstader? They would only do that if they could make a killing. No. That doesn't work. According to these reports, Hoffstader's empire is in trouble all over. There's no killing to be made."

"Are there other contacts he could make in Singapore?"

"Like what?"

"I don't know, you're the fucking investigator."

McNab shuffled the pile, yet again. "Well, what's around Singapore? Indonesia, Malaysia, the Philippines. Nothing there. Hah! Brunei!" Rico looked at him blankly. "The Sultan of Brunei. One of the richest men in the world. He has billions."

"He didn't go to Brunei."

"How do we know? He might have flown from Singapore to Brunei. He could have flown anywhere from Singapore. We don't have Hoffstader's schedule. We don't have any way of finding that out." McNab paused. "Besides, if he did go to Brunei, so what? He'd go anywhere to get money. He'd sell anything to get money, including his grandmother." He paused. "What if... Never mind."

"What, Grif?"

"It's just a crazy idea. Went nowhere fast."

"Tell me."

"What if he was working some deal with China. But these IMF reports say his proposed deals with the Chinese have foundered, they're off."

"So what if he was working a deal with China?"

"So, nothing. I'm just reaching for something, anything."

Rico rubbed his nose. "I don't know if I should ask something this subtle, but if he was working a deal with China, he'd go to China. Wouldn't he?"

McNab's eyes closed briefly, and he took a deep breath. "Yeah. He would." He paused a moment. "If it was a legitimate deal."

Rico rolled his eyes. "Jesus. Aren't we getting a little far out here? We're sitting here in a small town in the middle of fucking nowhere talking about international industrial intrigue as if 'A' we knew something about it, 'B' we could do anything about it even if we did know something about it, and, further, 'C', we would give a shit? Especially about Hoffstader? Get real, man."

McNab flopped back in his chair. "You're right. I just got caught up in this thing about Henry. More to the point, about Pat. I don't have anything to go on. It all revolves around Hoffstader, somehow. I just don't know how."

"Why would Hoffstader, multi-billionaire and world-wide public figure, want a street bum like Henry dead? Think about it. It just doesn't make sense. Get a new theory."

"There was the pie thing."

"Oh, right. I can see the headline now, 'Billionaire Commits Murder Over Peach Pie.' Give me a break."

"You're right. I'm reaching. I'm reaching because I don't have anything else."

"Go home. Eat pizza. No. Get laid, go home, eat pizza. By the way, I hear you're getting laid, again. Someone in pink?

Eh? Is that where you got those cuts and bruises? Or am I behind the times?"

"Right. Time for me to go home." McNab grabbed his jacket. "Look, I didn't want to tell you, but someone tried to take me out last night."

"What? What happened?"

"Don't ask. But if anything happens to me, call this guy. Tell him what we've done." McNab gave him the paper. "Just be careful, however you do whatever you do out there in cyberspace. Don't leave a trail."

"I never do."

Sixty-One

"You really like these burgers this much that you would fly four hundred miles to get one?" Doug tucked into his. Outside, a twin Otter was taking off.

"Like you said, finest burger in Elko." McNab wiped his mouth with the flimsy napkin that seemed endemic to coffee shops. "This is sort of a strange request. I'd like you to find out who someone is."

"Who?"

McNab reached into his pocket and pulled out the newspaper clipping he found in Henry's pocket. "This man." McNab pointed to the Chinese man circled in the photograph standing in a group in back of Hoffstader and Premier Lee.

Doug put down his disintegrating burger and wiped his hands on several napkins. He picked up the clipping. "This from one of our newspapers?"

"New York Times."

"Why?"

"It's the only thing that links Hoffstader and the murder of a friend of mine. I think it's important."

"How is it important?"

"I don't know yet. My hunch is that once I find out who this guy is, then things will start to make sense."

"You sure know how to pick 'em, Grif. I don't know. This is a bit strange. I'll check it with our political guys. I'm going back to Washington tomorrow."

"There's another thing."

"What?"

"Could you find out what you can on a Viet Nam vet named Saigon Duphet. Oh, Christ, what was his real first name? Uh," McNab snapped his fingers, "Courtney, that's his first name. Courtney Duphet. Inherited some telephone company in the mid-west."

"Is that all you have?" Doug had a piece of lettuce hanging out of his mouth.

"Please, Doug, soonest?"

"Why the rush?"

"I can't tell you all of it right now, you'd have me committed."

"I should do that anyway, just on general principles," Doug said.

"You may be right. If my theory is right, Hoffstader is so frightened about something that he had one man killed, had my friend beaten up, and tried to kill me."

Doug stopped in mid-bite. "Does this have to do with DOSAP? Because if it does, I need to be in on it."

McNab also stopped eating. "I don't know. It may have to do with that, but I don't have anything to go on right now except blue sky theorizing. It sounds good, but right now there's nothing to back it up."

"Tell me."

"Not right now. Let me work on this a little bit and let me bring you something you can sink your teeth into. Okay?"

"I don't like this, Grif. We shared some pretty sensitive stuff in our time. All of a sudden you don't trust me?"

"It's not that. It's that what I'm working on will get lost in the shuffle if what I think is happening is really happening." Doug cast a cynical glance at him. "I promise if I come up with anything that you can use I'll get it to you as soon as I know it. One last thing."

"Your middle name should be 'one last thing."

"I'm serious. If I disappear or something weird happens to me, go after Hoffstader, okay?"

Doug nodded. "Right." He indicated the check. "You pay."

SIXTY-TWO

McNab put his beer down and looked at the pile of papers again. All investigators know that the small details were what made the case. He just didn't know which ones. He started over again with the sheriff's reports. He sketched out the crime scene and put where the bodies were, where Otto had been hiding. Everything fit. Nothing stood out as not belonging there, except that it had been three well-dressed men killing two winos.

On to the autopsies. McNab started with Larry's. Straight-forward. Nothing out of the ordinary. Same with Henry's. He was turning the paper over when it caught his eye. He set the form down again. Under the heading of external injuries, McNab noted the description of lacerations on Henry's face. They were extensive and brutal. What had caught his eye was the line that said there were minute pieces of gravel or stones in the cuts. It went on to detail size and color. Then, and McNab hadn't read this far before, that samples of gravel from the alley were compared and did not match. Further analysis was recommended.

McNab looked through the papers. There was no further analysis sheet. He thought for a minute. Herman had sneaked these out to him. It was possible, even probable, that the analysis hadn't been done by the time Herman made the copy. McNab made himself a note about who had done the autopsy and to carefully check the report.

He pulled out the inventory of Henry's belongings. He fondled the crinkled papers again and tried to imagine what some of them were. He reviewed his notes and recalled conversations with Herman, Grogan, Bofford, Erk, and Otto. Something was missing. He couldn't find it. McNab put the papers back in the file, closed it, and sat in the chair, rubbing his eyes and face.

He took another pull on the beer, picked up the phone, and dialed the number of Erica Wallace, M.D., pathologist and sometime medical examiner in Euphrates. McNab remembered the name because he had seen it on a few of the community boards that Pat worked on. It took several tries to penetrate the protective barriers at the clinic where she worked. Finally, she came on the line, and McNab told her who he was and why he was calling. McNab explained that he was informally looking into the case because he had doubts about the official explanation. Doctor Wallace was direct and focused.

"Yes, I did receive the analysis, but I'm not sure I should be telling you about it. The report went to the Euphrates Health Department and to the sheriff. You can ask them."

"Well, Doctor, I have asked them to review the case but they don't seem to want to do that."

There was a long pause on the phone. "This exceeds my authority. I'm afraid I can't help you."

"Would it be possible to meet with you for a few minutes?"

There was another long pause. "I don't think so."

"Doctor, I'm not asking you to divulge any secret information. Mostly what I want is your opinion on a couple of things that don't make any sense."

Pause. "My schedule is rather full."

"Do you know Pat Morrissey?"

"Yes. We've served on a couple of charity boards together."

"I don't know if you know this, but Henry Bouchard was Pat's brother. My main concern is that Pat get the peace she needs about the death of her brother. If you like, I can bring her along."

Pause. "No. Don't bring her. I'll meet with you in my office. Give me an hour."

After the medical assistant had shown him into her office, McNab looked around. Graduate of Bryn Mawr with honors and then Georgetown Medical School. Board-certified in both Family Practice and Pathology. Several plaques honoring her charitable work and pictures of her in various locales in the third world. There were shots of her surrounded by African women, a large frame with several photos from a Peruvian village, and another compendium from what could only be backcountry Mexico. Doctor Wallace was African American, short, plump, with a broad smile. McNab couldn't quite reconcile her cool manner on the phone with these pictures of a seemingly ebullient woman.

The door opened, and Doctor Wallace came in. She stuck out her hand. "Erica Wallace. Please have a seat." McNab sat as directed. "What can I do for you, Mister McNab?"

McNab was mesmerized by her large, dark eyes. They looked directly through him. This was someone he knew he couldn't manipulate and didn't want to. "As I told you, neither Pat nor I think Henry Bouchard's death was as it appeared. She asked me to look into it, and I've been doing that. Right now, I'm at a wall. I know he was murdered and not by Larry, the other man in the alley, but I don't know by who, and I am fresh out of leads. I'm hoping you can provide some direction from the physical evidence."

"What does the sheriff's department say?"

"They have an easy solution which they took. Who cares if two winos kill each other?" I'm afraid I've made myself *persona non grata*."

"If it wasn't the other man in the alley, who do you think did it?"

"I don't have a theory about who actually killed Henry."

"Or the other man?"

"Or Larry, either."

Doctor Wallace sighed, looked down at her desk, then looked up again. "If your theory is correct, doesn't that mean that Larry was also killed by someone else?"

McNab paused. "Yes."

"So you are investigating two alleged murders, then, not one."

"Yes."

"And you think the Euphrates Sheriff's Department, with whom I work regularly, are incompetent?" She picked up a glasses case elaborately woven in South American colors and kneaded it unconsciously.

McNab shifted uncomfortably. "I think that may be too strong a word. I have also worked with them, transferring prisoners, and some informal investigative things. What I see is an overworked department that wants to clear cases as fast as they can. As you know, Euphrates, for its size, has a very high unsolved murder rate and clearing two cases can materially affect the statistics. It's an attractive temptation."

She continued to knead the glasses case. "How is Pat taking this?" Her voice seemed slightly softer.

"She's devastated."

"How are you involved?"

"Pat and I share a house. Over the last few years we have become good friends. In another incarnation I used to do some investigative work in the military, a fact I don't advertise. She asked me to help."

"Is she through with Tanya, yet?" McNab's eyes widened. Doctor Wallace put down the glasses case. "Please call me Erica." The mood suddenly relaxed. She leaned back in her chair. "Your first question was about the particle analysis of the debris found in Mister Bouchard's facial cuts. When I collected the material from the cuts it wasn't unusual except that the particles didn't seem to be the same as a random sample of the gravel in the alley near where Mister Bouchard fell. They were generally of a different color. Because they seemed dissimilar I sent a sample to a friend in a lab in San Francisco. Her preliminary analysis shows only that it is different. There wasn't enough to make a determination as to where it might come from. Just not from around here."

"By around here, do you mean within the city or a larger surrounding area?"

"I can't pinpoint the location for you, if that's what you mean. It's just a strange mix." McNab sighed. Erica got serious again. "But there is something else."

"Yes?"

"Not about the particulate matter." She frowned. "It's about the knife wounds." She picked up the glasses case again. "It bothered me at the time. I told one of the investigators, but he didn't seem to want to hear it."

"What was it?"

"After doing a lot of autopsies you get to know the particular savagery of battles to the death. I didn't see this here."

"What does that mean?"

"In most knife fight wounds I've seen there are a lot of slashes and grazing blows, if you will. When people are fighting they move. When they are struck with a knife they react. They may not react in time, but sometimes there is evidence of that reaction. A pulling away so that the last part of the slash isn't quite as deep as the first. Things like that." Erica kept kneading the case. "Here though, on both men, the wounds are almost all straight in, deep penetrations. As if they had been unable to avoid the knife coming at them. It didn't seem right. It didn't fit with what I've learned from other bodies." She paused a moment. "I also wondered why the facial lacerations were so brutal, so obviously the product of a beating, yet the knife wounds seemed so clean."

"You said you told the sheriff about this?"

"Oh, yes. I told Herman's new partner... Aaron Grogan? Yes, Grogan. He was acting as liaison for the case. He dismissed it."

"Did you talk to Herman, himself?"

"No. He didn't come down for a long time after that. Only Grogan. Then, you know, we were all busy on other cases and I forgot it. I figured if Herman wanted to know more he would ask. After all, wouldn't his partner give him all the information?" Erica looked at him earnestly.

"Of course."

"Is there anything else I can do for you, Grif?"

McNab was lost in himself and almost didn't hear the last question. "What? Oh. No. Thank you, Erica. You've been a great help."

"Please offer my condolences to Pat."

Sixty-Three

Cold canned corned beef was, well, awful when it was cold. McNab tried making a sandwich out of it with loads of mustard, but it still didn't cut it. The fire was almost going out, so he threw some more branches on it. Sounds of the river water running over the rills soothed him as the night deepened. When he first moved back to Euphrates, the memories would sometimes overwhelm him. Coming to this place on the river and camping for a few days would ease the pain, would open him back to life. Now it was his habit to come here when he needed to think.

He finished the bad sandwich, drank the last of the coffee out of his Thermos, and put them away. He cleared a patch of ground and rolled out his sleeping bag. He was just crawling into it when his phone beeped. "Yes?"

"Grif? Doug."

McNab closed his eyes for a moment. "Hi, Doug. Glad it's you."

"Well, old buddy, I'm glad it's me, too. Got a minute, or are you up to your ears in paperwork?"

McNab looked up at the myriad of stars and the bright moon. "No, Doug. No paperwork. What's up?"

"Got an ID on that picture you sent me."

McNab got up and went to the truck for his pad and pen. "Hold on a second, Doug." He got out his material. "Yeah, go ahead."

"This guy is named Chu Sha Lee. His official title is somewhat murky. Sometimes he appears speaking of rural development projects, sometimes it's forestry projects. The intel boys say he's the premier's chief hatchet boy. He also runs errands for the premier when unofficial channels are preferred. 'Special projects' as they're known. He is rumored to have spearheaded the recent crackdown in Tibet and the other satellites in the area. Lots of people disappeared. Not a nice man, Grif."

McNab finished writing down the information and thought a moment. "Anything else, Doug?"

"Nope. Except he hasn't been seen in a few weeks. That sometimes means he's running one of those errands. On the other hand, I'm told we don't have many assets within China, so public appearances may be overrated as hard info. What does this have to do with, Grif?"

"I don't know, Doug. When I know, you'll know. Did you get anything on Saigon Duphet?

"Matter of fact I did. He was in country two tours. Volunteered both times. Purple heart, DSC. Was up on a court martial for drug dealing, but was acquitted. Went through a VA drug and alcohol program, twice. Got himself a tour on a locked ward for attacking the psych techs. Got a VA mortgage, listing his occupation as fork lift driver at Celestial Arts Jewelry. He lost his job a year later and defaulted on the loan. That's all the official stuff we have. Just disappeared from our screen." Doug paused. "Grif, I can't access any more civilian records without a national security reason."

"That's okay. Thanks a bunch. I'll keep in touch." McNab signed off.

He put his tablet away and threw another few branches on

the fire. Why would the Chinese premier's assistant for dirty work be of interest to Henry? And who was Saigon working for now? He climbed into his sleeping bag, checked his watch, and looked at the sky. Right on schedule, the international space station crossed the sky, a delicate faint star in man's firmament.

Sixty-Four

"What is it?" McNab barged into Pat's office. "Your message said it was important."

"Grif, I'd like you to meet Jamyang Rinpoche. Jamyang, Grif McNab, my good friend."

McNab shook hands with the tiny monk. Red and yellow robes looked decidedly odd in Pat's mostly Victorian office. "Pleased to meet you. Jamyang?"

"Yes." The monk bowed with his hands pressed together.

McNab did the same. "I have always admired the Dalai Lama."

Pat gestured to the seats in front of her desk, and they all sat down. "Grif, Jamyang and I were talking about the incident when his friend, Ongdi, was killed."

McNab looked to the monk. "I am very sorry for your loss." Jamyang nodded.

Pat went on. "We finished up the jurisdictional details early and found ourselves talking about it." McNab nodded. "I think you might want to hear this. Jamyang agreed to repeat it to you. Jamyang? Would you mind telling your story to Grif? Could you start with your arrival in Euphrates?"

"I will. Thank you." He bowed again. For the next forty

minutes, Jamyang told, as best he could in his less than perfect English, about their mission and all their misadventures, including their trip to Mountain Lumber and their disappointment via Brian Bofford, their meeting Derek McGuinty and their tragic visit to the forest when Ongdi died.

McNab's attention was awakened by the story of the accident. He questioned the monk closely. "Yes. It was a large vehicle. One of the wings was green."

Pat interrupted. "Fender."

"It did not slow down. Then it crashed into our car. When I got out of the car the vehicle was gone."

"You're sure it had one green fender?"

"Yes. I don't forget that. It get very large as it come to me."

"What color was the rest of it?"

The monk thought for a minute. "Not red. Not brown. Like both."

McNab looked at Pat. "Otto." She nodded.

Sixty-Five

"Doctor Wallace, please. Tell her it's Grif McNab calling." He waited a few moments, then she came on the line. "Erica? Grif McNab. Do you have a couple of minutes? Can I come by and see you? It'll be very short, I promise. Thanks. I'll see you in about ten."

He jumped back in the truck and drove toward her office. McNab changed lanes, and looking in the rearview mirror, he saw an SUV with one green fender change lanes, too. He looked up ahead. Quickly he turned right, cutting across two lanes, sped down the block and turned left, and pulled into a hauler's yard he knew. He pulled around behind a dump truck, got out, and sidled up to the side of it. A few moments later, the green-fendered car drove slowly by. Two men were in it. The one in the passenger's seat looked overly large. They moved on. McNab returned to the car and carefully drove side streets to the doctor's office.

"Come in." Erica ushered him into her office. "What can I do for you?"

"Sorry about the rush. Just a couple of quick things. You remember our talk about the gravel, or whatever, you found in Henry's wounds?" She nodded. "You said it wasn't from around here."

"That's right."

"I know this is going to sound weird, but could it have from off of this planet?"

Erica looked at him for a moment and then started to laugh. "You mean ectoplasm, or little green men slime?" When McNab didn't join in, she slowed down and stopped. "You're serious?" McNab nodded. "Okay. What I collected was a bit of gravel, sand granules, even, whose color didn't match the alley. That's all I know."

"Did you check the chemical composition?"

She leaned forward. "This was a case of two men who in all probability killed each other in an alley. There was no reason to check it out. What I did informally was just my own curiosity."

"Are the samples still around?"

"I believe so."

"Can you get the chemical composition checked out for me?"

"Why?" Erica had picked up the woven glasses case and started kneading it.

"I have a theory." When Erica didn't respond, McNab went on. "It's a strange theory, and you might think I was off my rocker."

Erica thought a moment. "Maybe you'd better not tell me. Besides, it wouldn't do any good. The kind of testing you want could only be done at the FBI lab or some large university. They would have to use a mass spectrometer, maybe do gas chromatography, and have other equipment far beyond our capabilities. The order for that kind of test would have to come from the sheriff's department. Am I still to understand you are reluctant to go through the sheriff?"

McNab nodded. They sat silently for a few moments. "Can you get me the samples, or some of them? I think I know where I can get them tested."

"Why would I want to do that?"

"Good question. A sense of justice, perhaps?"

"Why wouldn't I trust in the sheriff's department that I work for?"

"I'm not sure it's a matter of total trust. We all know the things that happen in bureaucracies. Ego is often more important than truth." She didn't respond. McNab sighed. "Promise not to call the guys with butterfly nets?"

"If you don't get violent."

McNab sat back and folded his hands in his lap. "Okay. Remember I told you that Henry Bouchard was Pat's brother?" She nodded. "I've been tracking down every movement Henry had in the last few days of his life. Every trail leads back to Eric Hoffstader."

Erica started to shake her head. "If this is another case of everything wrong that happens here is only due to the evil Eric Hoffstader, you're wasting your time. I've heard all the fringe environmentalists. I'm not interested."

"Just listen to me, please? Let me tell you what's happened." She sat back, arms folded across her chest. For the next thirty minutes he talked. As he did so, she kept looking at his face. Slowly, her arms unfolded, and she listened. "That's the story. I don't know why Hoffstader would want to get involved in killing Henry, maybe his ego couldn't take some peach pie. That sounds like a pretty flimsy motive for murder. Maybe there's another, but whatever it is I think he did it. If those pieces of gravel are from the moon, then we have him. If they're not, I'm going to feel very foolish."

"How are you going to get them tested?"

"I have a friend in the Air Force who's connected. If he thinks this story holds water, he'll have them tested in a minute."

She kneaded the glasses case. "I'll have to have some pretext to get the samples." She was silent for a few moments. "Let me know where you'll be."

"I'd better call you."

She scribbled on a pad, "My personal cell."

SIXTY-SIX

"Doug?" McNab drove on the back streets toward the air express office, talking on his cell. "I'm sending you some pieces of sand and gravel. Yeah, that's right, sand and gravel. I want you to analyze them." He kept scouting the cars around him. No green fender. "I want to know if these pieces come from the moon."

Doug's voice was scratchy. "What are you talking about?"

"You having any luck with that espionage investigation, the guy that had my file?"

"No. The sergeant isn't talking and the trail ends with him, so far."

"You still think it's Hoffstader?"

"Of course I do. We know he was behind it, we just can't prove it."

"We can get him."

"How?"

"We can get him for killing a wino."

"What?"

"Can you analyze these specimens for me, or not?"

"I don't know."

"If you link it to the espionage case?"

"Well, sure. If it is linked to it."

"Let's pretend it is for now. Doug, if these are moon rocks I can nail him."

"Have you been drinking? Never mind. Send them to me direct."

"I'm on my way to the air express office now. You'll get them tomorrow morning." McNab hit the 'off' button and pulled into the parking lot.

In a few minutes, he had the specimens addressed and handed them over the counter. "When does the plane leave?"

The blue-clad middle-aged woman behind the counter kept entering the information into the computer. "Stuff leaves our office at 4:30, gets to the plane around five, loads, and is airborne by six. Gets to the city in time to be on the nine o'clock." She looked at the clock. "You could still make it, Mister..." she looked at the return address, "McNab. Say, are you the astronaut? My husband and I moved up here a few years ago. We heard there was a retired astronaut in town. Say, how was it there, out in space?"

He looked at his watch. It was 4:25. "Thanks," he looked at her name tag, "Dottie. It was great." He left the office quickly and got in his truck and left.

At five o'clock he was settling into the brush along the slough, about a mile from the airport. He had a clear view of the 'cargo area,' simply the tie down for the air express single-engine turboprop. The truck drove up, and two blue-clad men got out and started to unload packages. The pilot helped load the bins that were then loaded onto the plane according to their weight. Just as the pilot was about to close the cargo door, another company van drove up. The driver leaped out of the truck and ran to the pilot. He handed him a package. The pilot tried to refuse it, but the driver insisted, gesturing emphatically. Finally, the pilot took the box and signed the receipt book. He locked the cargo door and climbed into the cockpit. McNab could feel him doing his pre-start checklist.

Several minutes later, the plane taxied to the runup area, and at 5:58, the wheels lifted from the runway.

McNab put down his binoculars and sighed. He got up from the grass and started back up the faint trail toward the copse of trees and his hidden truck, binoculars hanging from his hand. Doug would get the specimens early, and hopefully, he would have the information that day. He shook his head. It would be at least several days before the tests were complete. It didn't matter how big an emergency he thought it was; the machinery would move at its own pace.

There was a movement in the brush. McNab froze. Out of the brush came a line of quail crossing the trail. He relaxed. It was a good reminder to keep careful. McNab started walking again. He felt a little lurch in his hand. He looked down and saw that the frayed binocular strap had separated, and now they hung by just one piece. He'd meant to get the strap replaced for the last two years. Rather than pulling up on the remaining strap and risking that it, too, would separate, he bent over to cradle the binoculars. It was that frayed strap that saved him. As he bent over, he heard what sounded like a loud bumble bee zoom past his ear. Instinctively he fell to the ground and lay still.

He lay immobile, his prone body hidden by the taller grass. He heard the deliberate swish of feet through the brush, coming slowly his way. One person. Slowly he pushed himself about five feet to the right side from where he fell. McNab looked around for any kind of weapon. Stone, stick, some-thing. There was nothing. He felt the strap of his binoculars. Would it hold if he swung them?

Slow-paced swishes kept coming toward the spot. McNab didn't dare chance a look at who was coming. Odds were the killer was holding whatever gun he had pointed toward where he thought McNab had fallen. If he could get himself launched just right, he could reach the man before he had time to swing the gun around. He wouldn't have time to swing the binoculars. It would have to be barehanded. McNab moved his feet quietly to get into launch position, trying to get some sort of purchase on the ground.

The swishing noise was increasing in volume but not pace. McNab calculated he had another ten seconds or so. He could make out a shape through the grass but kept his head down. As the shape got almost even with him, McNab tensed his muscles. McNab exploded with all his strength toward the killer, wanting to catapult into him. His feet slipped on the grass and instead of hurtling into the killer, he bobbed up out of the grass and fell back down on his face. Immediately he rolled to his right.

Saigon Duphet swung his silenced pistol and fired. McNab counted the shots. Then he realized he didn't know whether it was a five-shot revolver or an eighteen-shot automatic. He rolled again. Bullets plowed up where he'd just been. He kept rolling until he rolled off into a weed-filled ditch, landing so hard it almost knocked his breath out. The shots stopped. He didn't know if Saigon was out of ammo or was just waiting.

The ditch was deep enough to crawl in, and it led toward the trees where his truck was. McNab crept as quietly as he could. Just ahead, a fallen tree crossed the ditch. McNab had just enough space to crawl under it. He heard a grunt as Saigon found the ditch like he did. McNab started to get up to sprint for the trees, then stopped. Quickly he slithered up out of the ditch and lay behind the log. He was still hanging on to the binoculars, but the remaining strap was about gone after being dragged through the brush.

Saigon came down the ditch in a crouch. When he approached the log, he decided to go over the log instead of under it. As he raised his leg to climb over it, McNab rose and heaved the binoculars at him. At the same time, he leaped at Saigon. McNab was in the air when the binoculars hit Saigon in the temple. McNab belly-flopped onto an unconscious man.

"Christ, you're heavy for a skinny guy," McNab muttered to himself as he hoisted Saigon on his shoulders and carried him to the truck. When he got to the trees, he saw Saigon's blue four-door Toyota car. He rifled the man's pockets and got his keys.

McNab laid him down in the back seat of his own Jeep, then tied his hands with some rope. He checked Saigon's eyes. One pupil was larger than the other. "Shit." Severe concussion, maybe a subdural hematoma. The skull is particularly thin at the temple. He might have done more damage than he thought. McNab jumped in the driver's seat and sped toward the hospital.

SIXTY-SEVEN

"So, when are you moving?" Grogan asked Herman as McNab was brought into the interrogation room.

"Escrow closes in two weeks."

"What's the name of that place, again? I still can't get the names straight."

"Glen-Aire. It's going to be sweet."

Grogan finally chose to notice McNab when the pilot was seated. "Don't you ever get tired, McNab?" Grogan stood in front of the table where McNab sat. Herman sat in the corner.

"Yeah, I'm tired. I'm tired of you jerking me around. I'm the guy who almost got killed."

"Haven't I heard this one before?"

"Yeah, and you did diddly about it." McNab turned to Herman. "May I have a cup of coffee, Herman?"

Herman looked to Grogan. Grogan paused a moment, then nodded. Herman left.

Grogan paced back and forth. "That's right, McNab. I'm in charge now. So let's stop playing games. Who's your contact?"

"What are you talking about?"

"Don't give me that shit, McNab. You know what I'm talking about."

The door opened, and Herman appeared with a paper cup of machine coffee. "Black, right, Grif?" He put it on the table.

McNab picked it up and sipped some of the rancid brew. "Jesus, you call that coffee?" Herman shrugged. "Is this guy for real, Herman?"

Herman squirmed. "Grif. Aaron isn't who we thought he was."

Grogan interrupted. "I'm DEA, part of a program that helps communities with drug problems. The chief asked for our assistance a while back. The plan we worked out was for me to appear to join the sheriff's office. We had a unique situation here. Want to tell me about it?"

"About what?"

"Who's your contact, McNab?"

"Fuck you, Grogan. Contact for what?"

"You're in this up to your eyeballs. It'd be a whole lot easier on you if you would cooperate."

"Herman, what in the fuck is he talking about?" Herman shrugged.

Grogan kicked the table, spilling McNab's coffee. "Listen good, McNab, we know what you're up to. Want me to spell it out for you?"

"I would be so grateful."

"We figured you were in it when you took Manuel Tanaka up to Deak City. We almost thought Herman, here, was in it, too, but we cleared him."

"Who?"

"That half breed drug runner you transported to Hundray. The one you beat up in the plane?"

McNab thought a minute. "The scumbag who bled all over my seat? When the engine quit?"

"Yeah, him. Then when you hooked up with Saigon Duphet we were sure."

"What are you talking about?"

"We've been following Saigon Duphet for four years. He's a bag man and errand boy for Tanaka. We were hoping he'd lead us to the next higher-up, but Tanaka's been too crafty for that. When Tanaka got sent up, we thought we were on the right trail. With Tanaka in jail, he'd need a messenger boy to keep his operations running. Saigon's his boy."

"So it turned out. With Tanaka up here, it made sense for the cartel to move in on the local growers to finance the courier operations he'd need. Deak City's too small for someone not to be noticed. Headquarters would have to be in Euphrates. Got to admit, Saigon had a cute story about the nudist camps. Funny how all those camps were in the back woods where the dope grows tall.

"So you show up and fly him to El Cielo. We know El Cielo's been used for ferrying out dope. We know Tanaka's moving in. You show up there with Saigon Duphet in daylight. Not very bright, McNab. Tanaka would consider that danger-ously stupid."

McNab looked over at Herman. "Do you believe this shit?"

"Well, you got to admit it doesn't look very good, Grif."

"Jesus. Thanks for everything, Herman." McNab mopped his face with his hands. "Let me explain this in simple words. I was flying the plane. The engine quit. Tanaka, or whatever his name is, panicked. So, I hit him. He threatened to kill me. I didn't take it seriously and clearly I should have." He paused. "Ask Herman, he heard him threaten me. Didn't he, Herman?"

Grogan waved away McNab's explanation. "Obviously you were supposed to kill Saigon, take his place. Saigon had probably gotten too well known to us for his own good. A replacement had to be made. You didn't succeed at El Cielo, so you had to try again. How about it, McNab? Want to make it easy on yourself? Tell us how you were recruited. It was the plane wasn't it? You had no money, it was your only way out. Tell us your contacts, the whole ball of wax. We'll make a sentencing recommendation."

"Just what is it I am supposed to have done?"

"First degree murder, McNab. You killed Saigon Duphet."

McNab was on his feet. "That's bullshit. He was still alive when I brought him in."

"You're real good, McNab. He never regained consciousness. Died from brain damage from whatever you whacked him with." Grogan leaned across the table. "This autopsy's not going to help you, McNab."

McNab sat down. "I want a lawyer."

Grogan looked over at Herman. "What did I tell you? Fucking hero. Heroes don't need lawyers."

SIXTY-EIGHT

McNab sat still in his cell. The noise. Talking, yelling, radios, pounding on the bars. He hadn't slept at all. He wondered if he ever would if he stayed here. Exhaustion would undoubtedly club him down eventually.

There was a change in the noise level. Catcalls and obscenities rang out. He heard the ring of footsteps down the hallway. There were two of them, and they stopped in front of his cell.

Grogan nodded, and the guard opened the cell. "You're free, McNab, for now. Just remember that when you make a mistake, and you will, I'll be there." He turned and left the guard to shepherd McNab out of the jail.

He walked down to the release desk and stood as his belongings were pulled out of the sack. "Wallet, with twenty-six dollars in it, check book, fifty-five cents in change, pen, set of keys, second set of keys. What is it? You got a lot to lock up?" McNab shrugged. "Sign here." The guard pushed a clipboard in front of him. McNab signed.

.   .   .

Pat sat curled up in the bay window. McNab asked, "Mission accomplished?" Pat nodded and sipped the dark roast coffee. Bright sunlight cascaded in from the large windows.

McNab lay on the floor, looking up at the ceiling. "Thank God they were still there. Any trouble locating the gun and the binoculars?"

"Right where you said they were. Herman was almost disappointed. Creep."

"Did it take long?"

Pat stretched and yawned. "No. He just picked them up and put them in evidence bags and we went straight back to the station."

McNab nodded. "Will it be enough?"

Pat waved her hand. "They'll rule it self-defense. They just have to save some face first."

McNab rolled over on his side. "Yeah, but in the meantime it gives Grogan reason to mess with me." Pat grunted.

Suddenly he sat up. "What if Hoffstader is in it with Tanaka? Is that how he's going to bail out his companies?"

"Sounds pretty improbable."

He stood up. "Any more coffee?" Pat nodded, and he went to the kitchen to fetch a cup. When he came back, Pat was hugging her knees.

She turned her head toward him. "Remember the Delorean case? Cheeky car builder? Tried for selling drugs to finance his operation? Found not guilty?" McNab nodded. "Maybe it isn't so improbable for Hoffstader. After all, he does business all over the world. Lots of opportunity."

"Yeah. Could be. I don't see how the Chinese connection fits, though. China is death on drugs."

"Yeah. So is the U.S., except for the CIA."

"Point taken."

Pat smiled. "At least we don't have anyone running around trying to kill you anymore."

McNab walked slowly around the room. "I'm not so sure."

"What?"

"Remember when I told you about Saigon's ambushing me at El Cielo?" Pat nodded. "Something about that wasn't quite right. While I was in jail I had time to think. Saigon couldn't have cut the fuel line. He was in the mountains. The cut was done in Euphrates."

Color drained out of Pat's face.

SIXTY-NINE

McNab pulled the envelope out of his back pocket along with his checkbook. Darcy was at her desk behind the counter. "How's it going, Darcy?"

"Oh, hi, Grif. Just great."

McNab grunted. "I've got your fuel bills and Ed's invoice for the fuel line here. Is Ed around?"

"Let me check. He's either going to the city today or tomorrow." She went to look at a schedule book.

McNab looked out at the low leaden sky. "Not much flight instruction going on today, is there?"

"No. Not much. Terry's got one instrument student today. They're going to Deak City and practice approaches." She found the schedule book and was leafing through it. "I hope business improves. We've had only one student inquiry in the last couple of weeks, and he was kind of strange."

"How so?"

"He wanted to know all about the airport, like how many planes were on the field, what hangar space cost, what flying businesses were here. All kinds of stuff, but not much about learning to fly." McNab looked up from his checkbook. Darcy frowned. "Here it is. Ed's gone, won't be back for four days.

You can leave his check with me if you want." She shut the schedule book. "Big guy. Walked with a limp. I'm not sure he could have passed the physical. I don't know why he was asking about lessons. From the way he talked, it was like learning to fly wasn't that important to him. Oh, well, we get stranger folk than that here." She laughed.

McNab didn't. "Would you recognize him again, if you saw him?"

"I couldn't forget his size. Or the way his mouth curved down on one side. It hardly moved when the other part of his face did. It was kind of spooky."

McNab handed her the checks. "When was that, that he came by?"

"Oh, when was that? Let's see," she drummed her pencil on the schedule book, "must have been about ... Oh! I know. It was the day before you came in about the fuel line. That day you were weird and the cops came and all? I remember because I was thinking that if weird things happened in threes, I was going to take the next day off."

McNab forced a laugh. "Yeah, that was something. Tell Ed thanks for the fast service on the fuel line."

He went into his office and made a pot of coffee. When it was brewed, he took a large mug and wandered out onto the tarmac. The wind sock flopped weakly. Egrets coasted into the field opposite where the cattle were grazing. McNab walked around the line of small T-hangars where privately owned small planes were sheltered and over to the edge of the airport. The creek flowed slowly past on its way to the ocean, leaves floating on top. He squatted down in the tall grass along the bank. Across the water, four deer emerged from the grass and came down to sip. They looked at McNab, who didn't move, slaked their thirst, and melted back into the brush.

SEVENTY

McNab and McGinty stood in front of the hangar. "You're sure about this?" McGinty asked.

"Not completely. But I'd rather not take the chance."

McGinty nodded. "Yeah, I know what you mean." He turned to the two monks who were admiring the old plane. "Boys, I think it's a good idea. Grif is a good man."

Jamyang Rinpoche nodded. "Where are we going?"

McNab faced him. "To stay with a friend of mine for a while. He does some farming out in the woods."

"He is a good man, too?" There was a twinkle in Jamyang's eye.

McNab chuckled. "Yes, he is. Since he came back from war he has tried to live a peaceful life."

Jamyang nodded. "We know war, also. Very bad. The forest is a good place for meditation. We do *phowa* for those killed in the invasion. And Ongdi."

"Phowa?"

"It is a, how do you say it, practice for the dying, or for those who have died. It helps them to die well. It also helps them to find their path of rebirth."

Jamyang Rinpoche sat in the front, Tenzing in the back.

McNab chuckled to himself. There was something incongruous about the monks' orange and red robes and the green David Clark headsets. He finished the runup and taxied his airplane to the hold line, ready to take off. On the runway, the Hoffstader Industries bizjet spooled up its engines and started to roll for takeoff.

McNab spoke into his microphone. "We'll wait about three minutes before we take off." Jamyang nodded. "The reason we do that is little tornados come off the wingtips of that airplane in front of us. All airplanes. It's a byproduct of lift. The bigger the plane, the more lift, the bigger the tornados. It's called 'wake turbulence.' If we get too close they could roll us right over. If it happens too close to the ground, it would slam us in the dirt and grind us into dust. That's why I wait." They watched the Gulfstream IV climb effortlessly into the clouds.

Three minutes later, McNab pushed the throttle in on his Cessna, waddled down the runway, lumbered into the air, and turned inland. "There will be a tree for you," said McNab as they flew over the forest.

"When it is time it will show itself to us."

A while later, McNab descended, clearing Roy's tall trees, and landed in the pasture without frightening the monks. They climbed out into the meadow that was Roy's front yard. Craning their necks, they beamed at the tall trees surrounding it.

Roy scratched his head as he came out of the house. "What the——?"

"I need a favor, Roy."

"Sure, Grif. What is it?"

McNab told him.

SEVENTY-ONE

McNab closed the hangar door and slowly walked back to the office. He dialed the direct number. "Hello, Herman, it's Grif." He listened a moment. "Sure, I understand. You've got a job to do. I know that. I want to ask you a favor, Herman. I want to show you something. It will shed some light on the case of Henry's murder." McNab listened for a long time. "I know what you think of the case, Herman, but you should see this. It's something I found in Deak City. Where Otto was murdered." He listened longer. "I know, Herman, I know. Look, I promise you that if you come see this with me, it will be the last time I mention Henry to you." There was more chatter on the other end. "I know you're not supposed to consort with suspected criminals, Herman, but how long have we known each other? You know this is all bullshit. Tomorrow's your day off, right? Meet me here at eight in the morning and we'll fly to Deak City. On second thought, make it nine. I'm going to have a few with Mingus tonight. Tell Carol you're going fishing. Hell, we might even do some fishing. Thanks, Herman." McNab hung up. He had a lot of work to do.

. . .

"The counselor and the con!" Mingus turned to McNab. "Is this your last meal? May I suggest macaroni and cheese? I would have to send out for it, of course, but it would ease the transition to institutional fare."

McNab looked at Pat. "Why is 'fuck you' the only thing I can come up with for him?"

"It's what he deserves."

Mingus looked pained. "So unimaginative."

McNab sighed, "I was going to have a drink with him. Do you believe that?"

Pat smirked. "Then I came along and ruined everything. Thank God."

Mingus pointed to the bar. "You buy, I'll drink. Even with her. Later."

McNab and Pat went into the bar and found a table. Pat shrugged out of her coat. "Are you sure it's all right that I came?"

"Positive."

"Isn't this boys' night out or something?"

"Nah. I hadn't had a drink with Mingus in a while, that's all. It looks like he's pretty busy, though."

They had just ordered their drinks when McNab looked up and saw Herman standing in front of their table. "Hi, Grif. Pat. Mind if I join you for a minute?"

McNab pointed at a chair. "What's up, Herman?"

Herman looked around and signaled for Myrna. "I'm not supposed to tell you this." Pat and McNab looked at him expectantly. "It just seemed like a shitty deal. Grogan. You know." They both shook their heads. "Saigon's alive."

Pat's jaw dropped. "That asshole! I'll have his ass over hot coals so fast that…"

McNab cut her off. "Why are you telling us this, Herman? You were on Grogan's side last I saw."

Herman squirmed in his seat. Myrna arrived with their drinks. When she left, McNab continued. "Well?"

"I got caught up in it, Grif. Grogan was so persuasive. He had me believing that a guy I'd known forever was a bad guy. He made it sound believable. But the more I thought about it, the more bullshit it seemed. It was all reasoning, no evidence. I know you, I know you didn't do it. So I came."

Pat stirred her drink vigorously, her face flushed. "What about Saigon? What's he saying?"

"He's still in a coma. Haven't gotten anything out of him, yet."

McNab sat back and looked at his friend. "That hurt, pal."

Herman looked down at the table, then over to Pat, who wouldn't look at him, then to the wall, and finally back to McNab. "I'm sorry, Grif, I really am."

McNab sat still for a moment. "Tomorrow we'll do some fishing, after Deak City. Okay?"

"Yeah, that'll be great. Thanks, Grif." He looked at his watch. "Oh, my gosh, Carol will be worried. I'd better get on home." He took a quick, large swallow of his drink. "I'll see you at eight, Grif." He stood up.

"Herman. Nine."

"Oh, yeah. I guess I... it's eight hours, bottle to throttle. Right, Grif? Did I remember right?" He stood up.

McNab gave him a thumbs up. "You did, Herman, you did." Herman quickly left the bar.

Pat stirred her drink faster. "That little creep. Why did you let him off the hook like that? He doesn't deserve it!"

McNab took a sip. "It's a small town, Pat. You just move on."

They looked up simultaneously. Mingus stood before them with a bottle of champagne, singing, "You fought the law, and the law lost." They both groaned.

SEVENTY-TWO

At nine o'clock the following day, McNab was pulling the hangar door open when Herman arrived with his fishing pole.

"Hi, Grif." Herman's voice was tentative.

"Glad you got here on time. I wasn't. Help me get the plane out."

As they both pushed the plane out of the hangar, Herman said, "I guess I'm still a little nervous? About engines? I mean, this plane has only one?"

"Don't sweat it, Herman. It'll be just fine." McNab, it seemed to Herman, moved slower than usual. His pre-flight was a little sloppy. McNab noticed Herman's noticing. "Up late last night. Besides, I just flew it yesterday, nothing's wrong." He finished the checks and they took off.

Turning north as they reached the coastline, they were confronted with a low cloud deck. McNab frowned, then got out his instrument charts. "Should have checked the weather before I left," he muttered.

Herman looked uneasy. "Is it safe to fly? I thought you always checked the weather."

"Yeah, I usually do. But Deak City's only a hundred or so miles away." McNab found what he was looking for. He dialed new frequencies into the radios and filed an instrument flight plan for Deak City. A few minutes later, he had his clearance and corrected his course.

They flew on in silence for a while. The cloud deck showed some holes, with a glimpse of forest beneath. Herman asked, "You sure it's safe to be up here?" McNab just nodded. "What is it you want to show me in Deak City?"

McNab consulted his charts and instruments again. "How long have you been on Hoffstader's payroll, Herman?"

There was a stunned silence.

Slowly, "What are you talking about, Grif?"

"You know what I mean, Herman. How long has Hoffstader been paying you?"

"That's ridiculous."

McNab checked the gauges. "Aren't you moving out to that Glen-Aire subdivision?"

"Yeah. Carol's business has been doing good."

"Carol's business is in the tank, Herman. And you haven't made lieutenant yet."

"This isn't funny, Grif."

McNab looked down at the charts, then adjusted the VOR bearing selector. "No, Herman, it certainly isn't funny. I kept wondering how did Hoffstader know which of my clients to bully?" Herman didn't answer. "I've talked to you more about my clients than anyone, just like you've talked to me about Carol's business." Still no answer from Herman. "How did Grogan know I had an autopsy report? I didn't tell him. You were the only other person who knew about that. How much was it to set me up, Herman? In dollars?"

"I don't know what you're talking about."

"I think you do. You gave me incomplete autopsy reports on Henry. Why? Hoffstader knew all about my finances. How?"

"Come on, Grif. Lay off this stuff."

McNab reached over and changed the page in his new

GPS receiver. "Hoffstader's involved in Henry's death, Herman. He's also involved in the death of that Tibetan monk." Herman snorted in disgust. "I think he's also involved in Otto's death. If you're involved, Herman, it could be accessory to murder."

Herman was sweating now. "This is all bullshit, Grif. Just... bullshit."

"Then tell me how you got the money to buy a house."

There was a long silence. "Carol's uncle died, left her some money."

"Herman, please. Don't do this. Just tell me. How long and how much?"

Herman's face was bright red now. "Shut up! Just shut the fuck up! Take me back!"

"You aren't cut out for this stuff, Herman. You can't lie that well."

Suddenly Herman reached inside his windbreaker, pulled out a gun and pointed it at McNab. "Take me back, god dammit! Now!"

McNab didn't say anything but looked at his charts again. "You're not supposed to carry one off duty, Herman. Put it down. You're not going to kill me. Who would land the plane? Where would you land it? You see any airport down there?" McNab pointed down at the cloud deck.

Herman continued sweating. "Just take me home." It was more of a plea than a demand.

McNab just shook his head. "Tell me, Herman. Who is your contact with Hoffstader? Is it Bofford? Rosemary? Who?"

"I'm not telling you shit." The gun wavered. "Take me home now."

McNab consulted his charts. "Ever want to know how a plane flies, Herman? You're a curious guy." Herman was looking out the windows, trying to find a place to force the landing. "The tops of the wings are more curved than the bottoms. That means air moves over the top of the wing faster than the bottom. It creates a lower pressure on the top of the wing. The higher pressure under the wing presses up. That's called lift."

"That's fucking fascinating. Now get me home!" Herman poked the gun into McNab's face. McNab pulled the carburetor heat on, then pulled back on the throttle, bringing the engine to idle. The engine noise lessened, the nose of the airplane dipped, and the plane began to descend. "What'd you do?"

"You said you wanted to go home. If you want to land somewhere you have to descend." The airplane started to pick up speed.

"Stop it!"

McNab pulled back on the yoke, and the airplane came to a level attitude. "See, if you increase the angle of attack, that's the angle between the wing and the relative wind, the curvature of the wing effectively increases. That gives you more lift."

Herman didn't know quite what to do. "Just get me home!"

McNab went on in professorial tones. "But if you increase it too much," he pulled the yoke back some more, "the curve becomes too great. The air separates from the wing and causes turbulent air flow over the top of the wing. The wing loses lift." At that moment there was a small sound of a horn going off. "Ah, hear that, Herman? When that goes off, it means we are close to a stall. A stall doesn't have anything to do with the engine. A stall is when the wing loses all effective lift. The wing won't fly anymore."

"God damn you!" Herman was screeching now. "Stop it!"

McNab kept talking in a calm tone. "Now, if one wing loses all its lift before the other one, something interesting happens. The wing that has stopped flying will drop, but the other wing will keep on flying." The horn sound went up in pitch. "In fact, it will lift itself over the top and the airplane goes into a steep nose down attitude." He paused. "Give me the gun, Herman."

"Stop it! Stop it now!"

The horn was screeching now, and the airplane was starting to buffet. The nose began to dip. McNab abruptly kicked the right pedal with full force. Suddenly the view out of the window corkscrewed. Herman screamed. His gun hand hit the instrument panel in front of him. The gun flew out of his hand, dropped to the floor, and skidded under the rudder pedals on his side. The airplane was pointing down at what seemed to be a vertical angle, and it started to spin, picking up rotational speed by the second. There was a hole in the cloud deck below them. Heavily forested mountains showed through it. McNab continued conversationally. "This is how you get into a spin, Herman. You can't have a spin without a stall. Are you remembering this, Herman? Do you know how to get out of a spin?"

Herman was screaming louder. "Stop it! Stop it!"

"Who's your contact, Herman?"

"Please stop it! Please stop it now!" He was whimpering.

"This plane isn't rated for spins, Herman. I don't know how long she'll hold together. Who's your contact?" The clouds were rushing up at the plane, the hole in them getting larger and larger. Branches on individual trees were almost visible, except for the spinning. Herman shrieked, "Karl! Karl Vadner!"

They were in the cloud hole now, the tube of gray gyrating around them. "How much, Herman?"

"Twenty-five thousand!"

The plane plunged out of the hole into the clear air under the clouds. McNab neutralized the ailerons, then shoved the yoke forward, breaking the stall. He pressed the left rudder pedal, and the spinning stopped. They were now in a high-speed dive, heading down into a canyon. The airplane seemed aimed at a small boulder in a small stream. Fir and redwood raced as McNab pulled back on the yoke to pull them out and added power. Herman was weeping with fright. They pulled out of the dive about forty feet above the creek and headed downstream. McNab settled the plane and brought it back up to a reasonable low altitude. Herman was gibbering.

McNab wiped his forehead with his right hand. It was shaking. He consulted his charts and flew onward within the walls of the canyon. At the end of the canyon, he turned east into the valley. McNab looked around and picked his route. For a while they flew in canyons and valleys, hopping just far enough over the tops of ridges to get into the next valley. Occasionally McNab would see a cabin, a dirt road, and most often, the slash of a logging site.

Finally, they came up over the last ridge, almost clipping the tops of the trees, and McNab cut the power and put in flaps. There was a small dirt road ahead, with a cabin on the left side and a barn near the edge of the clearing. McNab saw they were high. He turned the yoke left and pressed on the right rudder. The plane dropped out of the sky, left wing low, nose pointed about forty-five degrees to the right of the center line of the road. Herman moaned and covered his face with his hands. McNab kicked the left rudder at the last moment so the plane aligned with the road and flared. The plane floated long. The three-point touchdown was perfect, but too far down the road. McNab braked carefully, holding full back pressure on the yoke. He didn't want to put the plane on its back. Just before the airplane reached the place where the road dipped down into the trees, McNab stomped on the right rudder, and the plane whipped around, dust flying every-where, and came to a halt.

SEVENTY-THREE

"Roy, you've got to top those trees," McNab muttered to himself. As the propeller stopped, McNab became aware, for the first time, of a strong odor of urine. He got out of the plane, went around to the passenger door, and got Herman's gun. Birdsong erupted from the trees, and insects buzzed in the meadow. A man came out of the cabin and walked down to the plane. McNab stretched as the man approached. "Hello, Roy."

Roy looked at his watch. "Right on time."

McNab pulled Herman along the path to Roy's barn at the end of the meadow. As he walked, McNab pointed to the trees.

"I know, Grif. I just didn't have time." Roy followed Herman.

"I almost didn't get in here." McNab looked over his shoulder. "Let's get him inside and then put the plane in the barn. Then I can look at it to see if it's damaged."

The three went into the back of the barn where Roy had made a bunk room years before when he could afford to have someone working for him. McNab sat the numbed Herman on a bunk, took some handcuffs from his jacket, and cuffed him to it. "We're going to stay here awhile, Herman." Herman just nodded.

Within fifteen minutes, the plane had been put into the barn, and the door closed. McNab and Roy came back into the room. Herman had regained some of his bearings. "You can't do this. I'm an officer of the law. This is kidnapping. You'll both get life!"

McNab pulled a chair over, turned it around, and straddled it. "Herman, you're already dead. You might think about that before putting your mouth in gear."

"What do you mean?"

"We were on an instrument flight plan. We were on radar. The radar tapes will show that we suddenly descended at a very high rate and that we disappeared from the screen over very hostile terrain."

"What?"

"When the weather clears they'll launch an air search for us, but as you can see, they won't find us. The ground search will concentrate on a valley miles and miles from here. In a little while we'll be declared legally dead."

Herman thought for a minute. "What do you want?"

"Who's Karl Vadner?" Herman hesitated. "Come on, Herman, who is he?"

Reluctantly, Herman forced it out, "He's Hoffstader's goon. Does the dirty work that Bofford can't do. That's all I know."

"I want to show you something." He motioned to Roy, who pulled out Herman's gun and pointed it at him. McNab went over to Herman and undid the handcuffs. McNab led the trio out into the barn where the plane sat.

McNab stopped them near the rear of the plane. "Did you tell Karl that we were going flying today?"

Herman didn't say anything. McNab opened the baggage

compartment of the airplane. He then pulled a screwdriver out of his back pocket and began undoing the screws that held the rear bulkhead in place. About fifteen minutes later, the bare aluminum inside of the airplane, from the back seats to the tail, was visible. McNab motioned for Herman to come over. "Take a look."

Herman looked down the narrowing aluminum tube that was at the rear of the plane. Halfway down on the left, taped onto the side with duct tape, was a parcel the size of a shoe box. "Bring it out here, Herman." Several minutes, and a couple of skinned knuckles later, Herman brought out the oblong parcel. McNab gestured toward a workbench. "Open it."

He placed the box on the bench and pulled the tape off it. Then he took the top off. Herman stepped back, stunned. Inside was some white doughy material, an alarm clock, and wires going from the clock to a cylinder pushed into the doughy material.

"Well, Herman, did you tell Karl we were going flying?"

Herman started to wobble. He made it to a bench and sat down. Finally, he just nodded.

"I figured out you might be feeding information to Hoffstader. But when you showed up at Luego's last night, I was sure of it. He did tell you to make sure I was busy, didn't he?" Herman merely nodded. "I got to the hangar about five this morning. The little traps I left showed someone had been inside. I just had to figure out what they were doing. It took me almost three hours to scour that airplane. Check the fuel tanks, oil, had to change the oil, all the engine mounts, control surfaces and cables. I started at the front and worked back. Should've gone the other way. But there it was, just like you saw it." McNab paused. "I took the batteries out, of course. You still want to protect Hoffstader, Herman?" Herman shook his head. "Tell me about Karl. How it got started."

Herman shifted his position on the bench, and the story came pouring out. "Carol's shop is doing terrible. We've had to put money into it for the last six months instead of taking any out. More each month. I was complaining to some of the guys at the station. It's been hard, you know. Last round of mill closings just gutted us. Folks can't even afford used clothes now. Anyway, one of the guys,"

McNab interrupted, "Who?"

"You don't know him. Jimmy Kay. Works in records. Anyway, he tells me I should talk to this guy he knows for some extra work. Rent-a-cop stuff. Turns out it's Karl. We have a couple of drinks and pretty soon it's clear he's working for ML. I don't have anything against ML or Hoffstader. So I work a couple of events and things for him. A lot of the guys do. It's no big deal. Then..." Herman stopped.

McNab motioned for him to continue.

"Then little envelopes started appearing in my desk. They had cash in them. Not much, but enough to help. I didn't know what to do. I didn't know who put them there. I knew it wasn't smart, but, Jesus, Grif, we were going down the tubes."

"Just keep going, Herman."

"Then one day Karl wants to see me. He says there is a group of monks from some weird place coming to town. He just wants me to keep tabs on them, let him know what they're up to. I ask what does ML want with monks. He gets very serious. He tells me the way to keep friends is to not ask too many questions. I get it. I passed a few pieces of information to him I'd heard about the monks, including that story about the peach pie on Hoffstader's head. He didn't seem to think that one was very funny. The envelopes got a little fatter." Herman shrugged.

"What about Henry?"

Herman shifted on the bench. "That was really strange. It was pretty clear to us that Henry and Larry just plain killed each other. Then Karl calls and starts *selling* me on the idea that Henry and Larry *must* have killed each other. I didn't get it. Then there was all this weird stuff about the autopsies. That's when I gave you a copy. I didn't really look at it. I sort of didn't want to know, you know? I just didn't get it. Then it got way strange."

"How?"

"Karl comes and says he wants me to report on your movements. I ask why. He tells me never mind why, just do it. Well, I don't just roll over because big, ugly Karl tells me to, I objected." McNab grunted. "It's true, Grif, I objected. Didn't do me any good. He reminded me of 'the Godfather.' He made me an offer I couldn't refuse, Grif. Twenty-five thousand to keep close to you and tell him everything or he cuts me off completely and tells the other guys I'm a rat." Herman averted his eyes and took a drink of his coffee. "It was my only chance. I'm not going to make lieutenant. Everyone knows that, even me. Carol's shop is busted. If we could get out of the lease we'd shut it down in a heartbeat. With the twenty-five grand we could get out of the shop lease and move to Glen-Aire. It means so much to Carol."

"Did Karl give you any indication why it was worth so much money to keep tabs on me?"

"No. I didn't ask. It was too much money."

"What does Karl look like?"

"Big. Real big. Ugly. Scary ugly. Droopy mouth on one side."

"Does he walk with a limp?"

"No. He walks just fine." McNab dropped his head and sighed. Herman thought for a minute. "Except the last couple of weeks he said he sprained his ankle." Herman chuckled a little, then stopped. "The rumor was that when that whole peach pie thing came down that Henry bit him on the ankle." He laughed again. No one else did. "He was limping a little the last time I saw him, but it was almost gone."

"When was that?"

"Last night." Herman looked down again. "After I left you at Luego's I saw him."

"What kind of car does he drive?"

Herman thought for a minute. "Buick. Big white Buick. He just got it."

"What about before?"

"Big piece of shit old Jeep."

"What color?"

"That's a good one. What color wasn't it? Mostly brown and red. Had one green fender. Looked like he didn't finish the paint job after replacing the fender. I saw him with that one maybe twice, three times. Before that it was a black Grand Prix. Muscle car. Before that…"

McNab cut him off. "Okay, Herman." He brooded a few minutes.

"Roy, you still in?"

Roy nodded. "Sons of bitches."

McNab turned back to Herman. "I don't know if you've figured this out yet, but you're dead whether you stay here or not." Herman looked confused. "You were supposed to die with me. If Karl finds out you're alive, you won't be for long. I have some work to do to find out just why they want us all dead, so you have to stay here for a bit."

"But Carol! She'll be … I can't let her think I'm dead."

"Better she thinks you're dead than you really be dead."

Herman put his head in his hands. "Okay."

They were silent for a moment. McNab focused on the defused bomb. "I can't believe you'd do that to me, Herman. We go back to sixth grade." The deputy stayed mute.

McNab turned to Roy, who shook his head. McNab sighed. "Come with me, Herman. Let's go to your quarters." He went to the deputy and helped him up. The three of them walked back to the bunk room. McNab pushed Herman in it and closed and locked the door.

Herman came back to the door and started to pound on it. "Hey! What's going on?"

"Can't trust you."

"Come on. I'll be good."

"I know you will."

SEVENTY-FOUR

"Thanks, Roy." McNab patted Roy's truck with the new axle. Roy pulled back onto the road. His headlights swept over the blue four-door Toyota that Saigon Duphet had driven. It was parked where he'd asked Pat to leave it, a quarter of a mile down the road.

McNab trotted to the car and unlocked it with the keys he'd taken from Saigon. As if in an unfamiliar aircraft, McNab took a few moments to identify all the controls. His last check was the registration. The car was registered to Celestial Arts Jewelry Company in Los Angeles. McNab started the car, and quickly he was on his way.

Twenty minutes later he was ringing the doorbell at a dilapidated cottage on a large lot tucked away behind a trucking yard on the outskirts of Euphrates. There was no answer. He tried again. And again. Finally, he heard shuffling sounds and an indistinct voice saying, "Hold on. I'm coming."

The porch light came on, revealing a sickly green door with peeling paint and a stained concrete stoop barely covered by a black mat that said 'W_lc_m_' in faded pink. The door opened and Dewey Phelps peered out. "Who is it?" The newspaper reporter was trying to put on his glasses with one hand while his robe was opening because the other hand had been removed from the robe to open the door.

"Obviously, a vowel freak made off with your stock in trade." McNab pointed at the mat.

Phelps finally got the spectacles on and looked at McNab. "Jesus Christ! You're supposed to be dead!"

"I'd give you the Mark Twain quote but I'd rather come in."

Phelps ushered McNab into the tiny living room and shut the door. The faded green shag carpeting was covered in pizza boxes and fast food wrappers mixed in with crumpled pieces of paper. The crumples led to a computer in the far corner. Empty soda bottles stood on every flat surface in the room. "Come on in. I cleaned up specially, hoping you'd drop by. Want a brew?"

"Yeah." McNab sat while Phelps rummaged in the refrigerator. He came back with two bottles of ginger brew. McNab remembered the story that Phelps had drunk himself out of a series of jobs from the Washington Post on down. When he landed on the bottom rung, in Euphrates, he finally quit drinking.

"So. How is it being dead?"

McNab took a drink of the spicy soda. "Better than the real thing."

"This is a great story already, and I don't even know anything. Mind if I get a tape recorder?"

"Aren't you ever off?"

"Give me a break, Grif. Half the National Guard is out in the mountains trying to find your body, and you waltz in on me at," he looked at his wrist and saw there was no watch, "what time is it?"

"One forty-one AM."

"Right. Early." Phelps sipped his drink. "Should I be obvious?"

"You mean, like, why am I here?" Phelps nodded ironically. "To give you the biggest story you've had in this town."

"Just by walking in the door you did that."

"No, Dewey. I mean a real story. One that could put you back on the media map. But I'm going to need some help."

"Ah. The catch."

McNab nodded. "Let me tell you a fable of our times." After an hour of non-stop talking, Phelps agreed to help, provided he got the exclusive. McNab stayed at the cottage for about two hours until Phelps returned. McNab climbed into his car just as the diesels in the truck yard were starting.

He drove to a place about a half mile from his own house and parked the car. He moved with great care through brush parallel to the road until he was across from their drive. No obvious surveillance. He quickly crossed the road and dropped into the creek beside the property's driveway. McNab sloshed as quietly as he could up the stream until the creek diverged from the way to the house. For about forty minutes he sat still and observed the land around the house. Finally satisfied, he crossed the open area and went up the back stairs. He'd just gotten inside the kitchen when he heard the sound no burglar ever wants to hear, a pump action shotgun being racked. "Hold it right there."

The lights in the kitchen blazed on. Pat was standing in the doorway to the hall, the gun pointed at him. Confusion crossed her face. She dropped the gun and ran to him, grabbing him in a bear hug. "Grif!" It was all she could manage before she started to sob.

SEVENTY-FIVE

They held each other for a few minutes. Then Pat disengaged and held him at arm's length. "You bastard!" She hauled off to hit him. McNab caught her arm in mid-air.

"How about some coffee? I've got a lot to do and not a lot of time to do it in. I'll fill you in as we go."

Pat scowled at him, then went to make some coffee. McNab raced to his room and returned to the living room with an armload of clothes. He threw them on the floor and went back for another load and his suitcase. He was packing when Pat came in with the steaming mugs.

"It's very important that I be dead for a while." Pat looked at him quizzically. McNab recounted the events to that point. "If Hoffstader thinks I'm dead then he'll relax. Maybe just enough. I'm going to be out of touch for a little while. If I don't contact you within four days it'll mean I'm really dead."

"Can't you…"

"No. It's too late to stop. Hoffstader won't stop until I'm dead. If I don't make it back, call this number, ask for Doug. Tell him everything you know." McNab stopped packing. "Tell him about the monks, too. I don't know how, but they're in this, too." He finished his packing. "I know it was shitty, but I couldn't tell you ahead of time because your reactions had to be real. For Hoffstader. It's very important you still act like I'm dead. And you can't tell Carol."

Pat nodded. "Anything else I can do?"

McNab thought a moment, then told her.

It was past noon by the time McNab pulled into Roy's place. After unloading his equipment and luggage, he put the car in the barn beside the plane. He listened to Herman complain, cajole, and threaten for about ten minutes, then went to the house and fell into an exhausted sleep.

As the sun went down, he awoke. When he came to the table the monks were already there. Roy brought in a pot of bacon and baked beans and they all fell to.

"I already gave your so-called friend his," said Roy.

After dinner McNab got out the tools he'd brought. He went to the barn and checked the airplane from spinner to tail. It took a while. Structurally the aircraft was fine. He finished tightening screws in some of the under-wing inspection plates. He saw a few popped rivets, none critical. McNab knew he had been quite lucky. Next, he altered the identification number painted on the aircraft's tail. He changed a six into an eight and an F into an E. Since Charlie's last paint job was a long time ago, it had the smaller numbers on the tail. The alteration would hold up under casual scrutiny. About midnight, McNab returned to the house, ate again, and fell into bed.

In the morning his luck held. The sky was clear. After talking to Herman and instructing Roy, McNab took off, again barely clearing the trees, and headed southeast. McNab kept off designated airways and flew low, but legal. Mountain forests slowly gave way to foothills, now turning brown, and finally to the hot central valley. McNab avoided the high traffic airport areas. A few hours later he was over the

Tehachapi Mountains and coming into the maelstrom of Southern California airspace, which contains one-quarter of all airborne aircraft in the United States at almost any given moment.

McNab contacted SOCAL Approach and put himself into the air traffic system. The controllers handed him off from one sector to another and finally to the Santa Monica Airport control tower, where he landed. The airport had changed radically since he'd been here several years before. The field, where a group of cloth-covered biplanes had departed on the first round-the-world flight in 1924, had succumbed to the sterility of upscale corporate aviation. McNab remembered when the last Fixed Base Operator, or FBO, on the field who still catered to small airplanes closed. He parked in the transient area. The rental van was waiting for him, and in a few minutes he was ensconced in a cheap motel in Santa Monica.

McNab spread out the photos from Dewey Phelps on the bed and reviewed them. He did the same with Rico's printouts. When everything was in order, he went out to dinner.

The Third Street mall was bustling. Some years ago the three-block-long section was dead, killed by the mega-mall built at one end of it. Shrewd investors had brought in multiplexes and restaurants, now one of the busiest areas for miles. McNab passed up the Wolfgang Puck pizza place and knockoffs of it, choosing a trendy establishment featuring Chinese-California cooking. There was little chance Hoffstader would think he was alive, much less near his corporate headquarters. Still, McNab decided to stay out of character. He sipped an expensive microbrew and checked his watch and the area.

Inside an hour McNab was in the Century City towers, the two triangular buildings that were the signature of this locus of business. It was the closest metropolitan center to the most exclusive suburbs of the sprawling city.

McNab entered one of the buildings as a non-entity in a cheap business suit, thin tortoise-shell glasses, and a cut-rate eelskin briefcase, one of hundreds and hundreds pouring up the escalators from the parking garage. The directory showed the name of the company just as it had been on Saigon's car registration, Celestial Arts Jewelry Company, Inc., suite 3144, where Saigon had ceased working many years ago, according to Doug. McNab noticed two other names as he scanned the rest of the directory, China Commercial Trade Association, Suite 3108, and Odin Electronics, Suites 3000 and 3100. There were no other offices listed for the thirtieth floor.

On the twenty-ninth floor McNab entered the law offices of Garland, McGuire, Riddle, and McManus. The receptionist put him into a conference room and asked if he would like coffee. He said, yes, please, black, and where is there a telephone? She pointed to the other end of the long table. As he dialed, his eye was caught by a broad line of slightly off-tone paint snaking its way down the inside corner of the room. It took a moment to remember. He wondered what it would have been like at 4:31am, high in the tall building during the Northridge earthquake. These buildings, he knew, had been built on giant rollers so that when the temblor hit, the structures rolled rather than shaking themselves apart. Two days of inspection had showed only cosmetic damage, like the crack he saw, and the workers returned just in time for two giant aftershocks.

There was no answer. As McNab was putting the receiver down, the conference room door opened, and Jim Riddle walked in. "Grif! Good to see you! Come on down to my office." Riddle was tall and beginning to bulk out. They walked down the lushly carpeted hallway. "Got your information, Grif." Riddle showed him into an office with a spectacular view of the city's western reaches and out to the ocean. As he sat behind the desk, Riddle gestured around him and said, "Beats the Air Force!" In the Air Force, he and McNab had formed a friendship while collaborating on cases years ago. Riddle, the lawyer; McNab, the investigating officer. Now one of the city's most successful lawyers, he still remembered the friendship. He reached into a drawer and pulled out a bound report. "All here."

"How about the Reader's Digest version?"

"Okay. Celestial Arts Jewelry, Inc. was formed in 1971 by a group of Viet Nam vets for the purpose of importing Thai, Laotian, and Cambodian jewelry into this country. Now they also deal in Burmese and Malaysian. They had contacts in Thailand from being stationed there. Company has been reasonably successful, selling medium to low end earrings, bracelets and trinkets. Ah, let's see, forty-one employees. Last year they did a little over twelve million in sales. One serious brush with the law about six years ago. They were claiming to import disassembled parts, low tariff, when they were actually shipping in fully assembled pieces. Much higher duty. Customs service takes very unkindly to this kind of practice. Top guys almost went to jail. Some deal was made, and they paid big fines, but no jail time. Since then, nada. Just your small time vanilla import company."

"Foreign ownership? Say Chinese?"

Riddle looked at him quizzically. "No. The stock is closely held. The original four investors, equal shares."

"What about them?"

Riddle opened the report. "William G. Gifford, former army captain. Lives in Holmby Hills, president. Hiram L. King, former sergeant major, and VP, lives in Malibu. Leroy Washington, former corporal, VP marketing, lives in, ah, Beverly Hills. Enzio Montaldo, former PFC, VP finance, also lives in Malibu." He looked up at McNab. "You thinking what I'm thinking?"

"You mean, how does a company that does twelve million in gross sales with forty employees support four people living in the most expensive real estate in the country? And top floor Century City offices?"

"You want credit and bank checks done on these guys?"

"I don't think so." McNab thought. "Were these guys in the same outfit or something?"

"I don't know. I don't think I can get that kind of information."

McNab waved it away. "That's all right, I can find out."

"Could you tell me what this is about?"

"Believe me, you don't want to know."

"Can it compromise the firm or my employees?"

McNab was silent for a moment. "I don't think so. Not if you've been careful in your investigations so far."

Riddle smiled. "All public record. So far."

"I need one more favor, if you can do it."

"What's that?"

"If it becomes necessary, can you say I'm working for the firm as a process server?"

Riddle drummed a pen on his blotter. "You sure you don't want to tell me what this is about?"

"When it's over?"

Riddle sighed and nodded. "I'll let personnel know."

SEVENTY-SIX

McNab left the office building and drove to a retail store in Torrance that Rico had told him about. By the time he returned to Century City, he was wearing a maintenance worker's outfit. He took a step ladder out of his rental van and proceeded to the thirty-first floor.

After checking the angles from several places, he set up his ladder under an 'Exit' sign near the end of one corridor. McNab climbed the ladder and carefully removed the sign. People came and went, paying no attention. A maintenance uniform was almost as good as an invisibility cloak. Out of his canvas bag he pulled a small box and cable and pushed it into the cavity in the ceiling left by the base of the sign. Carefully he extended the antenna. Out of his bag came another 'Exit' sign. Hooking up the small cable, he installed the new sign in place of the old one. He checked the view from the top of the ladder. The hidden camera in the sign would show clearly who came and went from suites 3100 and 3108 and the unmarked doors that were obviously part of those offices, the only two on this corridor. McNab figured 3100 was Hoffstader's personal office, with the rest of Odin's operational staff on the floor below. Celestial Arts was on another triangular leg, the two corridors meeting near the elevators. He repeated the same actions with a sprinkler head camera pointed at Celestial Arts Jewelry Co. He now had full coverage of both halls and the intersection. With the small amplifiers he had attached to them, the 'signs' would broadcast the pictures up to three miles away, where he could receive them in the comfort of his van. Satisfied, he folded up his ladder and retreated.

McNab went to an upscale takeout place in the shopping mall of Century City. He ordered a couple of sandwiches to go and coffee. Fifteen minutes later he was parked on a residential street in direct view of the triangular building and watching two screens. It was very dull TV. He kept a recorder going on both cameras for the times he would have to move the truck. He didn't want to appear suspicious to the neighbors.

The next forty hours were an education in boredom. Monotonous legions of people came and went in both corridors. McNab became convinced that Odin Electronics must employ fifty thousand people in that office alone. The China Commercial Trade Association was visited regularly, though far less, and primarily by what he came to recognize as staff. Hardly anyone went into Celestial Arts, and no one he recognized. He began to think this was not such a good idea.

At last, he decided. He would watch the tapes in search mode to see if anyone was interesting, then slow it down to look more closely. This way, he could walk and eat and not go crazy in the enclosed van with the sounds of traffic around him all the time.

Hoffstader came and went regularly, but only to Odin. Karl, the big man who accompanied Hoffstader on their flight to Two Forks, and Herman's contact, was almost always with him. Often Hoffstader would greet people in the hall, waving and smiling. Whenever someone came to the office of the China Commercial Trade Association, McNab slowed the tape. Often he stopped the video to compare images. Dewey

Phelps had given him the pictures the newspaper photographers had shot, but not printed, from the peach pie incident. At his request, Phelps had enlarged several of them. Two showed a car driving away from the Mountain Lumber headquarters. Greatly enlarged, and very grainy, the face of an Asian man was recognizable behind the wheel. McNab constantly checked the images from Phelps' photos against those on the tape. No luck.

By the end of three days the van was full of wrappers from McDonald's and Burger King, the Colonel's buckets, leftover pieces of bagels, two partially empty cream cheese containers, little pieces of French fries, dozens of empty Starbucks coffee cups, napkins, paper towels, and sandwich bags from Louie's Pastrami Palace.

McNab had just about decided that he was pursuing the wrong path. As far as he could tell, there was no cross-pollination between Odin Electronics and the China Commercial Trade Association. Nor was there any connection between Celestial Arts Jewelry and either of the other two. He kept watching tapes. Scanning evening and late at night was very fast. Few people, other than routine security patrols, came down either corridor, and none entered the offices he was concerned with.

He decided to give it one more day. After that, he would figure out an approach to an Odin staffer. If that didn't work, he'd take a bigger risk and go after one of the Chinese Commercial Trade Association people.

Thursday, McNab sat in the parked van drinking lousy coffee, eating a wretched breakfast roll, and adding more to the packaging pile that was his transportation. It was just before 7:00am and he was reviewing the tapes of the previous night. Even on fast scan it was boring, empty halls. While they were running, he picked up the special cellphone and dialed.

"Doug, Grif."

"Grif? What the hell? Aren't you supposed to be dead? 'Course it was too good to be true."

"How did you know up there in DC?"

"You forget, old buddy, you were once upon a time a public person. It's been all over the news."

"Yeah, well, I'd be grateful if I stayed dead a while."

"You ready to tell me what's up yet?"

"Hoffstader."

"That's it? Just Hoffstader? Come on, old buddy, you've got to give up more than that."

"Can't right now. Have you gotten the lab results on the gravel samples?"

"Yeah, I have them right here. Hold on." The phone went silent for a moment. "Here we go. Well, old buddy, you've got yourself a fine sample of good old American river bottom gravel."

McNab, stunned, couldn't speak. "You're sure?"

"Yep."

"Not from the moon?"

"Nope. Moon rock looks just about the same as Earth rock. I mean, after all, the moon is a piece that was knocked off from the Earth. Difference is that some isotopes are present in different ratios in moon rock. The ratios show it's from good old mother Earth." When McNab didn't respond, Doug went on. "If you're thinking—"

Suddenly the screen in front of McNab went to snow. "Shit!" McNab said. "Got to go, Doug. I'll call you."

"Wait, Grif—"

"No time, Doug." He hung up the phone. He noted the time on the tape and continued the scan. All snow until the end of the video. He rewound the tape to where the malfunction was and looked at it. The time was 1:21am. No one in the corridor. He rewound the video until he could see the last people in the hallway. At 12:44am the security guard he had seen on many other occasions wandered down the hall checking door knobs and sauntered back. Then no one until the camera ceased working.

McNab drummed his fingers on the table. Should he venture up there to repair the camera? Was it an actual malfunction, or had someone discovered it? He rewound the tape further. The last people out of the Odin suite were some secretaries, then, finally, Hoffstader. Karl locked the door and tested it. Then he paused a moment, unlocked the door, and went in, for less than a minute, to retrieve a briefcase. He then locked the door, and he and Hoffstader left. About five hours later, the camera stopped.

McNab needed the information. He couldn't just station himself in the corridor for twelve hours a day. The camera had to be fixed. He looked at his watch. He would wait for the morning rush to be over so he would be noticed by fewer people. He tossed down the last of the rancid brew and prepared.

Just after 9:30 he set up his step ladder in the thirty-first floor corridor. He'd seen no one from the tapes looking at him. In fact, the hall seemed unusually empty. He went up the ladder and worked the sign loose. He was about to detach the cable from the sign to the transmitter when the cable slithered out of the hole and hung down. Just as this was registering, there was a blow to the ladder, and McNab was falling through the air, carpet rushing up at him. As he hit the floor, he rolled over in time to see Karl's face and the colossal fist coming at his face. He went black.

Seventy-Seven

McNab groaned and tried to feel his face. That's when he found out his hands couldn't move. Slowly he became aware that he was sitting on a chair. His vision cleared, then clouded. He was in an office, tied to a chair with plastic cuffs. He looked over a long, highly polished conference table, surrounded by comfortable chairs, to a view of West Los Angeles, Santa Monica, and the foothills. The view had a greenish tint. It was close to sunset.

He heard the door open behind him. In his peripheral vision, Karl loomed. The big man came up to him and grabbed his face in a hand that seemed to McNab the size of a catcher's mitt. McNab tried to think of some snappy lines, but his head ached too terribly. Karl peered into McNab's eyes, dropped his hand, and left the room.

A few minutes later, the door opened again, and Karl came in, accompanied by Hoffstader. The mogul went around and sat at the desk facing McNab. Karl pulled up another chair and sat beside McNab.

Hoffstader just looked at McNab for a few minutes. Then he put his elbows on the desk. "What are we going to do with you, Grif?" McNab didn't respond. "You are so ungrateful. I offer you a fine position in my organization. You refuse me. You accuse me of terrible things. Because of your fine service to this country I make allowances for your rude behavior I wouldn't make for anyone else. I even offer you a way to build your own business without investing a cent. And you repay me by spying on me." McNab said nothing. "Odin Electronics is the constant target of sophisticated industrial espionage. Your pathetic attempt using such crude methods disappoints me. I would have thought that with your investigative experience you would show more flare. I admit we were confused at first. We were searching inside our offices for the source of the transmissions. When it became clear they were coming from the hallway, well, Grif, you forgot about the emergency exit door to the stairs just behind the sign. After all, that's what the sign points to."

McNab said nothing.

"Where is Deputy Herman Pecheur?"

McNab opened his mouth to speak. All he could croak out was, "Water."

Hoffstader motioned to Karl, who went behind McNab and got a glass of water from a wet bar that McNab couldn't see. "The drugs Karl gave you to keep you under do tend to dry the mouth." Karl came around, fed McNab some water, then sat beside him again.

"So. Where is Deputy Pecheur?"

McNab worked his dry throat. "He didn't make it."

"What does that mean, exactly?"

"Your bomb wasn't totally successful. The tail didn't blow completely off. I managed a controlled crash. I made it, Herman didn't."

Hoffstader said nothing for a while. "You know, Grif, it doesn't have to be like this. I like you. We could be a great team. We could do a lot for each other. I could get you where you've always wanted to go: into space. Now, there's no use kidding you that you could actually fly the Shuttle.

NASA is very fussy about that. But I could get you there as a mission specialist. And I have some very special missions that could use a man like you, Grif. What do you say? Let's let bygones be bygones. Get on with life. Fulfill your dreams?"

Hoffstader waited a full minute, then addressed McNab, again. "What is it you think you know?"

"You tell me." McNab coughed.

Hoffstader nodded at Karl. The big man slapped the back of McNab's head so hard that the chair rocked, and he almost fell to the floor, chair and all. Spots of color filled his vision. His headache exploded.

"No more rudeness, Grif. I haven't got time. Why are you coming after me?"

"Get off it, Hoffstader. You know why. Otherwise you wouldn't have tried to kill me."

Hoffstader nodded to Karl. When Karl's hand connected, McNab's head snapped forward so hard it felt like a vertebra popped. Blood trickled out from the corner of his mouth where the force of the blow had made him bite his tongue.

"Tell me."

McNab was reeling. He faced Karl, "You're real good with women and hog tied people, aren't you, you asshole." McNab turned to Hoffstader, "I thought you killed Henry Bouchard."

"Who?"

"The guy who put the peach pie on your head."

Hoffstader paused, "Very funny, Grif. Why would you be interested in a wino?"

"He was Pat's brother."

Hoffstader paused. "What else?"

"That's all."

Hoffstader was silent. "Are you sure?"

"Yeah, I'm sure."

"I'm not sure. Tell me more."

"There's no more to tell."

This time McNab didn't see Hoffstader's signal. Pain flared, and he blacked out.

Voices filtered through. "God dammit, Karl. I need the information."

"Sorry, Mister Hoffstader. I'll go easier."

"Ah. He's coming around." Hoffstader's voice was hearty. "Grif. Grif. You really need to tell us everything."

"Fuck you." Hoffstader held up his hand, and Karl stopped in mid-swing.

"Grif, if you can't cooperate I'm afraid we'll have to use other methods." He made a sweeping gesture around the room. "Did you notice the green tint in the glass? It's five inches thick. Bullet proof, random vibrations so lasers can't pick up sound. Speaking of sound, it's sound proof. This is a special conference room we use when discussing our confidential bids and deals. Very similar to the SCIFs the CIA uses. Nothing in, nothing out. No one can hear us, Grif. Am I making my point?"

"Look, Hoffstader. I thought you killed Henry. I thought I had you nailed. Gravel in Henry's wounds looked like it came from your ring. I had it analyzed. The gravel in Henry's wounds isn't moon rock. I made a mistake."

"Surely there's more?"

"I couldn't figure why you wanted him dead. That's all. I was trying to find out."

"Why did you persist after you analyzed the gravel?"

"I just got the results this morning. The same time I noticed the camera was out."

Hoffstader was silent for a while. "You know, Grif, I think you're holding out on me." McNab shook his head. "Yes, I think you are. Karl...?

Karl left the room. McNab started to sweat. "Look. Hoffstader. This isn't necessary."

"Then, tell me, Grif. What else is there? You've been spending a lot of energy prying into my life and I think I have a right to know. Would you like your privacy invaded, Grif?" When McNab didn't respond, Hoffstader went on. "I don't mean to belabor the obvious, Grif, but, well, you're already dead."

McNab tried to think. If he told Hoffstader about Saigon, and they were in it together, he was dead. If he told him about Chu Sha Lee, the Chinese premier's man, and they were doing something, he was dead. More than that. If he told about either of them, Pat was in danger, too. If he told him about the Tibetans... what did they know about his knowing? There probably wasn't anything there that couldn't be explained away.

"Maybe I was wrong about you, Hoffstader. Somehow I got it into my head that your security people got too zealous with those monks. I thought it might be connected with Henry since he hung out with them. But since you didn't kill Henry, then the Tibetan thing is, well, an accident. My interest was strictly Henry. It's over now."

"Ah." Hoffstader made a non-committal noise. Karl came back into the room carrying a small black bag. "Tell me more about these monks."

"Uh. There's nothing much to tell. Henry took them around a little, then he had his run-in with you. I mean the pie thing. Then, well, nothing." In the meantime, Karl, in full view of McNab, was bringing out a syringe and a vial.

"Is that it?" Hoffstader leaned his chin on his hands almost as if he was praying.

McNab was still sweating. "Yeah. That's all of it."

Hoffstader motioned to Karl. "You make it difficult to believe you, Grif. What about your meeting with the monks in Miss Morrissey's office? Why didn't you tell me about that?"

Karl finished filling a syringe. He squirted a few drops out of the needle and waited. McNab turned back to Hoffstader. "It wasn't important. It didn't concern me, really. I was just going by there and Pat had them in her office. She does a lot of pro bono work and—."

Hoffstader waved him silent. "No matter. You will tell us all about it, I'm sure." He nodded. Karl moved in. McNab struggled, but with no effect. Karl shoved the needle into his arm and pushed the plunger down.

"You've got this all wrong, Hoffstader. There's nothing more to tell."

Hoffstader wasn't listening to him. He got up and went to the door. "Karl, I'll be back in a few minutes." Hoffstader opened the door. McNab opened his mouth to scream. Someone in the office should hear him. But his mouth wouldn't work. His voice wouldn't work. As the door closed, he managed a small croak and went into darkness.

McNab became dimly aware of a popping sound. It was close. The sound was getting louder. As his eyes opened, he saw that Karl was standing in front of him, rhythmically slapping his face. Suddenly it hurt.

"You gave him too big a dose, you stupid prick. He isn't any use to us unconscious."

"Sorry, Mister Hoffstader."

McNab looked around him. Outside, the sky had darkened. The bright lights of the city sparkled. "Grif."

"Hmmmm?"

"Where's Herman?"

"Herman, Herman, Herman. Herman is a hermit." McNab started to sing, "I'm Hen-ery the Eighth I am, En-ery the Eighth I am I am—"

"Okay, Grif." Hoffstader wiped his brow. "Tell me about the monks."

"Oh. They come from a little tiny country. You know they aren't really Tibetans. Did you know that? They... can I have some spaghetti? I'd really like some spaghetti. I bet the Chinaman would like some noodles, too, don't you? Spaghetti is a noodle, you know."

Karl started to hit him, but Hoffstader stopped him. "Who is the Chinaman, Grif?"

"He likes noodles. Or maybe it's pie. He missed the pie, you know. He just drove away."

"Tell me about the Chinaman, Grif. Now!"

"I dunno. I dunno." McNab started to sing, "Ching chong Chinaman sitting in a tree. Do you remember that one? I don't remember the rest of the words. Do you?"

"Tell me, McNab."

"China is next to Saigon, you know. If you look on a map, do you have a map here. China's in pink and Vietnam is green. It's really pretty. Do you know Saigon? I used to know Saigon."

"God dammit, tell me!" Hoffstader was starting to yell.

"I bet you know Saigon. I do." McNab nodded a self-satisfied nod.

Hoffstader nodded, and Karl smashed his fist into McNab's face. There was a terrible crunching sound. Blood spurted from McNab's nose, and his head dropped forward. From a long way off, McNab heard Hoffstader yelling.

"You sonofabitch! I told you to go easy. He'll be out for hours, now. You're so goddam stupid. Ignorant fucking animal. You want to keep this job? You listen to me when I tell you something. Stupid ape."

"Sorry, Mister Hoffstader."

"Obviously this isn't working. We'd better take him..."

McNab strained to concentrate, but the words swirled away.

SEVENTY-EIGHT

He struggled to surface. He thought he heard jet engine sounds, then went under again. He became dimly aware of bouncing around on the floor of a van or truck. Then there were hands under his arms, and he was dragged out of the vehicle. He smelled sage and dust. He identified the sound of his feet dragging through dirt. His nose throbbed and his head ached.

A yellow rectangle appeared. There was a room. Threadbare green carpet, vintage 1979, overstuffed chairs. A narrow hall with a patterned runner. Quick view of egg yolk-colored concrete block walls, a single bed, and a wash basin before he was dropped on the floor. The door closed, cutting off the light. He let go into unconsciousness.

The door opened, and he heard the footsteps of two men come in. They picked him up. He saw cuffs of blue jeans and scuffed white New Balance under khakis. They dragged him down the hall and into another concrete block room. McNab came to as they strapped him into a metal chair. As he looked down at the floor, McNab saw dark brown stains that surrounded the drain just visible beneath him. His nose started to throb. A very bright halogen lamp came on directly in his face. The light bored into his skull. He thought his head would split open from the pain. The two men left and closed the door.

It could have been minutes or hours later that the door opened again. McNab turned his head to see a man bringing in some boxes. He had thick glasses, a scraggly gray mustache, a long ponytail, and blue jeans. The man shoved the boxes against the wall under a table. He came to the chair and bent over McNab with all the interest of an entomologist. McNab started to say something, but the man turned and left.

After another indeterminate period of time, Pony Tail came back in and inspected him. McNab managed to say, "Water," before the man left. Several minutes later, he returned with a tumbler of water and a straw. He held the glass until McNab drank it all, then went.

When the door opened again, it was Karl. He smiled. Then he slapped McNab across the face. Karl's huge bulk gave the slap the force of a massive blow. McNab's head snapped around, and the bright colors danced in his vision again. Karl slapped him again and again. The big man seemed to be enjoying himself. McNab felt the welts rising on his face. Karl kept slapping him. The skin on his cheeks started to tear. Blood trickled out of the corners of his mouth. Karl kept on slapping. McNab wondered when the questions would begin. Just as he was about to lose consciousness, Karl quit slapping him.

McNab thought he heard the door open several times, but no one appeared over him. Finally, Pony Tail came in and brought three other bright lamps and set them up at chair level facing McNab. He turned them on. McNab tried to turn his face to the wall. Pony Tail set up several more chairs in the back of the lights and then went to sit at the table. A short time later, McNab heard several people walking through the door. Metal chairs scraped on the cement floor as the visitors took their seats.

It was Hoffstader's voice that came through. "Grif, I don't think you understand exactly how serious we are about you telling us everything you know."

"I don't know anything more than what I've told you." The light felt like it went completely through his head.

There was some murmuring in the back. Hoffstader came back. "I'm afraid we don't believe you, Grif. You're going to have to do better than that."

"Fuck you, Hoffstader."

Karl blocked the light as he stepped in front of McNab and started slapping him again. The force of Karl's blows punched McNab's teeth into his tongue. Blood flowed more freely down his chin now. Then Karl shifted his attention to McNab's midsection. After several powerful punches, McNab vomited. Karl stopped.

"Tell us what we want to know."

McNab was only sitting upright because of the straps. His head hung down to his chest. He pulled it up to look right at Hoffstader. "Go to hell, you piece of worm shit. I'll bet you looked cute with that peach pie all over you."

At that, Hoffstader jumped out of his chair. He pushed Karl out of the way and hit McNab in the face, his ring gouging a chunk of flesh out of McNab's left cheek. Hoffstader hit him again and stopped, breathing heavily. "Out with it."

McNab spit some blood out at Hoffstader, then laughed. "I just got it, Hoffstader. You're such a piece of bullshit I bet that ring isn't real. I bet you made it all up. Moon rock. Like hell. You can try to fluff up your sorry ass image all you want, but you're still just a piece of poor white trash trying to pass."

Hoffstader screamed, "Fucking faggot! You talk to me like that?" and swung to hit McNab in the face and head. The ring tore McNab's left ear and temple, just missing his eye. Hoffstader was swinging wildly, swearing. A voice from the back of the room called out something. Karl came over and pulled Hoffstader off, still swinging at the air and cursing incoherently. McNab coughed up blood, which ran over the dark stains on the floor and dribbled down the drain.

Karl put Hoffstader down. Hoffstader turned around and kicked Karl in the shins. Karl winced. "Don't you ever do that again! You work for me, not the Chink. You understand that?" Hoffstader's breathing slowed. He motioned to Pony Tail. "Okay. Do it."

Pony Tail unloaded the boxes onto the table. McNab strained to see what was in them but couldn't. Karl sat in a chair next to McNab and just looked at him with a slight smile on one side of his mouth. After a few minutes, Pony Tail nodded at Karl and sat down in a chair by the table. The big man got out of the chair, went to the table, and picked something up. As Karl came around in front of the chair, McNab saw a pair of wires with alligator clips attached to the ends.

McNab strained at the plastic straps that held him down. He thrashed, but nothing moved. After several tries, he gave up. Karl bent over him, grabbed his shirt, and ripped it open. Then he attached one alligator clip to each of McNab's nipples. As sharp teeth dug into the flesh, McNab sucked in his breath.

Karl nodded at Pony Tail. Pony Tail did something at the table. McNab screamed.

SEVENTY-NINE

The smell of medicine, oily and pungent. McNab tried to turn over. Pain brought him fully awake. He blinked several times. Sunlight poured through large windows. Sagebrush, mesquite, and sand stretched out to rugged mountains. He lay under soft white sheets, an ivory down comforter. Impressionistic pastels hung on the cream-colored walls. Another bed, a couch, a round table, and several chairs upholstered in soft earth tones completed the furniture in the room. An open door that must lead to the bathroom was near the window. Vases of flowers sat on the table at the end of his bed and on the end tables of the couch. McNab looked at himself. His wounds were covered in gleaming white bandages, just barely stained with the yellowish unguent.

He tried to remember how he got here and couldn't. McNab moved his legs, grimacing with pain. He decided to get out of bed. Just as he was pulling back the covers, the door opened. "No you don't, you naughty boy." The slightly Southern lilt came from a petite red-headed nurse. She smiled brightly as she came to the side of the bed. "You just lie right back down there. You need your rest." McNab hesitated. "Come on, now. You got some healing to do." Gently she pushed him back down in the bed and pulled his covers back up.

"Where am I?" McNab just managed to ask.

"You're just fine!" She patted him gently on the head. "I'll be right back. Don't go away!" Out the door she went.

McNab lay back on the soft bed and took a deep breath. He looked out the window. Probably California high desert. "Here you are." She came bustling back into the room. "You can call me Romy. Here." She held a bowl of hot steaming broth. "Take some." She took a spoonful and held it in front of his mouth. "Come on. It's good for you."

McNab opened his mouth and winced. Bandages on his cheeks and head moved, stretching the torn skin. He swallowed the delicious broth. "Where am I?"

Romy spooned up some more broth. "Sierra Vista. Now have some more."

McNab turned his head. "What town?"

"You are a stubborn one, aren't you? Well, we're right near Ridgecrest. Well, not that near. Open up."

McNab took in the next spoonful. He could feel the nourishment starting to flow through him. Romy fed him the rest of the bowl before he said anything else. "Near China Lake Naval Air Station?"

"Don't you worry about that, now. We're going to have some medicine. A little later we'll try to get you up and walking."

McNab nodded weakly. Romy reached over to the table. "Take these." Romy pushed a paper cup at him containing three blue and two yellow pills. "Use this." She held a glass of water for him. McNab paused a minute, looking at Romy. He blinked and took the pills.

"Good boy!" Romy took the paper cup and empty glass from him. She put them on the table next to the bed, then arranged his pillow. "You're looking a lot better than when you came in."

"When did I come in?"

"Couple of days ago. You're doing so well! What would you like for lunch? We have barbecue and pizza. Salad, French fries, ice cream. Say, you like corned beef? They just got some great corned beef in. Direct from New York. Think about it, let me know." She walked to the door and opened it. "They said you could even have visitors."

"Wait!" McNab called out. His voice trailed off as Pat walked in.

"Hi." Pat's voice was subdued. She came and sat by the bed.

McNab reached for her hand. "Thank God. How did you find me?"

Pat didn't answer. She started to cry. He realized she looked tired and haggard. She pulled her hand away from his to grab a tissue from the side table. She wiped her eyes, then blew her nose. "I'm sorry, Grif." Tears filled her eyes. "I should never…"

"Pat…"

"It's all my fault."

"Don't talk that way." He tried to sit up, wincing. "Could you help me get to the bathroom?" He tried to push back the covers, but Pat had to help. Finally, McNab was sitting on the edge of the bed. He only had shorts on.

Pat gasped. Great purple and yellow bruises punctuated his midsection. Burn marks were visible around the edges of the bandages over his nipples. Other dressings showed under the bottom of his shorts. Scrapes and blue and yellow bruises decorated his legs. "My God, Grif, what have they done to you?"

He heard the door open. In walked Hoffstader and Karl. "We thought you'd like some company." Karl stationed himself by the bed next to Pat. McNab could see a bandage on Karl's cheek. Hoffstader stood on the other side of McNab, smiling broadly.

McNab tried to stand up, but fell back on the bed, "Hoffstader, no. Please, no." Pat stopped crying and pulled herself together.

"We knew Miss Morrissey would be worried about you. Weren't you?" Hoffstader gestured to the room. "Well, as you can see, Grif is fine. He wants for nothing. Am I right, Grif?" McNab's face sagged. "I believe we are about to reach an agreement, aren't we, Grif?"

"Hoffstader, please..."

"We could show Miss Morrissey our special discussion room, if you like, Grif."

McNab turned his head toward the door. Two other people came into the room and stood in the back, near the couch. One was Pony Tail, the other McNab recognized from the picture: Chu Sha Lee, shadowy assistant to the Chinese premier. McNab turned to Hoffstader. "No. You don't have to do that."

"I thought you'd see it my way." Hoffstader turned to Pat, who regarded him expressionlessly. "He is an intelligent boy. Why don't you sit over there?" he indicated the couch. Pat went stoically to sit next to Pony Tail, who preceded her to the sofa.

Karl brought up chairs for Hoffstader and Lee. Hoffstader sat, looked over at Lee, and then addressed McNab. "You're on, Grif."

McNab looked at Pat. He turned to Hoffstader. "I couldn't figure out why Henry had to die. It was obvious that he was murdered along with Larry. Otto saw Karl kill them. He didn't know who Karl was, but he knew enough to leave town. Then I found him, questioned him, and told the cops. Then the cops told you. Otto died. Because of me.

"What happened was that Henry saw Lee there, at your headquarters. Henry sent you Lee's picture with a lot of crazy stuff attached. I think that's why Henry had to die. Lee wasn't supposed to be there, then.

"So, I asked myself, why not? What's wrong with a trade delegate seeing an industrialist? Nothing, unless they're not supposed to be seeing each other. Negotiations with China over the forest products deals had broken off. So why not restart them? You don't restart if you don't want a public link between the parties. Henry, much to his detriment, found the link.

"Lee spearheaded the crackdowns in Tibet and Lo Mulang. The monks from Lo Mulang were in Euphrates to get a tree to rebuild a monastery. They had official permission. But not approval. Human rights are important to the US. China is up for renewal of Most Favored Nation status in a couple of months. They have to appear to be loosening up. So the official word from Beijing goes out to loosen up. The unofficial word is to hamper at every turn. Lee turns up in Euphrates, a monk dies, the quest for the tree is postponed until if falls off the front page and the nightly news."

"Brilliant, Grif. I kept telling you to join my team. Go on. Please."

"Lee's coming to screw up a one tree deal in a backwater town doesn't make sense. What else is going on? Just down the hall from Odin's offices is Celestial Arts Jewelry Co. They import cheap jewelry from the countries that form the 'golden triangle.' Drugs. I wouldn't have figured that out unless Saigon Duphet hadn't tried to kill me. You're trying to refloat your sinking empire with drug money. Mister Lee over there is your partner in that. He does supply, you do distribution along with Manuel Tanaka, silent partner in Celestial Arts Jewelry. It seemed ironic to me: the opium wars were fought so that the British could sell drugs to Chinese. Now the Chinese were going to sell drugs to our children using one of our prime defense contractors as pipeline."

Hoffstader looked at him. "That's amazing, Grif, just amazing." He turned to Lee. "Isn't that amazing, Mister Lee?" Then Hoffstader started to laugh. Lee smirked and almost suppressed a high-pitched giggle. Pat looked at the floor. Pony Tail and Karl just sat at their stations. Finally, Hoffstader stopped laughing and wiped his eyes with his silk handkerchief. "That is most ingenious, Grif." Hoffstader turned to Lee. "We will have to talk with Mister Tanaka, don't you think? This is a most serendipitous moment." He turned back to McNab. "What else, Grif?"

"What's so funny?"

"We don't have a relationship with Mister Tanaka or his jewelry company. Nor did we know of Celestial Arts' profitable sideline. Until now, of course. I wonder if it's worth exploring. What do you think, Mister Lee?"

Lee spoke for the first time. "An interesting idea. It isn't the first time we've heard of such a plan. But, not at this time, Mister Hoffstader."

"Somehow I thought you would say that." Hoffstader turned back to McNab. "Nice try, Grif. What else have you got for us?"

McNab, trying to recover from this turn of events, looked at him helplessly. "I don't know. That's it."

"Come, come, Grif. Surely there's more? You don't think I'd go to all this trouble just to remove a wino?"

"There's nothing else, really."

Hoffstader drummed his fingers on his knee. "Karl, take Miss Morrissey down the hall."

McNab shouted, "No!"

"Well, then?"

Pat burst out. "No. They're going to kill us, anyway. Don't tell them anything."

Hoffstader looked at Pat, then back at McNab. "She's right, Grif. It's not a matter of whether, it's a matter of how."

McNab heard himself say, "DOSAP."

Hoffstader blinked. "What about it?"

"You tried to steal it."

"I developed it."

"You lost the bid. Then you tried to steal the Littlefield Technologies data because it is a better system."

"And?"

"You were going to sell it to China to bail out your rotting empire. But they caught your guy."

"They caught one guy." Hoffstader smiled at McNab's shock. "Right. There is another. You don't approve, do you, Grif?"

"Approve of treason. No, not really."

Hoffstader laughed. "Grif, how can it be treason? Our own government approved the sale of missile technology to the Chinese. Why should I second guess our own government?"

"They didn't approve this."

"Call it anticipatory approval." Hoffstader stood up. "Our country needs a strong defense and defense industry. Odin is a part of that. I'm simply ensuring the survival of our country."

"By betraying it."

Hoffstader leaned over his bed. "You think so simplistically, Grif. Your way of thinking is nineteenth century. You think in terms of geographic nations. There are no nations. There are only economic interests. Today these economic interests are Exxon, Apple, Intel, Microsoft, Google, and so on. They have no homes. They are global. War, in today's world, is fought in economic terms, for markets. China is the largest underdeveloped market left in the world.

"Mister Lee represents China. He still has some quaint ideas about nations, but, like all reasonable men, he will come to understand the true nature of the world. I admit that for a little while things could be uncomfortable. They will attempt to curry favor in the third world by allocating stealth detection technology to their client nations or coerce them with Belt and Road. But look on the bright side. Odin will have to come up with better stealth technology!" Hoffstader laughed. "But right now he has what we want and vice versa. We make a deal. Everybody is happy. Of course, some primitive thinkers could hamper the inevitable somewhat. It's more convenient if they don't. So, Grif, who else knows about this? You certainly didn't get to know about the Littlefield thing by yourself."

"No one."

Hoffstader grabbed McNab's bandaged wrist tightly, causing him to wince. "Last chance, Grif. Or Miss Morrissey..." He let go of the wrist.

McNab sighed. "Doug Matthews. He doesn't know for sure. He gave me raw information, I pieced it together."

Hoffstader thought a moment. "Ah. Yes. Colonel Matthews, as I recall. Good man. But not a friend of ours. How many others?"

McNab hung his head and whispered. "No one." It was the best acting job of his life.

Hoffstader smiled. "Good. I knew you were smart." He went to the back of the room to confer with Lee and the others.

Pat got up from the couch and came to the side of the bed. She took McNab's hand and held it gently. They tried to tune out the drone of voices.

Hoffstader's voice rose, intruding on their reverie. "This isn't Tiananmen Square. I don't control Euphrates. There have been too many deaths and disappearances there already. It's too small a town. All they want is a god damned tree! Let's give them the damn tree! Sink the ship it sails on if you want to. Whatever." Hoffstader and Lee were standing toe to toe, both angry. "You take care of the monks *after* they've left my part of the country. I'll handle Matthews."

Lee said something they couldn't quite hear. Hoffstader motioned them all toward the door. He stopped Karl and whispered something to him. They all left.

Pat sat on the side of the bed. "Doesn't look very good, does it, Grif?"

McNab shook his head. "I'm sorry, Pat. I just didn't know when to let go."

"I should have never asked you to do anything about Henry." McNab waved the remark aside. "I mean it. He was dead. He was out of his misery. I should have left well enough alone."

"We all have great hindsight."

"We're a couple of fuck ups, McNab."

He laughed. "Yeah."

There was an uncomfortable silence. Pat brushed the hair from her face. "I'm sorry, Grif." McNab shook his head. "I mean it. We're going to die and it's my fault."

"Personally, I think it's Hoffstader's fault."

"You know what I mean."

"Maybe we should think of some memorable last words. You know, like, uh." He was silent a minute. "Well, you give it a try."

Pat grunted. "I'm not feeling very eloquent." She stood up and walked to the window. "Maybe if I'd given up on Henry..."

"Instead of yourself?"

"Too close to home, McNab. I always told Cindy that: 'Don't try to fool him.' Yeah, instead of myself. I always put him first. Not just after his death."

"'You could've been a contendah'," McNab parodied.

"Yeah. For sap of the decade."

"You loved your brother, Pat. There's nothing wrong with loving someone."

"Oh, yeah? Look where it got us. What about you?"

McNab thought a minute. "I guess if I really got honest about it I'd have to say that Cindy and I weren't completely idyllic. Truth is, the cracks were showing. I just didn't want to see them." He paused. "After she died it was easier to canonize her than to look at her. Or me."

"We both canonized her. Saint Cindy, savior to us all." Pat came back and sat on the bed. "Was it all bad, though?"

"No. I got a best friend."

Pat nodded. "Me, too." She brushed her blouse self-consciously.

"One good piece of news, though." McNab looked up at her. "Saigon regained consciousness. You're cleared."

"How did that happen? I'll bet Grogan loved that."

"He was a bit sheepish when he called. Your plane was already missing. He said that according to Saigon, Tanaka got enraged when you hit him in the airplane when the engine went out. You hurt his machismo. Tanaka was serious when he called you a dead man. He became obsessed with killing you. Saigon's orders were to kill you or else." McNab shook his head. "Now they've got Tanaka on another attempted murder charge, along with Saigon."

"Well, what do you know? I'm not the attempted murderer."

They sat in silence for a while. There were muffled sounds, perhaps engines, through the thick panes of glass. Neither paid much attention.

A little while later, the door opened. Pat turned as Karl and Pony Tail entered. They carried plastic restraints, those McNab had been bound with. Karl motioned Pat over to the couch. She hesitated. Karl moved toward her. She went. He gestured for her to hold her hands in back of her. Karl bound her hands and sat her down in the chair. The two men moved toward McNab. He was too weak to resist. Karl pulled him out of bed, spun him around, and cuffed him. McNab bit off a cry of pain.

Karl and Pony Tail pushed McNab and Pat down the hall. They came to the end of the corridor to a locked door with a keypad on the wall. Karl stood behind the prisoners as Pony Tail stood in front of the pad, blocking McNab's view, and entered a code. He pulled open the door. Sunlight blasted them as they came out onto the desert hardpan.

They were prodded along a path that led to another building. McNab's body stiffened as he flashed that it was where the interrogation room was. Karl now held a gun on them as they walked. Instead of entering the building, Karl indicated they go left, around the back of the flesh-colored concrete block structure. As they rounded the corner, McNab saw a backhoe beside a trench. A bag of lime leaned against the building.

Pat's knees buckled. Pony Tail pulled her up, pushing her along to the berm of sandy dirt next to the trench. Karl pushed McNab, and he fell by the ditch. Pony Tail moved back behind Karl. The big man smiled his lopsided smile and raised the pistol.

Suddenly there was the sound of a door slamming open, feet running, and shouting, "Stop! Don't do it!" Around the corner, sliding on the sandy gravel, came a small man. In that zone where time slows down, McNab noticed the man had his black hair parted on the left side, a hooked nose, khakis, New Balance shoes, and several acne scars on his right cheek. He saw Karl turn slowly toward the shout. The man lost his balance and hit the ground on his right side, hands flung out in front of him. "No. Hoffstader said no!"

EIGHTY

"What did it look like out there, when they brought you in?" They were back in the infirmary room, McNab in bed.

"I didn't get that close a look. Grif, I was so scared. Hoffstader's men grabbed me at home, took me in a van to the airport and loaded me on his jet. All I saw before we landed was a lot of desert."

"How long a ride was it from the plane to here?"

"Not long. Ten minutes, maybe. We went through several gates, though. One with sentries."

"Could you give me some water?" Pat got up and brought him some water. She held it for him to drink. When he was finished, he collapsed back down on the pillows. "Let's make a run for it," McNab laughed weakly. He gestured to the window. "Take a look out the window. Tell me what you see."

Pat went to the window and looked out. She craned her head left and right and stood on tip-toe. When she was finished, she came back to her chair by the bed. "Desert. Lots of desert. The fence..."

They both turned their heads as the lock clicked and the door opened. Karl came in and stood to one side. Romy rolled in a covered cart. "I hear you're both staying for dinner.

That's so nice. We have chicken cordon bleu from our own kitchen, salad and peach cobbler. There's soft drinks and coffee. If you need anything else, just press the little green button." Romy pointed to a wall plate next to the door. "Bye, now." She left, Karl exiting behind her.

"Cute." Pat went over to the cart and took the cover off. "Well, if it's a last meal, it could be worse." She looked over at McNab. "Want to try and sit at the table?"

McNab nodded and threw back the covers. He slowly moved his legs over the edge of the bed and put his feet on the floor, breathing hard. Pat went to the bed and helped him stand, his arm over her shoulder. They moved slowly over to the table and sat down. McNab was sweating. Quickly Pat served the dinner and sat down to eat.

McNab chewed delicately on the chicken. "They want something else from us."

"I wonder what it is?"

They continued the meal in silence. When they were done eating, they drank coffee and waited. A couple of hours later, Karl and Romy returned to fetch the cart. Romy was her sunny, cheerful self. Karl effectively blocked the door. When they left, the sun was setting.

McNab tried a few stretching exercises, gasping with pain. Pat went again to the window to look out. McNab gave up on his efforts and slowly came to the window. He tapped it. Thick as he imagined. Desert swept away as far as they could see, all the way to the mountains. The tall fence was barely discernible off to the side, fading away to the mountains. He went back to his bed. Long after night had descended, Pat, exhausted, finally collapsed onto the other bed.

They were awakened by Karl opening the door. Pony Tail was behind him, holding a gun. Karl gestured, and they were handcuffed and led out into the darkness. This time they went to the right and headed toward a gate in the fence. Pat looked wildly at McNab, who was just managing to stumble along.

Just as they approached the fence, headlights swept around a turn. A long black limousine pulled up and screeched to a halt. Pony Tail opened the door, and they were shoved into the spacious back seat.

Karl and Pony Tail kept them covered while they rode. Neither McNab nor Pat said anything. Less than ten minutes later, the limo stopped. The two men got out and motioned them to exit. They got out as best they could with their hands tied behind their backs. McNab looked around. Standing before them was a gleaming white Gulfstream IV business jet, the Hoffstader Industries logo emblazoned on its side. Karl gestured them up into the plane.

Hoffstader was in the luxurious champagne leather seating group. Grandly he motioned for them to sit down. "Karl. These are our guests. They don't need to be restrained." With no expression, Karl cut their bonds. McNab and Pat rubbed their wrists and sat in the plush seats. The twin fanjets spooled up, and they were rushing down the runway into the night.

Once airborne, Hoffstader turned to Pony Tail. "Champagne for our friends."

Soon they all held Baccarat crystal champagne flutes filled with Taittinger Blanc de Blanc. "A toast to your homecoming." Hoffstader raised his glass. "It's a miracle you survived your ordeal in the forest, Grif." He drank. McNab and Pat just held their glasses.

McNab put his flute down on the oiled wood table. "What do you want, Hoffstader?"

Hoffstader pursed his lips. "I think we need to come to an understanding. Somehow Colonel Matthews found out you were our guests. It took a while to negotiate an understanding with him. The points are these. You and Miss Morrissey are to be returned. In exchange neither he nor you will make any further efforts to embarrass me. On any level." He looked at them. "Agreed?"

Pat started to object. "What about the spying? What about...?"

McNab put his hand on her arm. "The government doesn't want a messy spy scandal right now. Especially one that they can't prove. Am I right, Hoffstader?"

"You should really reconsider my offer, Grif." He chuckled. "Yes, you're right. At this moment it would all be your word against mine. It would slow the development of DOSAP and just create a lot of messy press the government doesn't need right now."

Pat started to stand, "But what about..."

McNab pulled her back into her seat, wincing with the effort. "So the deal is we get released, we don't talk, ever. Right?" Hoffstader nodded. "Our silence is our protection. If we break it, Hoffstader sends Karl, or someone like him. If an 'accident' happens to us, the government goes after him."

"Very astute."

He turned to Pat. "We can't prove anything, Pat. About Henry, or anything. It's all will o' the wisp. At a trial it would all be circumstance and conjecture, no corroborating evidence." He turned back to Hoffstader. "Lee. He approves?"

"He'll accept it."

McNab picked up his glass. "Deal." He drained his glass.

EIGHTY-ONE

"Great burger." McNab tucked into the juicy hamburger.

"For breakfast?" Pat had settled for eggs. Both ate voraciously. Doug, bemused and unshaven, drank his coffee. They were in a coffee shop near the Air Force Space Command in El Segundo, just south of LAX.

"Not as good as the ones in Elko, though. I owe you one, Doug." McNab said through a mouthful of fries.

"One? Like hell, old buddy. You'll be buying burgers 'til hell freezes over."

McNab nodded. "Tell me. How did you manage it?"

Doug put down his coffee. "Got a call from a fella named Rico. He said you told him to call me if anything happened to you."

"Good man."

Pat looked up. "How did Rico know?"

McNab picked it up. "That cellphone that Rico got for me? It was actually a satellite phone and had a special GPS function. With each call, sent or received, it sent the geographic coordinates directly to Rico no matter who was on the call. We had a plan. If I hadn't made a call for eight hours, Rico would call me. Even if I didn't answer it would activate the GPS and it would send him the fix." He turned to Doug. "That how it worked?"

"Yep. Got a call from him with the coordinates of your van. You left the phone in the van. Made it a lot harder." McNab nodded. "You were damn lucky, old buddy. We got to the van a few hours later. Had a look at the tape machines. One had gone down. I guess that was when you hung up on me." McNab nodded. "Just when I was going to give you something juicy."

"What?"

"You know that so-called moon rock you sent me? You thought it was Hoffstader's? I was trying to tell you that NASA doesn't give moon rock souvenirs. Hoffstader had a ring made up to look like one. Uses it to impress his buddies. It's a big joke in NASA. But no one wants to be the one to call him a liar publicly." McNab just nodded. "Well, back to the van. The other machine was still running tape. A while later, in the evening, guess who showed up in the elevator area? Hoffstader, that goon he runs with, and you, all trussed up in a wheelchair."

Pat looked at them. "This is incredible."

Doug smiled. "The next part wasn't so easy. I had to go outside the chain of command a bit." He poked McNab in the shoulder. McNab winced. "Sorry. But you will buy me burgers forever. I lifted a couple of frames of the tape and emailed them direct to Hoffstader. We didn't hear from him for a while. I was getting pretty worried."

"So were we," said Pat.

"Finally he started to palaver. Well, the brass got in on it. It took a lot of dickering but we got the deal. They almost flayed me alive. But, they figured they got some good information on Hoffstader from me, courtesy of Rico. Leverage they called it. Think they can squeeze him on the next bid."

"He's a murderer!" Pat was enraged. "You mean you're still going to do business with him? I can't believe this!"

"They'll keep him from bidding on the super classified stuff." Doug said lamely. "It's not my choice."

McNab put down his coffee cup. "He's got another guy on the inside. And he has a customer." He told Doug about Lee.

Doug whistled. "That's a horse of a different stripe, old buddy. Hoffstader wasn't quite as straightforward as we thought. Like that should surprise me." Doug thought a minute. "Can you prove any of it?" McNab shook his head. "Well, it won't make much difference, then. Hoffstader's got his fingers in too many pots. We got too many contracts with him and he's bought too many Senators. He'll just deny it and we'll keep on giving him business."

Pat said, "Isn't there anything we can do?"

McNab turned to Doug. "Do you have that tape? The one from the van?"

"Yeah."

"Can we take a look at it?"

"It's still in the lab."

A half-hour later, they were looking at the tape. Doug pointed, "See? Here comes Karl, pushing you in the wheelchair. Right behind him comes Hoffstader. Hold it." The technician froze the tape. "These are the frames I sent to Hoffstader. They're the ones that most clearly show your face and his face. After this, it's less dramatic. The elevator door opens. You get angled off to the side a bit, so your wheelchair holds the door open. Hoffstader stands outside for a bit."

"Why does he stand outside?"

"Waiting for someone else."

"Who?"

"I don't know." Doug motioned to the tech, who started the tape. As Doug had said, the elevator door opened, and Karl pushed McNab over to prop it open. Hoffstader stood outside the door for a minute. Then another figure walked into the frame.

EIGHTY-TWO

They stood in the lobby of the office building. McNab leaned against the cool marble and wiped the perspiration off his forehead. Pat handed him the briefcase. "Are you sure you're up to this?"

"Yeah. It's now or never."

"You haven't told me what you're going to say to him." McNab thought a moment, then told her. Pat gaped. "But it's not true." She paused. "You're trying to bluff him!"

"Let's just say I don't think he's as familiar with our legal system as he could be." McNab took a deep breath and walked to the elevators.

"Did you tell Doug?"

"No. And he doesn't need to know."

"But, Grif, that isn't the deal."

"Do you really want it to end like that? I don't." Pat had nothing more to say.

A few minutes later, McNab limped into the sparsely furnished office. The delicately pretty receptionist looked up at him. She saw a man dressed in a maintenance man's uniform, torn in many spots, bandages soaked with pungent yellow medicine on his face and ears, limping.

"I want to see Mister Lee."

"Do you have an appointment?"

"No."

"May I inquire what this concerns?"

"A matter of great importance to Mister Lee."

She tried to be very diplomatic. "I'm afraid Mister Lee's calendar is full for today. May I schedule you for another time?"

McNab sighed. He pulled an envelope out of the incongruous eelskin briefcase he carried. "Please give this to Mister Lee. I think he'll want to see me."

"Why don't you leave this with me and I'll see..."

McNab leaned over the desk at her. "I guarantee that he will want to see this right now. Please give it to him." The tone brooked no refusal. She took the envelope and retreated through the door into the inner office.

A few minutes later, she came out. Right behind her was Lee. He took a look at McNab and beckoned him inside.

Lee offered him a seat in front of the ornately carved desk. He put the envelope on the desk in front of him. On top of it was the picture of Hoffstader, Karl, McNab, and Lee taken on the surveillance camera. Lee said nothing. McNab opened his briefcase and pulled out the notebook that Pat had assembled for him. He pushed it over to Lee.

"I think you'll find most everything there." Lee didn't move. "When you do look at it, you will find that we have quite a strong case against Hoffstader for kidnaping, murder and espionage. That picture," McNab pointed, "implicates you."

Lee shrugged. "All I see is some people waiting at an elevator."

"If that's all that is, you wouldn't have seen me." McNab sighed. "Please review this evidence carefully, Mister Lee. Let me explain. No politician would ever approve this deal that Hoffstader says he made with the military. Somehow, somewhere it will leak. So this is how it might happen. I could turn this notebook over a federal prosecutor. A politically ambitious prosecutor."

Lee glanced at his intercom.

"Don't even think about it. There's copies. Allow me to continue. They could arrest Eric Hoffstader. The prosecutor would want everyone involved in this to be convicted and put in jail. If there is a political angle to it, especially international spies, so much the better. It would serve him well in his pursuit of higher office. You know politicians, don't you, Mister Lee?" McNab shifted in his seat. "So. The prosecutor would offer Hoffstader a deal. A plea bargain we call it. Hoffstader would get a reduced sentence for his total, repeat total, cooperation." Lee remained impassive. "Names, dates, places, amounts. Co-conspirators. Everything would come out. Everything." They both were silent for a moment. "I seem to recall that the Senate is considering a very large trade treaty with China, even as we speak."

Lee sat very still.

McNab continued. "I'm sure there will be no trouble. After all, your progress on human rights is remarkable. The Trangmar monastery, for instance. Its rebuilding will be so beneficial for China's image, don't you think?"

Lee paused, then inclined his head slightly, stiffly. "May I offer you some tea, Mister McNab?"

McNab stood up. "Thank you for your generous hospitality, Mister Lee. Please forgive my rudeness. I have another appointment."

EIGHTY-THREE

Roy knew that noise. He'd heard it a thousand times in Nam. He ran out of the house in time to see the big green helicopter land in the meadow. As the blades came to a stop, the door opened, and McNab slowly got out. Behind him came Doug Matthews and two men carrying rifles, all in uniform. McNab walked over to Roy, who almost felled him with a slap on the back.

Roy pulled back and looked over at the armed men. "You invading someone?" He looked back at McNab. "God. You look like shit, Grif."

"Thanks, Roy. I'd say the same to you if it were true." They laughed. "Our boy okay?"

They all started to walk toward the barn. "Yeah. He's not very happy, though. Keeps complaining he's hungry."

"Is he?"

"Yep."

"Good man." McNab clapped Roy on the back. "Where are the monks?"

"I don't know, somewhere in the woods doing their monk thingee."

They all went into the barn. The sound of the men

walking echoed in the large structure. As they approached the pen where Herman was kept, they heard his voice. "Hey, Roy. How about some real food? What are you trying to do, starve me? Jesus Christ, Roy. What'd I ever do to you?" McNab walked up to the little barred window. "Grif! You're back! Jesus, you look like shit, Grif." Roy smothered a laugh. "Get me out of here, Grif. He's been starving me!" Then Herman saw the soldiers. "What's going on?"

"You look good, Herman. You must have lost fifteen pounds." McNab opened the door and walked into the small room. Herman backpedaled and was finally stopped by the wall. "Herman. The colonel has something to say to you."

Doug came in the door. The two armed men walked through the door and took up stations on either side. Herman looked wildly around the close room.

"Herman Pecheur?" Doug intoned.

"Yes." Herman was clearly bewildered.

"You served your country in the Army and then in the National Guard?"

"Well, yeah. It was a long time ago."

Doug took out a paper from his briefcase. "By order of the Department of Defense you are hereby recalled to active duty as of May 24th of this year, that is, ten days ago. Your commanding officer is Major Griffin McNab. Do you understand?"

Herman shook his head. "What's going on here?"

"Do you understand?" Herman said nothing. "I will take your silence as assent. Sign here." Doug held out a paper to Herman.

"What's that?" Herman's voice rose an octave. "You're Air Force, I was Army. You can't do that."

"Department of Defense. Sign here." Doug produced a pen and pointed it at the bottom of the page. Herman hesitated. Doug nodded, and the two soldiers stiffened.

McNab said, "I'd sign it if I were you, Herman." Herman signed the paper.

Doug put it back into his briefcase. "Everything that has happened to you in the last ten days has been classified top secret. Everything. Major McNab will brief you on what you will say did happen. Is that clear?"

Herman nodded, dumbly.

"If for any reason, you divulge anything not specifically approved by Major McNab, you will be subject to court martial on charges of treason against the United States of America. Is that clear?"

"Grif, what is this?"

"Herman, listen to the Colonel."

"Is that clear, Corporal Pecheur?"

"Yes, sir."

"Excellent. Your recall to active duty ends today at 5:00pm." He took another paper out of his briefcase. "Sign here."

Herman signed.

"Major McNab will report to me, from time to time. I expect that your name will never appear in his reports. Am I clear?"

"Yes, sir."

"That is all." He turned to McNab. "Carry on, Major." McNab saluted, and Doug left with the armed men.

McNab and Herman walked out of the cell. By the time they got to the door of the barn, the helicopter was lifting off. Roy was standing on the steps of the house. "Come on, Herman, we have some talking to do."

Clyde Barnham was planting trees. Down on his hands and knees, ass in the air, his job was to plant thousands of tiny trees in the devastation where Mountain Lumber had clear-cut hundreds of ancient giants. Soon ML would claim that there were more trees in their harvested lands than before harvesting had begun over a hundred years ago. The fact that few of those trees survived to maturity was hardly ever mentioned. Also not mentioned was that ML paid for the planting by the tree. Clyde knew too many contractors who simply buried thousands of trees instead of planting them. He and the two dozen on his crew were working the Two Forks reclamation project. The soil had been so damaged that the chances of any of the new trees surviving the winter were almost nil.

Only another hundred trees 'til lunch, Clyde thought. He used to be a logger on these same hillsides making three times the money before the layoffs. He'd given up a bed down at the mission to take this job. If his back lasted, he could make enough today to pay his part of the cabin rent and get a bite to eat. Just one tree at a time, he thought.

Clyde reached for another tiny tree when he looked up and saw two men staggering out of the brush at the top of the ridge. The two men practically fell down the side of the hill to get to him. The skinny one was holding up the one with all the bruises. They looked like shit.

EIGHTY-FOUR

"What do you mean he hasn't returned my call?" Hoffstader didn't wait for a response. "Call him again. I don't care what time it is in Beijing. The fucking bank wants an answer by noon, and I need his answer now." He punched his phone off and threw it on the seat beside him. "Karl!"

"Yes, Mr. Hoffstader?" Vadner was driving the limo down West Olympic Blvd. toward the Santa Monica Airport, where the ML jet waited. Traffic was heavy, and the going was slow.

"What's going on out there?"

"Where, Mr. Hoffstader?"

"Out there, numbskull." Karl looked out the left side of the car. "No! The other side. Christ, they're walking faster than we're driving. What's the hang-up?" A group of slender, black-haired men were strolling on the sidewalk and were, indeed, walking faster than cars on the clogged street were driving.

Suddenly, they turned toward the limo and pulled out guns. Hoffstader heard a popping sound. A bang from the left side of the car made him swing his head back the other way. A star pattern appeared in the window next to his head.

"They're shooting at us! Get me out of here!" Hoffstader

screamed. More popping noises and more star patterns in all the windows. "Karl! Move! Fuck!"

Karl's head whipped around. "Don't worry, this is bullet-proof glass."

"The fuck it is! It's not holding! Get me out of here!" Karl turned the wheel, smashed into the car in the next lane, and stopped. No momentum. He backed up, caving in the grill of the car behind, turned the wheel, and stomped on the accelerator, trying to push the car ahead of him out of the way. The sounds of squealing tires and grinding metal melded with the gunfire into an unbearable roar of chaos.

No luck. No car was moving. There was nowhere to go. Smoke from the overheated tires billowed all around them. Deep thuds of large caliber bullets hitting the body of the limo echoed throughout the interior. Hoffstader scrabbled, frantic. Now there were slender, black-haired men coming toward the limo from both sides, firing as they advanced. Puffs of paint and dust erupted off surrounding cars.

The men were closing in. "Karl" Hoffstader yelled. The window next to him was crazed, the cracks getting more and more numerous with each hit.

Karl opened his door and rolled out onto the pavement, gun in hand. He crouched down and scuttled away from the limo dodging between cars. He moved very fast for a big man.

"Karl! Karl!" Hoffstader was alone, screaming. There was a fast volley of shots, and his window exploded inward.

EIGHTY-FIVE

As they took off in the mist and turned north at the coast, McNab looked over at Pat. Towering cumulus rose over the mountains. Pat held the box in her lap. The plane bounced mildly in light turbulence. Several miles north, out over the ocean, the visibility was crystal clear. McNab slowed the plane. He put in some flaps to bring the speed down, then slipped the plane by banking to the left and using right rudder. This decreased the wind flow on the passenger side. He nodded at Pat, and she opened the passenger side window. Wind and noise filled the cockpit.

Pat held the box for a brief moment, and then leaned out the window and let it go.

"Freedom!"

Her cry filled the cabin as the white cardboard box fell. McNab got out of the slip, raised the flaps, and put the plane into a spiral. The box with Henry's ashes first stabilized, then started tumbling. The wind caught the flare of the box lid, ripping loose a small piece of tape that had secured it. A white plume came out of the box and then stopped. Immediately, another streaked out behind it.

"Look at that! It's perfect! It's perfect!"

They wheeled about Henry's ashes, descending in a spiral, watching the white dot grow smaller.

"Did you see that? It was perfect!"

They slowly circled until, finally, they saw the box hit the water. McNab turned the plane back toward home. A sudden updraft jolted them. They didn't speak for a while. He turned to Pat. "Are you all right?"

She looked down at the waves breaking on the rocks, the primordial forest, and the seagulls that swept by underneath the plane. She shook her head. Tears streamed down her face. He made the turn toward Euphrates, where the fog was lifting.

Miles away, Jamyang Rinpoche, Tenzing, and Derek McGinty stood in dappled forest sunlight before a giant fir tree, ferns surrounding them. The monks raised their heads, and their eyes followed the straight trunk through the branches to a mosaic of blue sky. They paused, then looked at each other and nodded. McGinty smiled. Jamyang and Tenzing turned to the tree and began to chant in low tones.

After parking the car, Pat and McNab walked across the Square toward Luego's. A bent old man pushed his shopping cart laden with dismal green garbage bags to Otto's old corner and stopped. He sat down under the replacement sapling, just planted by the city, and looked vacantly over the Square. One of the shop owners walked by on her way to open her store. "Morning, Jake," she said, walking on, not waiting for a reply. Pat looked quickly away.

Coming into the restaurant they headed for their favorite window table. Mingus came out of the kitchen as they approached the table and opened his mouth. Something made him look more closely at them. The wisecrack died before it was born.

They looked out at the gray bay. Small patches of blue appeared in the sky. Steam fog curled up from the still water. A line of five pelicans glided over the water parallel to the shore.

The TV over the bar was tuned to Channel 25, the local station. On screen, Brent Marlowe, news anchor, was commenting over the CNN video feed.

"So far, police have not released any names of suspects other than to say they appeared to be members of rival Asian drug gangs engaged in a turf war. The Chief of Police said he was relieved that no other members of the public had been injured during the gunfight.

"Jacquye Ormus, a local spokesperson for Mountain Lumber, had this to say." The video cut to Jacquye, standing behind a lectern. She wore a somber dark green business suit. The backdrop was a large aerial photo of a redwood forest. "The Mountain Lumber family wants to extend our condolences to Mr. Hoffstader's family and to our whole community? We lost a great man? Mountain Lumber will continue treasuring our local forests while providing great economic benefits for our community?" Marlowe came back on screen. "Our full coverage of the funeral services for Eric Hoffstader will continue after this."

Myrna came by with the pot. "Warm up?" Pat shook her head. McNab nodded. "Otter family's back," Myrna's eyes indicated a small clot of people standing on the wharf looking down at the water. She poured McNab's coffee. "Gonna clear up in the afternoon," she said, then disappeared.

ACKNOWLEDGMENTS

This book would not be here without much help and support. I'd like to thank John Baer for the finer points of Skywagons, Martha Longshore for sage publication advice and cover design, and Booklegger owner Jennifer McFadden. Thanks also to the readers and critics who offered valuable insights and suggestions: Nick Spicer, Howard Freiman, Brian and Laura Julian, Barney Benhoff, Becky McAllister, Laura Martignon, and Jill McCarthy. My apologies to anyone whose name I neglected to include here.

This book would not have been possible without the unstinting and untiring support of my wife, Nancy Short. Her keen editorial eye, relentless questioning, and endless patience in reading innumerable drafts were heroic and indispensable.

As always, any errors are mine alone.

About the Author

Stilson Snow, a native Angeleno, has written a newspaper column, penned articles for a literary journal, been an advertising copywriter, and produced educational films. He developed a diverse set of skills well enough to be paid as a sommelier, flight instructor, truck driver, stock broker, encyclopedia salesman, COO of a medical clinic, radio announcer, and fine art photographer.

If he can't be snorkeling off the Big Island, he is happiest engaging in his creative pursuits within sight of the redwood forest along the wild Northern California coast, where he now lives with his wife, Nancy, and dog, Laika.

Made in the USA
Middletown, DE
19 June 2023